THE RISING

THE RISING SERIES
BOOK FOUR

KRISTEN ASHLEY

ROCK CHICK
PRESS

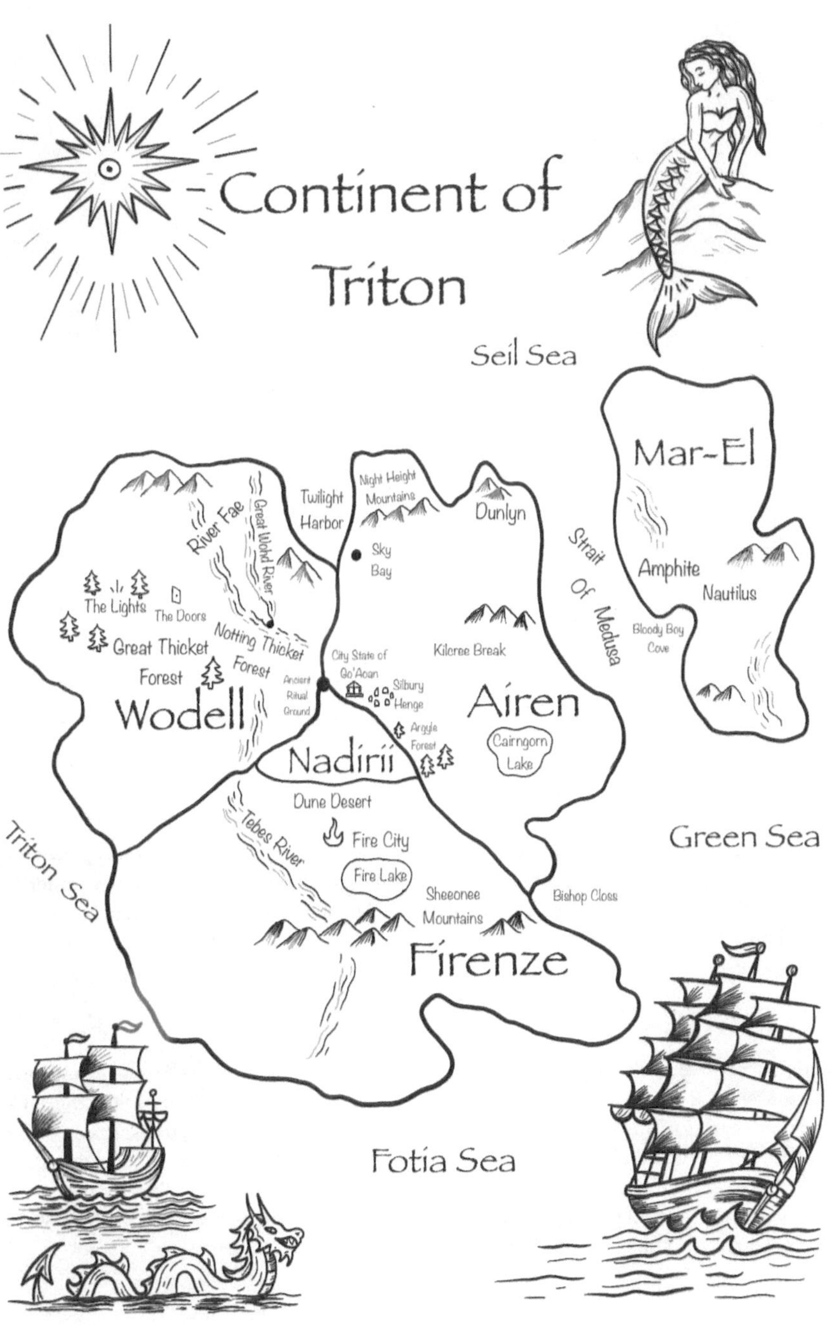

Continent of
Triton
Seil Sea
Mar~El
Amphite
Nautilus
Bloody Boy Cove
Night Height Mountains
Twilight Harbor
River Fae
Great World River
Dunlyn
Sky Bay
The Lights
The Doors
Notting Thicket
Great Thicket Forest
Forest
Wodell
Kilcree Break
Strait Of Medusa
City State of Qo'Aoan
Silbury Henge
Ancient Ritual Ground
Airen
Argyle Forest
Cairngorn Lake
Nadirii
Dune Desert
Fire City
Tebes River
Fire Lake
Green Sea
Sheeonee Mountains
Bishop Closs
Triton Sea
Firenze
Fotia Sea

THE RISING

 The Rising

A LOVE IS EVERYTHING SAGA BY

KRISTEN

NEW YORK TIMES BESTSELLING AUTHOR

ASHLEY

118

THE WORK

Marian
Farm Six Miles West of the Ancient Ritual Ground
WODELL

She was beginning to feel the pain in her back becoming an ache in her entire body, which was good.

Everything else was bad.

She lay on her side on the floor in the farmstead, peering into the lifeless eyes of the dead child not five feet from her as she heard the screams of the mother coming from the other room.

The father had already been consumed.

Consumed.

The screams stopped but worse started as she heard the noises of sobs and pleas.

And then noises of something else.

What have I done? she thought.

After some time, she heard the familiar sound of the Beast's release and the crying and moaning of the woman abruptly halted.

Marian tried to move her legs, and they moved, but it made the pain in her back excruciating, thus she was forced to stop.

She needed a draught for the pain.

She needed to rest.

She'd have neither.

Where is that bloody priest? she thought.

"We must be away, Daemon," Jellan stated in a voice of genuine obsequiousness, false calm, but still managing to convey not a small amount of urgency.

"Fetch me some of the man's clothes," the Beast ordered.

"Of course," Jellan murmured.

"You don some too," the Beast went on.

"As you wish."

"Pack more, and I want my female bathed. She is dirty. I do not like her dirty. Bathe her and dress her in the woman's clothes," the Beast finished.

"It will be done," Jellan, the arsehole, the fool, the duplicitous sycophantic *cretin* assured.

She heard steps ascending stairs as she heard others approaching her.

She also heard the rain coming down in sheets and sheets.

She saw his feet, filthy with mud and grass, before he crouched and she saw his member hanging between his thighs, large even flaccid, and now tainted with blood.

Marian's mouth filled with bile.

She then felt his gentle touch as her hair was pulled away from her face.

"Do not be angry at me, my witch," he clucked.

Don't be angry?

Her mind reeled for ways to play this.

Jellan could shove his nose right up the creature's arse.

She would be who she was.

"You might have broken my back," she snapped.

"You could have a broken back, but you would still have your magic."

She lifted her eyes to his and saw what she did not see all these months she had been with him.

He was still beautiful.

In this form.

But he was not innocent and docile and misunderstood. He was not simple and easily led.

He was devious and crafty.

She had been played.

By her Beast *and* Jellan.

"You connived with him against me," she accused.

He shrugged.

She turned her eyes away.

"I needed you both," he shared. "I could not ascend without your power, and his. But when I ascended, I needed a meal. And such it was."

"Will you do me like you did that woman in the kitchens?" she demanded.

"I like you willing. You have much exuberance."

Her gaze shot to his handsome visage again.

The new definition of twofaced.

"I can hardly be of service to you in that manner if my spine is snapped," she spat.

He fell to his arse, and Marian gritted her teeth against the moan welling up her throat wrought by the pain in her body as he pulled her into his lap.

He then smoothed her hair again before he chucked her under the chin.

"I will not hurt you if you do not earn it. You are too important to me," he told her.

"Important how?" she asked.

"There is more work to be done, important work, and I need you and our friend to do it."

Marian was not feeling joyous about this news.

"What work is to be done?" she inquired.

"I fear it would be foolhardy to tell you of this at this juncture," he shared.

She opened her mouth to speak but was interrupted when Jellan appeared at their sides, stating, "I have your clothing, Daemon."

Marian glared up at the fallen priest.

He was dressed in the dead Dellish farmer's clothing.

It was too big on him.

However, as fate would have it, it would fit *Daemon* perfectly.

"Heat water for Marian's bath," Daemon commanded. "We must soothe her aches. And see if this dwelling has medicine. She is in pain."

Jellan's eyes flashed his displeasure at his service, but he said nothing against it, nodded, set the clothing on the floor beside Daemon and moved away.

"And get these bodies out of here," Daemon added.

"I am but one man, Daemon," Jellan reminded him.

Daemon twisted his head to look at the priest. "Then we shall have to find you some assistance. But for now, it's just you, and your standing there, glaring at me is not seeing to the things I've asked you to see to."

No, this Beast was not simple, docile, innocent and easily led.

Jellan bowed his head and scurried off.

Marian would have smirked, but such was the direness of the situation, she could not even take enjoyment in Jellan's subjugation.

"He, well he..." Daemon began, stroking her cheek. "Black of soul, is he."

Marian lay still in his arms, held to his body, seated in his lap, and stared at his face for she felt something had changed about him and she'd experienced enough change from him that morn, she could take no more.

"You," he whispered, still stroking her cheek. "I regret you. You were guided to your darkness."

"I don't..." She swallowed. "What do you speak of, Daemon?"

"If I did not need you for what must be done for me to succeed this time, kill the gods, claim their kingdom, I would have used you like the one in the kitchen and then put you out of your misery."

Kill the gods?

What gods?

"Daemon," she whispered, "what do you intend to do?"

"They created us; they cannot forsake us. They will learn this time."

Us? she wondered.

Who was *us*?

"But you could have veered away from the darkness. You did not," he murmured, studying her face. "This was your mistake."

Oh, *Gods.*

"Daemon—"

"Thank you for releasing me, my witch."

After saying that, he stood.

And when he did, Marian rolled out of his lap, onto the floor with a painful thud that forced a grunt from her before she emitted a groan.

She watched him walk out the front door into the rain.

Then her gaze fell again on the dead child.

The child he killed.

The child was, perhaps, four.

Her Beast.

The one she'd helped ascend.

Marian closed her eyes.

"By the gods," she whispered. "What have I done?"

119
THE NEW

The Great Coven
Silbury Henge, Argyll Forest
AIREN

In the clearing of the forest, the first flash of light came before the first of the five standing stones.

The light was crimson.

The witch Nandra of Firenze.

The next was green.

Rebecca of Wodell

Then came marine-blue.

The witch Lena of Mar-el.

The last was coral.

And there stood Melisse of the Nadirii Sisterhood.

"Why did you bring me here?" Melisse straightaway snapped, and she did this angrily. "My sisters are—"

"There is something very wrong with the veil," Rebecca stated, openly concerned. "You must have felt it."

"Nadirii and Airenzian ride on the revolutionaries *as we speak*," Melisse returned irately. "Ophelia is lost. Of course, there's something very wrong with the veil."

"It is not that," Rebecca replied.

"It cannot be the Beast," Lena murmured, and Melisse's body shot straight at her words. "His ascendency would be more...dramatic. Don't you think?"

"It's something," Rebecca said.

"It is something," Nandra agreed.

"I must get back to the mountain," Melisse decreed.

"You are of the Great Coven now," Rebecca told her quietly.

"It should be Elena, though I am glad you did not pull her here at this time, for she is needed. And I might not be at my greatest strength, but I can still string a bloody bow with an arrow and that's needed as well."

"It is you," Nandra shared.

"Right. Fine," Melisse clipped. "Now release me, I must return."

"We must hold the ceremony," Lena said.

"Later," Melisse gritted.

"You are of the Great Coven now. In this time as in any time, but particularly in *this time*, we must be at our full strength. Thus, we must hold the ceremony."

"*Later!*" Melisse shouted, turned, rushed to her standing stone, touched it...

And she was gone.

120

THE MIRACLE

King True
One Hundred and Fifteen Miles over the Border
AIREN

They were riding east, rain streaming down, hell bent for leather in order to get as many miles under their horse's hooves before the necessity came to allow the steeds, and the men, rest.

And the next day they would do it again.

But as they rode, True was assessing the distance they had to cover, and the days that would take, and coming to unhappy outcomes.

Unless the allied militia was thoughtful enough to give Elena time for mourning, and Elena elected to do that mourning on the side of a mountain three hundred miles away from Sky Bay— both of these unlikely—the ambush could happen in the Night Heights any day.

Thus, True was coming to terms with the fact that the best-case but entirely impossible scenario was that somehow, Cassius with five hundred soldiers, Elena with the same, could defeat twelve thousand militia, and True and Farah would meet them on their victorious return to Sky Bay.

However, what was far more likely to happen was that he would lead his men, and his wife, to the sight of a massacre, deep in enemy territory, in five days' time.

To be of any assistance to his friends, he needed magic he did not have.

But even knowing this, he did not turn back.

He prayed to Gennara, the Dellish goddess of magic and protector of the charmed folk, but he did this with a sinking heart.

They were too far away.

They were simply too far...

He pulled back on Majesty's reins and lifted a hand up at his side.

He heard three calls of "Halt" around him, more down the line, as Majesty skidded to a stop, the steed's body shifting sideways at the quickness of it.

"By the gods, True," Farah whispered.

By the gods, indeed.

"I did not even know—" she began but stopped when the unicorn before them dipped her proud head, and when she lifted it, she did this away from True, as if indicating she wished them to follow her.

"Go to the back of the line," True told his wife.

"Sorry?" she asked.

He tore his eyes from the magnificent creature and looked to his queen.

"Darling, go to the back of the line."

She only studied his face a moment before she nodded, wheeled her mount and started to the back.

True looked the other way, to Wallace, who also nodded, turned his steed, and followed Farah.

True then returned his attention to the unicorn.

He dipped his chin to her.

She lifted her head and shook it as her way of saying his message was received.

She then turned and started galloping away.

"*Ride!*" True bellowed.

He felt Majesty's haunches bunch before his horse burst forward after the unicorn and then True heard the thunder of hooves behind him as his men followed.

They went perhaps a quarter of a mile when, for some reason, the unicorn's body adjusted as if she was intent to clear a gate in her path when there was nothing to clear as before them lay nothing but road.

She rose into the air.

Without guiding Majesty to do so, True and his mount rose into the air after her.

He heard cries and shouts and knew the line at his back rose as well.

There were more cries and shouts when all about them faded to purple and it felt like they were soaring through the air.

But within mere instants, the purple was gone.

And their horses landed with a thud someplace else altogether.

~

King Mars
On the Journey to Airen
WODELL

MARS WAS FORCED TO ADMIT, he was rather unnerved at the knowledge that his queen was a better horseman than he.

She rode at his side, in full charge, her body bent over her steed, her head tipped back, face determined, and she did not fear the breakneck speed they were using.

Indeed, it seemed she did not even feel it.

These were his thoughts, for he refused to acknowledge the dread settling like a weight in his gut at what they might be riding to.

He'd assessed their distance from Cassius and Elena, and even if they rode their mounts to a lather each day—something he refused to do, he was a Firenz after all, and horses (and animals as a whole) were not treated thus, no matter the reason—it would take them at best, ten days to reach the Night Heights.

It was likely more akin to fourteen.

And the closest being on this earth he had to a blood brother was Cassius. They'd known each other since youth. Cass had saved him during an attack and prevented him being violated. He was the only person outside his father and mother, and Silence, who had given Mars loyalty and love that was not attached in some way to duty.

Like his father, who had died nearly six years previous, and Mars still could not reconcile it, he could not imagine this earth without Cassius on it.

But there was no way, save a miracle, he was going to get to his friend in time.

He was praying in vain, he knew, but he was still doing it to all his gods, The Muse, The Grace and The Spirit, in hopes they would come to him and bestow a miracle.

He was doing this when he pulled so sharply on Hephaestus's reins, his steed did a full circle beneath him.

"*Arresto!*" he shouted.

He heard his men come to a halt behind him.

"Faith," Silence breathed from beside him.

Mars sat astride his mount and stared at the unicorn stallion in front of them.

The stallion had his head slightly turned in order to stare Mars directly in the eye.

"*Bellezza*, go to the back of the line," Mars said.

"All right, my love," she acquiesced immediately, and he felt her leave his side, but did not look away from the unicorn.

"Kyril," he called.

"He's already following her," Basil said behind him.

Mars gave his queen time to make her way to where she needed to be.

Then he jerked up his chin.

The stallion turned and galloped away.

Mars bent over Hephaestus's neck and dug his heels in his mount's sides.

They burst forward and followed the unicorn, and he heard the thunder of horses' hooves behind him as they did the same.

They could not have gone half a mile before the stallion curled his front legs and pushed off his back ones, leaping in the air in order to clear nothing.

Hephaestus followed suit.

There were noises of alarm behind him that Mars ignored, for all about them turned purple.

And then the purple was gone as they landed in wet turf in the middle of a blinding rain.

121

THE BATTLE OF THE HEIGHTS

Prince Cassius
Valley at the Base of the Night Heights Mountain Range
AIREN

They had several advantages.

The first was the element of surprise.

It was not a complete surprise. A thousand horses galloping down the side of the mountain made noise.

But when they arrived, the enemy had not had nearly the time they would need to prepare to face what they were about to face.

Not to mention, a thousand horses galloping down the side of a mountain, the sight that was, the noise it made, when you knew the men and women on those horses were riding in with the intent to do you harm, it was intimidating.

As Cassius planned.

The second advantage was a different kind of surprise, one for Cassius.

They had not fortified their position. They'd dug no trenches nor erected any barricades.

The way was clear, when he and Elena's troops arrived, for them to ride right into, and through, their encampment.

This was a boon he had not expected.

And they needed every boon they could get.

The third advantage was the Nadirii archers.

Nadirii archers did not let fly an arrow unless they'd taken aim. Their target might move in the interim, and thus be missed. But they did not waste ammunition on a barrage intent to daunt, not do damage.

Thus, when the front line, including Cassius, Elena, Macrinus, Jasmine, Serena, Hera, Rosehana, and their following line, including Antonius, Nero, and Cass and Elena's best cavalrymen got close, they bent low over the necks of their mounts.

And the Nadirii archers behind them took aim and let fly.

Thus, as the first line of the allied militia that had scrambled to meet them were on foot, and they had not had time to fully don any armor, they therefore collapsed as a whole before Cassius and Elena were within fifty feet of them.

It was the forward cavalry's job, as they rode over and through the fallen, to deliver damage with their swords and their horses' hooves that would make certain they did not get up.

This, they did.

The next advantage circled back to the first three. It was one Cassius had hoped to gain with this strategy and was pleased he did.

For it was impossible to miss the fact that a great number of the militia decided on the spot—with a surprise, full-frontal attack and legendary Nadirii archers in play—maybe they'd made the wrong decision on whose side they wished to take.

Deserters were racing into the forest beyond in droves.

In the thick of it, Cassius could not begin to deduce how many had fled.

He just knew it wasn't enough.

But at least it was something.

A further advantage was that they were all on horseback.

Cassius could cut through three men before they got close enough to do damage to him or Caelus.

Thus, this was how Cassius proceeded, with Elena doing the same at his side, cutting a swath of wounded or dead militia alongside their comrades who were doing the same.

And the last advantage to their preliminary attack was that, when Gallienus was king, the landed gentry were given the option of whether or not to send their militias if the king called them to service.

Some did.

Most did not.

Those who did not used their militias to keep the peace in their fiefdoms, this mostly taking the form of intimidating and bullying recalcitrant vassals, mutinous peasants or upstart merchants and freemen.

As such, the soldiers they were fighting were not well trained and had little to no experience.

Very different from the Airenzian and Nadirii warriors who they now faced.

But this was not all there was to that particular advantage, for some of these men weren't militia at all.

Just dissenters to Cassius's vision of the future of Airen.

So, they had no experience and very little training, if any.

And they realized, quickly, and for some it was the last thing on this earth they learned, how important it was to be trained to face battle.

The disadvantages, Cass noted immediately, started with the fact that the militias had trolls.

Trolls had skin tough as leather, bones strong as steel, and the worst, they felt very little pain.

They were not impossible to kill.

They were just difficult to kill and even more difficult to maim, for if a troll sustained an injury, even a mortal one, he would just keep fighting until he dropped.

The other disadvantage to Cass and Elena's troops was that there were just so fucking bloody many of them.

The trolls had been activated, and he knew some of his people were being pulled from their horses, when Cassius's next planned advantage was put to use.

As previously decided, when Nadirii and Airenzian began to get unhorsed, the Zees appeared as they were very good at doing—from what seemed to be thin air.

They attacked at the left flank.

And by "the Zees," it was not only the Patras.

Silvanus had talked six tribes into joining him and Fern's army with the intent to cause havoc in Airen. More land for them to roam, if it was made safe for them to do so.

In other words, more people for them to divest of their belongings in a charming way that was still thievery.

The tribes didn't need much talking to agree, Silvanus had shared.

They enjoyed causing havoc.

And thievery.

Which meant a good two hundred and fifty men were entering the fray to the left.

And it had long since been agreed by all realms that magic could not be used in battle.

This meant there had been much discussion the previous eve if this agreement amongst realms held true in a civil unrest.

In other words, would he and Elena allow the Nadirii to use battle magic.

In the end, Cassius and Elena had agreed to uphold the accord that banned magic in battle.

It was banned for a reason, as it offered such an unfair advantage, those that wielded it could easily use that power in a way that would get out of hand.

Silvanus had explained, for his part, it didn't matter.

He'd do what he wished for the Zees felt bound to no realm.

They were sovereign to themselves, each tribe.

Cassius did not give him permission, for Silvanus would not care. He did not attempt to talk him out of it, for Silvanus would not care about that either.

And thus, bright bursts of red or blue could be seen exploding to the left as the Zees' witches used their magic to freeze militia soldiers so their men could do to them as they wished.

This practice was distasteful to the point of repugnant to Cassius.

But the alternative in the now was him, Elena, and nearly everyone he loved ending that day dead.

Therefore, he'd find a way to live with it.

Eventually the onslaught became too intense and Elena tossed her leg over Diana's neck, sending her mount careening out of the melee, Cassius knew, so the steed would get to safety.

When she did, Cassius followed suit.

They fought back to back, and he determined, if a miracle happened and they survived that day, he'd encourage her to take up using a shield, for she fought with sword and dagger, whereas he fought with sword and shield.

He did not like her not having a shield when he was not in the position to act as such for her.

He did not like her in battle at all.

But, gods damn, if she wasn't good at it.

Indeed, they were an exceptional team, as he'd found when they'd beat back the siege.

She had his back and weaker left flank.

He had hers.

In the siege, they'd been unbeatable. Unstoppable.

But they'd had superior numbers in the siege.

That was not the same in the now.

However, in the now, it helped that Serena had set herself up as Elena's personal guard, and by default, his.

The enemy was coming at them from every quarter, he and Elena easily a focal point, making it clear they were the primary targets.

But Serena refused to be unhorsed, refused to lose her advantage. She brought down trolls with a speed and ease that was astonishing, and between the three of them, the fallen were piling up to the point Cass was slipping on their blood, tripping over their bodies or simply skidding on the mud caused by the rain.

It was when they were eventually overcome, Serena was dragged from her horse, and Elena let out an enraged, agonized shriek, that Cassius knew three things.

The first, he had to engage their final advantage, their last resort.

And second, he should have called in the dragons. He should have made the decision to extinguish the lives of twelve thousand of his countrymen to save his love, to save his friends, to save his life and to save his realm.

And last, he and the woman he loved were going to die on that field.

He could not have stopped her being there.

No, he never could have stopped her from raising her sword to protect his reign and free the women of Airen.

He also could not stop their daughters from facing more loss.

But if he had to die, he would choose doing it fighting for right with his woman at his back.

The rage, however, still consumed him as he thrust up his sword, roaring his wrath.

At this signal, he heard the feminine shouts as Fern's army invaded at the right flank just as a barrage of arrows screamed into the fray from Fern's archers that had positioned themselves high in the trees to their right.

They, too, were untrained, if not, Silvanus had shared, entirely unskilled.

As best they could, they'd been preparing for just this day.

Regardless, they only had such weapons as they could steal from the homes they'd left or their raid on Kilcree Break.

They had utterly no armor.

Their only advantage was determination and the burning rage of centuries of oppression.

Cassius feared they'd be cut down in little time, and those who survived, if the battle was lost, would wish they'd died on the field with what would befall them after.

This being why he held them to the last.

But in the now, they caused havoc, alarm and redirected attention.

And all of this was sorely needed.

He thrust and deflected, with sword and shield, the blood of his enemy and the rain from the skies dripping down his face and his leathers, as he bellowed to Elena, "*Use your magic!*"

Serena slipped and fell while he was shouting.

Elena dashed toward her sister, screaming through a backhand swipe she delivered that tore open an enemy soldier's shoulder and half his chest before the man could lower his sword onto her fallen sister.

Serena caught another blade aimed at Elena on her way up.

Gods, the enemy was so close, there were so many of them, he could feel their fucking *breath*.

"*Gods dammit, Ellie!*" he thundered, without Elena at his back, nearly taking a slice to the stomach before he got his shield in front of it. "*Use your bloody magic!*"

He did not know if she did or she didn't when, over the din of shouts, grunts, steel striking steel, cries of pain, moans of agony, he heard the rumble of hooves.

Many, many hooves.

And then suddenly Serena was joined by Chu, who immediately and clearly cast himself as her personal guard, and his cold, methodical, exceptionally skilled technique guided them out of a pit of bodies and into a freer battlefield which afforded better footing.

They were there naught but seconds before he heard the whoosh of an explosion of fire to the south, this accompanied by screams of agony and shouts of surprise as flames soared and men caught fire.

By the gods, that was...

Another hissing explosion.

Flaming arrows with attached bags of fuel was a tactic of the...

There was another.

Firenz.

Then came a heavy bombardment of arrows coming from the west but dropping from the sky over the south, an area covered entirely by the enemy waiting to take their turns.

Out of the side of his eye, Cassius noted these arrows had green fletchings.

Dellish.

Then another explosion.

And more arrows.

The din of clashing steel seemed to rise in a sound that could only mean more men entering the fray.

The field started to thin as the enemy started to bolt.

And then thin more.

Nero rode by them, striking out with his sword and circling.

"They're fleeing!" he shouted.

"Give chase! I want prisoners!" Cassius shouted back.

Nero wheeled his horse around and tore away.

Suddenly, a flash of white raced by them, around, and then Cassius saw Sky, his bonded male unicorn rise up to his hind hooves and strike the air with his front, purple sparks flying from his hooves when he did.

"*Nadirii!*" Elena shrieked, raising her sword straight into the air.

"*Nadirii!*" Serena screeched, doing the same with her weapon.

"*Nadirii!*" he heard all around.

Sky's front hooves fell to the ground and a purple ring shot out from where Cassius and Elena stood, this felling all of the enemy for ten feet about them.

The rest beyond who witnessed this turned instantly and *bolted.*

Cassius remained in position, knees loose, shield and sword up, his back to his woman, breaths coming short and fast, the rain he had not felt since it started making its presence known.

Death and blood and carnage littered the landscape.

And then Mars was there on Hephaestus, pulling his reins to the left, Hephaestus's rump going to the right as he stopped. After he arrived, not a second later, True's Majesty had to lift both front hooves half a foot from the earth when he stopped.

Their swords were bloody as were their horses' legs up to their chests.

"*Take your knees!*" Macrinus roared, orbiting his mount around the soldiers that had been felled, but were now pushing up. "*Drop your blades and take your fucking knees!*" Mac thundered, swinging his sword and severing the head from the body of one who did not comply quickly enough.

At that, Cassius felt his heart jolt, for that kind of viciousness was not in Mac.

The others instantly did as Mac had ordered.

Cass looked up to Mars, who was regarding Mac, before he felt Cassius's eyes and turned his gaze Cass's way.

He then looked to True, who was recovering from a wince aimed in Mac's direction, before he turned to Cass.

"It seems Ophelia gave you a parting gift, no?" Mars asked, tipping his head to the unicorn Sky.

"Sky and Star have been Ellie's and mine for some time," Cassius told him, focusing on this inane conversation rather than what lay all around, how the hell his friends had made it to them in time, what losses they'd suffered and what was next.

"Unicorns have great magic, beyond anything on this earth, including the Mer, but they can't do that," Serena declared.

All looked to her.

"If they could fell all about, they would not be threatened by man's greed for their magic and thus, they would be able to roam free," she said, "That was their magic, as instilled by a Nadirii yell, as given by a powerful witch. Our mother."

Cassius finally lowered his sword.

Elena did the same at his side.

Another Nadirii yell started about them, growing stronger and stronger.

This one not calling magic.

This one calling victory.

Gods.

They'd made it.

They'd survived.

She'd survived.

Cass sheathed his weapon and searched for Ellie's hand.

He found it.

And he held tight.

122

THE LOSSES

King Mars
Base of the Night Heights Mountain Range
AIREN

Mars walked with Silence held close to his side, Kyril and Basil at their backs, through the winding encampment that had struck up after the battle.

Silence was as her name and had been much the same since he'd come to her, drenched from the rain and bloodied from the battle.

Since, he had kept her from the slaughter of the battlefield that, for the last hours, his, True's and Cassius's men had been directing militia prisoners to clear.

It was time to report.

But Mars needed no report.

He had seen that battlefield. The moment he and his men had ridden up to it, his gut had dropped thinking that there was no possibility Cass and Elena could be surviving that bloodbath.

In other words, he already knew the losses were grave.

And until they had thorough assessments of the lay of the land about them, he had his sword at his back, his Trusted close, and his wife at his bloody side.

"Mars," he barked at the flaps of True and Farah's tent.

Then, without invitation, he pushed through them, drawing Silence in beside him.

"Mars," Farah said softly, rushing to him.

"Silence," True greeted, striding to her.

He let his queen go long enough for True to embrace her, Farah to embrace him, and then Farah to embrace Silence.

Then he pulled her close again.

He was not surprised when he saw True do the same to Farah.

"Did you call for Cassius and Elena?" Mars asked True.

"Yes," True answered.

"Would you like wine?" Farah offered.

"Please," Silence accepted and began to move, but Mars's hold strengthened.

He felt her eyes, so he looked down at her.

"I'll be right here, my love," she said softly.

He drew in breath.

And let her go.

"I'm assuming you were visited by a unicorn," True noted as the women bustled to a trunk.

Mars jerked his head up in assent. "You?"

"Yes."

"Thank the gods," Mars muttered.

"Yes," True agreed. "Even the damned caravans at the back that weren't keeping up came through whatever the hell it was we leaped through."

"Same," Mars grunted.

"Did you have purple?" True inquired.

"Yes," Mars told him. "Magic is back in Airen, this is certain."

"Of course," True replied. "The Nadirii are here."

Without a call, the tent flaps opened and both men turned to them, hands going to the hilts of their swords.

But they relaxed when Cassius walked in.

Without Elena.

"Where's Elena?" True asked.

"She is tending the wounded," Cassius answered tightly.

As he took in his friend's expression, Mars felt his wife come to him and press to his side.

For undoubtedly, she'd seen it too.

He slid his arm along her shoulders, and she called gently, "Cassius?"

"Jasmine was slain," Cassius said tersely, the words rough and edged with pain.

The reason Mac was uncontrolled at battle's end.

"Gods, Cassius," True murmured.

"Rosehana as well," Cass grunted.

Silence pressed closer to him as Farah emitted a pained mew.

"Elena's mother was just lost. Elena is...she is..." Cass began. They all gave him time, but he shook his head sharply and declared, "Antonius will not recover. He's in great pain, and it is unknown when that pain will be over if the end is to come naturally. He's asked for the soldier's poison."

"Fuck," Mars bit.

"I cannot brief you. I have agreed to give it to him, and he is taking time with our gods. I must see to Tone, and then find my woman," Cass finished.

Silence gave Mars a demanding squeeze.

He looked down to her.

"True will look after me," she whispered.

True would die for her.

Thus, Mars acquiesced to her demand.

"Do you want company?" he offered.

Cass barely met his eyes but that did not mean Mars missed the pain dwelling close to the surface of his friend's.

"Suit yourself," he muttered, bowed shortly to the women, then disappeared between the flaps.

Mars pressed a brief kiss to his wife's mouth and followed him, not even bothering to gesture to Basil and Kyril as he left the tent.

They stayed with their queen.

Cassius was walking fast, and thus it was a good thing Mars's legs were as long as his.

He caught him up and asked, "Mac?"

"He's torn apart," Cass grunted. "There was love between them."

"Yes," Mars murmured.

"She took a blade for him."

Fuck.

"Cass—"

Mars said no more, for Cassius stopped, turned to him, and Mars nearly reared away from the depths of black that had become his eyes.

Cass's eyes were normally sky blue.

When he felt emotion, the night sky could be seen in them instead.

Now, there was naught of any of that.

There wasn't even any white.

Just black.

Mars had never seen that, and he'd known Cassius to feel great emotion.

And he did not know what to make of it, except what he knew would not ever happen, even before he'd seen his friend's eyes as such.

He would not ever make Cassius Laird his enemy.

"My reign will be safe. My land will be free for all, Mars. They will not die in vain."

"They already haven't, my brother," Mars said quietly.

"She took a blade for him," Cass bit.

"My friend—"

"Ellie's sister took a blade for *my brother*."

"It is war."

"It is *obscene*," Cassius retorted. "For what? For what do they fight, Mars? How can you even begin to form the fucking *thought* that you'd take up arms to stop another from being free? Much less *kill* for it?"

"I cannot answer that, for I have not had that thought, Cass."

Cassius looked to the ground and wrapped his hand around the back of his neck.

Mars took them to the urgency at hand.

"It is certain he will not recover?" he asked carefully.

Cassius dropped his hand and looked to him. "Liam says it's impossible. He left some of his intestines and most of his lifeblood on the battleground. He could barely move his mouth to ask for the poison."

"Then do not delay a moment longer in giving it to him."

Cassius didn't.

Not even to nod his head.

He turned on his boot and jogged to a line of tents set up at the base of the mountains where the wounded were being tended.

Mars ran with him.

They went through the flaps of one and were confronted with a number of lanterns turned high, a deathbed, a dead man in it, and his two friends standing vigil.

"Did you give it to him in my absence?" Cassius asked Nero.

"No, he slipped away on his own," Nero replied.

"I should have given it to him," Cassius muttered, looking down to Antonius. "I should have ended his pain."

"He lasted perhaps five minutes after you'd left, Cass," Nero said, "Thus gaining the last thing on this earth he might want, not forcing you to administer the poison. Years ago, he told me he'd never ask that of you, no matter how bad it was. He did not know then how bad it could get, but I know, if it had to end like this, he would be glad the last thing he did, he did on his own."

Mars did not doubt this and suspected no one in that tent did, for all of them would feel the same.

Before anyone could say a word, Mac announced, "I'm taking Jasmine to The Enchantments."

"I'm sure that's a good idea. Let me speak to Ellie about it," Cassius murmured.

"I wasn't asking," Mac clipped. "I was telling you I'm taking Jazz to The Enchantments. We discussed it last night. And she said, if she was where she is now, she wanted to become one with the veil in The Enchantments. So that's where I'm taking her."

"And I'm saying, please do not leave until I can talk to Ellie so she can make her decision of whether or not she can go with you," Cassius returned quietly.

Mac scowled at his friend before he looked to his boots.

A moment was given before Cass called, "Mac."

Macrinus's head came up, and he seethed, "I want to kill something."

"I know," Cassius whispered.

"I couldn't even stop fighting so I could pull her fucking body from that pit."

"I'm sorry," Cassius said, his words heavy with the weight of the decision to attack that morning.

"You didn't gut her," Mac spat.

"It was my—"

"She'd fucking kick you in the arse if she heard you speak the words you're about to say. She was a fighter. She believed in what we did today. And now it's time to take her home."

Cassius fell silent.

"Before she was lost, she was gods-damned magnificent," Mac declared.

Nero moved closer to him, lifted a hand and wrapped it around the back of Mac's neck.

But Mac couldn't tear his gaze from Cassius.

"From the second I laid eyes on her, she was gods-damned magnificent."

"She was," Cassius agreed.

Mac's voice was much different, coarse with emotion when he asked, "Is this what you've been feeling all these years?"

"Yes," Cass answered.

"How do you...how did you...*breathe*?"

That was when Cass moved.

So did Nero.

Mars lifted his chin to Nero as he came his way and they began to leave the tent.

Cassius went right to Mac and pulled him into his embrace, cupping the back of Mac's head and shoving his face in Cass's shoulder.

Mars saw Mac's shoulders wrench once, and then he walked out.

They took several steps away and stopped.

They said nothing to each other.

It was Nero who first spoke.

"They should have bitched to their fires and got drunk in their taverns and picked fights with each other."

"Mm," Mars hummed in agreement.

"He has never engaged, not once," Nero said.

Mars turned his gaze from staring unseeing down an alleyway formed by tents to Nero.

"Not with this realm, not with his father, not with his brother, not in any battle he was forced to wage," Nero went on.

Mars held his eyes.

"In my knowing of him, I've seen him engage with four things. His wife, his daughter, his lieutenants, and Elena," Nero stated.

Mars said nothing.

"They should have bitched...to their fires...and got drunk...in their taverns," Nero said through his teeth. "For Cassius Laird unleashed about something he gives a shite about, they will curse for eternity their decision to force his hand this day."

Mars continued to say nothing, for he knew this to be true.

"Before," Nero carried on, "he was fighting for what was right, but mostly he was fighting because Ellie believed in it, and he'd shift the stars for her. But now..."

Mars nodded.

Nero continued to release it.

"Otho was his brother. Tone was his brother. And she was a pain in his arse, but he loved Jazz. But that is not what makes Cassius. For Cassius, it is not about what he wants or needs or feels. Thus, it is not that her loss hurt him. It is that her loss hurt Mac. It hurt Elena. And they will know how he feels about that."

"You've lost today as well, Nero," Mars noted cautiously.

"They're going to know how I feel about it, too," Nero bit, turned and strode away.

Mars watched him go even after he disappeared from sight.

Not long later, Cassius came out of the tent, but Mac did not.

"I am uncertain, *mio amico*, it is good you leave him in there with Tone," Mars noted.

"He asked to stay. He will not be at Tone's burial. He wants to take Jazz soon. He will wait for the brothers who shroud so I can go about my business and talk to Ellie. And then he will seek Hera and prepare to transport Jasmine and Rose."

Mars nodded and fell in step with Cassius as his friend began to move down the line of tents.

He'd forgotten about their shrouding ritual. How only some, who had been trained in the proper procedure of soaking the dressings in herbal liniments, before cleansing and wrapping their dead in them as soon as possible after death, could prepare a body for burial.

It was a process of caring that Mars always found surprising, considering Airen was not known as a caring land.

He felt, if there was care, it should be shown while the one you cared about was breathing.

He also felt it was somehow apropos, that the Airenzian only showed this after death.

"The Nadirii lost twenty-two, eighty injured. Thirty-eight Airenzian fell, fifty-four injured. The Zees are still assessing amongst tribes. Fern's women—"

"You do not have to report to me now," Mars interrupted him, though he did it thinking something Cassius never would.

From what he had seen, that number of losses for his side in that conflict were actually very low.

"I'm abolishing our feudal system," Cass decreed of a sudden.

Mars was so stunned at his words, he stopped them walking.

"Lords stripped of titles and lands," Cassius went on. "Castles will be claimed by the Regency and given to the citizens of my kingdom. They will be made into schools, hospitals, orphanages or colleges at my behest. Peasants will be awarded ownership of the land they work. If you eat, you earn the food you put in your mouth. You don't take it off another's back. If you own a home or a plot, you pay for that too. You don't languish in the spoils your forebears earned taking up arms for a king four hundred bloody years ago."

Nero was right.

They would regret, for generations to come—indeed until what once was, was lost to history—they would regret causing anyone Cassius loved to feel pain.

"This is great change, Cass," Mars murmured.

"This will be, Mars. They had to pay women a decent wage, keep their bloody hands off them, and let them go to school. None of this is asking much, except for them to be decent human beings. They will see that decision would have been the wise one to take. But they will see it too late."

"You will have our swords," Mars told him something he already knew.

And because it was, Cassius did not address that.

He asked, "How did you get here so quickly?"

"We had help from your unicorn, Sky. And True had help from his mare."

"Star," Cass said.

Mars beat back a smile, for this name was unsurprising, as named by Cass.

"Star," he said.

"And they...what?" Cassius queried.

"They took us through an ether, Cass. I do not know. I was in bloody Wodell this morning, and now I am here."

Cassius had no response to that, indeed, it seemed to take him far away, and Mars let him go there until he felt it necessary to bring him back.

"You did not use Frey's dragons," he noted.

"I did not wish to incinerate twelve thousand men I did not know, some who may be confused, or easily persuaded, or coerced, or caught up in the frenzy at the beginning of dissension, so they know not, truly, what they are fighting for."

Mars would not have made the same decision, but he did not share that. Cass's heart had always been softer than Mars's, even if he was adept at hiding it was.

"And now?" Mars asked.

"Now, I need to speak with my woman and see to her in her grief. Now, I need to assess the full losses. Now, I need to interrogate prisoners. I've sent so many gods-damned birds, it's a wonder the sky isn't black with ravens, for I need to know what's happening elsewhere in my realm."

"My men will be riding up from the border as soon as they receive my summons," Mars told him. "And we did not speak of it, but I would wager True is doing the same."

Cassius nodded his gratitude before he murmured, "I need an example."

Mars knew precisely what he was thinking.

"Do you know of a primary instigator?" he inquired.

Cassius focused fully on him. "I don't know if I care if they are primary. Every lord whose militia is here today will lose his stronghold to dragon fire."

Mars did not smile, even if he wished to, before he shared, "This would be my decision."

Cassius's face lost some of its intensity, though he did not smile. "I do not know if that heartens me or frightens me."

He clapped a hand on his friend's shoulder and didn't remove it.

"This day will be heralded in the tomes of history, that you prevailed against those odds. And I know that means nothing now, but it is the beginning of the end of a blight on our continent. Thus, there will come a time, I hope, my brother, that you and yours can take heart in that."

Cassius inclined his head.

Mars gave his shoulder a squeeze before he released him and said, "I'm also sending men to assist in securing the borders of The Enchantments."

"This is wise. I've no doubt this will be a target for them, and I've sent a raven to do the same."

"I will report to True. You go to Elena."

Cassius nodded again and started to turn to leave, but he stopped.

"Did you sustain losses?"

Mars shook his head. "A few injuries, but no losses."

"Thank the gods," Cassius murmured, and moved away.

Mars watched him go, and as he did, he thought for a moment of Antonius.

He then thought of Jasmine.

Bear them close to your bosom, he asked of his Muse god.

He then moved through the camp in order to reclaim his wife.

123

THE REJECTION

Princess Serena
Base of the Night Heights Mountain Range
Airen

"I will guard them. You rest. Your journey will be long," Serena said to Hera and Macrinus, both of whom were standing close to the bodies lying on the earth under the moonlight, shrouded in coral and purple cloth, covered with the dusting of pinecones and needles Serena had placed on them in order to surround them with symbols of nature.

"And you?" Hera asked.

"I may ride," Serena told her. "I do not know. I am at the calling of my queen."

Hera studied her.

"I will guard her, Hera," Serena said low. "I will guard them both."

Hera continued to study her.

Serena stood still and allowed it.

After a time, the Nadirii warrior turned to Macrinus.

"Let us go, my friend, and prepare for our journey," Hera urged quietly.

Macrinus didn't move, not his body or his gaze from the shrouded figure on the ground.

"Mac," Hera whispered.

"I find I cannot leave her," Macrinus whispered back.

"You need to pack your things, and hers, so you can be prepared to take care of her," Hera told him and reached out to touch his forearm, finishing, "So you will be ready to take her home."

"She should be here, and I should be there," he replied, dipping his head toward his woman's body.

"And if she were standing by my side, and you in her place, she would be saying the same thing," Hera returned.

Slowly, Macrinus turned his gaze Hera's way.

"There is no more honorable death for a soldier than to die protecting the one you love," Hera said softly.

"You have lost as much as me this day, how do you—?" Macrinus began.

"We will lie in each other's arms tonight and remember them. I will weep and you will absorb my tears. That is how. But this cannot happen until we ready their things. So please, Mac, come away. I need you."

Serena saw that instantly captured him.

He twisted his arm to catch Hera's hand

Hera closed her fingers around his.

And without a glance at Serena, connected in grief, they moved away.

"We will guard them," Gal called, coming out of the shadows of the forest beyond, moving with Brix toward Serena.

"I have promised," Serena told them, then bid, "Find somewhere and rest."

"We spent our day infiltrating enemy tents, disabling ammunition and cataloguing the names of treacherous gentry," Brix stated, coming to a halt and crossing his arms on his chest. "You spent your day in more onerous pursuits. You need sleep. Tomorrow will be busy."

"I have promised," Serena returned. "I will find rest when it is time to find it."

Her gnome friends were silent for some time before Gal broke it by saying cautiously, "You don't have to make up for the reputation you earned all in one day, my warrior."

"I know how I would feel if it was you lying there, Gal," she retorted, indicating Jasmine's shrouded form with her hand. "And I've known you but weeks. My sister lost her *true* sister this day. And I will *guard her*."

"There is naught around to harm her," Brix said gently.

"She is a lieutenant to the queen, fallen in battle. She receives this honor in her death, Brix. Now go. Find Cassius. Report what you learned this day. And then find somewhere to sleep."

"We've already reported," Gal told her.

"Right, then, just find somewhere to sleep."

Her friends studied her in an entirely different manner than Hera had done.

They eventually looked to each other before they made their decision.

Gal came forward and touched her hand before he moved away.

"You'll be all right," Brix said, then he followed his friend.

Serena watched them go before she assumed a stance of parade rest, standing guard over her queen's fallen sisters.

And although she found it difficult, she did not move a muscle when she saw his shadowy form approach, his visage blackened by the fires burning beyond him in a field covered in tents that had earlier been covered in bodies.

His features came into focus by the light of the moon when he got close to her and stopped.

"Little mouse," he said tenderly.

"Trusted," she returned neutrally.

She watched his face absorb the word she used to refer to him, and how much he did not like it.

And she also watched him move beyond that.

"The enemy is in full retreat," he shared.

"I know this," she replied.

He looked to the ground then to her.

"Nadirii custom when the queen's lieutenant has fallen," she explained. "She has a guard until she joins the veil."

"Ah," he murmured then shifted. "I will keep you company."

"I rather you did not."

She watched his frame string tight.

"Serena—"

"You need to see to your king."

"I need to see to you."

"I have no need for that."

"You do not speak truth."

You would know all about that, she thought.

"I am seeing to my duty and it is the duty of a Nadirii," she said instead. "You are not welcome to join it, Trusted."

"It would seem your sister and you have made amends," he noted.

That is none of your business, she thought.

"We are at war," she pointed out.

"It was more than you in battle I witnessed before I made it to you."

She shrugged.

He moved closer.

Her hand shifted to her dagger.

He did not miss her movement, thus he stopped.

"I am a Nadirii guard to Nadirii fallen, Trusted," she said low. "Respect that."

"We must talk. Not in the now. Later. When your duty is done."

"There's naught to say."

"There's much to say," he disagreed.

"It has been said."

"I was disappointed, my princess," he whispered. "I spoke rashly and acted the same."

"I was not referring to what *you* said," she retorted.

His head twitched before he asked, "And to what were you referring?"

"This is not respect, speaking of this over my fallen sisters."

"I understand that. Though I cannot imagine, if they were breathing, they would want their deaths to stand between two lovers."

"We were never lovers."

His head tilted to the side. "I'm sorry. Are you a different Serena than the one who moaned under me as we joined?"

"You fucked me, and you played with me, and apparently, you did both of those at the same time in various ways."

"Fuck," he whispered, coming swiftly to understand her meaning.

"Yes," she agreed.

He shifted as if to get closer, his hand rising as if to touch her, murmuring, "Serena—"

Her fingers curled around her dagger. "I swear to the goddess, Trusted, if you touch me, I'll take your hand and gladly accept whatever punishment my queen and your king choose to dole on me after doing it. We are done. As you said, we've had our end. You didn't allow me to reply in that time, so I shall do it now." She paused and finished, "Agreed."

"You must know," he said softly, "it started one way and became another."

"I know only two things. I got what I deserved, and my lesson was learned."

Chu took a step back, looked to the bodies, then to her.

"I will give you the night," he decreed. "We'll talk on the morrow."

"I will be at my queen's disposal tomorrow."

"And I have faith she will be disposed to make you speak with me."

"You would be wrong," she retorted. "She was much relieved you'd found yourself rid of me. She was not supportive of her man's scheme, even if she enjoys its success. Then again, that is my sister. Her first thought is always to heal, not harm."

"Then she will surely feel differently when she understands what grew between us," he returned.

"A seed needs fertile soil to grow, Trusted. You are most wise. Don't be foolish now. I will admit, that seed was planted. But without nurture, in the wasteland of me, it withered to nothing."

Chu shook his head. "I don't believe that. And I also do not like to hear you speak of yourself in that manner."

"And I'll repeat, don't be foolish now. You know better."

"I know today you fought like a sister protecting her sister, and I do not refer to the Nadirii."

"The earth can do without me. It cannot do without Elena."

"That is a sister speaking about her sister," Chu said gently.

"That is a woman who knows her place in this world, and her value to it. You taught me that."

His entire frame jerked at her words.

"Serena—" he growled.

"Please go."

"Little mouse," he murmured.

"You do more harm than good, remaining here, Trusted."

They locked eyes.

In the end, it was unsurprising when he dipped his chin to her and took a step back before he turned and began to walk away.

"Trusted," she called.

She heard the annoyed rumble come from his chest through his mouth when she called him thus again, this as he turned back to her.

"You were right," she told him.

"About what?" he asked.

"She was alive."

"Sorry?" he queried.

"The lady of the chalk. She was alive, falling through nothing, holding her dead lover."

With her hand, Serena indicated the bodies lying at her side and then she swept her hand out to indicate wherever Macrinus and Hera were.

But she stopped herself before she indicated him.

"A life of yearning, and then heartbreak," she finished. "And forever, they will hold them in their arms and have nothing."

"I was wrong," he returned.

"Look at them," she retorted, again indicating her fallen sisters. "You were right."

"I was wrong for I said those words to you, having never been falling in love before."

Serena felt her body turn to stone.

"Now I have," he went on. "And they have. And they will get past their despair and not one time for the rest of their lives will they consider what they shared with their lovers nothing."

And as usual, Chu got in the last word.

Before he walked away.

124

THE GRIEVING

Queen Elena
Base of the Night Heights Mountain Range
AIREN

I slapped back the flap, and for once, felt no succor upon entering Cass's spartan tent.

It held a wide but thin pallet that sat atop a frame that was but half a foot off the ground, that frame covered in black hides to insulate the bed from the cold earth, the mattress covered in the same hides and nothing else. Not even a single, slender pillow.

Two trunks, one his, one filled with supplies.

And a small, folding table, now unfolded and fixed, covered in parchments, where Cassius was standing right then, reading one of the parchments.

No, this no-frills accommodation that was so very Cass (before me), and thus always settled me upon entering, did not lighten the load borne by my heart.

His eyes came to me, and I felt no succor from the gentleness of his gaze either.

But I moved direct to him.

"Ellie," he whispered, dropping the parchment on the table.

And no relief from his deep voice saying my name.

I rounded him, to the front.

His hands came up, but before they could touch me, I pushed him.

Hard.

He stepped back on a foot.

I pushed him again.

Harder.

He stepped back again, and I followed him.

"Darling," he murmured.

I pushed him again and again, following him, until I got him where I wanted, standing at the foot of the bed.

"Elena."

Holding his gaze, remaining silent, I went for the buttons on his trousers.

He lifted his hands and cupped my jaw in both.

"My love," he said.

That was right.

I was his love.

He loved me.

This beautiful man...

This loving father...

This loyal friend...

This fearsome warrior...

He loved me.

He loved me, loved me, loved me.

I reached into his leathers and pulled out his cock.

He grunted and the pads of his fingers dug into my skin, but he did not move away.

I stared into his eyes as I stroked him until he was hard, and only then did I let him go. I did this in order to plant my hands in his wide chest again and shove.

He went down on his arse on the pallet.

He was barely settled there, knees high, when I climbed on.

Still gazing deep into his eyes, I reached between my legs, shoved aside the body stocking, grasped his shaft in my other hand, positioned him, and bore down.

He growled, his fingers curling around the cheeks of my arse.

I whimpered, gripped his neck in both hands...

And I rode.

I took him, and retreated, took him, and retreated, bounding on his cock, gazing into his eyes, not caressing, not kissing, not speaking.

And he let me.

Let me handle him.

Let me take him.

Let me use him.

On these thoughts, the tears came.

"Ellie," he whispered, his tone ragged, his hands gliding up my spine.

I moved one of mine away so I could shove my face in his neck.

There, I said, "I need you to climax."

One of his hands instantly changed direction, but as it came around the front, I caught it by the wrist and put it back to my arse.

"No." I lifted my head to look at him. "You. Just you."

"I can't."

He couldn't.

Goddess, I knew he couldn't.

He couldn't take from me without giving.

"Please," I begged, squeezing him with the walls of my sex, watching him bare his teeth at the feel, the sight of that making me automatically squeeze again, moving faster atop him.

His voice was thick when he replied, "I'll try."

I clasped his jaw in my hands and rode him, my face close, our noses brushing, our breaths mingling, our gazes locked.

"Darling," he gritted, his fingers digging into my arse.

"Yes, Cass," I breathed.

"*Elena*," he groaned, taking over, both hands moving to my hips, slamming me into his cock.

His grunt drove up inside of me as he released my arse to grasp my throat and hold me where I was as his neck arched back, and he jetted inside me.

I watched it move over his handsome face, feeling his powerful body spasm under mine, and when his head fell forward, his forehead resting on my shoulder, I pressed my face again into his neck.

And my body bucked with my sob.

Both his arms closed tight around me.

"Lamb," he whispered, making as if to move.

But I clamped tight on him with everything I had and cried, "No!" into his skin.

"All right, my love. All right," he soothed, settling in but doing it tightening his hold on me.

I wept into his neck for some time before the words bubbled out of me.

"It's like she's been gone for years, and I've been grieving her every second that has passed."

"I know."

"The last time I saw her, we were charging down the mountain. I turned my head, feeling her attention, and she grinned at me."

This, "My love," was guttural.

"How do I tell Dora?"

His arms grew ever tighter around me as he fell to his back, keeping us connected, but doing it letting me rest my weight into him.

"You will find a way. We will find a way," he assured.

"I'm angry."

"As am I."

"I feel....my insides feel..."

I did not know how to finish.

Cass did.

"Raw."

I started to lose him between my legs, and thus my head jerked up, and I said urgently, "You must remain hard. I need you inside me."

With brushing strokes, he pulled the hair out of my face and continued to do it even when it was away, murmuring, "I would wish this for you, my princess, but I'm afraid my anatomy doesn't work that way."

"I need to be connected to you, Cass."

"You are, Elena."

"I need you a part of me."

"I am, Elena."

I closed my mouth at the deep rumble of his words.

And I stared into his eyes, understanding instantly how very much he meant them.

"I have sent birds," he went on. "Your sister's gnomes reported beyond what we learned from the prisoners. With that, I have a firm grasp on who stood against us this day and caused your loss. I've demanded every being evacuate the holds of the traitors. The dragons will fly in but two weeks and whoever is left behind will be no more. In the meantime, Mac is intent on getting Jasmine back home as soon as possible. This is a promise he made her. I will try to communicate with Sky and Star. They somehow transported Mars and True here. I will request they transport us to The

Enchantments so your fallen can enter the veil there and do it without delay."

He said much in all that, the last of it I agreed with wholeheartedly.

The first of it, I didn't.

"You-you're going to incinerate the holds of the traitors?"

"Tone, Jasmine and Rose are dead amongst too many bloody others. Fuck yes, I'm going to incinerate the holds of the traitors."

I began to push up, but Cass again wound his arms about me and held me where I was.

"And I will hear no words against it," he growled.

I stared into his eyes turned black.

Pitch.

Not the iris.

The entire eye.

Oh dear.

"Sweetheart," I whispered.

"You have to tell Theodora that Jasmine and Rose are lost. I have to tell Aelia Antonius is lost. They killed Otho too. My daughter will lose no more. Dora will lose no more. And by the fucking gods, *you* will lose no more."

On his "you" he squeezed the breath out of me.

I pushed my hand from between us so I could pet his beard in a soothing manner, muttering, "We will discuss this when our losses are not so fresh."

"We will not, Elena."

I stilled for I had never heard that tone from him before.

Unyielding.

Completely.

"I could have lost you. You could have lost me. Our daughters, parent-less. All our friends, gone. For what?" he demanded.

I could not answer that.

"Right," he grunted.

"Cass—"

"You will not feel pain."

I stilled again, for the black of his eyes, which had been receding, snapped back, and it appeared the night in his gaze was stormy.

"And if you do, if someone causes that pain, it will be avenged."

"All right, my prince," I whispered.

"All right," he grumbled, the storm in his eyes retreating.

"Perhaps I shouldn't have led our evening as I did when I walked into this tent," I muttered.

"If you need to release your pain by taking a lash to my flesh, I will endure it."

I blinked down at him.

He was not finished.

"If it takes you out of your mind and your hurt to use my body, riding my cock, climbing on my face, yanking at my balls, fucking me in my arse, you will do it. You will turn your mind, ease your pain, and I will come for you, I will shoot for you again and again, I will bleed for you, whatever you want to take from me to give you what you need, I will offer it to you. You own me, Elena. I love you and I am yours in any way I'm needed."

"I love you too, sweetheart," I whispered, moved beyond reckoning at the power of his words.

However.

"But I'm not sure I'd take a lash to make you feel better," I went on to admit.

"I would never mar your beautiful skin," he growled, openly annoyed, as if I thought he might someday actually do that.

"Well, I wouldn't yours either," I returned.

I watched him calm as he murmured, "Just know you could."

"It will never come to that. I just needed to feel...I just needed to feel you alive, all around me, inside me. I just needed you."

His arms left me so he could capture my head in both his hands.

"I am right here."

I closed my eyes and dropped my forehead to his.

He shifted so he could press his lips there then he moved me to press my face in his neck.

He then resumed holding me.

After some time, I noted quietly, "You said the words." I paused and added, "Now, twice."

He gave me a squeeze and not quietly, replied, "I did."

"It is quite unfair, the first time you did that and then raced off into battle without allowing me to return them."

"I'm not racing anywhere now."

I lifted my head and looked down at him.

And without delay, declared, "I love you, Cassius Laird, my warrior, my prince, my future husband. And I love that you love me too."

A small smile quirked his mouth as he stroked my cheek tenderly with his knuckles.

"Jasmine, I think, would approve of me falling on your cock in my grief," I remarked.

Another smile quirked his mouth before he replied, "She would indeed."

I felt my face crumble as Cassius watched it, which was why it was again shoved into his neck and his arms went around me tight.

I wept even as I asked, "How's Mac?"

"Undone."

His word made me weep harder.

"She was loved, darling, and she knew it," he whispered.

I nodded.

And I was glad for that.

But it didn't make me feel the slightest bit better.

After a while, I calmed, but Cassius did not move, neither did I, even if I knew I must be heavy, and I also knew he was leaking from me and that had to be aggravating.

"Your seed," I muttered.

"Ignore it," he muttered in return.

This was easy for me to do, as it wasn't aggravating me.

"Cass—"

His voice was deeper when he ordered, "Ignore it, Ellie."

I sighed.

Cassius started twisting my hair around his fingers.

"She would agree with the dragons," I told him.

"She absolutely would."

"She was a warrior to her soul."

"She was. And she lived every second of every day of her life on this earth to its fullest."

"She did. And she was the best friend anyone could have."

"Yes," he agreed.

I burrowed closer into my prince.

"I love you, Cass."

"And I you, my Ellie. You own me, body, heart and soul."

I pressed deeper and the tears came again.

Because I loved he gave me that.

And Jasmine would love it too.

And through my tears, Cass held me.

I loved he did that.

And Jasmine would love that too.

125

THE BROTHER

Queen Ha-Lah
Amphite, Underwater Capital of the Mer
STRAIT OF MEDUSA

The table was long that separated my king and husband, Aramus, from my other king, Jorie of the Mer.

But as long as it was, it was truly even longer, for the two men sitting at opposite ends of it, scowling at each other down the length, were making it thus through obstinacy.

I sat at Aramus's side, waiting for him to say something.

But once he had regained consciousness after the Mer had dragged him down to their underwater city, he was not best pleased that he'd been pulled under without his consent.

Or that they'd magicked him unconscious.

Not to mention, also mer-napped me.

It took considerable time to calm him down, even though I agreed wholeheartedly this was not the best way for the Mer to begin relations between our two realms.

But we'd been in Amphite, the capital city of the Mer, now for hours.

Aramus's men were probably beside themselves with worry that we'd disappeared.

And Dora and Aelia were likely terrified.

We needed to move forward establishing relations and then get home.

And this would be any kind of relations (though, preferably good ones, however, I wasn't sure how that would happen with such an inauspicious start).

"My king," I whispered, reaching out to touch Aramus's wrist where it lay on the table, the better to give him the ability to irritably drum his fingers, something which he was doing.

"We will commence when I hear an apology," Aramus decreed.

Oh no.

"Then you might as well leave now," Jorie retorted.

"I have no issue with this," Aramus stated, beginning to rise.

I grasped his wrist and tugged to keep him seated, hissing, "*Aramus.*"

"We have done without them for centuries, my queen," he stated, his eyes not leaving Jorie, but fortunately his behind not leaving his seat. "We can carry on without them now."

"My darling, he is the king of *my people*," I pushed. "And we need all peoples allied, Aramus. Especially those with power. With magic."

My husband said nothing.

"And he is Silence's *brother*," I stressed.

Aramus grinned a wicked grin at Jorie. "Good luck getting through Mars to meet her, my friend."

Jorie bared his teeth.

Oh, but he wanted to meet his sister.

And that made me happy.

I just needed to get my stubborn king happy about it as well.

"She has no siblings," I reminded Aramus. "Her mother is as weak as the king who is her brother. Her father is—"

Aramus's head ticked, having sensed as we all did the kind of man (and more importantly, father) that Johan Mattson was.

But I knew.

In her missives to me, it was clear she had not been raised in a nurturing manner.

I did not share all with my husband.

But he was no fool.

I took instant advantage. "Can you imagine, growing up as she did, discovering your brother, your *blood*, is King of the Mer? Indeed, growing up alone in that house, for Silence was very much alone in that house, Aramus, and then coming to learn you have a brother at all?"

Neither man spoke for long moments, though Jorie now appeared even more unhappy upon hearing how Silence had been raised.

Aramus broke the silence.

"Your father, he also was king?"

"Yes," Jorie bit off.

Aramus's tone had warmed a shade when he went on to inquire, "And he is no longer amongst us?"

"No," Jorie answered shortly.

"I am sorry," I said to Jorie.

"I am as well. He was a good man, a good king, and a good father," Jorie replied.

"Silence, Queen of Firenze, is dear to my wife," Aramus declared. "I call her husband friend. At any time, but especially in times like these, I would not want to introduce anything into her life that would upset her."

"You assume I would upset her?" Jorie demanded indignantly.

"No, but you say your father was a good man, and yet he begot Silence, and this is unknown to Silence. I do not know for certain, but we suspect Silence not only is unaware she is Mer, now, I more than suspect she does not know the father who raised her is not her own," Aramus returned carefully.

Jorie lifted his chin.

And then fortunately, he gave in a little.

"My mother died. She was young. I was but seven years old. My father was most grieved. Amongst the Mer, when one's mate perishes, it is custom to go swim-about. A mate can be gone years in their search for solace after they lose the one they love. My father was gone for two. I know he went to the land, took his legs, traveled widely with the Zee people who are like many of us. They wander in schools, wherever they wish to roam. I did not, and he did not, know, in his meanderings, his seed brought forth a child."

Jorie took a breath and continued.

"That is, I did not know until word reached us that the new Queen of Firenze has silver eyes. No one but the royal line of Mer has silver eyes. My two aunts have silver eyes. My cousins have silver eyes. As you can see, I have the same. My aunts have not left the underwater realm to go to land. However, my father spent much time in the country of Wodell, and in his diaries, spoke of meeting, and lying with, the lady of the arbor. I did not know until I knew of Silence that the lady of the arbor was the *Lady of the Arbor*. And thus, Silence, Queen of Firenze is my sister."

Jorie's expression changed, grief seeping into it, before he cleared it and carried on.

"He was beloved, my father. By me. His people. He was generous and he was caring. He valued family above all else. My mother died on her third attempt to bring forth another child for him. In his last breaths on this earth, he apologized to me again, something he had done repeatedly since her loss, that he gave in to her desire to have more children and thus I lost my mother. This before he shared his love for me and called to her to tell her he could not wait to see her again."

My husband turned his head to look at me.

"Both of their fathers were kings, and both of their fathers are lost," I whispered.

"And now we know the foundation of what makes the King and Queen of Firenze," he whispered back.

He then returned his attention to Jorie.

"Do you know of the prophecy?" he asked the King of the Mer.

"We know much. Lena, your witch in the Great Coven, keeps us apprised of the follies of those on land."

I could tell by the tightening of Aramus's jaw he did not like the word "follies."

Fortunately, he did not dwell on this.

"Silence, as well as Ha-Lah, and myself, are part of this prophecy," Aramus shared.

"I know this too."

"The Beast rises."

"We feel the quakes here as well and know what causes them."

Aramus again looked at me.

"Make your request, Sea King," Jorie demanded.

Aramus turned again to Jorie.

"I have outlawed whaling," he shared.

"We know this," Jorie replied.

"I have abolished the binding," Aramus went on.

"We know this as well," Jorie said.

"And I have decided that any harm done to a Mer will mean the perpetrator's death, hanging from the yardarm, blood drained from the neck."

Jorie sat still and stared at my husband.

He did not know that.

"The law has been written," Aramus continued. "But it has not yet been enacted, for we will wait until such time as we can call to the Mer on land, and now at sea, to share they are safe. Now is not that time. No one is safe in this time. But when those prophesied make Triton safe, I will assure the Mer are the same. And I will garner oaths from every kingdom of Triton for their protection of the Mer. However, proclaimed or no, enacted or no, if word comes to me that a Mer has been harmed, the perpetrator will hang from a sirens-damned yardarm and be drained of their blood."

Jorie did not speak, but I did not fail to note he was watching my husband very closely.

Aramus stood and looked down the table at his fellow king.

"My wife is your people. But this is not the only reason your people are my people," he stated. "I am the Sea King. I will protect the Mer in promise and deed, with my armies, my armadas and my life."

Jorie remained silent.

Aramus did not.

"Now you may wish to involve yourself and your people with the happenings on land, or you may not. That will be your choice. I will not make a request for your might, your power and your magic. It will be up to you to give it. I will not negotiate you doing the right thing. I will not hold your sister from you. Not for you, but Silence adores her cousin True and she has much love to give. I would not keep a brother from her. Thus, Jorie, King of the Mer, it is up to you what you and your people will do. When you are ready to meet your sister, we will make that so."

Jorie still did not speak.

Thus, Aramus continued.

"Now, my wife and I are going home. There are two little girls who have already lost too much in their young lives who are undoubtedly frightened beyond reason Ha-Lah and I have gone missing. We must return."

"You seem to think much of yourself that you, at long last, have made just decisions for the beasts of the sea, and the beings in it," Jorie returned.

"I think only that I must thank the gods for my wife. For in truth, if they had not guided her to me, I would have sailed and raided and whaled and not considered any of these things."

"That does not say much for you," Jorie retorted.

"Indeed," Aramus returned. "But it says a great deal about my wife."

"My king," I whispered, warmed to my core at his words.

He looked to me, and when he saw my expression, his face grew soft.

"You are my conscience. You know this, so do not look as if my words surprise you."

"You are a fine man, a great king," I replied. "For you did not have to listen to me and more, do something about it."

"How about we settle on the fact we're both bloody wonderful?" he teased, a twinkle in his brown eyes.

Oh, but that twinkle.

I grinned at him. "I can do that."

"Though, you're more wonderful," he muttered.

And I warmed anew.

"Perhaps we can steer your conversation away from mutual admiration and back to matters at hand," Jorie suggested, and my husband and I turned our attention to him only to see his brows draw together as he looked beyond us.

I looked that way as well, to see another bare-chested, iridescent-leather-trouser clad mermale moving swiftly our way.

Not exactly our way, he went straight to Jorie.

Jorie, taller than this brethren by at least half a foot (I had not seen many of the Mer having taken their home in this realm, but of the ones I saw, and the ones I knew on land, I noticed that Jorie was taller, broader and more powerful of frame than all of them), and thus, he bent his head so the mermale could have his ear.

In short order, he jerked upright in a manner that had both my husband and I tensing.

Or it could have been the expression on his face.

Either way, it caused Aramus to rap out, "What is happening?"

Jorie's gaze came our way, and when he spoke, his tone had softened.

"I am sorry to say, the war in Airen to free their females has begun in earnest this day."

"Oh, my gods," I breathed.

"The rebels cornered your friends on a mountainside. The Regent's troops were outnumbered at least ten to one," Jorie went on.

My heart lurched.

Aramus immediately grasped my hand and started dragging me to the door, which would take us to the island in the middle of the grotto, which was, as far as I could tell, a part of Jorie's palace.

"We must get to land. Then to my ship, for we must make haste to Cass," Aramus declared.

"They won," Jorie called.

Aramus stopped dead.

I ran into him.

And we both woodenly turned back to Jorie.

"Who won?" Aramus asked, his voice dead.

"Your friends."

His fingers tightened so deeply around mine, the bones in my hand might have broken, if my fingers weren't tightening so deeply around his.

"They're alive?" I asked, my voice husky.

"There were losses, but the Prince of Airen and the new Queen of the Nadirii were not amongst them," Jorie reported.

"Do you know aught else?" Aramus asked.

Jorie shook his head.

I tipped mine back to catch my husband's gaze.

"We must send ravens. Cass may need you to engage. He may just need you. Thus, we need to get home," I told him.

He nodded and began to drag me again.

"We will all go to them, together," Jorie decreed, and again, Aramus and I stopped and gave him our attention. He continued, "There are rumors the King of Firenze is at the battlefield, with his wife, even though this couldn't be so, as yesterday, they were in Wodell and Cassius and Elena are at the base of the Night Heights. But regardless, I won't meet my sister here, in Amphite, not anytime soon. So I go with you."

"Then come along and don't dally," Aramus bid.

However, I was stuck on what Jorie said.

"How do you know so much?" I asked.

"Mer have powers," he answered.

"I know, I am Mer," I reminded him. "But that doesn't answer my question."

"Some have some powers, others have other powers," Jorie shared, which also didn't answer my question.

"And what powers allow you to know so much that is happening on land?" I demanded to know and felt Aramus, who I could sense was keen to be away, settle in at my side, for the now, keener to know this.

"There are many of us who have exceptional hearing," Jorie explained.

"Ah," I murmured.

"And there are others of us, a smaller number, and all of them of noble blood, who can cloak ourselves," he went on.

Aramus grew very still.

I stared at my brethren, saying through stiff lips, "Cloak yourselves?"

"Disappear. Become shadows. With only those who have let us into their hearts, those who we are connected to as mates, this coupling smiled upon by the gods, able to see us."

"In other words eavesdrop," I snapped.

"Spy," he returned.

"You've been *spying* on my queen and I?" Aramus clipped.

"We spy everywhere," Jorie stated unconcernedly.

"You say this as if this is not a detrimental matter in diplomatic relations," Aramus returned.

"And how is this?" Jorie replied confusingly, taking up his trident and walking our way. He passed us, murmuring, "If you would, follow me."

We followed him out of the consular chamber to the open area of the island in the grotto.

There were Mer floating in the water. Some lazing with fins flapping in the water on smaller islands set around.

All attention came to us when we emerged.

"Stand back, please," Jorie instructed.

Aramus stood back.

As for me, I stood behind Aramus who stepped in front of me.

Jorie watched him do this, and he did not attempt to hide his approval of this maneuver.

Then he turned, lifting his trident at the side over his head, and he ran across the sand.

But as he would throw it, he executed a graceful leap into the air and twisted his body around...

I gasped as he disappeared in a swirl of shimmer that eddied around the trident staff as it soared through the air.

The three points imbedded in an unoccupied, small island some thirty feet away, the shimmer burst the moment it struck land, and Jorie reformed.

"Well, I'll be sirens-damned," Aramus muttered.

I fought applauding, but I could not stop clenching my hands to my chest in delight, at the same time wondering, if I had a trident, if I could learn to do that.

"In this cavern," Jorie called from across the water, "I cannot show you the full power of the trident. However, rest assured, not only if you're touching the holder of a trident will you travel with him, it can traverse far. Not from Mar-el to Airen. But, say, for instance, over a mountain range." He was silent a beat before he asked, "Now, how is that for diplomatic relations?"

Neither my husband nor I moved.

Then Aramus did.

To speak.

"Can you take things with you?" Aramus veritably barked. "Weapons? Supplies?"

"If it is carried on your person, yes," Jorie answered.

"Do you need to pack?" Aramus went on.

Jorie looked down to his attractive, but decidedly Mer trousers which were all he was wearing, then back to us.

When he did, he grinned.

I preferred bald, bulky, marked and midnight, like my husband.

But smiling, Jorie was not difficult on the eyes.

"I have a feeling I'll be found out as Mer if I don't at least change," he jested.

"Go, now, then follow us," Aramus ordered. "We'll leave word at the castle you're to be treated like a king until my wife and I can attend you. We will not take long, however, and then we shall be away."

"Well I hope they treat me like a king, since I am one," Jorie retorted.

Aramus didn't bother to reply.

He looked down at me.

"Let's go home, baby. It's time."

I nodded, guiding him to the edge of the water.

Before I led us in, I halted as my husband spoke.

"It was an unusual start," he called to Jorie and got the other king's attention. "But from here on, Jorie, King of the Mer, you have my vow to ally our kingdoms for the good of all who make a home in or by the sea."

Well, that was well said.

Pride swelled in my chest.

Jorie dipped his chin into his neck.

Aramus dipped his into his neck.

And then, I led my husband into the water so I could take us home.

126

THE LEGENDS

Queen Farah
Base of the Night Heights Mountain Range
AIREN

"I cannot begin to explain how, at this juncture, a renegade witch with an untrained army running amuck in my realm might do irrevocable damage to a mission we both share that it is crucial, in going about it, we find victory," Cassius stated to the woman standing before him, and he did this through gritted teeth.

I stood by my husband who, I noted after a sidelong glance, agreed with Cass for he did not appear as angry as Cassius, but I could see he was not happy.

"Rest assured, Fern has the best interest of this mission at heart, my prince," the woman, her name Elsa, replied.

"I'm fully aware of that," Cassius retorted. "That is not at issue. At issue is the renegade part of my earlier statement."

Elsa looked uncomfortable.

"Where is she?" Cassius demanded.

"I am not in the know of that," Elsa answered.

"It's my understanding you're her ranking general here," Cass replied.

"Her mission is top secret," Elsa shared.

"From her Regent?" Cass bit out.

"Sire—" she began.

"Find out where she is. Find out what she's doing. And *report it to me*," he clipped. "We are at war, Elsa. As such, I am not only your Regent, I'm your commanding, gods-damned officer. And there is one thing I do not countenance in my troops. Going rogue."

Elsa stared up at Cassius in shock before her face split into an enormous smile.

For a moment, I did not understand her reaction.

And then it struck me she was delighted to be considered, and treated, as a soldier.

"Right away, sir," she stated crisply.

"Dismissed," Cassius muttered.

She nodded, began to curtsy, stopped herself, instead saluted, and hurried away on her booted feet, wearing trousers, and it was a ridiculous notion on my part in that moment, but she made me want a pair of trousers.

Cass turned to True and I, as well as Mars and Silence, who were standing with us.

"They had three hundred and twenty-two women here. They lost three yesterday," Cassius said. "Bloody *three*."

"You did say they entered the battle closer to the end," Mars noted.

"All told, we stood approximately fifteen hundred against twelve thousand. And they lost only three," Cassius returned, and I knew his comment was not about disappointment (obviously), but surprise...and respect.

"Apparently, one must not underestimate the concept of right equaling might," my husband murmured.

"Three dead, True. But one hundred and seven were injured," Cass told him.

"I will assign Luther to them," True offered. "They're motivated and they're organized. If they hone their skills, they could be formidable."

Cassius appeared to think for a moment, before he replied, "This might appeal to Nero. He needs something to turn his mind. He can work with Luther."

True nodded.

Mars broke in.

"This is a good idea, but in the now, we must decide the course for us all," Mars said. "With your warriors, you and Elena heading to The

Enchantments, mine coming up from Firenze to do the same, resources would be too concentrated there if True's men and mine accompanied you."

"I've called for more men from Wodell to go to Sky Bay. I can take Farah and Silence and we'll add to your numbers there," True put in. "Mars and his men can go with you, Cass."

"Lahn shared that things had deteriorated in Dunlyn, and reports from my men verify it. I sense it might be a stronghold. Aramus has sent ships there and—"

Cassius stopped talking when we all turned to a clamor happening in the makeshift horse corral close by.

In it were a number of battle mounts.

But also, Sky and Star, Cassius and Elena's unicorns.

Both were fretting.

Star, the mare, was cantering this way and that, as a human would pace.

Sky appeared to be charging the gate, turning at the last moment before he'd break it, as if saying he wanted free.

"Open the gate, let out the charmed ones!" Cassius called to the page who it was clear saw to the corral.

The boy rushed forward to do as told, and I wondered—when the unicorns could magically leap through space, and in a trice, land hundreds of miles away—why they didn't not-magically leap the fence of the corral.

The page let them out, swiftly running the gate closed before any of the other horses could get free.

However, the unicorns did not rush away to find exercise.

True crowded me and Mars pulled Silence close as they rushed Cassius.

The stallion paced a circle agitatedly around the five of us as the mare went right to her prince, dipped her neck and butted his hand with her nose.

"What is it, love?" he murmured, stroking her muzzle.

But it was the stallion who answered, tossing his head back and braying.

"What are you saying, Sky?" Cassius called to the stallion, still rubbing Star's nose.

True suddenly tucked me close when Sky reared up, striking the air with his hooves.

This, just as Elena came running.

"*Diana!*" she shrieked to the page. "Saddle my mount!"

The boy rushed into the corral.

Cassius rushed to Elena.

"*What?*" he barked, instantly on the alert.

"The Enchantments," she said, her voice naught but a pant. "Cassius, *we have to get to The Enchantments!*"

Oh no!

Sky came up behind her, and before Cassius, or anyone, could ask that first question, she whirled on the unicorn, capturing his jaw in her hands.

I was shocked the creature didn't pull away at her panicked movements, but he did not.

"Will you take us to The Enchantments?" she asked.

The unicorn jerked back his head in clear assent.

"Caelus!" Cassius shouted, running toward the corral.

"Do you need us?" Mars boomed.

Elena's head whipped around. "We need everyone."

"Oh, gods," I breathed.

Mars looked to True, but it was my husband who spoke.

"We cannot leave them," he said.

"We cannot take them," Mars finished.

They were talking about us.

Silence and me.

"Bloody hell," True muttered, then pivoted on his boot and shouted to a loitering Dellish squire, "Saddle Majesty and Regina!" he ordered.

The squire hopped to.

Regina was my steed.

I glanced at Silence who was being dragged away by Mars.

And I received an answer to my unasked question when I heard Mars order a Firenz soldier in Firenzii, "Saddle Hephaestus and Epona. Break camp. We ride!"

Epona was Silence's mount.

It seemed we weren't going to Sky Bay after all.

As the purple cleared and Regina's hooves struck land, at what befell my eyes, it felt like my heart would explode.

We were galloping full bore toward hell.

The Enchantments were under attack.

Hundreds of troops were taking aim with fired arrows shot into the forest, but instead of them soaring through the air and exploding amongst the trees, they detonated against an invisible shield.

Worse, there were dozens of catapults and trebuchets raining fire against the shield. Buckets of fuel set aflame were detonating against the Nadirii's protective veil in great swoops of blaze. With each powerful strike, a wave would reverberate, and an opening would form, giving a glimpse of sun and green that was starkly different than the chill, gray, late-autumn day in Airen.

Our horses had barely taken two dozen strides when, as if they had practiced it, True and Mars broke off in formation, curving to the left, taking Silence and my mares with them, forcing us to the back of the phalanx of Dellish, Airenzian, Firenz and Nadirii warriors who had traveled with us.

They guided us up a hill and True's Majesty circled me, my husband's head whipping this way and that to keep hold on my eyes, as he ordered gutturally, "You stay here, and if danger approaches before I can get a guard to you, you *flee!*"

He then rounded Regina, dug his heels into his steed's sides, and shouted, "*Heeyah!*"

They raced forward, with Mars following them.

Breathing heavily, Silence and I sidestepped our mounts so we were closer to each other, and we stared down at the mayhem below that our beloved husbands were speeding toward.

The others had engaged in battle and we could hear the clangs of steel and shouts of combat.

"Not to worry," Silence decreed, her voice quiet and small, betraying she was not taking her own advice. "The Enchantments have never been broken and our husbands are the greatest warriors of our realms."

I did not wish to worry. I knew both of these things, and they should have heartened me.

But as missile after missile struck the shield and some of the shouts of combat became noises of a different kind, I tried to keep my gaze glued to True and felt my heart squeeze when I lost sight of him in the confusion of the melee.

My True, so true, charging in without hesitation.

He was an example of right being might too.

And in that moment, weakness struck me, for I wished suddenly that he was just a little bit less true in order to keep himself a lot more safe.

"Oh, balls, *no*," Silence murmured, and my attention shifted to her then back to the action and I shot straight on my steed.

A rift had opened in the veil protecting The Enchantments that not only did not close but also did not hold the missiles at bay.

They were getting through.

And with the intensity of the onslaught, The Enchantments were catching fire.

"This cannot be," I whispered.

"Yes, it can. For it is not man doing that," Silence stated, and I again turned to her to see her gaze no longer to the battle but it was looking beyond me. "It is magic."

I twisted my neck and felt my eyes narrow, for along the crest of the hill, some ways away, but still visible, was a line of sorcerers.

I knew their bent for they were in full chant, precisely placed, arms raised, heads tipped back, calling on their magic to aid the villains' operation.

And there had to be fifty of them.

Further, in the confusion below, our people had not noticed them.

I turned back to Silence, and the instant I did, she proclaimed, "Your wind. My fire."

My wind?

Her...*fire*?

I had no chance to ask after this.

She'd dug her heels in her mount and started charging toward the sorcerers.

Without thinking, I followed her, and as I did, as an automatic precaution, I called upon my magic, feeling it gather in the small of my back, a tingle, an itch, a burning.

Silence was bent over the neck of her horse, but as we grew closer to the line of sorcerers, she sat back, raised both hands, palms open but fingers slightly curled...

And to my amazement, in them formed two balls of fire.

She hurled them both toward the first sorcerer.

His robes caught fire, and on a shriek, he plummeted out of the line, snaking this way and that before throwing himself to the ground and rolling.

By the gods.

Silence had command of fire!

She turned her head and looked down her body at me, shouting, "You!"

Now I knew what she meant by "my wind."

I had something to command too.

And in this dire time, I had to command it.

I sat up, brought my hands crossed before me at my chest, then flung them out to my sides.

The next sorcerer in line whirled up into the air in a twirl of damp leaves as if caught in a wind funnel.

I then swung one of my arms to the right and he went flying through the forest.

"I did it!" I cried with excitement.

Silence did not share in my excitement.

She was focused.

Thus, the next wizard took Silence's fire.

I needed to focus as well.

I did this and the next I sent careening into a tree.

More fire from Silence, this time, one of her projectiles hit the next wizard in line and another projectile, the one after.

The skin all over my body raging but my breath coming calm and easy, I caught the next three up in a mighty gale and sent them soaring over the naked treetops, trailing dead leaves in their wake.

At this juncture, the line of conjurors had noted our attack, thus they started to break formation and scatter.

"What the bloody hell are you doing?" I heard Wallace shout from behind me.

"*My queen, stop!*" Silence's guard Kyril bellowed.

We both ignored them with Silence again looking back, down her body to me.

I jerked my head one way and pulled my reins in that direction.

She went the other.

"Gods dammit!" Wally yelled.

I chased the sorcerers, leaning left to right in my saddle as Regina dodged the trees, all the while hearing Wallace bound behind me at Regina's heels.

Sending forth a gale, I caught several of the fleeing men, forcing them back to whence they came, where a wall of fire was opening in a circle.

I carried on, grateful to Wallace, who noted my gambit and broke from his chase of me in order to bear down on our foes to force some of the wizards into my line of magic.

We caught as many as we could, which drattedly wasn't all of them, before Silence and I passed each other on our mounts, and she closed the ring of fire.

Then Silence, without pause, again tore off on her mount.

I watched, marveling at her seat on a horse, which was exceptionally skilled, and I noticed she was intent on tracking the sorcerers we had not caught in her corral of fire.

Kyril raced after her, but as I would do the same, Wallace rounded in front of me, cutting me off, shouting, "Have you lost your bloody mind?"

"No!" I shouted in return. "We captured twenty of the enemy and incapacitated nine!"

"They could have turned their magic on *you*."

"They did not get the chance," I told him what he had to have seen. "And now we must help Silence find the rest."

But I had lost his attention. Two Dellish soldiers had approached.

"Guard them," Wallace ordered the men, jerking his head to the sorcerers caught in the flaming circle.

I took that opportunity to turn my attention back to the battle.

I was not a military genius, but it was not difficult to see that the surprise arrival of the a four-nation contingent was unexpected, as was the incapacitation of their sorcerers.

Two catapults and three trebuchets were ablaze, scores of enemy soldiers were on their knees with their hands held behind their backs, True and Mars with some of their men were racing after enemy cavalry that was trying to escape, and Cassius and Elena, with their unicorns in the lead, were galloping into The Enchantments at the edge of a blazing forest fire.

Florian approached us, and had not stopped before he shouted my way, "Can you bring the rain?"

I looked to the fire building not only in The Enchantments but spreading into Airen.

And doing this quickly.

Good gods.

"Farah! Can you bring the rain?" Florian repeated urgently.

I could not.

I nevertheless pulled the reins of my horse, and touched her sides with my heels, taking her speeding directly towards the flames.

"What are you about?" Wallace, riding at my side, yelled.

"I cannot bring the rain, but maybe I can blow it out," I told him.

"Wind feeds fire," he reminded me.

Still racing that way, I looked to him at my side and suggested, "Then maybe I can smother it."

"Maybe?" he asked.

I felt the heat of the blaze and pulled back at my mount. Regina halted, skittish and unsure under me that close to the growing, and spreading, inferno.

"We must ride out, evacuate," Luther, approaching us, called.

I said nothing.

I was concentrating.

If I could bring the winds, perhaps I could also take them away.

"If True sees Farah this close to the flame, he'll have all our balls!" Bram, joining us, shouted. "We must *go*!"

I ignored him too.

I closed my eyes.

I then visualized the fire.

The area around it...

And that was when it struck me.

The earth.

The leaves.

The sensations came again at the small of my back, up my spine, radiating, spreading.

I placed both hands on my belly.

Pressing in, I expelled all the breath from my lungs...

And then on a rush, I threw my arms out and up, opening my eyes, and sucking in as much air as my body could take.

Doing this, a great blanket of wet leaves rose from the forest floor and swooped out and up, to the pinnacle of the burn.

I brought my arms down and the leaves, and the flames, collapsed in on themselves, and with a great whoosh of hot air, a cloud of billowing smoke and an almighty screech that scored at my ears, the leaves returned to the earth.

And the flame flashed out.

Upon which, I slid out of Regina's saddle and fell to the ground.

～

I REGAINED consciousness in the arms of my husband.

I could smell scorched earth. I could feel his strong, solid body all around me, his warmth penetrating my heavy clothes.

But all I could see was his face.

And I could not read it.

Though his eyes were ruptures of green so intense, it was as if they were alive.

"We had to do what we could," I defended myself (and Silence) before he could say a word.

"You...that is *you*, my Farah, singlehandedly saved The Enchantments, and much of the Argyll Forest, I suspect, from burning to the ground."

Although I was most pleased with what I'd been able to do, this might be an overstatement.

"It is wet. It rained just yesterday."

"Not in The Enchantments."

I blinked up at him.

"You saved the home of all Nadirii," True went on.

"I—"

"Today, you became legend."

I shut my mouth.

True smiled at me.

"I then collapsed off my horse," I whispered ashamedly.

True stroked the hair from my face with his fingers, telling me, "Elena shared this is because you used much magic to douse the blaze. She has some potions you can take, rituals you can do to assist in building it again in you. And she advises you must rest. These things you will do. For although what you accomplished today saved homes and probably lives, I sense it will be important that you nurture the power within you."

I sensed he was correct.

"You must know, you have been unconscious for some time," he shared. "My men reported you did not hit your head when you fell from your steed, but Elena said that this is also not unusual after an effort the magnitude of which you gave today."

"How long have I been asleep?" I asked.

"Perhaps three quarters of an hour."

Oh my.

"I..." I trailed off, studying him before I stated quietly, "I thought you might be angry at me."

The surge of green dimmed in his eyes, even if the pride remained in his expression, as he said, "If I had my chosen world, and I could safeguard you in it, we would be in Wodell, preparing for winter, the festivals we have then, which are joyous and heartening and break the monotony of cold, short days that seem, as time passes, like they will never end."

He gathered me closer where he sat on the leaves in the Airenzian forest with me in his lap.

"But I do not have my chosen world, and I cannot safeguard you from all you might see, and all you might need to do. That said," he gave me a squeeze, "knowing the beauty of your bravery and power fills me not with anger, but with pride."

"Then now you know how, every day, I feel about you."

The green surged in his eyes again as he curled me up at the same time he bent into me in order to take my mouth in a deep kiss.

When he ended it, I had my arms around his neck but slid one hand to his jaw.

"What was lost today?" I asked.

"No warriors, several treehomes of Nadirii that were situated close to this border, though, the sisters who lived in them were unhurt. There was some loss of life on their side, none on ours. In the end, mostly, we just have a great number more prisoners."

His gaze went vague in a manner I called questioningly, "True?"

It took him a moment to speak his next words, and I would know why when they came.

"Two of the sorcerers at whom Silence hurled fire perished. Several others are forever maimed."

Oh gods.

I was uncertain how Silence would cope with that.

"And...my wind?" I queried.

"The three Wallace reported you sent soaring over the treetops, darling..."

He trailed off but I pressed my fingers into his jaw and urged, "Tell me."

"Two sustained significant injuries it is likely they will not survive. One died, landing upon his head." He shared this and then rushed to say, "Farah, they meant to—"

"I know what they meant to do, True. Do not forget, I am proud to be Queen of Wodell as I am thus, standing at your side. But I am born Firenz and we do not vacillate in doing what must be done to those who have earned it."

"You can say this to yourself, and perhaps it is true," he replied gently. "But if thoughts come up in you, know to your soul what I hope you know in your heart. As you have been for me, I will be there for you."

As you have been for me...

I smiled at my husband.

"I would hold you forever, no matter where I am, even sitting on wet earth in Airen. But there is much to do, and we must get on doing it," he remarked.

I nodded and my husband tightened his hold on me as he took his feet, before he put me on mine.

And before we set off to do what was next that we needed to do, I caught him at the sides of his neck with my hands and held tight when he gazed into my eyes.

"I love you, True," I whispered, knowing it was felt, in times like these, that these words needed to be spoken so they were understood, when in truth, this sentiment should be expressed in all times.

True was not ignorant of this, which was why his face softened and his hands came to mine at his neck, not to remove them, but to curl his fingers around mine and hold them warmly against his skin.

"And I love you, my Farah."

We held each other's eyes.

We took our moment.

And then we turned in order to set about doing what there was next to do.

Queen Silence
Northeastern Border of The Enchantments
Airen

"Leave us," Mars ordered on his approach to where I stood not far from the smoking circle I had doused when soldiers had arrived to take custody of the captured sorcerers.

I watched men and women from four different armies scatter at my husband's command.

As for me, I waited until he got close before I lifted my hand, palm out his way, and demanded, "Don't even start. I am fine. Farah is fine. We—"

I said no further words, for I was up, and then I was down, my cloaked back to a blanket of wet leaves, my husband atop me.

"Mars," I whispered.

"Kyril told me the lot of it."

Balls and begorrah.

Bloody, big-mouthed Kyril.

"Mars," I repeated.

"I am the Fire King," he stated.

I opened my mouth, though I did not know what I would say.

Regardless, whatever it would be, I didn't get to say it.

"And you," his hand spanned the side of my face, "are *the Fire Queen*."

I stared up into his eyes that were twin sparks of red flame.

"No thought," he said. "No hesitation. *No fear*. Kyril saw you ride. You dug your heels in your mount and did what had to be done."

I did what had to be done?

That was all?

"Y-you're not angry with me?" I asked.

"*Mio ardente, mio amore*, today, you...became...*legend*," he declared

Legend?

"A man does not get angry at a legend for doing what makes her thus," he finished.

"I-I just...well, I didn't do anything more than what Elena does all the time."

His brows shot together. "And that makes it less important, what you did today?"

I didn't have an answer for that.

"The veil protecting The Enchantments was falling. The Enchantments would have burned. With the veil down, the parts that didn't would have been vulnerable to attack along the entire Airenzian border. If you and Farah had not intervened, even if we routed their warriors easily, we could not have saved a nation," he decreed.

"Well, I guess that was pretty...excellent of me and, erm, Farah."

He grinned down at me. "Yes, it was *pretty excellent*."

I didn't think it was a good idea to remind him of my next, but much had happened that day, and the day before, and the months before that, and I knew we were likely not close to done.

Thus, I wanted it all to be out now, rather than have Mars rethink his reaction to this occurrence, which would mean we would revisit it.

"You did not want me close to danger," I reminded him.

"I did not, I do not," he agreed. "And I did not when I did not know you could wield fire, also when I knew. You are treasured by me, and if my choice was omnipotent, I would have you live your life reading your books and concocting your extraordinary gowns and the most vexation you'd experience is attempting to design a seating chart for a royal dinner that won't have warring clans spilling blood in our dining room. I am not omnipotent. But I *am* fortunate. There have been many times, my Silence, since I met you that you have surprised me about *me*."

"I have surprised you about...*you*?" I asked.

"Indeed, for one year ago, if you told me my heart would be taken by a petite, raven-haired beauty with skin as pale as pearls and eyes of mercury, who was smart enough to observe before speaking, think before doing, except when it came to chasing through the forest after traitors, I would call you mad. Indeed, but a week ago, if you told me my wife would go chasing through the forest after traitors, I might have been moved to find some way to intern you so you would not harm yourself. But now...now..."

The banking flames burst anew in his eyes as he dipped his face closer to mine.

"Now, my Silence, you must answer me. Do you matter?"

I felt my throat close as I stared up into his flames.

"Tell me, my love, do you?" he pushed.

"Yes," I whispered.

"You did before," he stated. "I am just glad now you see the strength of it as I have always seen, and yet it grows more day to day, from the first moment I laid eyes on you."

"I very, very much love you, my darling husband," I told him with no small amount of fervor. "And you must know, you are treasured by me too."

"This is good, for I very, *very* much love you, my beautiful, brave wife."

Beautiful and brave.

I smiled up at my king right before he kissed me.

But he was Mars. As much as we both enjoyed the kiss, I had my back to the damp leaves, and being Mars, he had a mind to that.

Thus, he finished the kiss all too swiftly, pulled us both to our feet, and murmured there were decisions that needed to be made so we must join the others.

However, as he walked us to where they were huddling, I noticed something I'd never quite noticed before.

It had been there, it just had not dawned on me.

As my husband moved with me tucked close to his side, he did this with a pride of bearing that had a great deal to do with who he was, what he was, and how he was.

But he also did it because he had me on his arm.
He was proud of what I did that day.
But truly, he had been proud of me since our beginning.
Because there was something of which to be proud.
And this something was...
I was me.

127

THE WOMEN

Tedrey
Abandoned Stable, Twenty Miles West of the Ancient Ritual Grounds
WODELL

Tedrey stood next to Moira, one of the young women who had been rounded up by Fenn and Thom to sacrifice in order to surface the Beast. She had been the one who had first helped him release the other girls.

And they were all still with him, seven in total, either because they were far too terrified to find their homes by themselves after what they'd experienced, or smart enough to know that traveling together was safer.

He wished to escort them all safely home.

But with the Beast unleashed, Tedrey not only had no coin, they had no horses. He further had no weapon in case they ran into trouble (and with the way things were in all realms these days, Zees or highwaymen could be the least of their worries).

And last, he just simply did not have the luxury of taking the time such an endeavor would require.

He had to get to Notting Thicket. He had to get to Birchlire Castle. He had to find some way to gain an audience with King True and share the dire news.

He worried naught could be done.

This was, of course, *the Beast*.

But they must try, and he did not have the power to do it himself.

First, however, he had to find someone who would see to the women. Their families had to be worried to distraction. If he could find one soul he sensed he could trust who would take charge of them, he had no doubt they would be safe at their own hearths in little time.

With the Beast risen, he just had even less than "little" time to give.

In that moment, in a stable that Tedrey had noted on the way to the Ritual Ground (so he'd led the women there in the rain after they'd fled, and at least it had provided shelter, if not warmth, and they'd spent the night there), Moira had hold of a long stick.

She was using it to draw a rough map of eastern Wodell in the dirt.

"We are here," she pointed with her stick. She then moved it what Tedrey considered a disheartening distance away and dug a little hole in the dirt, finishing, "Notting Thicket is there."

"Yes, Moira, but as I shared with you, I need you to guide me to someone you can trust who will take in these women and see to it they are safely home. I have to do that first, before I head to the Thicket. But it must be done quickly. So please, tell me if you know of someone who is close that you would trust with this task. Or, perchance, there is a temple nearby where there is a priest or priestess who would take on this duty?"

"I live in the Lesser Thicket, Tedrey," she replied. "Northeast of here. It's at least fifteen, perhaps twenty miles beyond where we started. I do not know this place at all."

That was not stellar news.

Further, her home was at least two days' walk, if they could manage a good pace and do so for hours and hours without even a morsel of food amongst them.

Which would take him four days' out of his way.

He glanced at the other women.

Moira knew what he was thinking, all of it, for she said, "We will go with you."

He looked back to Moira and replied quietly, "You know we must get them home."

"I know those men had you for whatever purpose they had you, though as they seemed to be saving you for last, I can only imagine it was worse than what they did to those girls, which is impossible to fathom," she retorted.

He did not know if she was right. The Beast seemed to dispense with the men without delay.

Whereas what Thom and Fenn had done to those women…

"You got yourself loose," she continued, "and you did not run. You helped us. And after you'd freed us, you made sure we'd escaped, positioning yourself to block the path between them and us. But when you returned to us, you looked like the Beast had been awakened and you shared with me you had to make haste to Notting Thicket."

He blinked at her, for her words took him aback as he had not shared the Beast had, indeed, awakened.

It came to him slowly that this was what many people said. It was akin to, "you looked like you'd seen a ghost," but worse.

And as sayings go, that one was true. He'd cope with a thousand ghosts before he again had to witness the Beast risen.

"Tedrey?"

He came back into their conversation when Moira called his name.

"Did you hear me?" she asked.

"I'm sorry?" he queried in return.

"I was saying, as those villains were there for nefarious purposes, it obviously must be reported immediately as they are Go'Doan and they must be of this Rising."

"They were that," he affirmed.

She regarded him closely. "If this is so, I do not know why we need to go all the way to the Thicket when we can find a local constabulary and report to them. That is what King True wishes us to do."

"They were, er…higher ups in The Rising." He was pleased with the words he shared that he did not have to lie.

"And who were those who came up from the ground?"

And again, he was pleased he did not have to lie.

"I do not know two of them, but one was a Go'Doan priest."

He had found in the short time he'd been in Moira's company, she was most canny, and she demonstrated this again by asking, "Is there something you're not telling me?"

And now Tedrey found that he could no longer utter an untruth.

But for her sake, should she actually believe the true, but fantastical tale he had to tell, he could prevaricate.

"I do not know who the woman was. But the man was not…*right.*"

"Not right?"

"I do not think he's of magic. But I also do not think he's strictly of the earth. What I think is, if you ever see him again, you must flee."

Her eyes flashed with what he was coming to know was an unusual display of fear from her before her shoulders straightened and she declared, "We will go with you."

"Moira—"

"I was heading to market when they took me," she announced.

Tedrey felt his heart squeeze at the thought she was simply going about her business and she was thrown into a nightmare.

She was not finished speaking.

"Constance was in her own kitchen, baking bread. Terra and Irma were together, making apple butter and canning preserves for the winter. We were not safe in our own homes, living our own lives. The queen was killed at her son's wedding. Our prince, nay...*King* True, who is the fairest man in all four realms, had a conspirator publicly disemboweled. I cannot say I disagree with this choice. I also cannot say I agree with it. I simply cannot say. My mother was not executed at my wedding. She died after being run over by an apple cart. She will never see me wed. But I someday wish to be wed, Tedrey, and I do not know what was happening in that clearing, what is happening in our realm. All I know is that the only place I feel safe right now is at the side of a man who could witness those atrocities, and when he has the chance to flee, he does not. He puts himself at risk and saves my life and those of others. That is where I have to be. So I am going to Notting Thicket...with you."

Tedrey stared at her, his system coursing with such profound shock at her words, he was unable to do anything but just that.

When he had recovered enough, slowly, he turned his head and saw six other women staring at him.

Not Moira.

Him.

And slowly, they all nodded that they agreed.

"I have no coin," he told them. "I have no weapon. We have no mounts, no food."

"You are good and right in a topsy-turvy world, and for now, that is enough for me," Moira stated, apparently speaking for all.

They were going to Notting Thicket.

Tedrey and his women.

As the decision had been made and there was no time to waste, he didn't waste it.

"Everyone, find a stone," he instructed. "Then go to the wall. Quickly carve your name in it and state you are well, you are heading to Notting Thicket, and they can find you at Birchlire, seeking an audience with King True."

"Anyone who reads such a message will think us mad," Constance noted.

"Anyone looking, and I am certain loved ones are looking for you, Constance, will not care if you're mad. They will simply see you are alive, and they will know where you're going. And that will be all they will need not only to help them find you but give them hope."

Without another word, Constance did what the others were doing.

She started searching the ground for a stone.

Tedrey found his own stone and went to a section of dilapidated wood.

He thought hard, but not long, about what he would write.

And then he wrote:

Faunus, The Rising is done. But the creature has risen. I hasten to Birchlire to tell King True.

That was going to be the end of it, but he found himself turning back.

Thank you for seeking me. I hope you find me, for I very much hope to see you again.

He was not certain that Faunus was seeking him, though knowing Faunus, and Lorenz (as well as Nyx), he felt sure someone was. That noted, since he knew someone was, he was in little doubt it would be Faunus.

He also wished he had not written that last part, at the same time he was glad he had. But once he did, he found he could not stop himself from going on.

If something happens to me before you find me, know you had a place in my heart, tell Saturn he did too, and tell Lorenz and Nyx I died the man they made me, thus I did such with a clear head and a full heart.

"Are you writing a tome?" Moira asked over his shoulder. "Or should we be away to Birchlire Castle?"

"We should be away," he said. "Please tell the others to prepare to go."

"We have naught but the clothes on our backs, Tedrey," Moira pointed out. "We do not need to prepare."

"Teddy," he corrected.

"Pardon?"

He glanced at the "tome" he wrote on the wall before he looked back to Moira.

"My friends call me Teddy," he told her.

Her lips quirked and then she said, "Shake a leg…Teddy."

He smiled at her before he turned back to the wall, carved in a hasty "Teddy," and then he gathered his women.

After scanning the area outside with some intensity, they left the stables and Teddy took the lead.

But as they moved out, Moira fell in step at his side.

"I am sorry to hear your mother met with an accident that took her from you," he murmured.

"Good and right," she mumbled in return.

"Pardon?" he asked.

"Nothing," she replied, but then wrapped her fingers around his and walked much closer to his side.

Teddy felt the warmth of her hand, but also so much more through her touch.

Thus, he felt his head was positioned higher as he led them through the trees in the direction of Notting Thicket.

He also curled his fingers around hers.

And they were away.

128

THE INK

Queen Elena
Northeast Border
THE ENCHANTMENTS

I stood in the sun and stared at the open rift in the veil that we had not yet mended since it was rendered yesterday.

It would be mended that night.

I saw the new day was gray again in Airen, and threatened rain.

I also saw the contingent of warriors guarding the fissure.

Not their side and our side.

Mingled.

Nadirii warriors in their battle tunics and leg casings and Airenzian soldiers in their black leather.

And last, I felt his approach.

Only when he stopped to stand at my side did I turn my head to look up at him.

"True," I greeted.

"Ellie," he replied.

We stared into each other's eyes.

I suddenly knew not what to say, and I blamed this on the fact that the last time True and I stood under the sun in The Enchantments, we were in love and hoping against all the odds that we would find some way to live our love in a world where that wasn't possible.

Not much time had passed, but much had happened in it.

I was still in love, as was he.

But not with each other.

True broke our silence, whispering, "I would take you in my arms, your losses this grave, this fresh, to assure you of my friendship and support, and yet I feel I cannot."

"And now you know how I felt when you lost your mother."

He turned his body to me, lifting his hand to run his knuckles along my cheek.

"True," I whispered.

And then I was in his arms.

We held each other tight and it was again True who spoke first.

"Ophelia will be missed."

"Mercy will be missed."

"Jasmine was...well, *Jasmine*."

A bubble of laughter surged up my throat and out my mouth, and I took my cheek from his shoulder to tip my head back and catch his gaze.

"She was *Jasmine*," I agreed.

There was humor in his eyes, but it ebbed away before he said, "Tonight, during the ceremony, when it is released from its bounds down here, her spirit will restrengthen the veil that protects her sisters and she would be glad of that."

"I...I..."

I could not believe I was about to say what I was about to say.

But in that moment, the concept of the "us and them" that had been so long was extinguished now, as our soldiers stood intermingled after two days of battle side by side.

As my heart was owned by their future king.

And his heart was owned by my sisters' queen.

And for more reasons than the warmth and friendship I needed that I felt from his arms about me, I also needed True, the King of Wodell.

A man whose instincts and integrity I admired.

"I am thinking of not closing the rift...but creating two more."

True stared down at me.

I continued, "Another to the west, to Wodell. And another to the south, to Firenze. And perhaps, if they find their ways to heal the wounds they have thoughtlessly rendered in their handling of The Rising, also a third to the north. To Go'Doan."

"Elena," True murmured, openly astonished.

"We cannot...we cannot..." I shook my head. "We cannot call on other peoples to change, to grow in hearts and minds, to accept each other, to accept *us*, without building our own bridges. Or in our case, breaking down barriers in order to create gates that can be closed, but they can be opened as well."

"This would speak a profound message, but I am not certain how it would be received by your sisters," True remarked.

"I would not keep them open for anyone to come in at will," I told him, the plan taking shape as I spoke of it. "At least not in the beginning. We could create a sort of system. Documents required for entry. Petitions made where we will know the travelers' reason for being here, and either grant it, or deny it. We could vet them. We could establish some kind of communication with Airen, Wodell, Firenze. Assess if someone has some kind of unsavory history with your constabulary or...something."

I petered out in the end, deciding he must think I sounded quite mad.

"This would take a good deal of organization before implementation."

I gently pulled from his arms, turned, and standing in the warm sun as I looked to the rift between realms to see the gray beyond, I muttered, "It is foolhardy."

"I wouldn't say that."

I again shifted my attention to True.

"I'm simply saying it would be an onerous endeavor to take on, but not an unworthy one."

"I, well I feel like, something of this magnitude, I should, well...I should..."

I was speaking to True.

But I was also speaking to a king and what I was thinking of saying was outrageous.

And would seem more so to a supreme ruler of a realm.

"You should?" True prompted, his expression open and interested and so very True.

"Put it to a vote," I blurted. "Of the Sisterhood," I went on to explain. "To see if they agree and support my plans." When he said nothing, I murmured, "I sound mad."

"I've already begun forming a parliament," he announced.

I felt my lips part.

"And so I can say in all earnestness that you do not sound mad, Ellie," he told me. "You sound like you have been but days the queen of your people and yet you're demonstrating precisely why your mother decided on you to guide her realm into the next generation."

"Do you believe she would be supportive of it?" I asked.

"I feel she would have trusted you to do right by her sisters. And if you feel this is right in this time, yes. Definitely. She would have been supportive of it." He glanced at the rift and back to me, and when he spoke on, his voice had lowered. "And it is right in this time, Ellie. Trust your instincts. Your mother did."

I drew in a deep breath, released it and settled in the relief his words brought before I looked over his shoulder to see Cassius approaching.

True caught the direction of my gaze and twisted that way.

When Cass arrived at us, he muttered, "True," True muttered, "Cassius," and then my intended not only claimed me in a hold about my neck which was strong and fitted my front to his side, he kissed the top of my head.

Once he was finished laying this claim on me, I tipped that head back.

"All right?" he asked me.

"Yes," I answered, my eyes narrowing on him.

His lips twitched but he said no more and looked at True.

"Any news?" he asked.

"Of what?" True asked in return.

"Of anything," Cassius replied.

"Naught. You?" True said.

"Naught," Cassius murmured.

Cassius then sighed.

I tried to pull a hint away, and Cass allowed it.

A hint.

Thus, it was then I who sighed and wrapped my arms around his middle.

"What are you expecting?" I queried.

"Two days, two campaigns," Cass responded. "For the most part, they are not trained. They are not skilled. They have limited intelligence of our allegiances and our force, and that does not deter them. But they are organized, and they clearly have a plan."

"Calm before another storm?" True suggested.

"My guess, yes. Thus, we also must plan," Cass declared, his arm around my neck tightening for a moment before it relaxed again and he went on quietly, "Today is Jazz's. It is Rose's. Tomorrow, we will sit down and make decisions."

True nodded before he said, "Then now, I will leave you. Cass. Ellie."

"True, thank you," I replied.

"Any time, my friend," he murmured, warmth in his gaze on me.

He then jerked up his chin to Cassius, turned and strolled away.

I watched but stopped doing this when Cass asked, "Why did you express gratitude?"

I had my own question thus, I did not answer his and asked mine instead, "Was it necessary you lay claim to me in front of True? I mean, really, Cassius. I am yours, he is Farah's. This possession you feel it necessary to relay—"

"Cease speaking," he ordered.

I stood still in his hold, mostly so I wouldn't do something stupid, like break free and punch him in his arm (or elsewhere), and instead I shared my ire at his command by glaring up at him.

"Accept this, woman, it is the way it will be," he declared.

"Every time we're around True?" I demanded.

"Every time you are around a man."

Every time I...

What?

I could not believe what my ears were hearing.

"Have you gone mad?" I asked.

"No."

"Every time I'm around a man you will stake your claim," I stated to be certain I was hearing correctly.

"I will amend," he returned. "Every time you're around a man who might wish to be between your legs, be that in the past, the present, or I might have some inkling he would consider this in his mind in the future. Others, such as those who prefer their own gender, those too old to remember what to do with a stiff cock or those too young to know how to use one, no."

"You *have* gone mad," I decreed.

He shrugged.

I began to pull from him only to find myself pressed closer, but now we were front to front.

"It is me, Ellie," he informed me. "And you love me. So let it be."

"And what if I were to do this around every woman who might conceivably find you attractive, which is about seventy percent of all the realms, not including women who prefer their own gender, or little girls who have not yet learned the uses of men, but definitely including older women who likely never forget what a man can do with a stiff cock."

He grinned wolfishly down on me. "I invite your claiming at your leave, my queen."

I could only hold my glare for approximately three more seconds before I burst into such gales of laughter, I found myself collapsing against his chest.

When I was finished, and I felt his lips against the top of my hair, his hold about me, it came to me he had not laughed with me, and I realized what he was about.

He wanted me vexed, or frustrated, or amused.

He wanted me anything but grieved.

Oh, my Cassius.

I turned my head and pressed my face into his chest as I rounded him with my arms.

"Ellie," he whispered into my hair.

"It was good while it lasted, sweetheart," I told him.

I then burrowed into him.

His arms tightened.

We stood that way for some time before he gave me a squeeze and said something his tone told me eloquently, he very much wished he did not have to say.

"Hera shared that they are soon to begin building the pyres, my darling."

I nodded, my face rubbing against his leathers.

"After, I would ask that you attend me as I ink Jasmine into Mac's flesh."

I closed my eyes tight but did so nodding again.

I loved it that Mac intended to do that.

"Nero will then ink you into me."

I opened my eyes, dipping my head back, and caught his.

"And it would be my plan that you and I return to Sky Bay, with Mars, Silence, True and Farah," he continued. "For I will have you inked into me and then I will have you wed me without any further delay, no matter what these insurgents plan. You are my queen, but I wish you to be princess of my realm, my bride, and at long last, *my wife*. And when I make you just that, I want our friends about us. All of them." His face softened, "Or all of them we have left."

I felt my own face soften as I whispered, "I vote for this plan."

"We will return to the Bay when you feel you are ready."

"In my stead, I'm leaving Lucinda in charge of The Enchantments. She will protect it and she will keep the sisters calm and focused. Julia will remain with her to assist. But in this time of strife across Triton, I'm keeping Melisse with me."

"And Serena?"

"She is my top general, Lucinda was Mother's. Thus, my sister will stay with me and Agnes will be at her side to assist."

"Decisive," he murmured.

"You don't agree?"

"I think your mother chose you for many reasons, my warrior. And one of them is that you are just that. Decisive. Another is that you're able to delegate. We all have much happening, too much. Not a one of us can take it all on. It is only the wise who understand that with a depth that they do something about it and share the load."

I nodded and did so not hiding how his compliment made me feel.

"So, we have our plan," he said, his tone now gentle, which was a tender reminder that we did indeed have our plan, and as such, I had other things on my agenda for that day and I needed to see to them.

"We have our plan," I agreed.

"I felt you find some rest when your mother slipped into the veil," he noted in the same tone.

"The veil is a part of us, all of us," I told him. "Even you, though you are not attuned to it. But as we are, the Nadirii, those who are charmed, those who hold magic, we feel it more. She is a part of me as she made me, but when she slipped into the veil, she became a part of me in another way. So yes, Cass. It brings me peace."

"So, it will be good we can release Jazz and Rose and give you that," he murmured.

"Yes," I replied, coming up to my toes to touch my mouth to his. "Now I must set about preparing my friends."

In turn, he touched his lips to my forehead before he gave me a squeeze and let me go.

I walked several paces away before I turned around, still walking, but backward, and called his attention, which had shifted to the rent in the veil, back to me.

"Just so that you know," I said loudly, "I accept your invitation to claim you against all who might wish your stiff cock."

His body gave a mild jolt before he tipped his head back and roared with laughter.

And there...

For in all his care of me, I had not forgotten he had lost too.

Thus, a smile playing at my lips that I had managed to return the gift of a short respite that my man had given me, I turned again and headed with dread, but less of it than I could have felt, to where we would build the pyres.

~

Princess Serena
Northeast Border
THE ENCHANTMENTS

AFTER THE TASK WAS COMPLETE, as she strode from the pyres, she saw Chu where he had been sitting for some time, cross-legged in the grass, his back against a tree, his sword across his lap.

His eyes on her.

In fact, his eyes had been on her the entire time she helped her sisters erect the pyres.

She ignored him through this (as she had been ignoring him since their conversation the evening after the Battle of Heights, though it was hard to do so, especially when he fought at her side the day before—fortunately, that battle had been short).

Serena also ignored him as she strode toward the tent where she was sleeping, as her treehome was in the heart of The Enchantments, some forty miles away, and she was sticking by her queen, and her queen was not moving from the rift.

This was disappointing, she wished to show her treehome to Gal and Brix.

But as her queen was here, this was where Serena would be.

She did not, however, ignore Heloise, her lieutenant who, along with Genia, her other lieutenant, and Darma, her mentor, had ridden to the border upon hearing it had been breached.

And now, they stood huddled, some twenty feet away.

Serena did not ignore Heloise for Heloise broke off from the others and approached.

She stopped and waited for her friend to arrive.

It was with a heavy heart, but not surprise, when Heloise did not delay launching right in.

"You build Jasmine's pyre?" she asked snidely.

In her thirty-two years on that earth, Serena had learned very recently she did not know very much.

But in that moment, she knew that did not matter.

For she knew she needed to act solely on what was important in the now.

Her mother was dead.

Her only remaining blood, her sister, faced grave challenges on multiple fronts.

And her sister had not only forgiven profound affronts, even with the history Serena had created between them, without delay and without hesitation, she had settled her trust on Serena's shoulders.

Indeed, before they began building Jasmine's and Rosehana's pyres, Elena had taken Serena aside and said, "We will travel to Sky Bay soon, to regroup after these battles but also for my wedding. And if you will have the post, I would wish you to be my top general in this war we wage with the Airenzian against the Airenzian. And as such, I would have you by my side."

Serena hesitated nary a second in assuming that command.

She knew instantly her decision was the right one, for she watched her sister's eyes grow moist before Elena nodded and moved away.

And Serena no longer felt confusion or alarm at the feelings that came to her in the new bent of decisions she was making.

For her sister had lost a sister.

And Serena was giving her a new one.

And that felt right.

So, she was moving on, choosing family and nation above all else.

As her mother would do.

As her sister would do.

Thus now, *this*, with Heloise, she would not do.

And as such, her reply was simple, and obvious, for Heloise, with the others, had watched her do it.

"Yes. I helped to build Jasmine's pyre."

With that, she turned to regain her path to her tent.

Heloise moved to stand in front of her, forcing Serena again to stop.

"She died fighting with Airenzian *for* Airen," Heloise stated.

"I know. I was there. Fighting *with* Airenzian *for* Airen," Serena returned.

Heloise's face twisted before she hid it and asked, jerking her head in Chu's direction, "Who is that man who follows you?"

"He was the love of my life before he was lost to me."

Heloise did not attempt to hide her disgusted shock before she whispered, "The love of your life?"

"Yes," Serena confirmed.

"A man?" Heloise queried.

And Serena's patience slipped. "Yes, sister, your eyes are not deceiving you. He is indeed a man. Very much so."

"Who you loved," she stated with disbelief.

"Who I loved," Serena stated with conviction.

Heloise now appeared confused. "How is he lost to you when he's sitting fifteen feet away?"

"It's a long story," Serena mumbled.

"As it is clear you do not wish to share it, fine then," Heloise retorted. "But now tell me, why do you travel with gnats?"

Oh no.

Bloody no.

Serena's back shot straight as fire scorched through her veins.

This reaction must have registered on her face as well as in her body for Heloise took a step back.

"Those males are my friends," she clipped dangerously. "And when I could not trust you to call upon to be at my side, at my back, involved in my life, for you would not comprehend my mission and my purpose, *they were*. It was dangerous, Heloise. I could have been discovered by The Rising, and in their machinations, they shared clearly they did not mind dealing hostilely with those they thought were enemies. And a royal title made those dealings all the sweeter to them."

She drew in a deep breath, and with it a slender thread of patience, before she leaned toward her friend and finished.

"And if you...*ever*...refer to my friends, or any fucking gnome any-fuck-ing-where, Heloise, as a gnat again, I will challenge you, and I will unhorse you and then I will draw my sword and I will humiliate you in a way that you will *never* forget it."

Heloise knew Serena could do just that, and this was why her face paled before she started, "Rena—"

Serena leaned back with a snap of her spine and interrupted her.

"I serve the Nadirii Sisterhood. I serve Queen Elena. I serve my blooded sister as she takes her crown as the Princess Regent of Airen. And if you, Genia and Darma do not share these philosophies, I am honor bound to report that to my queen. I will advise her that she then relieve you of your duties in the Nadirii army. However, rest assured. Elena is fair. She will find you something else you are adept at doing."

It was Heloise whose spine snapped straight at that.

"I will remind you, I've been at your side since training," she declared.

"And I did not invite you to leave it," Serena retorted. "I simply told you the terms you must accept to remain at it."

Heloise glared at her.

Chu was watching, Serena was keenly aware of that, so she did not have time to allow Heloise the fullness of her glare.

She also did not have the patience for it.

She thus walked around her and resumed her path to her tent.

A tent Gal and Brix were now standing outside, also watching her.

Goddess, she hoped they were too far away to hear that gnat comment.

But seeing them, knowing why they stood where they stood, their gazes upon her, she thought it was funny that she knew them such a short time, but she felt their strength at her back far more thoroughly than she'd ever felt Heloise's or Genia's.

Or Darma's.

And she'd been to battle with them so many times, she'd lost count.

By the goddess, she'd been a fool.

It was with blatant design that Chu had positioned himself as such that he was not only close enough to watch her work at the pyre, but she'd have to walk by him on her way to the tent.

This she did not looking at him.

Even so, this did not deter Chu speaking.

"That was well said."

She ignored that and continued walking.

She also shot a look to Gal and Brix that shared without words she was in no mood for the mood she saw on both of their faces before she slapped the flaps back on her tent and entered it.

Gal and Brix, as they were wont to do, ignored her mood and charged in behind her.

"We must speak," Gal stated.

"We must not," she replied, throwing herself down on her pallet and casting her mind about for something to do, anything that would make her appear busy enough they'd leave her be.

She should be meditating before the ceremony.

One look at her friends and she knew there was fat chance of that happening.

"He's pining for you," Brix began, darting his arm out behind him to the tent flaps, finger pointed, indicating Chu, "in direct vicinity *to you*."

"And?" she asked.

Brix's brows shot up before they darted together.

"We must hear this story of what happened between you and him," Gal declared.

"We need hear no story," Brix put in. "He's a Trusted. Trusted are *trusted*. He wears the green and red against the black on his mantle. He has Mars's ear." He tossed his hand to indicate Serena. "And he fights gallantly at her side not only for this righteous mission, but in protection of her person, and she walks by him without looking at him?"

"Maybe he hurt her," Gal returned to Brix.

Brix made a chuffing noise, but then his eyes shot to Serena.

"You are strong," he said.

"Even a strong woman can be hurt by a man," Gal declared. "For the Green Man's sake, Brix. Hurt comes in a variety of forms. And the worst of it is the kind that does not leave a bruise that can be seen."

Brix's eyes, still on her, went squinty as he demanded, "Did he hurt you?"

"Brix—"

She got no more out.

He made his own (correct) assumptions, thus turned on his boot as if to march out, she knew, to confront Chu.

Bloody hell.

Except he did not get to do such.

The tent flaps slapped aside and instead they were all confronted with... Chu.

She cast her gaze to the ceiling of the tent, praying, *Goddess, deliver me.*

Chu's deep voice sounding brought her attention back to the tent.

"I would have words with Serena."

"And I would have Sinchella, the fairest maid of The Doors, take my cock," Brix retorted. "But she prefers gnomes with a great deal more coin than I have, so there's little chance of that. As there's less chance of you speaking to Serena if she does not wish to be spoken to."

It was at that, Serena was again surprised at her reaction for she not only wished greatly to burst out laughing, she wished even more to rise, walk the four feet of the tent to Brix, and give him a hug.

"Serena," Chu called.

"We have said all there is to say," she reminded him.

"And that says all that needs to be said in the now before you leave," Gal added, speaking to Chu.

"Little mouse," he murmured, eyes glued to Serena.

It was the wrong thing to do.

Gal's silent anger filled the tent.

Brix's filled it with words.

"Never pick a fight with a gnome, Trusted," he spat. "We have a direct line to your balls, so we do not consider it a low blow."

"Calm," Chu growled. "It is my pet name for her."

"She is no mouse," Brix retorted.

"She's *my* mouse," Chu returned.

"That's absurd," Brix shot back. "Think of another pet name. Like firebrand."

"Or maiden warrior," Gal suggested.

"Or minx," Brix went on.

"Hellcat?" Gal asked Brix.

"Works well, brother," Brix muttered.

Serena was listening to them prattle, an error on her part.

For when Chu's rich laughter filled the tent, it took her by surprise.

And his face softened with humor felt like a punch to the chest.

She dropped her head, focusing her efforts on keeping her heart beating, instead of it refusing to withstand the severity of the blow.

Gal most certainly noted her reaction, for his tone was much changed, conciliatory, calming, but beseeching when he said, she knew, to Chu, "You really must go."

"I cannot go, for I'm in love with her."

Her head dropped even farther.

"Then *we* must go," Gal whispered. "Brix," he prompted, for clearly Brix was not of the same mind.

"I'm not going," Brix proved her correct.

"Brix," Gal warned.

"Gal," Brix returned.

"*Welbrix.*"

"*Galbdor.*"

Serena opened her eyes and said quietly, "Go. I will speak with him and I will be fine."

Both her friends turned to her.

"You are certain?" Brix asked.

She nodded.

Both gave her a thorough assessment before they made their moves to leave.

"If she's upset any further…" Brix issued this open-ended threat to Chu before he moved through the flaps.

Chu gave it a moment before he said softly, "They are good males."

Well, at least they agreed on that.

"Yes."

"Serena—"

She stopped him before he could start.

"This is not happening."

"My beautiful warrior," he whispered.

Another shot direct to the heart.

"Please, don't," she begged.

He studied her, and as he did, he appeared to be getting angry.

This was proved correct when he bit out, "Why?"

"I loved my mother, and she is lost."

"I am sorry about that, my mouse, but—"

"She was lost before I could show her what I had learned. What she would wish to know. She left this earth, she joined the veil, not knowing she could be proud of me."

Chu stood at the flaps of the tent, apparently frozen by her words.

"And I lost you by—" she began to continue but interrupted herself as she had only the time to brace for impact before she was on her back on her pallet, Chu's weight atop her. "Chu," she wheezed, partly because of his weight, partly because, bearing it was so beloved by her, she could not process it.

"She speaks my name again," he murmured, staring down at her and shifting so some of his weight was held in his forearms and his hands could frame her face.

"I—" she began.

"You did not lose me, I am right here," he pointed out.

"I cannot—"

"You can."

"We cannot—"

"We can and we *will*."

Of a sudden, staring up into his eyes, feeling him there, the only thing in her world in that moment, the only thing beyond that moment, in weeks past and into a bleak future that she wanted most in her life—outside her mother's return to this earth—something started happening deep within her.

The strength of it, the foreignness of it so frightened her, in a panic, she bucked against his weight and started to fight him, for he was there, and she could not fight *it*.

The unknown happening to her with Chu right there...*right there*...made her clumsy and inept, thus he quelled her struggles with laughable ease.

But Serena could not dwell on that.

It was overwhelming her, whatever "it" was.

And she feared she could not defeat it.

"Let it go," Chu whispered in her ear right before she shoved her face in his throat and an excruciatingly painful sob wracked her entire body.

She was crying.

She had not cried in...

Goddess, even as a little girl, she did not cry.

With a hand cupping the back of her head, keeping her face against his skin, his other arm curled around her and he slid to the side, holding her tight to him as she wept.

And wept.

And *wept*.

Through her tears, she heard the tent flap open and she tensed.

But she needn't have worried.

Chu adjusted, hiding her with his big body, even as she felt his neck twist to look to the opening.

"She mourns," he murmured.

"I'll come back," Serena heard Elena say softly. "Erm, thank you for, um, seeing to her," she finished awkwardly.

Chu made no reply.

Serena only knew Elena had retreated when he settled at her side and started stroking her back.

When she had a handle on her tears—not a firm one, but a handle— Chu said tenderly, "Your mother was proud of you."

"I gave her no reason."

"I am of the understanding there was many a battle she sent you to win to keep your people safe, and you rarely failed her, or your people."

Well, there was that.

"Do you lament not being named queen?" he asked.

She tipped her head back to look up at him. "I have no patience for foolishness, stupidity or weakness. I also do not like my time wasted. I'd make a terrible queen."

His lips quirked.

"I lament she died disappointed in me."

"You simply lament, Serena, that she died."

She pressed her lips tightly together, for he was correct.

The air did not feel right, knowing her mother was not somewhere, breathing it.

He took his arm from around her to run his fingers along her jaw.

And doing thus, he murmured, "I have missed you."

She tucked her face back in his throat.

"Pride," he said over her head, his fingers gliding down her neck, over her shoulder, down her back, and he was holding her again. "It was torture, knowing you worked the Shanty without me at your side. I worried for you, day to day, hour to hour, minute to minute, held back from returning to you by my pride." She felt his lips at her hair. "We must be aware of this, my maiden warrior. We both have much of it so we must guard against giving in to our pride."

"As you know, I am no maiden."

"Thank all the gods."

She found to her surprise she was grinning at his throat.

"I quite like hellcat," she muttered.

His humor was not audible, but his body shook with it.

Serena closed her eyes tight and took a chance telling him something that made her vulnerable, but that he should know.

"She would have liked you. She would have found you most interesting. She would have enjoyed listening to the fables you carried to this land from your own. She would have admired your beauty and your skills. She would have...she would have been pleased for me with you."

"She was a great ruler and a good mother so I would have liked her too."

At his reaction, Serena took another chance with something that made her even more vulnerable, but he definitely should know.

"I would have liked to give you a good mother."

Chu's reaction to that was to squeeze the breath out of her with his arms.

She allowed this and it lasted long, almost to the point her need for air meant she could no longer allow it, before he relaxed and replied, "I will take her through your sharing of memories."

Serena turned her head to press her cheek to the base of his throat.

"Serena?" he called.

"Yes," she whispered.

"Thank you for forgiving me."

And she closed her eyes yet again.

Her reply, "And thank you, Chu, for forgiving me."

He shifted in order for his lips to find her forehead, where he pressed a kiss.

He then settled them, front to front, in each other's arms, on her pallet, and he fell silent.

Thus, Serena meditated in preparation for a rite in a way altogether new to her.

And in doing it, regardless of all the uncertainty, hostility and mayhem that swirled about four realms, she experienced the most beautiful time of her life.

Suspended in quiet mourning.

With Chu at her side.

~

Queen Elena
Beside the Double Pyres, Northeast Border
THE ENCHANTMENTS

IT MADE it a might bit easier this time, for Cassius now knew the ritual, and his part in it, so he took the decision to stand behind me, his arms around me at my chest, his chin resting on my shoulder, as we watched.

And the support he offered, both emotional and physical, was heartening.

Though what was not easier, witnessing Mac, with Hera standing at his side, her hand clasping his tight, as he stood beside Jasmine's body, gazing down at her, sorrow and regret for times that would never be shared, words that would never be uttered, love lost that ended too soon suffusing his handsome features.

Having already had our moments with her, along with myself, Jasmine's mother and two blood sisters watched him as did hundreds of Nadirii.

"I would..." His voice was croaky, he cleared it, looked down to Hera at his side then over his shoulder at me. "With respect, I would like to expose her face."

I clenched my teeth against my own emotion, looked to Jasmine's mother, who gave her assent with a nod, and thus I gave the same to Macrinus.

Hera let his hand go so he could reach to Jazz and expose her features.

She looked asleep.

So beautiful, my friend was so beautiful.

And seeing her visage again, my frame reared gently with the effort it took to hold back my sob.

Feeling it, Cass, my prince, held tight.

It was then I felt a new presence come to stand at my side.

I turned my head and saw Serena there.

She was close.

Very close.

But she did not touch me, nor did she look at me.

"You were bloody minded."

Mac's voice regained my attention at the pyre.

"So bloody minded, I would have died for you, but no. You wouldn't allow that. Instead, you did it for me."

I again clenched my teeth.

"And you were hilarious. It was almost as fun to fight with you as it was to make love with you," he carried on.

I watched as his ear dipped to his shoulder, his neck twisting, before he righted his head.

"Almost," he whispered.

I swallowed.

"We would have made beautiful children," he said.

I closed my eyes, forcing the tears to fall so I could see the sad beauty before me clearly, quickly reopening them so as not to miss another second of it.

This because I needed it.

I needed to know, before she was lost, my glorious friend had that kind of love.

"Tonight, I will ink you into my skin and carry you with me," he vowed.

"Through my life. To my grave. And as I lie in my shroud and the earth reclaims me, you will be with me, until I am no more. One with the earth, becoming that, with you."

I took one hand from grasping the arms Cass had around me and reached to my sister.

Part of me thought her fingers would not find mine, and I knew I would be fine with that, for that was Serena.

But all of me felt profound gratitude when I was proved wrong and my sister's fingers curled around mine, warm and sure.

Thus, connected with two of the most important people in my life, we all watched another of those, Mac, lean in and touch his lips to Jasmine's.

He left her face unshrouded as he took Hera's hand and guided her around to Rosehana.

Without asking, Hera exposed Rose's face, and without speaking, she gazed at it.

And after long, solemn moments, she whispered, "Tonight, I will ink you into my skin, my little bug, my sweet warrior, and carry you with me," she vowed. "Through my life. To my death. And until I am released into the veil, you will stay with me. And when I am no more, I will become that, with you."

I did not know Hera had made the decision to do this, and perhaps she had not.

Perhaps she heard the beauty of Mac's vow and decided to make it her own.

It did not matter which way it was, I was pleased she intended to do this.

For her.

And for Rose.

I squeezed Cass's arm and Serena's hands hard.

They both squeezed back.

Even Serena.

Hera and Mac moved around Rose's pyre toward Cass and me, joining the inner circle as Cass shifted to my side and took my hand and also Hera's.

I allowed Hera to begin the rite, and she did not delay in doing that.

And when my beloved friends joined the veil, the damage done to our realm was repaired.

They would like that.

They would wish that.

And I would give them that.

For now.

∼

I SAT on a mat beside the campfire, my eyes riveted to what was happening before me.

Cassius, bare chested, his trousers partially undone and open, exposing the newly shaved area above his cock on which was a fresh mark that denoted me, my ownership of him, and thus...*us.*

Also bare chested, with a new mark in the now I could not see for Hera's position was hiding it, one that was over his heart, was Mac. He was on his arse, his legs spread, his knees bent, and between them, resting back against his chest, her own torso fully exposed, was Hera.

Cassius was on his knees beside her, bent over her, inking Rose into her skin at her inside left breast.

Hera had her head resting on Mac's shoulder, his arms were about her, hands flat on her belly, and her chin was tipped down, watching Cass at work, as Mac's chin was on her shoulder, and he was doing the same.

I had not missed that they had found each other after their losses. Hera was not of that bent it would become more, but I felt there was great beauty that they would not mourn alone. They both had someone they could turn to who understood.

They were, in a way both beautiful and sad, each other's unicorns.

"It is discomfiting to wonder why I so loathed these men for as long as I could cogitate," Serena, sitting at my side, muttered her thoughts into mine.

"Some of them are pretty magnificent," I muttered in return.

"This I see," she replied. "And with the way our sisters are watching this ceremony, and Hera's participation in it, I foresee ink spreading across The Enchantments."

It was my opinion this would not be bad.

"I did not think there was anything good about that realm," she admitted.

"Perhaps we are not the sum of our parts," I suggested.

"Mm," she hummed.

"Though, if it makes you feel better, there are some of them who are significant arseholes," I shared.

I heard my sister chuckle, and I felt magic fill me at the hearing of that, wondering if that magic came from her to me, or if it came from Mum and Jasmine happy that she gave it to me.

"Can I trust this, uh...*Trusted*?" I asked.

"I...he is...that is, we..."

At her struggle for words, something that was most unusual from her, I tore my eyes from the ceremony before me and looked to my sister.

When I caught her gaze, she said, "I would race to the moon for him. And I would fall through the skies for eternity with him in my arms."

"Serena," I whispered, stunned at the poetry of her words.

"I know not how it happened, Elena," she replied. "It just...did."

"It has a habit of doing that."

"It just did for you too, with Cassius?"

I nodded but said, "Well, he sort of earned it."

"In Chu's case, he sort of *demanded* it."

Demanded it?

Of Serena?

I raised my brows.

"Do not ask how that happened either. It just...did," she muttered

I grinned at her.

She stared at my mouth like she'd never seen such before, then, hesitantly, she gave it back.

"You are incomplete."

Cassius's announcement had us both looking back to the firelit ceremony.

We had heard these words, and the ones we knew were to follow, before.

Nero had said them to Cassius when he finished his ink, Cassius said them to Mac when he'd finished Mac's, and now, her marks finished, Cassius would say them to Hera.

"Your story continues," he went on. "These marks honor your body. Your body honors these marks. You have taken the ink never to forget this part of your tale. You have taken the ink always to remember the importance of your life's whole story. You have taken the ink to honor what it represents. You have taken the ink vowing to hold in reverence this story of your life throughout your life, to your death, to your pyre, until you become one with the veil. Honor these marks, Hera, for they honor you."

"I will, Cassius Laird," Hera murmured.

"To your death, to your pyre, until you become one with the veil?" he demanded, rather belatedly if you asked me. The deed was done. But who was I to say how they should conduct a centuries-old ritual?

"To my death, to my pyre, until I become one with the veil," Hera made her oath.

"You are incomplete," Cassius repeated. "And Hera," he went on. "Regardless of the sorrow that taints this ceremony, rejoice in the beauty of that."

Rejoice in the beauty of that.

I'd first heard Nero say that to Cassius some time ago after my man's marks were done

But I'd been so intent on the act of his marking me into his skin, I had not considered those words.

Rejoice in the beauty of that.

Rejoice in being incomplete.

Rose was complete.

Jazz was complete.

My mother was complete.

I was incomplete.

And regardless of the sorrow that had settled in my soul.

I had more story to tell.

And I rejoiced in that.

"I will, Cass," Hera whispered.

Cassius smiled at her then set his instruments aside for someone to clean up and pushed back on his feet.

I lost track of most everything as I watched his hips swaying, his opened trousers moving with them, as he made his way to me.

Indeed, his movements mesmerized me to the point I also missed Chu joining us by dropping behind Serena and surrounding her with his body.

I vaguely noted acute attention to this act coming from all around, but only vaguely as Cass, and his opened trousers, was crouching in front of me.

I forced my eyes up to his.

"Please tell me after taking that mark where you took that mark that you're not out of commission," I begged.

And at my words, I received my second wolfish grin of that day from my prince.

"Absolutely not," he told me.

"And please tell me your gnome friends do not share a tent with you," I heard Chu murmur at my side.

"Absolutely not," I also heard Serena reply.

I pushed up, reaching out my hand to grab Cass's to pull him up with me, announcing, "Time for bed."

Cass chuckled.

I looked down at my sister who did not look entirely comfortable resting against Chu in the nest of his body, doing so for all eyes to see.

But she also didn't look like she intended to move anytime soon.

"Until the morrow," I bid.

"Until the morrow, sister," she replied.

I shifted my gaze to Chu. "We haven't officially met. In truth, it is unnecessary, for I know you, and you know me. That done, I will now share, if you hurt her again, I will crush you."

Chu simply smiled.

Cass got close to my back and said in my ear, "Let us go, lioness."

His words raced down my spine and detonated somewhere pleasant.

I gave Chu a strong look, my sister a goodnight look, then we moved to Hera and Mac whereupon I embraced both my friends, Cass clasped Mac on the shoulder and embraced Hera.

And finally, we made our way to our tent.

Another day not quite done, but close to it.

In a life that was joyously incomplete.

129
THE VENGEANCE

Lord Johan Mattson
McGarrity's Teahouse (a Brothel), The Arbor
WODELL

He liked the addition of the looking glass in this particular chamber.

Very much so.

And he studied himself in it, thinking he was still most virile and fit, before he felt a movement below him that took his attention from himself down to the body prostrated on its knees before him.

Oh yes.

That was what he was doing.

He liked that arse. It was curved and generous, the skin smooth and creamy.

Pegeen had always been his favorite.

He had no issue with the other two.

But he only used them when he wished some diversity of diet.

He grasped onto that ass, thrusting in her cunt, and then he smacked a cheek.

"Who's my whore?" he demanded.

"I am, milord," she replied, and he did not like the way her words sounded.

Thus, he bent forward, wrapped his hand around her hair and yanked it back, enjoying very much the noise of pain she emitted when he pulled her from her forearms up to her hands.

"Who is *my whore?*" he demanded.

"I am, milord," she panted, her body now moving to meet his thrusts.

"Yes, you are," he gritted, driving more forcefully into her, fancying she'd never had it that good. "Say it."

"I am your whore."

"Say it," he demanded.

She gave him what he liked.

"I am naught but a whore, *your* whore, Lord Johan."

Oh yes.

Yes.

"Say it," he gritted.

"I am a whore," she whimpered.

"*Say it,*" he bit.

"I am a whore," she whispered.

And he burst, slamming inside her, spilling his seed.

He again yanked back on her hair, enjoying the noise she made, before he fell forward, his forehead resting on her spine.

"You are...you are..."

His eyes had closed in his climax, but hearing these stammered words come from the direction of the door, they shot open.

"*Vile.*"

He shot straight and turned his head, feeling his eyes widen as he saw his wife standing there, her face ashen, her expression filled with hurt, staring at him in shocked agony.

"What on—?" he began, quickly pulling out of Pegeen to turn to his spouse.

"*Vile!*" Vanka cried.

Snatching at the bedsheets, Johan tugged them around his hips.

"Vanka—" he started again but was unable to say more.

"This one, this one you *pay,*" she said, throwing a hand toward Pegeen, who was scuttling away. "You installed her in *your daughter's home.*"

"Vanka," he said, struggling with the sheets to find his feet beside the bed.

"The others, they work here too. *They take you too!*"

"Wife, get a handle on yourself," Johan snapped, having found his feet, and thus his equilibrium in this ridiculous turn of events.

"You've been unfaithful to me," she returned, then shrieked, "*Repeatedly!*"

"Vanka," he approached her, "quiet down."

"No!" she snapped, shuffling to the side to escape him, but not the room. To his astonishment, she stood her ground. "You...you...you made her say she was your—"

She'd heard.

"Stop speaking," he commanded.

"You do not get to tell me what to do anymore, Johan," she returned, her pale face now turning red. "It is not simply that you took prostitutes. It is not simply that you hired prostitutes to attend your daughter's home. It is that you hired *your* prostitutes that *you* use to be unfaithful to me to attend your *daughter's home.*"

"She is not my daughter," he retorted.

"She is," Vanka spat, and Johan saw, and ignored it, as Pegeen scurried out of the room. "You commissioned her, you do not get to renounce her."

Johan decided a change of subject was in order.

"How did you know I was here? Are you following me?"

"You have made an enemy you should not have made, Johan. But you could not help it for you are..." she shook her head in short angry shakes, concluding, "*you.*"

"An enemy? What enemy?" he demanded to know.

"Only you," she said, her voice breaking.

"Make sense, woman," he bit.

"Only you," she repeated. "Only you would make an enemy of not only your daughter's husband, but the bloody *Fire King.*"

Johan's insides seized.

That animal.

That gods-damned animal!

That fucking *swine* had instigated this.

He would pay.

Oh, he would...

"You will not," Vanka declared.

Johan focused on her and saw she'd noted the direction of his thoughts.

"You will not tell me what to do," he spat.

"No," she said. "He will."

And with not another word, but he did hear her swallowed sob, his wife swept from the room.

She was gone nary a second before a tall, straight, good-looking young man in Dellish constabulary greens walked into the room.

Johan pulled the bedclothes tighter about him and announced, "I will have privacy."

"You will have notice, sir," the man returned, "that there is irrefutable evidence, as witnessed by me, your wife, and another member of the constabulary." He tipped his head to the opened doorframe, in which stood another man, less tall, less good-looking, but also wearing constabulary greens. "Of committing adultery."

Johan's blood ran cold.

It was not strictly against the law to commit adultery.

However, it was significantly looked down upon.

And if the betrayal was repeated, or longstanding, and a spouse wished to press matters, and had proof, the law there was could make it financially inconvenient.

"Your wife can press dissolution of the household," the constable told him something Johan knew. "Which she has already charged us with doing. And if you do not understand what that means, it means, with the extent of your infidelity, which management and workers of this establishment alike have shared has lasted years, your wife can petition as her wont for restitution."

As her wont.

This meant, if his adultery was proved, the length and the extent of it especially, which had been witnessed, and discussed, thus it would be proved, Vanka could make the wildest demand.

And he would be forced to grant it.

This did not happen very often.

Mostly because it was difficult to prove and that was mostly because establishments such as this did not often share about their clienteles' penchants. If they did, they would find themselves without a clientele.

Something this particular establishment might not have to worry about, if those in it were compensated by the wealthiest bloody king on the gods-damned continent.

Johan fought seething and opened his mouth to try speaking, "I—"

"This, however, is the least of your worries," the man carried on.

The least of his worries?

The constable continued, "For we are here not only on that errand, as charged by your wife, but on the report that you hired three women, who did not wish to take on this task, but had no choice due to life circumstances, and pressure from you with your title in your position, to spy on the king and queen of a nation allied with Wodell. And that, sir, is an act of treason."

Johan's entire frame froze.

"Now, it would be good of you to get dressed and come with us," the man finished.

"I...they...I..." He pulled himself together. "They, the whores, had no issue taking my money."

"You can share your version at the tribunal," the man said. "Now, please, dress."

"I cannot stand tribunal," Johan whispered.

The shame alone...

"If King True is feeling charitable, he could simply demand restitution in return for a guilty plea. Though, with a charge as serious as this, it could mean the relinquishing of the Arbor, after, of course, you make other restitution to your wife."

"The Arbor has been my family's seat for nine generations," he whispered.

"Again, please dress, sir."

"I cannot lose my seat," Johan told him.

"We can haul you out of here in that sheet," the constable at the door entered the conversation. "Your choice, milord. But you got about a minute to make it before I do."

It was no choice.

Johan hurried to dress, feeling anger and shame burning equally as neither member of the constabulary showed the slightest respect by even averting their eyes as he did it.

He had a handle on himself as, fully garbed, he walked their way.

"I demand a message sent immediately to my solicitor," he declared.

"Sure," the man in the door stated, shifting out of his way.

Johan stopped before he moved through it. "I also demand a word with my wife."

He would talk some sense into the stupid woman.

"We can make the request, but she's free not to grant it."

He tipped his head back. "She'll grant it."

"To save you a burning disappointment," the man in the door began, and Johan decided he did not like him very much, "she watched your performance through the window."

"The window?"

The man pointed across the room.

Johan looked there to see the mussed bed overhung with the new looking glass at the wall at the head.

"You can see yourself on this side, we can see you on the other," the man said.

Johan's throat closed.

"And she could too," the constable finished.

Vanka had...

Watched?

He felt his skin start itching.

He ignored this sensation and snapped, "Is this magic?"

"Nah, just a certain kind of silver."

"This cannot be legal," he bit out.

"I know no laws against it," the constable that had entered the room tired of the conversation and shared this by coming to Johan and taking his elbow in his hand. "Though there are laws against spying on a visiting monarch for any reason not condoned by the king. That's frowned on rather seriously," he stated, leading Johan forcibly from the room.

"I can walk on my own," Johan sniped. "And I wasn't spying on Mars. I was keeping watch on my daughter."

"Isn't she the queen of an allied realm?" the first constable asked the second.

"Yup, heard she visited orphanages and rode in the royal wedding procession and everything," the second constable answered. "I'd say that constitutes a 'visiting monarch.'"

"I do not find this amusing," Johan stated, trying to jerk his arm free.

He did not succeed.

Instead, the fingers around it tightened painfully and he was jerked to face the first constable. The one who had entered the room.

"We do not find this amusing either. And it is known wide our king particularly favors his cousin, Queen Silence. And thus, I also don't think he will find it amusing. My advice, I would start being smart, and I would start being that right about now, *milord.*"

Johan gulped.

The man resumed guiding him down the hall, but it could be more described as dragging him.

His humiliation, he would find, was not yet complete.

This, when he was not taken out a back way, or similar.

But instead, he was paraded through the social parlor of the brothel.

And it was a busy night.

He kept his head held high even in the silence that descended when he entered the room, and through the attention he received as he was pulled through it.

However, before he was drawn through the front door, he saw a large, dark man in sandstone leathers, a black mantle edged in red falling from his shoulders, his black eyes homed in on Johan.

He was leaning against a wall with his arms crossed on his chest. And he was clearly not there to look over the girls and find one to use.

One side of that Firenz animal's lips ticked before he pushed from his spot and then he walked through a door Johan had never used, but he knew it led to a back hall that would lead out a back door.

By the time he'd stepped up into the constabulary's carriage, Johan was shaken.

Thus, he looked down at the officers and stated, "I believe there's been a terrible mistake."

"And his plight dawns on him," one muttered.

"How about we let your solicitor sort that out, hmm?" the other one suggested.

And without another word, or allowing Johan to have one, they shut the carriage door right in his face.

And Johan Mattson's blood turned to ice as he heard the bolt turn.

130
THE REPORT

Sir Alfie Henriksson
The King's Informal Study, Birchlire Castle, Notting Thicket
W*ODELL*

Alfie did not like sitting behind True's desk, though when he received reports like this one, both Tor and Apollo (Tor being a king himself, Apollo being head of a House in his land, that being titled gentry, with command of his queen's army) advised him he should.

And True told him to make his study Alfie's own when True was gone and Alfie was acting in his stead.

So he sat behind the desk and listened to the reports of the swiftly waning power of The Rising.

"Thus, there are only two priests still at large," the sergeant sitting in front of him stated. His name was Holder Mikaelsson. He was a capable man, all business. So much so he reminded Alfie of himself, when he was whole. "We've concentrated our efforts on them and sent our best trackers after them. We're confident they'll be in Crittich Keep very shortly."

Alfie nodded.

Mikaelsson shifted in his seat in a manner so unlike him, Alfie went alert, along with Tor and Apollo, both of whom were sitting opposite him, across from Mikaelsson, their attention on the sergeant.

"Is there more?" Alfie prompted.

"There has been...a massacre."

Alfie straightened in his chair, Apollo leaned forward, Tor sat back.

"A massacre?" Alfie asked quietly.

"Women, thirty-two of them to be exact," Mikaelsson stated.

"Bloody hell," Tor swore.

"They had been debased, and then stabbed and finally had their throats slit. This in a remote area at the base of the Lesser Thicket Forest. There was another, found farther away from the area. She was discovered not wearing any clothes, stakes tied to her wrists and ankles. She perished of exposure, we're assuming, during an attempt at escape. We, um..."

When Mikaelsson hesitated, Alfie impatiently rolled his hand at him to continue.

"We have had a message from the local constabulary. An irate one," Mikaelsson shared. "Apparently, they sent repeated notices to the king over the years that women had gone missing with regularity, never to be found, and asked for investigators from the Keep to be dispatched. These notices were either downplayed or ignored by the crown."

"*Corporal!*" Alfie bellowed the instant the man ceased speaking.

One of the soldiers standing outside the door opened it and stuck his head in.

"Request King Wilmer grant me an audience at his earliest possible convenience," Alfie ordered tersely. "This being, please impress upon him, *now.*"

"Right away, sir," the man said, then disappeared behind the closed door.

Alfie cast his gaze through Tor and Apollo, both of whom appeared incensed, before he returned his attention to Mikaelsson.

"I wish to see this message from the constabulary in Lesser Thicket immediately," he demanded.

"I will have it couriered to you the moment I get back to my desk," Mikaelsson stated.

"And I wish every notice sent to the king found and delivered to me," Alfie continued.

"It will be done," Mikaelsson told him.

"Is aught more known about this situation?"

"Only that, over time, it was one girl here or there, within what is now understood is about a two-hundred-and-fifty-mile radius around this area where the recent bodies were found. Not knowing what this area was, for it is nothing but a clearing, though it would appear from the marks on the bodies, and the girl who was found, that all the women were staked to the ground in it with, perhaps, some ritual being held, and with that large of an area that covered several districts in two counties, it took some time for the local constabularies to realize that they all had a similar problem. However, it was only upon a great number of women going missing at once very recently that the locals established large search parties and came upon the pile of bodies."

Alfie felt his jaw would crack, he was clenching his teeth so tightly.

He forced them to loosen in order to query, "Were all the women who had recently gone missing killed?"

"They are uncertain if they have all the information, but as of now, at least five more women who had gone missing were not found with the bodies at the clearing. Though, their whereabouts are still unknown."

Fucking hell.

"There were also the bodies of two men," Mikaelsson went on, shifted in his seat again, alarmingly having trouble meeting Alfie's gaze, before he pulled himself together, looked right at Alfie, and stated, "One had had his head crushed by what appeared to be a great force, but it was caved in on both sides, not a weapon or a rock striking him in one. And there are no markings a weapon or a rock were used at all. The other was mauled, astonishingly brutally, indeed, his head was severed from his body by what appears to be the swipe of a claw, as if by an animal. A very large one."

"A bear?" Alfie queried.

"Bear do roam the Lesser Thicket, especially in unpopulated areas, but I have not seen the body, so I do not know."

"Are these men known?"

Mikaelsson shook his head. "They have not yet been identified, no."

Alfie drew in breath and sat back.

"Although there was much confusion and other reaction after the bodies were found," Mikaelsson went on, "thus tracks and footprints in the dirt were disturbed, it is thought that a number of people fled the area in all directions, men, and some women, one of the women barefoot, which, in tracking, was how they found the last victim. And there did seem to be some animal tracks. Hooves, like a horse. But they were odd. They were only found in a small area of the clearing, no horse tracks leading to or from that area, and there were only hind hoofprints.

However, it could be other tracks were destroyed in the commotion of finding the bodies."

"I'm assuming none of those who might have fled have been found," Alfie guessed.

"Not yet, though they are searching."

"Is there some indication this is of The Rising?"

He shook his head again. "It seems unrelated, sir. Though we've sent a variety of investigators to that area with due haste. Those who would aid in the search if some had escaped whatever happened. Those who would aid the locals in investigating what happened. And last, those who would determine if this atrocity happening in this time is a coincidence, or part of the larger issues we face."

Yes, Holder Mikaelsson was capable, all business, and fortunately thorough.

Alfie nodded and asked, "Is that all?"

"On that, yes. There is one other small matter, which I think you would be interested to know."

"It is?" Alfie queried.

"A priest, of this Rising, now in the Keep. His Go'Doan name was G'Seph. His given name is Joseph Durie, of the Airenzian. He has repeatedly told guards he was quite high up in that organization and is willing to share the inner workings of The Rising if a reduced sentence would be considered. There are, as you know, several prisoners who are attempting to make this same request. I report this one for he is the most vociferous in his requests, and he has recently mentioned the names G'Thom and Golden Thomas, which, as you also know, the guards were instructed to note and report if a prisoner cited them."

"We have ample prisoners in the Keep who can, and are, sharing the inner workings of these miscreants," Alfie replied. "And this one isn't the only one who's mentioned this Golden Thomas."

"I'll talk to him," Apollo cut in.

Alfie turned to Apollo. "I don't imagine True will be of a mind to be lenient with anyone in that faction."

"I won't make any promises," Apollo assured.

"Then as you wish," Alfie said.

"I'll go with you," Tor murmured.

"Excellent," Apollo replied.

Alfie looked again to Mikaelsson. "Are we finished?"

Mikaelsson nodded. "Yes, sir."

"Then, dismissed."

Mikaelsson nodded again, stood, dipped his chin to Apollo and Tor, then he left the room.

Alfie sat back in True's chair and turned his gaze to the two men.

But it was Apollo he addressed.

"You have an instinct about this priest?"

Apollo shook his head, but said, "I have heard that name before. In other reports. He is the man who had his hands shorn off by his own comrades."

"I remember," Alfie replied. "He also is the man who led Melisse into a trap and nearly got her killed, this *after* they'd shorn free his hands. My feeling is that indicates a rather extreme level of zealotry."

"Thus, it would be interesting, whatever he has to say," Apollo replied.

Alfie could see this.

Apollo put his hands to the arms of his chair and murmured to Tor, "We'll be away?"

"Once I talk with Cora. Tell her where we're going," Tor said.

"I shall also talk with Maddie. Half an hour? On the front steps?" Apollo suggested.

"I'll call for our horses to be brought 'round," Tor offered.

Apollo nodded.

They both stood, said their goodbyes to Alfie and left the room.

When the door closed behind them, Alfie looked down to his sticks that were resting on the floor by his chair, hidden from view.

He had been practicing on them as frequently as he could. However, he was finding to his frustration that his lower half was heavy and unwieldy, which made progress slow-going and tiring, so that frequency wasn't as frequent as he'd wish.

He could navigate across a room.

He could not get himself from True's study to his chambers without resting in chairs placed along the hall the entire way, this being done for the purpose of allowing him just that.

And stairs were impossible.

But navigating that hallway, under the carefully averted eyes of soldiers he once commanded, was a mortifying enough daily occurrence.

He couldn't even think on attempting stairs.

He closed his eyes, lifted his hand, and pinched the bridge of his nose just as he heard a knock on the door.

He dropped his hand and opened his mouth but closed it when he heard the latch turning and knew who it was.

He sighed and ignored his stomach warming.

This before who he knew would walk in without waiting for him to call his leave for her to do so, walked in.

Bronagh.

She closed the door behind her and bustled his way, asking, "Is your meeting done?"

Gods, she had far too many curves.

And too much hair.

And those bloody freckles.

"Alfie?" she called, and he started, lifting his eyes from her bosoms to her face.

Her cheeks were pink, but her manner was efficient.

He had, after insulting her gravely, managed to force her to listen to his apology, which she had accepted.

He had then managed to talk her into considering him as friend, which was harder to make her accept.

It was also hard for him to accept.

That said, all he had to do was look at his bloody sticks, his fucking useless legs, and it became a good deal easier.

"Is your meeting done?" she repeated.

"Yes, but I'm waiting on some missives I need to look over," he told her.

She appeared crestfallen, which was a rather dramatic reaction to his reply.

What on earth?

"I'm uncomfortable in True's chair, Bronagh," he reminded her of something he'd shared before in one of their many conversations, for she kept him company in his chambers often, now no longer simply as his nurse. "But I've spent so much time in that damned chamber, that damned bed, I'd rather be here than there. If you wish to stay and keep me company, get your book or your knitting, and be here with me."

"I'd hoped to talk you into going on a carriage ride."

He blinked slowly, nonplussed.

"A carriage ride?"

She threw herself in the chair Mikaelsson had vacated and Alfie again found himself gritting his teeth as she did, for much of her jiggled (and it was enjoyable to watch) while her hair bounced (and that was enjoyable too).

"Yes, Alfie, a carriage ride. You know, those wheeled conveyances, led by horses that—"

She would be outrageously annoying if she wasn't so adorable.

"I know what carriages are," he said with a sigh.

"Yes, well, the day is crisp and cold, but we could get a rug. And I know this bakery that does these vol-au-vents filled with the richest, meatiest stew you've ever tasted—"

"I can't go on a carriage ride with you, Bronagh."

"Why not?"

He refused to look down at his sticks.

Even if he did, she knew the direction of his thoughts.

"We can have the vol-au-vents brought to the carriage and eat them in there, Alfie," she said softly.

"I have things to do."

"It's always work with you," she huffed.

"This is because there's always work to do," he retorted.

"You have not been out of this castle since you were carried into it."

He did not like the reminder, but he kept his mouth shut on that.

"And again, this is because there is much work to do, Bronagh."

"You must enjoy life, Alfie," she returned.

"I enjoy life fine," he lied.

And she hooted, rolling her eyes, before she pinned him with them and stated, "Farah told me even before those horrible, *horrible* men did what they did to you, you were all about work and duty."

"I made an oath," he told her.

"I did too," she shot back. "Nurses take their own oaths, Alfie. To care with kindness. To maintain a steady hand. To ever have a listening ear. To never cease in learning. And that is not only my vocation, it is my calling. But it's not *my life*."

"Well this," he spread his hand over the desk in front of him, "is my life."

"It shouldn't be."

"Why not?"

"Because...because..." She bounced in her chair with agitation, and *gods*, his cock jumped with the same as she did, but his reaction was caused by something much different. "*Because!*" she finished.

"Bronagh, much is happening," he said low.

"And it will happen whether you sit in that chair or leave it for a few hours to enjoy a delicious vol-au-vent and then it will be here when you get back!" she declared hotly.

Bloody hell, it was irritating how clever she was.

It was especially irritating when she was clever during an argument.

He scowled at her.

She glared at him.

The door opened and King Wilmer swept in.

"I am now reduced to being summoned by a bloody knight," he groused instead of saying a greeting. "A crippled one."

Alfie's hands curled into fists.

Bronagh leapt from her chair.

When she did, Alfie's attention instantly shifted to her.

"Bronagh," he warned.

"No," she snapped, looking over her shoulder at him, her eyes wild with anger.

And *gods*, that look in her eyes...

If he had legs...

"What he said was not all right," she finished.

Fuck.

"Honey, no," he said gently.

Her eyes warmed considerably at hearing his endearment, something he had never given her, before she seemed to struggle and do it mightily.

But thankfully quietly.

She then declared, "*King* True will hear of this. And *we*," she pointed a finger rudely, but adorably, at Alfie, "are not done."

With that, she flounced from the room, slamming the door behind her.

"You should not accept that behavior from a nurse," Wilmer advised.

It would be a snowy day in Firenze before Alfie took Wilmer's advice.

"There was a massacre in the Lesser Thicket Forest," he announced. "Thirty-two women had their throats slit after they were violated and stabbed. The bodies of two men were found with them. This in an area that beseeched the crown repeatedly, as women with some regularity for some years had gone missing."

Wilmer blanched.

Seeing it, Alfie seethed.

This bloody imbecile.

"You know of this?" he pushed.

"Carrington told me he dispatched investigators. They were found to be runaways."

"I'm certain it is now unsurprising to you, but Carrington lied."

"By the gods," Wilmer whispered.

Indeed.

For if Carrington lied about this, it could have to do with his caring naught about the citizens of Wodell.

It could also have to do with The Rising.

"Do you remember aught else about it?" Alfie asked.

"I really...I just really..." Wilmer's shoulders sagged as he muttered, "I did not pay much attention."

"Thirty-two women are dead, and it is an assumption, but whatever number of girls went missing before them, they might be in the same state, for they have never been found. Does this not penetrate with you?"

The man's shoulders straightened as he admonished, "You are still speaking to a king."

"It is a title True left you with because his mother would wish it. But it has no meaning. And I would assume, by your reply, that the deaths of your citizens by such appalling means actually doesn't penetrate. Which, in turn, indicates *you* have no meaning."

Angry red rushed up Wilmer's neck to his face.

"We are done," Alfie muttered. "I have things to do."

"I would go to Bishop Cross," Wilmer suddenly declared.

Alfie stared at him.

"Gallienus told me I had an open invitation to holiday there," he continued. "It is warm at the Cross. And far from *here*. I will take my manservant and enough staff to manage the castle situated there and I will stay for the foreseeable future. This...all these..." he threw out a weak hand, "goings-on. They weary me."

Alfie did not remind him that Gallienus was no longer in the position to invite anything.

Nor did he share Wilmer was no longer in the position to requisition staff to take anywhere.

But as True would likely not hesitate to demur, Alfie didn't.

Thus, he asked, "Will you sail, or will you ride?"

"I see I will not be missed," Wilmer sniffed.

"No, you won't," Alfie affirmed without hesitation.

"You will find, the longer this war lasts in Airen, and True is away fighting it, how onerous is the mantle of rule."

The Airenzian war, if no ravens had gone astray that provided conflicting information, had now officially lasted all of four bloody days.

Alfie didn't get into that either.

"On the contrary," he replied blithely, "I find incarcerating those who caused harm and moving forward in bringing them to justice, righting a troubled treasury, and overseeing the expansion of the scope of our economy in an optimistic manner the likes of which this realm has not ever seen quite rewarding."

"Yes, and you have the luxury of one day stepping down when all that goes to hell."

"So did you," Alfie reminded him, watching Wilmer's body jerk. "Though, for my part, as my king's counsellor, and after swearing an oath to protect my land that I intend to keep, regardless I am now crippled, I don't intend to do that until I retire to a hearth and my books at a day when I am gray with age."

"I tire of this conversation," Wilmer decreed.

"This is good, for so do I."

After giving Alfie a long, hard look, Wilmer whipped his head around before his body in a manner that made Alfie nearly burst with laughter, before he flounced out much like Bronagh had done.

The door again slammed.

And Alfie put Wilmer out of his mind, and doing so, Bronagh entered it.

A carriage ride.

What was that woman thinking?

Alfie then had to force Bronagh from his mind (a much more difficult endeavor), and he did so as he picked up his sticks, hefted himself out of his chair and moved to the fire.

Carefully, he balanced on one stick as he quickly fed fuel to the irons.

He then maneuvered himself to the chair by the fire and settled in, equally pleased with himself he got where he was without a tumble, just as he was frustrated that was something he considered a victory.

He picked up the reports True had commissioned on how the counties and groups of charmed folk were reacting to the idea of a parliament. Files he'd abandoned when Tor and Apollo had arrived after he'd called for them when Mikaelsson came to make his report.

He was in the depths of reading them when another knock came at the door.

Calling leave for entry, a trainee soldier quickly delivered a bundle of parchments wrapped in military green ribbon that was sealed by a sergeant's wax mark.

He opened it without delay.

It took him an hour.

And he had to drag himself back to the desk to search through the drawers to find a calendar.

Thankfully, Wilmer's secretary had noted the dates of the quakes in the king's agenda.

But in making the connections, that was the only thing Alfie was thankful for.

He stared at the parchment on which he'd jotted all the dates with connecting lines.

He then bellowed, *"Corporal!"*

131
THE NEW AIREN

The People of Airen
The Royal Grazing Fields, South of Highgate, Sky Bay
AIREN

The cow herders in the fields and the soldiers that guarded the gate atop the cliffs were the only ones who saw them.

But at what they saw, the news would travel quickly as that news was *two unicorns* galloping into view *from thin air*, behind them riding their Prince Regent and his betrothed.

And then...

Then...

Oh, the spectacle!

The King and Queen of Firenze.

The King and Queen of Wodell.

The Dragon Commander and his Ice Bride of Lunwyn.

The Princess Serena and a man with the coveted mantle of a Firenz Trusted.

And finally...

Vast armies, including men, women, horses and supply carts.

Just as the ravens had heralded.

Just *so*.

Led by Prince Cassius and his golden-haired Nadirii queen, they entered the steep-graded, switchback avenue that climbed the face of the cliffs that marked the southern boundary of Sky Bay, riding toward Highgate.

The tall gates were open for day entry and the long procession rode right through.

And thus, it was the citizens of Sky Bay who witnessed what seemed to be a never-ending parade of royalty and military might making its way through the paved streets of the city, not dallying, but riding straight toward the lane that would take them to the Sky Citadel.

But birds had travelled far and fast since the Battle of the Heights five days ago, and the Battle of the Veil, which was just four.

Whispers had become open talk about the vanquishing of the Allied Gentry by their Regent in two places far away from each other, one battle which was described much more as a thrashing.

And these rumors, many found humorous.

Oh, those many Airenzian who clung so tightly to their traditions finding their just desserts in humiliation and defeat.

Really, what manner of man was threatened so by a woman?

She could cook and clean and mend and fuck, but not teach?

Not heal?

Not build?

Not guard?

The Nadirii warriors who assisted their Regent in trouncing the Allied Gentry proved all that so misguided, it was laughable.

And many, *many*, now free to do so, *laughed*.

Then again, the Nadirii had been doing such for centuries.

It was just now, those nitwits got a direct dose of it.

Oh yes, the veil had been ripped from Airen these past five days as unicorns rode and right prevailed.

And nowhere was it more evident than Sky Bay.

For those who had long since kept their mouths shut under the reign of kings who would shut it for them in unpleasant ways through their oppressive laws no longer had to hide behind closed doors and whisper amongst those like-minded about the impossibility of change.

Now, as their Regent and his bride rode through their streets behind unicorns, their royals openly noted surprise and even shock, when not only did many of the citizens rush to the edges of the streets and cry their "*Huzzahs*" when the heroes returned home...

Since they'd left on the heels of the king being sentenced to prison for decades, those of the New Airen proudly, gratefully and ecstatically *finally* were able to display their colors.

From sky-blue to heather-purple to Nadirii coral, and some with all colors in one, pennants could be seen everywhere.

Hanging proudly from windows. Draped over doorways. Flying from poles on roofs.

And those who had the time, inclination and coin to do it, painted their doors in New Airen.

These being any color of the sky, from dawn to midnight.

Or Nadirii purple or coral.

This was not all.

Oh no, indeed.

For men wore New Airen ribbons on the lapels of their frock coats, or neckcloths the colors of New Airen, doing this proudly to share openly the bent of their beliefs.

And women made quick work of dying petticoats all manner of blue, purple and orange.

And those women with the means had blouses made of those colors.

Indeed, down at the docks of Twilight Harbor just two days before, when news arrived the Battle of the Veil was won by their Regent and his queen, the innkeepers and pub owners opened taps and the doxies heated vats in the streets.

The whores then stood delightedly in the cold in their skivvies as they tossed their skirts and underthings in the vats. The same vats where men and women's hands and arms and chests and legs and faces were drunkenly dyed the colors of the skies it was told in ancient times their kings had commanded, and they were dyed thus in celebration.

It would be remiss not to note that the news their future princess had become a queen at her mother's passing had been observed by the citizenry.

And this was the only thing that stopped the procession on its way to the Citadel.

It had to halt, for across the lane that led up to the castle, a three-foot high pile of flowers, coins, scraps of purple or coral silk, broken arrows and white oak leaves barred their path.

Prince Cassius and his queen had to round their horses and jump the tributes to make the lane of the Citadel.

And at Cassius' command, the carts at the rear of the procession were unloaded at the base, their contents handed over the barrier and reloaded on empty ones to carry the belongs up the grade in order not to disturb the Bayzian tribute in honor to a lost queen.

The message had been made clear in Airen there was an Allied Gentry who would do its worst to maintain the status quo of the only land on Triton who clung to ideals that were not only outmoded, they were insufferable.

But the statement was also being strongly made, against them stood the New Airen Citizenry, and not only in Sky Bay.

And they had very different ideas.

132

THE INTRODUCTION

Queen Silence
Sky Citadel, Sky Bay
AIREN

To say the mood was hushed as we all strode into the grand entryway of the Citadel after our ride through Sky Bay was an understatement.

Distractedly, I noted the plethora of coral-colored spiked gladiolus in a large vase atop a grand, gleaming round table sitting on a lovely carpet, all this under a daunting candelabrum in the middle of the space.

But mostly, I was stunned silent.

Everyone was.

Even Farah, who had never been to Sky Bay.

But clearly, she'd heard about it.

And it had profoundly changed.

I looked up to my husband to see he was studying the gladiolus and he did not appear staggered.

He looked in danger of bursting with laughter.

I opened my mouth to ask after what he found amusing but closed it when the humor swept clean from his face, he moved to stand closer to me, and his attention snapped to the stairwell.

I peeked around him and saw a woman appear at the top.

She lifted her long, full skirts that consisted of a swoop of material over the front that led to rosettes at the side of her nipped waist, a cascade of graceful falling ruffles at the sides and in the back, and a tightly fitted bodice. All of this a bright shade of tangerine (save the ruffles, which were a fade of peach to tangerine) with accents of black.

She was racing down the steps.

She did this crying, "Elena!"

"Who is that?" I whispered to Mars, watching as the woman made the bottom, dropped her skirts and dashed to Elena.

I also noted Cass's man, Ian following her far more sedately.

"That is Domitia," Mars murmured.

"King Gallienus's last wife?" I asked.

"Mm," Mars hummed his affirmative, his gaze closely watching the women across the room.

Thus, I did so too.

Elena broke the embrace Domitia threw herself into but only did so holding the woman's hands out to their sides and demanding, "What are you wearing?"

Domitia's face fell. "Do you hate it?"

"I adore it," Elena replied.

Domitia's expression brightened so much, her dress stopped blinding me and her smile took over.

She then tossed a look over her shoulder at Ian, demanding, "See? Elena doesn't think it's too loud."

"I don't either," Ian drawled in reply. "Now that it's burned my retinas into dysfunction."

"Ian," Elena whispered in stunned surprise.

"You're obnoxious," Domitia accused over Elena's whisper.

Elena blinked and Cass did not hide his shock at her words, though I got the impression it was not about her rudeness, but her courage in uttering them.

"I'm honest," Ian returned. "You'd be prettier in pink."

She let go of Elena and rounded on Ian fully.

"I don't like pink."

"Then red."

"Red is too bold."

"Then anything that isn't the color of fruit," he returned.

"There are pink fruits," she retorted.

"Name one," he challenged.

"Berries!" she snapped.

"Berries are sweet and succulent and very good to eat. Citrus is tart and acid and *not you*," Ian fired back.

Oh my.

At that, Domitia herself turned very pink, clashing with her gown.

She then whirled on Elena. "He's been a scoundrel the entire time you've been away."

"She did not think me thus when I took her shopping for that bloody material she's drowning in, in the now," Ian told Cassius.

"You do know, we just survived two battles, one of which we were outnumbered, ten to one," Cassius reminded his friend.

"And I can say with all honesty, deep respect, and equal grief at all I know was lost that for many reasons, I would have rather been there with you than here...*shopping*," Ian retorted.

"I might laugh," I muttered out the side of my mouth to Mars.

"Don't," Mars ordered. "I'm uncertain who's going to blow first, Cass or Ian, but it would be very bad if you were in that firing line, for I would not like it."

That cured my humor instantly.

"Perhaps we can receive a report?" Cassius suggested drily.

"I'd be delighted," Ian replied.

"Are these your friends?" Domitia asked, eyeing the rest of us, now that the drama was done, appearing timid.

I also noted at this juncture, Dax Lahn and his Circe were coming into the room from a hallway off to our right.

Elena introduced us to Domitia. She did it warmly, but she did it swiftly.

She then held her hand so as not to indicate Domitia was dismissed when she turned to Ian and said, "Where should we talk?"

"Wouldn't you like refreshments after your ride?" Domitia asked.

Elena looked down at her. "If you could see to that, we'd be very grateful."

"It'd be my honor," she replied, before she grinned at Elena, bobbed a shy curtsy to Mars and me, Farah and True, Frey and Finnie, then she floated on a waft of tangerine silk and ruffles toward a hallway off to the left.

"The Great Hall has the seating," Ian said.

"Let's go," Cass called to Elena, reaching out to her with a hand.

She moved to him and took it, and we all walked into the Great Hall, which was truly a delight with silver velvet couches, low round pots tufted with tight-packed snowy carnations on conveniently placed tables, and thick, midnight-blue rugs covering the floors.

And I realized upon entering it, I had a rather dire, fixed idea of what the Citadel was like. So much so, it colored my memories of the Bay, which I remembered as nothing but cold and austere.

Mars grunted when he moved into the room.

"All right?" I asked him.

"Some time ago, Cass and I spoke of miracles," he answered. "It would seem Elena has a variety of magicks at her disposal, for I see she has wrought some."

"What are you talking about?"

"This room, under Gallienus, was designed to intimidate and call notice to him, forcing courtiers to compete for his attention. So far, *mia bellezza*, with some flowers, rugs and sofas, Elena has swept this place clean of him and the rule of his forebears in very little time. Thus, a miracle."

"These are not miracles, Mars," I educated him.

As he was seating me on a couch, he raised his brows in question.

"I learned from Mercy before she passed, the power of females takes many forms."

He grunted again as he sat beside me, slouched down in his seat, stretched out his long legs, crossed his booted ankles, and dropped into me, draping an arm around the back of the couch behind me.

My husband comfortably resting against me, all was right in my world.

For the now.

We waited as the others, including Serena and Chu, Hera and Macrinus, and Nero took their seats before Ian started talking.

"First, Elena."

He said no more. Simply looked at her with an expression on his handsome face that had a frog forming in my throat.

"Speak not, my brother," she whispered.

He nodded, looked to Mac.

"She is in the veil," Mac grunted. "And we will talk no more of it in the now."

He nodded and looked to Hera.

"She liked you very much," Hera said softly.

"And I liked her too," Ian replied gently.

Hera's lashes swept down.

He looked to Cass. "Tone?"

"He will be here soon, and we will lay him to rest by his father with his mother and sister at our sides."

A muscle danced in Ian's jaw before he nodded one last time and he said, "Right. You should know, I've received reports that there's a stronghold of Allied Gentry in Dunlyn. I've sent word to Navagio. He's randomly inundating low-populated, high-financial-loss areas, like warehouses, wharves, piers, jetties and merchant offices with cannon fire to provide cover for our operatives to infiltrate and find their headquarters."

"Excellent," Cassius murmured.

"Though, it has come to my attention just hours ago that Fern and her women have already infiltrated Dunlyn, and she is about that same errand."

"Fuck," Cassius bit.

"I've returned word to her to stand down," Ian went on.

"Good," Cassius said.

"She is not the only rogue faction at work, brother," Ian warned his prince.

Mars made a growly noise.

I put my hand on his thigh and he relaxed.

"There are reports of skirmishes breaking out all over Airen," Ian continued. "They're calling themselves the 'New Airen Citizenry.' And apparently, if groups of Allied Gentry are identified, they're being attacked or besieged in their own manors and castles. Not only that, in those places that are AG strongholds, NAC factions are marching in protest, which makes them return targets and *they* are being attacked and imprisoned in the dungeons of AG castles."

Cassius sat back on his couch, draping his arm around Elena, who was grinning.

"This is not good news," he groused to his intended.

"Civil unrest isn't always bad," she replied.

"And how can I ask Frey to call his dragons to incinerate these Gentry bastions if my own supporters are in their dungeons?" Cassius asked her.

"I'd forgotten you intended to do that," Elena murmured.

Cassius sighed.

"I will say, Cass," Ian cut in, "that once you heralded that notice, reports increased that NAC supporters, or simply Airenzian going about their business, mostly women, have been abducted and confined, thus if the dragons rain their fire, it will be gentry property that is destroyed, but our supporters will be the ones who perish."

Cassius's gaze sliced to Frey.

I glanced at Frey to see his jaw tight.

Ian continued, "I have sent peace-keeping squadrons out to areas that are not known AG strongholds in order to attempt to keep the NAC in those places under some semblance of control. And I've sent messages to AG strongholds where it is reported hostages have been taken, demanding their release. Your secretary has a full reporting of this you can look over."

Cass nodded.

"Can we talk for a second about what was happening between you and Domitia out in the entryway?" Elena requested of Ian.

At that, Ian's jaw got tight.

"For fuck's sake," Cassius muttered.

"You have to admit she's much changed," Elena said to Cassius, then turned directly to Ian. "Is it you we have to thank for that?"

"I've just been seeing to her," Ian lied.

"Uh-huh, just seeing to her. Right," Circe mumbled.

"*Kah fauna, rayloo*," Lahn murmured.

"Right, *raylooing*," Circe said, directing wide eyes to Finnie.

Finnie dropped her smile to her lap.

"What does *rayloo* mean?" I whispered to Mars.

"I've no bloody idea," Mars didn't whisper to me.

I swallowed down my giggle.

"Look! Isn't this lovely?" The woman under discussion cried from the doorway, and all turned to her as Domitia entered the room. "More company. I'm glad I ordered many refreshments brought up."

"Ha-Lah!" I cried, jumping up and dashing to my friend.

She opened her arms.

I ran into them, curving mine around her as she closed hers around me.

"I'm so glad you're here," I whispered into her ear.

"I am too, my—"

She didn't get to finish, for I was torn out of her embrace.

I then found myself behind Mars's back and he was retreating, taking me with him.

"Mars!" I snapped. "What on—?"

"Aramus, explain," my husband growled.

"Mars! Stop pushing me!" I hissed.

"Trust me," Aramus's deep voice came.

"You ask a lot, brother," Mars rumbled.

I shoved against his back at the same time preparing to sidestep him.

But suddenly, True was at one side of me, Cassius at the other, fencing me in.

"Maybe we should talk in the other room," True stated.

And at my cousin's chilly, enraged tone, I stopped moving, for I had not ever known True to be chilly *or* enraged.

"Cass," Mars bit out on a warning.

"Domitia, can you please take our new visitors to the red room?" Cass inquired.

"B-but, of course, Cassius," Domitia stammered.

"What's going on?" I whispered to the back of my husband's head.

"Not a word," Mars said, to whom I did not know, though I knew it wasn't to me.

"But, Mars—" Ha-Lah began to reply.

"Not a bloody, fucking *word*," Mars demanded.

"Of course," Ha-Lah whispered.

With that, Mars turned to me, bent so his face was in mine and said simply, "It is my duty to protect you, and you must allow me to do that."

I blinked.

What was he on about?

"Yes, my love?" he prompted.

"Yes," I breathed.

He pressed a hard kiss to my lips before he turned and prowled out of the room, Cassius, True, Lahn, Frey, Ian and Mac going with him.

Chu remained behind.

No doubt to see to me.

Aramus was nowhere to be seen.

I looked left to right, begging to know, "Please, someone, what's happening?"

"It will all be all right," Ha-Lah assured, coming to me.

Elena appeared to my one side, Farah to my right.

"But, what's happening?" I repeated.

"Soon you will know," Ha-Lah said, then laid a gentle hand on my cheek, and I saw her beautiful crystal eyes were warm. "And you will be happy."

~

King Mars

Informal Salon, "Red Room," Sky Citadel, Sky Bay

AIREN

"WE DIDN'T KNOW you were here," Aramus stated. "You were last reported in the Night Heights, which is a many days' ride away. And I'll wish to know how you were even there, for before that, you were reported in Wodell, which is a many *weeks'* ride away."

"We rode through the city in procession not an hour ago, Aramus," Mars growled, scowling at his friend.

"We did not ride in procession. We did so with some care, and more stealth, for we did not know the leanings of the Bay," Aramus replied. "We learned quickly but thought it best to carry forward cautiously."

Mars decided to let that go in order that he could find out what the fuck was going on and not leave his Silence wondering and worrying.

"And who is he?" he demanded of Aramus, referring to the tall, power-fully-built, *silver-eyed* man at Aramus's side.

"*He* is standing right here, and you can direct your questions right to me," the silver-eyed man said.

"You have her eyes," Mars clipped to him.

"She has mine," he retorted.

"You do know who I am," Mars stated.

"I do, but you don't know who *I* am," he returned.

"You do not understand my meaning," Mars said slowly. "When I say, you do know who I am, my meaning is, *I am her husband.*"

The silver-eyed man fell silent, with that, Mars suspected, under-standing his meaning.

"You share blood," Mars bit.

"Yes," the man grunted.

"And you know she exists," Mars continued.

"Yes," the man replied.

Mars felt blood roar in his ears and watched the man's eyebrows go up when, Mars knew, he caught the flames in Mars's eyes.

"And you and yours left her to neglect and abuse?" he whispered sinisterly.

The man took a step back as if Mars had delivered a physical blow.

"Neglect and abuse?" he whispered back.

But achingly.

At that, Mars fell silent.

"What's happening?" True, at his side, demanded to know.

Mars turned to him.

"Johan of the Arbor is not Silence's father. He cannot sire a child, but desired one, so he sent Vanka out to lie with someone for the purpose of conceiving." He ignored True's expression assuming a look of shock before it melted to anger and turned back to the man. "Your father? Uncle?"

"Father," the man said low.

He turned back to True. "His father is Silence's sire."

True instantly looked to the man and demanded furiously, "And why is *he* not here?"

"He has passed," the man answered. "And before I endure any more of your ire, I did not know, and *he* did not know, we had blood on land until I heard reports the new Queen of Firenze had silver eyes."

"On land?" Frey asked.

The man looked to Aramus.

Aramus nodded with what appeared to be encouragement.

The man looked to Mars.

"I am Jorie. King of the Mer," he declared.

The air in the room went static.

Mer?

Fucking hell.

Aramus's voice cut through it as he asked carefully, "Mars, does Silence know she's a mermaid?"

Her advanced hearing.

Her shadow.

Were these Mer traits?

He did not ask that.

He answered tersely, "No."

Aramus took in a visibly deep breath and let it out.

"She is a Princess of the Mer," Jorie said.

"She is *the* Queen of Firenze," Mars returned.

"I am not your enemy," Jorie replied. "I am, in the now, solely a brother who seeks an introduction to his sister." He took a step toward Mars, stopped, and finished, "I have no siblings. My mother and father tried..."

He didn't finish.

"Mine as well," Mars grunted.

"Without fortune?" Jorie asked.

"I had a sister, she passed," Mars shared.

"My mother died in the trying."

Mars felt a vein throb in his temple.

"What would you do for a sister?" Jorie queried quietly.

"Find one, grow up beside her, then marry her to one of the finest men in all realms," Mars replied, jerking his head to True.

Jorie glanced at True before saying to Mars, "I don't understand."

"It will undoubtedly be explained eventually," Mars muttered. "For the now," he did not mutter, but he did take a deep breath before he concluded, "It is time to meet your sister."

"Mars," True said low.

He looked to his friend. "She would wish this."

"I urge you to think of all that has happened in the last days, with her a part of it, and know she must now withstand this."

"She has a silver soul, my brother. It is bendable, but it very rarely breaks," Mars returned. "You treat her with care, which I respect, and I am grateful for. But she is much stronger than you think."

True held his gaze before he nodded, but he did so still communicating he did not like it.

"I would know…"

Both men turned to Jorie at hearing his voice.

"What you meant by abuse and neglect," he said to Mars.

"This man, at my side, until she met me, is the only man in her life that has shown her love and affection," Mars explained.

Jorie's eyes cut to True.

"She had but one friend," Mars went on, and Jorie looked back to him. "Her maid. Until she met the women in the other room."

Jorie's face grew hard.

"She was an outcast in her own home," Mars continued. "The man who raised her knew she was not of his blood, and treated her thus, even if she did not understand it. Though she knows it now. Regardless, he is of an ilk, if she *was* his blood, it would likely not be much better."

Jorie's voice was rumbling when he stated, "I would meet this man and have words."

And it was at that, Mars finally fully calmed.

"That is not your duty."

"I am her brother."

"And I am her husband and I'm seeing to it."

"How?" Jorie demanded.

"How else when my wife would be upset if I cut his throat?" Mars asked. "I'm taking away everything he holds dear and leaving him with nothing."

Jorie studied him a moment before he muttered, "I approve of this."

Mars didn't much care.

"Would you like to meet Silence?" he asked.

"Why in the seas did they name her Silence?" Jorie queried in return.

"I do not know and care even less. But there is great calm and beauty in Silence, both the absence of noise and the uniqueness of my wife."

Jorie's eyes narrowed on him before he noted, "It is my understanding your marriage was arranged."

"Yes, it was, thank the gods," Mars muttered.

"You are keen on her," Jorie observed.

"No, I love her."

Jorie smiled largely. "This brings me great gladness."

"That's all well and good, now would you like to *meet her*?" Mars demanded.

Jorie's body locked for a brief moment before he turned to Aramus and asked, "Why am I suddenly filled with unease?"

"Because her husband is maniacally protective?" Aramus asked in return.

"Tell me you would not do the same for Ha-Lah," Mars clipped.

Aramus grinned at him before he looked to Jorie.

"You feel unease, my man, because she is your sister and you wish her to like you." Aramus clapped him on the shoulder. "She is reserved of character, but warm of heart. And when you have a place in hers, as my wife has attested to you, her affection knows no limits." He squeezed Jorie's shoulder and dropped his voice. "Now, go. Meet your sister."

Jorie nodded to Aramus, to Mars, looked to the room and turned to the door.

As Mars moved to follow him, True stopped him.

"I would be there, True," Mars said impatiently.

"Silence is a mermaid," True whispered, fear bleak at the backs of his eyes.

With all that just occurred, Mars had not fully taken that in.

He did now.

By muttering, "Fuck."

"The Mer are...they have not been treated at all well, as you know,

Mars," True went on. "And Silence..." He shook his head "I'm protective, yes. But this is a great deal for her to take in."

"No one will harm her."

"If known, she will be a curiosity."

"No one. Will. *Harm her.*"

True nodded but said, "I believe you, but I urge you to ask her brother not to share all and control the flow of information. In other words, *slow it.*"

"Gods, you're an overbearing brother," Mars muttered.

True reared back in affront. "Pardon?"

"My queen rained fire on traitors but days ago, True. She has a soul of silver. A heart of gold. A candied mouth. A cunning mind. And a spine of steel. I know you don't underestimate her. What you must come to understand is, she is now a woman, a wife, a queen, and will, when things calm, be a mother. Allow her to grow up."

"I have," True clipped. "Of course I have."

"She is no longer in their clutches, my brother," Mars said quietly. "She is amongst those who love and respect her. You do not have to twist yourself into knots to be all to her in the limited time you have with her. Protect her from every hurt you can manage. In another time, I will express my gratitude to you for looking after her as best you could since her birth. In the now, just know, *she is loved.*"

Mars watched True swallow as he allowed Mars's words to penetrate.

He then watched his brother nod.

After that, he clapped him on the arm.

And then both of the men who loved Silence Laches the most in her life made haste to introduce her to her brother.

Queen Silence
Parapets, Sky Citadel, Sky Bay
Airen

"They loiter," my brother—*my brother*—muttered.

I looked from my view of studying his handsome profile as he leaned forward against the railings, gazing from the ramparts to the night lights of

Sky Bay, to where Mars and True stood, ostensibly talking, undoubtedly listening, some five feet away.

"My husband and my cousin tend to think I must be looked after."

"They are correct," he stated, turning his head to me.

I lifted my chin. "I am woman, but I am not powerless or stupid."

"Do you look after your husband?" he asked.

"Of course," I stated tartly.

He grinned and became all the more handsome. "You do know, if you love someone, that automatically happens. You look after them."

"Oh," I mumbled and turned to the Bay.

"You have great beauty. My father would be proud he had a hand in creating that," he declared.

Slowly, I closed my eyes.

I had known him but hours, and already, he told me I was beautiful.

I had known my father all my years, and he'd never said such.

"My sister," he called gently.

I opened my eyes.

"Thank you," I whispered. "And you are most handsome, and please know I do not say that only to return the compliment."

"You appeared in pain a moment ago."

I turned my head to see his silver eyes, *my* silver eyes, gazing at me.

"I hope you never know how it feels to have mostly nothing, and then be given everything. It's most overwhelming."

"My sister," he said, his tone edged in distress.

"Let us not dwell on these things," I suggested. "Can I ask you questions?"

He twisted his upper body toward me, leaning on an elbow on the railing, and answered, "Anything."

"If I am a mermaid, and you a mermale, why do we both have legs?"

"You are on land," he said. "When you are in the sea, the salt sea, my sister, you will transform." His face turned severe. "Though you will not do that unless you have myself or Ha-Lah with you. I do not know a single Mer who has lived their life unknowing they are Mer. But I know babes must learn to use their fins. I will not have you drop to the bottom of the sea your first time as who you truly are."

"Oh faith, that would be terrible," I muttered.

"You can breathe under the sea, Silence. Gills will form on your neck if you are out in the depths when you duck underwater."

"Oh," I whispered.

He smiled at me. "You have aunts and you have cousins and they will be most delighted to meet you. We lost my father, and we grieve. Having you is like having a part of him back."

"I...I...that is a lovely thing to say. Erm, how long has he been gone?"

"Naught but a year."

Naught but *a year*.

My father, my *true* father, had been gone naught but *a year*.

"I missed him by a year," I whispered.

"Yes."

We held each other's gazes.

Jorie broke our silence.

"You have his eyes. And you have his nose. And you have my grand-mother's stature." He leaned toward me and winked. "She too, was wee."

She was wee.

The knowledge I'd never meet my real father, and so many things about me I didn't understand explained, Jorie's seeking of me, his handsomeness, his wink, his *existence*, I could not cope.

"I am sorry, Jorie, but I..." I looked this way and that, then began to wave my hand in front of my face before I mumbled, "may need to freshen..."

"By the sea beasts," he muttered and pulled me into his arms.

They felt strong about me and he smelled fresh and salty and *lovely*.

I pressed my cheek to his chest, carefully wrapped my arms around his trim waist, and took in deep breaths.

"You may weep," he offered. "I have two female cousins. They get their hearts broken on a regular basis. My chest is their favorite cushion to absorb their tears. In other words, I have much practice."

He was the kind of male who allowed his cousins to use his chest to absorb their tears.

I emitted a strange hiccup that made me squeeze him with my arms.

His arms squeezed back.

I closed my eyes tight.

"I want to swim in the sea with you," I whispered.

"I cannot wait to take you there," he whispered back.

"I want to see your home," I told him.

"I hope you find it beautiful," he told me.

"I want you to see my home, Catrame Palace, it is lovely."

"I will journey there."

"I was always a princess, wasn't I?"

"Yes, but now you are queen."

"But I was always a princess, wasn't I?"

Jorie fell silent, as if understanding his answer had grave import, and thus he must consider it carefully.

He then said, "He would have spoiled you, his love for you would have been so great, giving you your every heart's desire. And I would have thought you were an awful brat. You would probably steal my dolphin friends and charm octopi, which are surly, which would make me jealous so I would have had to play tricks on you to get mine back. But now I am jealous of the men down the ramparts, especially your True. For he loiters there, due to the history of the love he has for you. And I find myself needing to build it new. For even if you grew up a terrible brat, you would be my sister, my princess, thus you would have my love. And the only heart I can take in not knowing you until now, is that even far apart, you always were."

Another hiccup came, lurching my body as I gave forth a little sob.

"You have made her cry," True accused, suddenly, so True, right there.

"True," Mars murmured low.

"I've got her," Jorie said.

I peeked to my cousin through spiky eyelashes, but I moved not another inch of my body.

"He has me, True," I whispered.

"True," Mars said again.

True glowered at me.

"And I'll always have you," I went on.

Only that made his face soften.

He nodded, then moved away.

I sniffled.

My brother held me.

I sniffled again.

He continued to hold me.

Then I asked, "Can we go swimming soon?"

I heard his smile in the single word he spoke.

"Absolutely."

133

THE ADRIFT

Jellan
Easternmost Edge, Argyll Forest
AIREN

They were lost.

He knew it.

Daemon just would not admit it.

And Jellan was loath to approach him about it, considering the fact he did not wish to know what response the creature would have to such a discussion.

Marian did not seem to have trouble with meandering aimlessly, seemingly cast adrift.

She also didn't seem to have trouble going head to head with him, Jellan had noted. She had not changed her manner in regards to the Beast at all.

And for all intents and purposes, considering he'd been utilizing obsequiousness from the beginning, Jellan hadn't either.

It just chafed, raw, watching those two together.

Along their meandering, Daemon had stolen not only clothes and food, warm, woolen blankets and some twine and tarp for a makeshift tent, but the steeds they now rode.

However, he'd only stolen two, for Daemon rode with Marian tucked close to his front and they whispered together as they journeyed.

Though there was no whispering when they fucked under the tarp at night.

Jellan did not like it.

Not any of it.

Not one bit.

He further did not like it that the creature seemed to listen to Marian. Take her advice.

Jellan would not admit it was *good* advice, say, sharing with Daemon that he might not wish to leave a string of bodies in their wake. Not after what they had left behind at the Ancient Ritual Grounds. What Daemon had done to that family at that farm. Telling him that all of that would eventually be found, and questions would be asked, and they would be sought, and they didn't need to leave a trail to make it easy to find them.

Daemon had, rightly, argued it mattered not if they found them as he had much power, so let them find them.

"You have work to do, do you not?" she'd queried cuttingly, causing Daemon to look chastened. "Do you wish to delay in that by having to murder investigating constables or angry townspeople? Only in doing so, having *more* seek you, causing further delays?"

Daemon had seen the wisdom of this and thus his short killing spree had ended.

Which was what Jellan suspected Marian wished.

And Jellan had further suspicions Marian wished them to be lost.

Indeed, with some of the routes Daemon selected (about which, Jellan was not finding it surprising, Marian gave no guidance), that took them nowhere, he suspected she was *making* them lost.

For, as the days passed, even though it was clear Daemon was seeking something, and it was clear she still had his ear and he listened to her, she did not make that first effort to discover what he wished to find or where he wished to go which meant she did not put herself in a place where she would need to assist him in getting there.

At least not that Jellan had heard.

Then again, they excluded him much of the time and he could not hear most of their whispers.

What concerned Jellan most of all, however, was this "work" Marian referred to.

What work?

In the legend of the Beast, he had ravaged the continent haphazardly. He killed. He raped. He pillaged. He destroyed. He tortured.

There was no rhyme or reason to it. This being one of the varied reasons he was terrifying.

Evil with a purpose was ugly. But understanding that purpose, tempering it, eradicating it, gave hope.

Evil run amuck with *no* purpose was chilling.

Of course, that was many years ago and there was no true and accurate accounting of it, and although there were numerous mentions of him, this deficit of knowledge included what was recorded in the tomes of the Go'Doan.

So perhaps there had been some purpose to it.

Some purpose that, when the Beast was imprisoned under the earth and his reign of terror halted, did not come to fruition.

Jellan wished to know.

Jellan *needed* to know.

But to attempt to find out, he'd have to separate those two and it did not seem he'd be able to.

On this thought, Jellan felt it and his head automatically tipped to the side when he did.

And as he was thinking on Daemon and Marian, and thus riding behind them and partly to their sides, he had their eyes on them.

As such, he saw Daemon's head give a slight twitch.

By the true gods.

He felt it.

He felt it too!

Did he feel all the others that had happened recently?

Jellan could not see much of Marian, but what he could see, it did not appear as if she had.

"It's the veil," he called, blurting it right out.

Both Daemon and Marian turned to him.

Bloody hell.

"I wish you would make him speak only when spoken to," Marian complained.

He barely spoke at all.

The bitch.

For once, Daemon ignored her.

And in so doing, Jellan took heart.

"What is the veil?" he asked.

"What you felt. It is the veil. The magical veil. It shrouds all of Triton. Even the seas and Mar-el. And it is disturbed, continues to be so and has for some time."

Not *disturbed*, as such.

Growing.

Amassing power.

Daemon stared at him.

Marian glared at him.

Jellan put his heels to his mount and cantered closer to them.

"We should find news of what is happening on Triton," he advised when he was riding at their side.

"Why would we need that?" Marian asked snidely.

"Because," Jellan said to her calmly, "there have been a number of impacts on the veil these past days. Witches are ascending."

She continued to glare at him, but Daemon asked, "Witches are ascending?"

"Dying," he told him. "Powerful ones. And in their deaths, they ascend and the magic they wield on earth joins the veil."

Daemon appeared very interested in this.

But Jellan did not have the opportunity to press it, for Marian demanded, "Why are they dying?"

"I do not know," he answered. "This is why we must seek news about what is happening in the realms."

He turned his gaze to Daemon to see the creature appeared contemplative.

"You feel it, yes?" he pushed. "When there is a tremor in the veil."

"I did not know what it was," he muttered.

"I feel it too," Marian said swiftly.

"But you cannot read it," Jellan returned, just as swiftly.

"It is not important to us, witches dying," she retorted.

"It is important to us why the veil shifted just now," he declared.

"Another witch dying? That must happen all the time, and I know it does for I felt this *veil shift* as you say, repeatedly."

"It is not only when witches die that it trembles, Marian," he shared haughtily.

"And why else does it tremble?" Daemon cut in.

Should he tell him of the prophecy?

Jellan did not know, and in truth, had reflected on this question much these past days.

He did not have control over the Beast. He was not even certain Marian did.

He was struggling with the answer to that question and was seeing now, he should not have alerted them to the messages of the veil before he'd made a decision.

"Jellan, answer," Daemon demanded.

"Powerful witches at work. Powerful spells cast. Powerful rituals held," Jellan dissembled. "For instance, the rituals conducted to awaken you caused more than a tremor of the earth. It was felt in the veil."

"Hmm," Daemon hummed, then queried, "Do they know I have ascended?"

Jellan shook his head, his reaction honest this time.

"I don't know. Though, I would assume if they had, we would not have been unmolested as we have been since you made the surface."

Daemon appeared also to be thinking hard on that.

But Marian was watching him closely and Jellan's heart beat hard in his chest for he sensed she knew he was not being completely forthcoming.

He felt certain she'd expose him and was utterly stunned when she did not.

Instead, she looked forward and stated, "He might be right. Perhaps we should know what's happening in the realms. Understand these messages of the veil."

Jellan was not sure the decision he was making was the right one. He did not know if he could gain the trust, and control, over the Beast to do his bidding, not Marian's, not Daemon's own. It did not seem in the now he could, though it did seem he was useful to the creature, if not useful to Marian.

But he did not feel he had firm footing in their little trinity.

Thus, he decided not to tell them the lovers had united in one place.

And they were not only together, something in and of itself that increased their strength.

They were *lovers*.

The prophecy had been completed. They were at full force. Their power was disrupting the veil, regularly, mightily.

It wasn't just powerful witches dying (although he sensed that was also happening, and he was keen to know why this was occurring so often), it was more.

Much more.

He feared what either one of them would do if he held this information from them, only to share it at a later date.

But if he could not gain control over Daemon, set him to do Jellan's bidding, not his own, definitely not Marian's, it would be essential that those prophesied remained at the height of their strength.

And that those powers grew.

Because if he could not control the Beast, someone had to eradicate it.

In the meantime, he had to find a way to ingratiate himself with the creature.

He had to find a way to lessen Marian's hold over him.

And he had to discover what this "work" was that Daemon wished to do.

Thus, he had to have information. He had to know what was happening in the realms. He had to have time.

He had to plan.

He had his own work to do.

And in the now that work meant he was allied with Marian in one thing...

He had to delay.

134
THE FINDING

Teddy
Westernmost Lesser Thicket Forest
WODELL

"I think we're far enough away, we can seek a road," he said to Moira.

"I think we need to continue to be cautious," she replied.

He shifted closer to her. "Moira, as I've said, we have *much* more of a chance of running into someone who can help if we travel the road."

"Yes, and *they* know we've escaped," she returned. "They were very intent on what they were doing, Teddy. *They* could be seeking us, and *they* can also find us on the road."

She was frightened, as were all the women, and they had reason. He understood this.

Thus, he held tight to his patience, something he was learning well to do these past days.

"We have passed many a farmstead where we could have stopped and asked for succor," he reminded her, still uncomfortable that they had, indeed, stopped, but not to ask for succor.

To take it.

They were now thieves.

Of course they would not have eaten in this past week if they had not stolen a cooling bread loaf from a window sill, several jars of preserves and pickles from a canning locker, a bag of shelled pecans left on a back stoop after the sheller was called away from their task, and a slab of cured ham from a meat stall.

But need was no excuse.

By his estimation they were still a three to four week walk away from Notting Thicket.

At least.

Not taking the road was adding to that and who knew what that creature had been up to in the meantime.

They needed to run into somebody.

They needed a conveyance.

They needed to be at Birchlire Castle three days ago.

"What do you think?"

Moira's question brought him back to their conversation, and when it did, he saw she was asking the women.

They had, over the days, created a democratic way of going about their business. Although Teddy and Moira were looked to as leaders and to make final decisions, everyone had a chance to have their say.

And sometimes, like now, when Teddy and Moira could not decide, it was put to a vote.

"I'm not going on the road," Terra said.

"Me either," Kate added.

A number of the rest of them shook their heads while those who did not, did not seem averse to staying off the beaten path, they simply looked undecided.

This meant they would remain hidden by the forest and sneaking through fields, maybe adding weeks onto their journey.

While the Beast walked the earth.

Teddy sighed, but inside was a controlled panic that was coming more and more uncontrolled as the days wore on.

He also considered, once again, for perhaps the two-thousandth time, sharing with them.

Teddy knew for (relative) certain The Rising priests that had fled, if they had escaped the Beast, were not looking for Teddy and his women.

They were finding safety wherever they could find it.

But unless he shared the far more frightening information of why they needed to make a great deal more haste, he could not tell them they had nothing to fear from the men who took them.

This he found tremendously upsetting for, like in the now, the echoes of the terror of what they'd experienced, what they'd witnessed, and what might have befallen them if they had not escaped interfered with their common sense.

He wished them to know they did not have to live every second, petrified that they would be dragged back to that place.

But he did not wish to replace that fear with one altogether more paralyzing.

"We will carry on as we are," he muttered.

"Teddy," Moira called, and as he was beginning to resume their journey, he stopped and looked back to her to see his friend grinning at him with reassurance. "We'll get there. Prom—"

She stopped mid-word, frozen, and she was not the only one.

Teddy heard it and he had frozen too.

For half a second.

Then he hissed, "Stay low, stay quiet, and follow me."

He got low himself, while scanning the trees, looking for fallen logs, hollow ones, wide trunks, anything that would hide them.

He did this as the distant, but approaching, sound of horses' hooves got ever closer.

The steeds were not on the road, which was some ways away.

They were coming *through the forest*.

Toward them.

"Kate, Terra, duck behind that log," he clipped, pointing to a fallen log that was thick, so it rose high from the ground.

Kate and Terra bustled that way and disappeared behind it.

With cautious haste, he continued guiding the rest through the trees and searching for hiding places.

But he could hear the horses getting closer.

Damn it!

Could he have been wrong about The Rising priests searching for them?

"Hattie, Constance," he whispered urgently. "Over there. Big tree. Hide behind it."

"Minnie, Irma…behind that log. Lie on the ground. Side by side. Everyone, pull leaves over you," Moira instructed, indicating a fallen log that was not tall, but would provide the two women cover if they did as told.

And the horses continued to get closer.

He turned to Moira.

"Go to Kate and Terra. Hide with them. If it is us they're searching for, I'll draw them away," he ordered Moira.

"I'm staying with you."

Gods!

Why was the woman so bloody *stubborn*?

It suddenly felt like the thundering hooves were shaking the trees.

Damn it, how many of them were there?

There hadn't been that many before.

Had they gone to find reinforcements to chase down seven women and him?

"Go!" he snapped to Moira.

"I'm staying with you!" she snapped in return, grabbing his hand and starting to pull.

He looked into the distance and he could see the first horses through the dead trees.

"Moira!" he tried to pull away. "Go hide!"

"Teddy!" she snapped. "Run!"

"*Teddy!*" he heard roared.

When he did, he stood immobile, staring at the trees, his heart beating fast, his skin warming, his throat itching to shout his elation.

"Teddy!" Moira was pulling urgently at his hand. "*We need to run!*"

"Go!" he heard whispered loudly from one of the trees, he thought from Constance.

"Please, Teddy. Take Moira and *go!*" he heard cried from behind a log. Terra.

"Faunus," he whispered.

"Teddy!" Faunus shouted.

"Faunus!" Teddy yelled.

He whipped to Moira, caught her face in both his hands, yanked her to him and kissed her smack on the lips.

He pulled away and exclaimed, "We are saved!"

"What?" she breathed, eyes wide and staring at him.

But the large, proud Firenz horses were upon them, all around, galloping grandly about them and Teddy had let Moira go, had turned and was running to one of them.

Faunus dismounted before his steed was at a complete stop and he only had to jog five steps before he and Teddy ran into one another.

They embraced, Teddy shoving his face in Faunus's neck, taking in his scent, feeling his strength, before Faunus grasped him on either side of the neck, pulled him back, and his head came down.

His kiss was wet and punishing and *fantastic.*

When he pulled away, in return Teddy took his head in his hands and stated, "I knew you'd come." He yanked Faunus to him, pressed his lips hard against Faunus's, pushed him away but didn't let him go, and he cried, "I knew you'd come!"

"Many thanks for the message about where you were headed," Faunus replied, grinning.

Teddy recalled what he'd written in that message and fought the heat hitting his skin.

"Though it would have saved time if you'd taken the bloody road," he went on.

"I have...we have..." He blinked and mumbled, "We." He brightened and shouted, "We!"

He pulled from Faunus and spun around.

"Ladies!" he yelled. "It's all right! Come out! It's safe! These are my friends come to rescue us!"

He caught sight of Saturn, standing by an astonished-looking Moira, and he bounded over the dead leaves to his friend.

They embraced, Saturn pounding him on the back stoutly many times, before he pulled away and looked severely down at Teddy.

"You are skin and bones," he declared.

"I've been abducted and then on the run," he returned.

"We need to fatten you up," Faunus stated, coming to stand by their sides.

Just the word "fatten" made him discontinue ignoring the gnawing hunger in his gut and his mouth began to water.

"Actually, if you have food, my women need feeding," he told them. "The ham we stole ran out yesterday evening."

"Your women?" Faunus asked, before his dark gaze moved toward Moira, as if he just noticed she was there.

Teddy shifted around, noting Firenz warriors everywhere, at least twenty-five of them, and many were standing beside or behind where his women were hiding, but had not come out.

"Truly!" he yelled. "It's all right! These are my friends!"

"How are you friends with Firenz warriors?" Moira asked quietly.

He looked to her and saw she was not only stunned, she looked worried.

"It is a long story, which I will tell you later. In the now, I am being most honest with you," he whispered, reaching to her, taking her hand and giving it a hearty squeeze. "You have naught to fear from these men. They look fierce. But they are most gentle. Especially with women."

"Yes, I am *most* gentle with women," Saturn decreed earnestly.

Teddy looked to Saturn.

He then saw how Saturn was gazing upon Moira.

Teddy turned back to Moira, and of a sudden, it was as if he was seeing her for the first time.

She did not have the lush beauty of Nyx, but he saw she was rather lush, especially when it came to curves.

And she had quite a bit of rich brown hair that probably looked rather lovely when it hadn't been days since she washed.

"Saturn," Teddy called.

"Yes?" Saturn asked, not looking from Moira.

"Saturn!" Teddy clipped.

"Yes!" Saturn answered, tearing his eyes from Moira.

"We have been through hell," he said softly.

It was then he sensed the others coming out of hiding.

He shifted and watched them scurrying toward Teddy and Moira. The women got close, very close to Teddy, shuffling Faunus and Saturn out of the way so they could form a tight huddle.

Indeed, Irma and Minnie, the most timid and those Teddy had assessed had suffered the greatest in their minds at what had been done to them, ducked and burrowed so close to Teddy, their frightened eyes surveying the tall, dark, formidable warriors surrounding them, he had to curve them in his arms and pull them closer.

As they did this, Teddy noticed the expressions on Faunus's and Saturn's faces change from jovial and relieved at having found their friend, to forbidding and furious as they sensed something very bad had happened to the women in Teddy's huddle.

He wished they would not look like that, for it only made them appear even more frightening.

"We *all* have been through hell," he said. "And we need a hearty meal, warm baths, a good night's sleep." He focused on Faunus. "And I need to speak with you. Urgently."

"*La creatura?*" Faunus asked.

Yes. He had read Teddy's message.

"Yes," Teddy answered.

Faunus gave a tight nod then he looked over their heads and barked in Firenzii, "Ride back. Secure every room in that inn we passed. Have them start a meal. Much meat, thick bread, butter, many potatoes. And have them heat water for baths. Make haste."

One of the warriors strode off to his horse and Faunus's eyes came back to Teddy's huddle.

They skimmed over the women, before they leveled on Teddy.

"We cannot go back," Teddy told him as calmly as he could when he regained Faunus's attention. "I need to take care of my girls. And then we must get to Notting Thicket without further delay."

Faunus said nothing to him, simply looked again over his head and ordered in Firenzii, "Procure eight horses. Good quality. They must be able to withstand a long day's swift ride."

When he replied, Teddy continued to speak in the language of the Vale, for he did not want the women to worry about what he said or think he was hiding anything from them.

"They need to go home, which is the other way, not to the Thicket."

"We stay with you," Moira declared.

Teddy gave her gentle eyes and murmured, "Poppet, we are saved."

All the women pulled in tighter.

"We stay with you," Moira repeated.

He held her gaze before he tore his away and looked up to Faunus.

"All right, they stay with me."

Both Faunus and Saturn were again taking in Teddy and his women.

They had tight jaws and fiery eyes.

Finally, Faunus decreed, "Let us ride."

FRESH FROM HIS bath (he had taken the last) and checking on all the women (save one, where he was headed right then), Teddy nodded to the warrior who stood at the end of the hall in the upper floor of the inn and received a nod back.

Then he stopped at a door and knocked.

"Yes?" Moira called.

"It's Teddy," he called back.

He heard the lock turn and the door opened.

Then, his new, clean tunic was fisted at his chest in her hand and he was pulled into the room.

She shut the door and locked it behind him.

"Moira," he murmured, peering beyond her to see she had a single room with a slender pallet atop a nondescript base, a small table and chair, a chest, a tiny fireplace with iron, and naught else.

Though the pallet looked fluffy, there was a clean pillowcase over the pillow and many woolen rugs to keep out the chill. And the fireplace might be tiny, but a robust fire burned there, warming the room.

"The others?" she asked.

"I have checked on them. Three and three, next door and across the hall from you," he told her.

"They are well?"

"You ate with them, Moira. And demanded to take the penultimate bath."

She glared at him.

He gave in.

"They are fed, as you know, and all have had baths, as you also know. Faunus has managed to get them clean nightgowns, and you know this too, as you are right now wearing one. And with the bag of coin he laid on their desk, the innkeeper's wife is searching for clean, warm gowns and cloaks for all of you for our journey tomorrow, and my guess, to get that coin, she will find them. They are settled in, they know the Firenz guard this inn, and they might not be fully restored, but they are in decent spirits."

She seemed to deflate after he reported this, and he remembered why he liked her so.

She was stubborn but she was also strong and most of all, she was caring.

During their journey, in the night, exhausted from walking, the women had slept as best they could, pressed together for warmth under the stars.

Not he and Moira. They took turns staying awake and keeping watch.

And it was she who should have had the last piece of ham.

But she gave it to Terra, who was the slimmest, and seemed to get slimmer by the day, thus Moira declared, needed the sustenance more than she.

Yes, she was stubborn.

But mostly, she was kind.

"We will request they get word to your families," he said carefully.

"Yes," she replied.

"Moira—"

"Is he your lover?"

Teddy suddenly felt a sickness in his stomach.

But he lifted his chin and said, "Yes."

"He is very tall, and he is very muscled," she decreed, rather than turning snide or looking repulsed.

"Um...yes," he agreed to her obvious assessment.

"And exceptionally handsome, in a Firenz way."

He was that.

"Moira—"

She gave a terse nod. "He cares deeply for you. You are his love. We can trust him. Trust *them*."

Teddy wasn't sure he was Faunus's *love*.

But yes, they could trust him. And *them*.

And he could not quite put his finger on understanding the feeling he was feeling at her reaction to discovering who Teddy was, or rather, *how* he was.

He did not mention that.

"Of course you can trust him. And all of them. I would not lead you astray." He then took her jaw in both hands and dipped his face to hers. "And as such, I am sure I can speak to Faunus. He will give you and the others a guard. Keep you safe as they take you home."

"What did you see back in that clearing after we ran away, Teddy?"

Her stubbornness was an obstacle too much.

Her intelligence was just plain annoying.

He dropped his hands, but she caught both of them and shook them.

"What did you see?" she pressed.

"Poppet—"

"All right, you don't wish to tell me that. But tell me this. We are safer with you and your warriors, whatever you saw, are we not?"

No one was safe.

But anyone was safer surrounded by thirty Firenz warriors.

"Yes," he said quietly.

"Then we will send messages to our families and stay with you. They can come to get us from wherever we go...with you."

He knew there was no talking her out of it, so he did not try.

"All right, love," he muttered.

She squeezed his hands. "Teddy."

He focused on her again.

"I don't care who you love, and I don't care who loves you. I know the man you are. Do you understand?"

He nodded, so much happening around the region of his heart, he did not trust himself to speak.

"All right," she whispered, and again squeezed his hands. "Sleep well and I'll see you in the morning."

"You too, poppet."

She smiled at him.

He bent and kissed her cheek.

They let go and he turned, but before he unlocked the door, she called his name.

He looked over his shoulder at her.

"Thank you," she whispered, then lifted a hand slightly at her side to indicate the warmth and shelter about her.

"We all survived," he reminded her.

"Because of you."

He gave her a soft look, she returned it, then he set about unlocking her door, leaving her room, and he heard it lock again behind him before he'd taken one step down to the chamber he would share with Faunus.

Saturn had the only other accommodation in the inn. Another single on the other side of Moira.

The rest of the warriors were either guarding the inn or hunkering down in tents around it.

He opened the door to his room, which was much larger, and saw both Faunus and Saturn at the table before the window, their big bodies sprawled in chairs designed for the Dellish, which meant they dwarfed them. A fire was raging in the iron in the grate, making the room warm.

And with a full belly, a clean body, seeing his friends sitting there, a bed but a few steps away, of a sudden, he was worn through and all he wanted was to climb in that double bed, pull the rugs over him and sleep for a month.

Alas, he could not do that.

"Sit here," Faunus demanded, arising from his chair. "If you sit on that bed, you'll fall into it and not tell us the words that need to be told."

Teddy went to the now-vacant chair while Faunus sprawled himself on the bed, his head in his hand, elbow to the bed, close to the foot, so he could see better, Teddy in his chair.

It was altogether too pleasing of a view, but fortunately, Teddy was too exhausted to waste time appreciating it, and definitely could do nothing about it.

"Start from the beginning, *il mio amore*," Faunus urged.

Teddy looked to Faunus.

He then looked to Saturn, who was pouring wine into a pewter chalice. This deed done, he slid it across the table to Teddy, who took it up, swallowed a healthy dose, and put it down.

And then he started at the beginning.

There were many times the room grew close due to the weight of their combined fury, or stagnant due to their shock at what Teddy told them.

But neither interrupted him all the while he spoke, sharing his story from the moment Fenn took him at Nyx and Lorenz's back step, to when they met in the forest just hours before.

He ended with his eyes on Faunus.

"We need to find an aviast. We need to get birds to King Mars, King True, King Aramus, Prince Cassius, Queen Ophelia. They must know. They must prepare."

"First, Teddy, this earth has lost Queen Ophelia. Princess Elena is now Queen of the Nadirii."

"By the gods," Teddy murmured.

"Second, Airen is in the throes of a civil war. It started but days ago and all the rulers of all the realms are there now, fighting it."

Teddy just stared at him.

Bloody hell.

How long had he been captive and then on the run?

The world had turned over.

"And last, this creature you mention, you are sure it is the Beast?"

"It transformed from man to...to..." He shook his head and looked between the two men, though he settled on Faunus again. "It is impossible to describe. Hideous. Fearsome. Powerful. In the form of a man, he crushed a man's head between his bare hands. As the Beast, his claws severed Fenn's head and he drank from the neck. He was not a troll. He was not a gogmagogg. I do not know of anything in magic, of this earth, even in lore to describe him. Except the Beast."

Head still in hand, Faunus tipped it back to catch Saturn's gaze.

Teddy looked to Saturn and saw the end of his shrug, and when he noted he had Teddy's attention, he wrapped his fingers around the wine bottle, reached across the table and poured Teddy some more.

He then poured himself more and got up to add some to Faunus's goblet.

They were all silent and they drank.

It was Teddy who spoke.

"I understand you do not wish to appear like you've lost your mind by sharing this with your ruler."

"We will share it," Faunus decreed. "Though, Teddy, it is not that I do not believe *you* believe what it is you saw. But we will just describe it rather than saying the Beast has risen. It is not outside the realm of what we know of this Rising to do whatever they will to get what they want. To call forth a creature. Create one. You said yourself a Rising priest was with the thing when it emerged from the earth. Perhaps they did something with dark magic, using those women as sacrifices, that they can no longer control. Whatever it is, Mars must know. They all must know. Yes?"

Teddy nodded. Relieved.

It was the Beast, he knew it to his bones.

But even if they didn't think that true, they were still going to send their warnings.

"Because of this, it is unnecessary to go to the Thicket as True is not there," Faunus declared. "You must talk to your women. Get them to allow us to escort them home so that we can make our way back to ours."

Teddy shook his head. "We still must go there."

"Why?" Saturn asked.

Teddy looked to his friend and dipped his voice low when he told him, "Because they slaughtered all those women. We must go to Crittich Keep. We must report what was done, so if those girls' bodies have not yet been found, they will be, and they can be given their pyres and their families can know. Knowing will bring great sorrow. And I do not know, I can only assume, but my assumption is, not knowing would be worse."

Saturn nodded.

Teddy looked to Faunus and he nodded.

"And if the others that ran away are still out there, they must be caught. They must pay for what they did to those women."

He did not receive nods from either man to that, but the intensity of their stares communicated they were in hearty agreement.

So, Teddy finished it.

"And if we're in the Thicket, if we're at the Keep, which is the administrative base of all constabularies around Wodell, not just a prison, my girls might feel safe enough for me to leave them."

"You have done well by them," Faunus said quietly.

"I have done nothing no other man would do."

"You are wrong."

Teddy pressed his lips together.

Faunus held his gaze.

Teddy fought squirming under the warmth of pride and affection Faunus was giving him through his look.

"It is time for me to find my pallet," Saturn muttered.

Teddy broke from Faunus's hold and looked to his friend.

He was up and grinning down at Teddy. "I am glad we found you and you are well. I imagined many things when we found you, too many of them not good. Though, discovering you with a harem was not amongst them."

Teddy chuckled.

Saturn came to him and chuffed him on a shoulder with the side of his fist.

He turned and dipped his chin to Faunus before he left the room.

Slowly, Teddy took a large swallow of his wine before he set the chalice down just as slowly and with even less haste, he looked to Faunus.

The instant they locked eyes, Faunus whispered, "Come to bed."

Teddy was on his side and Faunus was the same, behind him, moving inside him, his arm about Teddy, stroking his cock.

His strokes in both places were deep, thorough, intimate.

And it wasn't until Faunus's work at both front and back had gathered in Teddy's balls, drawing them up, causing his head to arch back and hit Faunus's shoulder, that Faunus's hand around his shaft tightened, drawing the climax out in a violent gush.

He then rolled Teddy to his stomach, straddled his thighs, and Teddy closed his eyes and memorized the smooth, deep, rough strokes up his arse before Faunus grunted quietly and gave him his seed.

He remained buried even as he fell to his forearms on either side of Teddy and pressed his lips to Teddy's shoulder.

"You will sleep well now, no?" he whispered in Teddy's ear.

"Yes," Teddy murmured.

"Like Saturn, I imagined many things in the finding of you, and they were *all* not good."

"Faunus," he whispered.

"I am glad I am not a seer."

"Thank you again for finding me."

He slid out gently, pushed away, but only to roll Teddy to his back and settle atop him.

And then he said, "*Mio amore*, I'd ride to the end of the earth to find you."

He then kissed Teddy tenderly before he shifted from the bed, brought a wet cloth to cleanse his seed from Teddy's arse, before he took it away and brought a dry one to spread over the bed so neither had to countenance the wet.

Faunus then tangled Teddy up in his long limbs and pulled the covers to their shoulders.

He had never slept as such with a lover in his life.

It was beautiful.

Teddy settled into Faunus's strength and warmth, the soft bed, the aftermath of good sex, the release of what felt like an eternity of fret and worry and fear, letting over to his exhaustion, and was nearly asleep when Faunus muttered, "This Moira does not have feelings for you, does she?"

"In that way?"

"I do not know the bent of your question, but I mean in the way she wants a cock that is mine."

Teddy grinned even as he gave a slight tremble at Faunus's claiming of his cock.

Faunus misinterpreted his tremble and pulled him closer before he pulled the covers up higher.

Ah, Faunus.

His Faunus.

"No, she does not have feelings for me in that way," he answered.

"This is good, for Saturn intends to win her."

All fatigue left him, and his head snapped back.

"Faunus, that cannot happen."

Faunus looked down at him through the dark. "Why no?"

"Because she's just been through hell."

"Not because you are overprotective of her because you guided her out of that hell and due to this, you now consider her your kin?"

His kin?

Well...

"Perhaps a little."

"Calm, *bello*, Saturn will handle her with care."

"Saturn fucks like a bull," he clipped.

Faunus chuckled before saying, "He won't do that the first time."

Good gods!

"He cannot court Moira," Teddy decreed.

"I will let you tell him that."

Teddy blew out a breath.

Faunus chuckled again, then fell forward, now trapping Teddy with his body as well as their tangled limbs.

"Sleep," he urged.

Teddy let out another breath.

And in no time, he was asleep.

135

THE TRAINING

Queen Farah
Guest Bedchamber, Sky Citadel, Sky Bay
Airen

I should have known my husband would not allow it for long.

And he didn't.

No matter how much I enjoyed moving atop him with him inside me, my gaze on him lying before me, his smooth, muscled chest, his eyes a vibrant green, the vines our combined magic created snaking up the bed.

No, True did not allow this for long.

He knifed up, took my mouth, rounded me with an arm at my hips, the other hand going to cup my breast, his thumb rubbing my nipple.

"True," I gasped against his lips.

"Mm?" he murmured, his arm about my hips taking over, lifting me and bringing down upon him much faster.

And harder.

"True," I whimpered. "Lie back, I like to watch you as I take you."

He did not lie back.

I cried out softly in protest as he lifted me off, shifted us, coming to his knees behind me. He grasped my hips in both hands, tipping them. Then he took his cock in one hand to guide it to me and thrust inside me again.

I arched into him, my head falling back, and he drove inside, both his hands gliding over the skin of my belly, one heading up, to my breast, one down, to work between my legs.

My hips jerked as he found my nub.

"*Amore*," I whispered.

"Damn, you're beautiful," he growled.

His finger between my legs combined with his shaft there…

"*True*," I panted.

"Why do you always hold back, darling?" he asked, sounding amused.

"Because…I like…how…you feel…and…I don't…want it…to end," I answered, my voice a staccato, each thrust of his cock pushing out the words.

"Mm," he murmured, taking his hand from my breast to pull my hair from one side of my neck so he could run his tongue all the way up it.

The ivy was coiling up our legs, binding us to the bed as the sensations gathered, my sex clutched his, he groaned his pleasure in my ear at the feeling of it, and I could hold back no more.

I climaxed before him.

When it left me, he was still thrusting inside, his hand between my legs now cupping me there, his other arm about me, fingers curled around the side of my neck.

I listened to his quiet grunts in my ear until it overtook him, and his hand moved to under my jaw, pressing my head back, as he shoved his face in my neck and rumbled his climax into my flesh.

I knew it left him when he slid his hand to the middle of my back, pressing me gently down so my cheek was to the bed. And then—so True, all True, but this part only *my* True—he continued to take me as his fingers glided over my skin at hips, bottom, waist, the small of my back, our vines receding, until he started losing his hardness.

Only then did he pull out, roll me to my back, and settle upon me, lifting the covers up to his hips, but he was my blanket.

His body was hard, but it was warm, and it was the best blanket in the world.

I ran the fingertips of both hands over his beautiful face, his cheek-bones, his eyes, his jaw, his lips, his temples and forehead as my eyes watched.

When he was done allowing this, he captured one of my wrists, turned his head, and pressed a hard kiss in my palm.

After he released me, I slid my arms around him, and my husband dropped down and took my mouth in a slow, soft, wet, lovely kiss.

When he finished it, he touched his lips to my nose before he looked into my eyes and asked, "What do you do today?"

"Elena has a gown fitting."

"Ah," he said on a grin.

"Have you heard tales of her gown?" I asked, having seen a fitting the day before, and having been shocked to my core at the frothy wonder of it.

Elena was not frothy.

But her wedding gown was a vision.

A vision of beauty.

A vision of hope.

"No, though maybe I have, and I ceased listening due to experiencing profound surprise after I heard she would wear a gown to her wedding. I felt certain she'd wear a Nadirii battle tunic."

"You've seen her in a gown before, True."

He looked perplexed. "I have?"

I studied him then reminded him. "Yes. At Catrame. That night. Early on when we all had just met. She came down wearing that stunning black gown."

"Oh. Right. Yes, she was wearing a gown that night."

She wasn't wearing *a gown* that night.

She was wearing a *stunning* gown that night.

He had been in love with Elena then.

He had...

I felt my eyelids get lazy for he had.

But now he was in love with me.

"You look like a cat who got her cream," he murmured throatily, his tone telling me he enjoyed my expression.

"This is because I am indeed a cat, my love, who just got her cream."

For a second, his body stilled over mine.

Then he burst with laughter.

I smiled at him as he did.

He continued laughing as he shoved his face in my neck.

When he stopped, he worked his mouth there.

I liked the feel of this so much, indeed I simply liked my True so much, I held him tighter with my arms and added rounding his thighs with my legs.

"What do you do today?" I asked.

"There was an attempted prison escape yesterday."

My limbs tensed about him.

Sadly, he lifted his head out of my neck. Not sadly, he looked into my eyes so I could again witness the green of his.

I would never tire of looking into his eyes.

Then again, I would never tire of anything that was True.

"Some supporters of Gallienus tried to free him," he shared. "They failed. It very much did not go well to the point two of the eleven conspirators lost their lives. The other nine have now joined Gallienus in his accommodations."

"And what does this have to do with you?"

"Cassius jailed a lord before he left to take Elena to Ophelia prior to..."

"Yes," I whispered when he trailed off.

True cleared his throat, and along with him in that moment, I quietly lamented all of our loss, so much of it, in so short a time.

True continued, "He has asked for an audience with Cass. Apparently, he is one of the instigators and feels that the best way forward in hostilities at this time is to enter negotiations."

"I'm sure he does, ambushing Cassius and Elena, only for them to ride out of the mountains fighting, to be joined by two nations' armies. Unicorns transporting all of us to thwart their evil doings at The Enchantments. Your soldiers now camped out on the grazing fields outside Sky Bay. Mars's approaching The Enchantments to assist in guarding them, his others running roughshod through AG strongholds in the south. Aramus's ships blockading every harbor and bombarding Dunlyn with cannon fire. If I was so thoroughly losing a war I should not have waged within barely a week of starting it, I'd wish to enter negotiations too."

True was grinning down at me throughout my diatribe, and he gave it a few moments before he replied.

"Well, I go with him and Aramus to Slán Bailey to speak to this Lord Felix."

I frowned.

"If we can manage it swiftly and without more loss, it will be good to have it done, Farah," he said. "Cass and Ellie's wedding is in a few days. And I wish to take you home. I wish to have some quiet time with you. I wish for some calm before we face another storm."

"I wish for that too," I said softly.

"Speaking of that, I need to ask your advice."

"Hmm?"

"I've received word from a constabulary in the Arbor."

"Yes?"

"They've arrested Johan on suspicion of treason. Apparently, he hired some prostitutes to spy on Mars and Silence when they were there."

I blinked up at him, thrown by this extraordinary, and extraordinarily stupid news.

"He was arrested in a brothel, after having sex with one of the prostitutes. All three who were paid to spy, as well as management, attest that he is a regular, and even frequent visitor and has been for years. As such, although infidelity is not a criminal offense in Wodell, it does carry penalties if a spouse wishes to press it, it is proven, and it has been long established. As such, Vanka has petitioned for the dissolution of the household. Which means they will remain married, but they no longer will reside under one roof, he has no claims to her, her bloodline or her progeny's person, properties or monies, and she can demand restitution. She has. In an astronomical amount that will be crippling to Johan."

"Er..." I mumbled, uncomfortable, for I had a feeling this befalling Johan was not a coincidence.

"I know Mars is behind it, Farah. I also know Johan did not spy on Mars and Silence for Wodell or other reasons regarding state affairs or personal ideals, but so he could find some way to drive a wedge between them. It was a faulty play and if Mars was not Mars, and he did not feel as he does about Silence, upon discovery, it could have made things very touchy between our two realms."

At least I could agree to that.

Thus, I did, saying, "Yes."

"So, what do I do?"

I was confused.

"What do you do?"

"It has been made clear I'm overprotective when it comes to Silence. It's also now known that Johan is not blood to her. I know what Mars will say if I ask him, since he maneuvered this, but I want to shield Silence from hurt. And because of that, I do not want to ask her. So, do I get behind Mars's play? Or do I show leniency in order not to upset Silence further than she already is about her father...and mother?"

"You get behind Mars's play," I stated instantly.

His brows rose slowly. "You answered that quickly."

"What does it mean, fully, to do that?"

"The missives are from ravens, so they are not thorough, but he is admitting to the spying, and why. And there is no recourse about the infidelity. It was witnessed. Even by Vanka."

My heart sunk for Vanka and my expression must have shown that for True spoke on.

"He has always been arrogant and acted like he could do anything he pleases. He had a more kingly manner than my father, and not in noble way. If she did not know this was a good possibility, she is a fool. Vanka has been turning the other cheek far too long. It sounds unkind, but I do not have much sympathy for her."

I could not argue that either.

Thus, instead, I noted, "True, you are king."

His brows inched together. "Pardon?"

"Take Silence out of this equation. If another member of your gentry spied on a visiting monarch without your knowledge or approval, what would you do?"

His lips thinned.

"Do that," I said.

"What I would do is relieve him of his landed title, Farah. Which means relieving him of his land."

"Do that," I repeated.

"It is only just recently we've come to know he is not Silence's father. She has grown up thinking he is. And he is my uncle."

"He spied on a visiting sovereign, True. It doesn't matter the reason. It cannot be abided. And, yes," I conceded, "this is precisely what Mars has maneuvered for you to do. But *Mars* didn't spy on himself and his wife. *Johan* did it. And you, as a monarch, who I have personally seen work very hard, very long, and with not a small amount of frustration to establish healthy alliances with the other nations of Triton, cannot have a member of your gentry for *any* reason imperiling that."

I took a breath while I watched True reflect on this.

Then I went on.

"Actually, it's worse. For it's so bloody foolish as to be obnoxious. It was not for crown and country. It was simply to be horrid. As you say, if Mars was not Mars and he did not feel as he does about Silence, you know how he'd react to being spied upon. His warriors would ride. It could have had very dire consequences, including the loss of life, just because Johan is an arrogant bastard."

He seemed to be studying my ear.

"Silence will understand," I whispered.

His gaze came to mine.

"You are certain?" he asked quietly.

This was his issue.

He did not wish to cause harm to his cousin.

I laid a hand on his cheek. "I am certain."

His body moved with the deep breath he drew in and it moved again when he released it.

"I hate this time," he said.

I was confused. "Sorry? What time?"

"This time, of a morning, when we have to leave our bed and let the world into our lives."

"Oh, *mia vita*," I murmured, lifting up to press my lips to his. I dropped my head back to the pillows and told him, "Me too."

"But I suppose we must do it."

"Yes, and in just hours, we will retire back to this bed and it shall be you and me."

He touched his lips to first one eyebrow, then the other, my nose, and then he said, "Until then, my beloved."

And alas, he pulled us from our bed.

~

"Bravo!" I cried, clapping my hands.

"My little sister is a markswoman!" Jorie boomed, moving with his big man grace to his sister to engulf her in a massive hug.

I glanced at Ha-Lah beside me, who was looking at the brother and sister dotingly, before I turned my attention back to Silence, who had her head well back to beam up at her big brother as he squeezed her in his bulky arms.

"It is funny, do you not think," Ha-Lah began, and I looked again to her. "How, when this journey began for all of us, we had so very little, and even if we have lost so very much along the way, what we have gained is beyond measure?"

How right she was.

"Yes, funny," I murmured. "In a very lovely way."

She cast a smile to me.

I returned it.

"Can I learn to throw daggers now, Ellie?" Dora asked.

She, along with Aelia, had returned to Airen with Ha-Lah and Aramus.

And she was now sitting on a low, stone fence at the side where we were in a courtyard amongst the expansive citadel grounds.

In my short time there, I had noted someone along the line in the history of Airenzian kings wished for beauty in this dark place.

Thus, amongst the twists and turns of the sprawling edifice that was designed to daunt, there were surprises. These included small, secluded gardens, courtyards and large balconies, as well as ornate fountains tucked in hidden corners or thin beds of tidy shrubs along walls.

Though, the most recent king clearly wished order. All outside space was formal to the point it was regimented. Shrubs, trees and potted plants were clipped precisely, with only pyramids, spikes and spirals as choice. There were no flowers, and this was not only because it was winter.

Although spartan, there was still beauty.

It could, as True told me Elena had accomplished inside the citadel, sharing she'd made great change in a short time, use a woman's touch.

I had no doubt, come spring, Ellie would see to that as well.

"And me!" Aelia cried. "Can I learn now too?"

"You will begin to learn daggers when you're twelve, like all Nadirii," Elena said to Dora and then turned her eyes to Aelia, and I saw her face was soft with having to deliver bad news to the girls. "Which means a long time to wait for you, sweets."

Both girls assumed expressions of mutiny.

"I'm afraid I haven't practiced near as much as Silence," I said to Serena, who was standing at my other side.

By "near as much," I meant "not at all." But I did not share this.

"Mm," was all Serena said on a dip of her chin across the courtyard.

She then headed toward Silence.

I looked across the courtyard and saw Chu move from where he was there, standing by Kyril.

"If you'd step to the edge, Silence," Serena requested as she walked past her, heading to the large, upright target some feet away, where all of Silence's five daggers were very close to the middle circle.

She pulled the daggers out, and without preamble, started running about the courtyard.

As, without warning, Chu started throwing stones at her.

They were not large, they were not small, and he darted about as he did it while Serena bobbed, weaved, ducked, rolled, was sometimes hit by the stones, and intermingled with this, she threw the daggers at the target from a variety of positions. Side arm. From resting on her knee. Even one of them she let fly while flat on her back.

When she was done, all but one had hit the center circle.

She turned to a wide-eyed Silence who was standing beside a frowning Jorie.

"Was it necessary for you to show off to diminish the excellent display my little sister treated us to?" Jorie demanded of Serena tetchily.

"I wasn't showing off, I was making a point," Serena replied to Jorie then looked to Silence. "It does not take away from your practice or that you have honed your skill admirably," she stated. "But in battle, you do not stand alone, throwing at a target. Perhaps in future, you can practice with some distractions."

"If you think I'm throwing stones at my queen while she tosses daggers, you've lost your mind," Kyril called.

Everyone laughed, and even Serena smiled.

But her attention went back to Silence.

"Though I would say, this is not what you should be practicing. *This...*"

She suddenly started sprinting toward Silence, and Jorie moved to round his sister in order to put himself between her and the approaching Nadirii warrior.

But just as suddenly, Serena leaped in the air, twisting at the waist, doing this flinging out her arm.

A fizzing line the color of lilacs shot from her hand, and in a sizzle as the line scored across it, the target was shorn into two parts, the top teetering for a moment before it fell to the ground.

Serena came out of her leap with her eyes on Silence.

And she finished, "Is what you should be practicing." She looked to me. "And you." Her eyes moved to Ha-Lah. "And you." She returned to Silence. "You were exceptional in the Battle of the Veil. Consider what you could do if you honed your skill."

"I have heard you and Silence helped in extraordinary ways with the winning of that battle," Ha-Lah muttered out of the side of her mouth. "Well done."

"Thank you, *sorella*," I replied. "But in the doing, I nearly depleted my magic. I now must take potions day and evening. Potions that Elena has tried to mask the taste with mint and rose, but they are still most vile. I also must meditate every day over a card Elena draws for me to help replenish it," I told her. "This, she prescribes me to do, for at least an hour. I have found, through the doing of it, I am not much skilled at sitting still."

Ha-Lah turned her head and grinned at me. "I suspect it was worth it."

I grinned back. "It bloody was."

"I'm not sure they should be depleting their power," Elena, also across the courtyard from us, called to her sister.

"And *I* am not certain my little sister will be close enough to another battle to throw her fire bombs," Jorie declared, having heard the tales told over a dinner of an evening, and even when he did, not liking them (and it should be said, many tales were told on both sides, including the fact that not only Silence, but Ha-Lah too, was Mer). But after he said this, he instantly looked down to Silence with a gentle expression on his face and stated, "Though from what I have heard, they were most remarkable, and your aim was exceptional."

"I'm a powerful witch, Jorie. But Serena is correct. I should sharpen my skills," Silence told her brother.

"You are a *wee* witch, Silence." He lifted one of his big hands and held out his forefinger and thumb about an inch apart.

Silence's head ticked as her eyes dropped to his fingers.

"Oh dear," Ha-Lah whispered.

I pressed my lips together.

Jorie dropped his hand. "And as such, you should be protected from matters such as these."

"I need to do my bit," Silence replied.

"You have done your bit," Jorie retorted. "Now let others do their bits."

"Hmm," I hummed, thinking this was not the course he should take to win his little sister.

Or at least not *this* little sister.

"I can't let everyone else take all the risks," Silence declared.

"You very well can," Jorie rejoined.

I could sense that Silence was beginning to become heated with the tone of her, "I will do what I must."

"You will keep yourself safe," Jorie returned.

"You do not have charge of me, Jorie!" she snapped, with that, sounding *just* like a little sister. I knew this for, in growing up, I must have said this to Mars five hundred times when he was being overbearing. "Thus, I will do what I please!"

"Fine."

Silence stared up at him in surprise at his capitulation.

However, he was not finished speaking.

"I will speak to your husband and cousin about this."

Silence slowly turned her head toward Ha-Lah and me.

Her cheeks were very pink.

I tried very hard not to laugh.

A stifled noise coming from Ha-Lah beside me shared she was doing the same.

"Let us move on to how you use a charging warrior against himself," Serena called into this verbal tussle, thankfully.

Then, for the next ten minutes, Serena sent Chu flying half a dozen times in half a dozen ways as he charged her. Though I noted immediately, she tended to send him careening over her back by ducking a shoulder into his approach and letting his momentum do the rest of the work.

Using a charging warrior against himself, indeed.

Each time this happened, Serena offered Chu a hand to pull him to his feet and they exchanged a look that made my skin heat.

Ha-Lah was clearly of the same mind, for she whispered to me, "I wonder what sex is like between those two."

"I shan't wonder, for my husband is on an island in the harbor and not close to me," I replied.

We both giggled as Serena called, "Farah, Ha-Lah, Silence, it is your turn." She pivoted to Kyril and requested, "Will you help?"

"I'm not charging a queen," Kyril declined. "*Any* of them."

"I will not either."

Serena whirled to Chu when he said these words.

"Why not?" she asked.

"This is a foolish question I will not answer," he said.

"You charged me," she pointed out.

He smiled a smile at her that also heated my skin before saying, "I am physical with you in numerous ways, my warrior. But I will not touch my queen, nor will I touch any of the others."

"I'll do it," Elena entered the discussion before it, too, became heated. "I could use some physical activity. I'm getting tight."

"Their majesties can throw me!" Aelia volunteered. "I'll charge them all day!"

Ellie shot a grin at her. "Maybe a bit later, all right?"

Aelia clapped excitedly.

"Um, I do not know if I could throw Elena," I said.

"I'll be fine," Elena assured. "We've been taught to land soft."

I widened my eyes at Ha-Lah.

Ha-lah just laughed and entered the turf area of the courtyard, declaring, "I'll start."

She did well, notwithstanding having to maneuver her heavy skirts and cloak, which Serena didn't have to do, as she wore a short tunic with long sleeves and thick leg casings.

"We need trousers," I told Ha-Lah as we switched places when it became my turn.

"I've already decided I'm commissioning a wardrobe of Finnie's breeches," Ha-Lah replied.

I made note to do the same before I concentrated on the matter at hand.

Serena showed me the steps. How to plant my legs but not lock them. How to protect my head and neck. When to engage my arms.

Elena was only able to clash bodily with Ha-Lah twice in the charges they'd done.

Elena was able to wrap her arms around me four times.

"I don't think I'm good at this," I muttered.

"You will not encounter charging soldier after soldier," Serena said, coming to stand close to us. "But if there is one, you need to keep your head about you and know what to do. Tomorrow, we will go over some of those hand-to-hand maneuvers I taught you in the Thicket. In any combat, you will likely be mounted and out of the way, using your magicks. What I am teaching you is just in case."

I nodded.

She gave a curt nod back that was not dismissive, it was just Serena's way of sharing she was ready to move along.

I resumed my place beside Ha-Lah and watched as Elena attacked Silence repeatedly while Jorie scowled thunderclouds at them.

We then watched Elena playfully tussling with both Dora and Aelia.

"Would all this business was over so that I could give Aramus a daughter," Ha-Lah murmured wistfully.

"Not a son?" I asked.

"Oh, I would take a son," she turned dancing eyes at me. "But he's keen on daughters."

"Are all women on land this comely and spirited?" Jorie boomed his question to Kyril and Chu, who were again standing together at the side, watching Elena with the girls.

Though, I was complimented to see that he swung his long arm out to include Serena, Ha-Lah and me.

"No," Kyril answered.

"This is good," Jorie stated, crossing his arms on his chest. "For I would wish I had taken my legs far more often if they were."

"Do you not have a special someone, brother?" Silence asked.

"I have one who is new who has all my attention, little sister," he replied, then hooked her about the neck and yanked her to his side. "And she is right here."

"I think I might love him," I muttered.

"Aramus is quite lucky that he is all he is, or I would not wish to be Queen of the Seas, but Queen of the Mer," Ha-Lah replied.

We giggled again.

Elena flopped on her back in the turf and demanded of the skies, "It *must* be time for biscuits and tea!"

Aelia flopped on top of her, making Ellie emit an "*oof*" noise, at the same time crying, "It is! Let's take them in that room that used to be all black and gray and sad but now is all yellow and gay and happy!"

"Let us do that, my little red princess," Elena agreed.

Aelia hopped up, shouting, "I want the biscuits with the chocolate on top!"

"I'm going to have lemon ones," Dora said, coming to help Aelia pull Elena up, each girl having a hand.

"Ooo...I want a lemon one too," Aelia declared.

"I'd take redhead, if True and I weren't destined to have a daughter who was dark," I muttered.

"And I'd take a blonde, if Aramus and I had any earthly hope of such a thing," Ha-Lah replied in her own mutter.

We again looked at each other.

And smiled.

～

Princess Serena
Guest Bedchamber, Sky Citadel, Sky Bay
AIREN

"I AM SWEATY, and have smudges of dirt all over me," she declared. "I shall change and meet my sister and her girls for—"

She didn't finish that for she found herself pressed against black stone and had Chu growling in her ear.

"Hands to the wall."

Her pussy pulsed.

"Chu—"

"Hands to the wall, little mouse."

They had not played since they'd reunited.

Oh, how she had missed this.

Serena placed suddenly trembling hands to the wall.

Other parts of her were trembling after he pulled up her tunic and then ripped her body stocking in two at the crotch.

"Chu," she said, this time in a moan.

"Speak only when spoken to," he ordered in her ear, driving two fingers up her cunt.

She went up on her toes and her eyes rolled back into her head.

He fucked her like that and then slid his fingers out, gliding them to her clit and rolling.

Her head fell back.

"Rub yourself against me," he commanded.

She did as told.

"Did you miss this?" he asked.

"Yes," she breathed.

"I only touch you."

"Wh-what?"

"It would not be sexual, what you requested earlier, but I only touch you."

"I—"

He thrust his fingers inside her and her eyes drifted closed.

"Fuck yourself," he demanded.

Serena did.

"It is of my people," he continued. "It is respect, to your chosen one. In my land, a man does not only give his heart. He gives all of himself. Unless it is a daughter, a mother, a sister, one of direct blood, his fingers never even brush another woman's skin. There are regions where a man will not even raise his eyes to another woman once he has bound himself to the one he loves."

Listening to his words, having him inside her, she started fucking herself faster on his fingers.

"I touch no one but you," he growled into her ear.

"Al-all right."

"And the daughters we will make."

She shuddered.

He withdrew his fingers and replaced them with his cock, fucking her against the black Airenzian stone, finger at her clit, face in her neck, his breath heavy and hot against her skin.

This he did until she climaxed for him, and then he did the same in return.

He was fucking her gently, his arm about her belly now, but his mouth was still at her neck.

"We will have only daughters. You can magick this, yes?"

He wanted to make babies with her.

And knowing that, she wanted to make babies with him.

"Yes," she whispered.

"Then you will give me daughters."

But I want a son who looks like you.

The thought entered her mind unbidden, and even if it astonished her, the having of it instantly made it a yearning.

"If we should have a son, we will teach him to love his brother, like your brother loved you, and you loved him," she said.

He slid out, turned her to face him, then pressed her to the wall with his body, his face close to hers.

"If we had a son, he would have claim to my brother's throne. We will have no son, Serena."

"We would teach him—"

"You are Nadirii, you wish a boy?" he asked.

I want a boy just like you, she thought.

"I want you to have what you want," she said.

"Then give me girls with copper hair and freckles."

"I can magic the sex," she muttered. "The rest is up to the goddess."

His eyes smiled. "Then I shall pray to my gods for copper hair and freckles." And with that, he kissed her quickly, then moved away, heading toward the door, tucking himself in his trousers as he murmured, "Clean up and go have tea and biscuits with your sister. I will see you here again as we ready ourselves for dinner."

"Chu," she called.

At the door, his trousers rebuttoned, he turned to her.

"Why?" she asked.

"Why?" he asked in return, his head tipping slightly to the side, his expression puzzled.

She swallowed.

And all she could say to explain her question was, "Me."

"I did note the copper hair and freckles," he answered immediately.

She swept her gaze away.

"My princess."

She looked back.

"Why me?" he queried.

"Sorry?"

He studied her then inquired, "Why have you convinced yourself you are unlovable? Why do you ask yourself why my heart belongs to you and you do not ask yourself why you gave yours to me? What makes me worthy?"

"You are...Chu," she stated lamely.

His lips tipped up. "I am that."

She felt his seed gliding down her thigh, not to mention she felt entirely uncomfortable with this conversation she, herself, foolishly instigated, and thus she murmured, "I must clean up."

"And you are Serena," he called after she'd begun to turn away.

She turned back.

"I have fucked many women. I have mastered many women," he announced, and her stomach twisted. "Not one of them was like you."

"I don't know what that means."

"It means, when she is the one, she is the one, and when she is, she becomes known as just that. You are the one, my princess warrior. I do not question why. Why I love gazing upon you. Why I love the feel of your cunt. Why I watch you use your magic on a target and it makes me fight my cock getting hard. Why I watch you offer your sister your version of kindness in her loss and it makes my heart tight. Why I like the smell of your hair when I sleep. I do not question why because there is no answer, but one. It is the one you gave to me. The answer to why for you is that I am your Chu. And the answer to why for me is that you are Serena. And you are mine."

"I think I wish to fuck again," she declared.

He gave her an entirely different smile as he began moving in her direction.

"No tea and biscuits?" he asked.

She shook her head. "No. Just Chu."

When he was close, he dipped low, caught her belly with his shoulder, and powered her back until she fell on the bed.

He pulled himself over her and whispered, "You need to be cleaned. We'll start with that and see where we go."

Chu didn't give her the opportunity to respond.

He slid down her body.

And thus, there was no tea and biscuits for Serena.

In fact, they almost missed dinner.

King True
Informal Salon, "The Red Room," Sky Citadel, Sky Bay
AIREN

"THEY ASKED FOR CONCESSIONS?" Ha-Lah inquired, her brows up, her face incredulous.

"They've demanded I roll back my proclamations and sit down with the gentry to hammer out a ten- to fifteen-year plan instituting the changes in a 'much more manageable and palatable manner,'" Cassius answered.

He then tossed back a large measure of whiskey.

True felt Farah's hand on his thigh give him a squeeze.

He looked down to her where she sat at his side on the sofa.

He then gave a short nod that this was true.

Her mouth grew tight.

True sighed.

Suffice it to say, their trip to Slán Bailey had been a waste of time.

Thus, they were all here, in the red room, having drinks prior to dinner, and those drinks were much needed.

"And your answer was?" Jorie asked.

"I gave them an option of where they could shove their ten- to fifteen-year plan," Cassius drawled.

Jorie roared with laughter.

Still in the midst of it, he turned to Aramus and queried, "How did I not know these landed had such very big balls?"

"Because prior to Cass, there was Gallienus, and he only used his balls to think, and considering the way he managed his rule, it is clear they were very small. And prior to True, was Wilmer, and he didn't have any balls at all." Aramus then looked to True and said, "I hope you take no offense, my brother."

"Would that one day I would find I am also of the Mer," True muttered in answer, before he lifted his glass and drew in his own large measure of whiskey.

He heard chuckles about him, but he used his concentration to swallow.

"True," Farah whispered.

He looked to her.

"I am not offended, sweetling," he assured, and it was not a lie.

She studied him a moment before she nodded.

"Negotiations rather broke down after that," Cass finished.

"Because you walked out of the room," Aramus reported, smiling broadly at Cassius.

"Thus," Ian entered the conversation, "I had the honor of sharing with Lord Felix that Cass is disbanding the feudal system and that, should he survive his term for treason against the crown, he will have no castle to return to. But regardless, in the now, he should endeavor to spend less time attempting to communicate with the AG in this ongoing conflict and more time trying to find someplace for his wife, sons and daughter to live for they're soon to be turned out and their home made into an orphanage."

"I'm certain that went over well," Silence noted, her eyes twinkling, her wee monkey hiding in the fall of her hair at her shoulder.

"He not only damned Cassius and Elena's line for eternity, but mine too," Ian replied to Silence.

"Oh no, does he have magic in his blood?" Silence asked worriedly.

"There has not been any real magic in the royal lines of landed Triton since the Sky King clashed against the Fire King," Jorie declared.

Everyone looked to him.

"They were both stout. Both mighty. Both had magic. And both fell in love with the same woman," Jorie intoned. "She was an extraordinary beauty. Born," he turned his eyes to True, "to the green."

He looked about the room, saw he had everyone's attention, and carried on.

"The firstborn, the Fire King, who had dominion over their realm, felt, as the firstborn, and as the true king, he should be able to lay claim to her. The second born, the Sky King, who ruled at his brother's behest the northern regions of their realm, felt they should play out a challenge, the victor winning her. The Fire King refused the challenge and spoke loud and much, which reached far, about how he would not do so as he did not wish to humiliate his younger kin. This infuriated the Sky King, and he demanded satisfaction. The Fire King responded by abducting the fair maiden from her green land, imprisoning her in his castle of sand and showering her with jewels and love and affection until she was utterly besotted with him."

"That sounds like one of your forebears," Silence murmured, and Mars grinned down at her unrepentantly.

"Stealing through the dunes," Jorie went on, "the Sky King infiltrated the castle of sand, and in his turn, seized her and took her to his keep on the black cliffs by the sea. There, he taught her the names of the stars and manipulated the clouds to form visions of her beauty in the sky. And he promised her their love would be written, her name on the sun, and his name on the moon, forevermore. Which, of course meant she became utterly besotted with *him*."

True noted Cassius staring at Jorie with an inscrutable expression on his face.

While Elena gazed at Cassius with easily read devotion.

And concern.

"The Fire King was beside himself with fury at her loss," Jorie continued. "He vowed he would lay waste to everything in a blaze of fire until she was returned. This meant the Green King felt he had to intervene. She was his subject. He claimed dominion over her and demanded her return to the green land so he could speak with her and know her desires."

"I've never heard this story," Ha-Lah whispered to Aramus.

"I haven't either," Farah whispered to True.

"Do you know this story, Frey?" Finnie asked.

"Not at all," Frey answered, his gaze on Jorie.

Circe was regarding Jorie with avid attention.

Lahn was looking into his glass like he wished there was more liquor in it.

Or the liquor that was in it was stronger.

"The kings agreed to meet in the place where all their realms touched, what is now," Jorie nodded to Elena, "known as The Enchantments."

"Did you know that?" Ha-Lah asked Elena.

"It was why that location was chosen to be the home of the Nadirii," Elena told Ha-Lah. "It was already steeped in magic."

"Yes," Jorie said. "Fools for love."

"What happened then, Jorie?" Silence asked.

"Have you not heard this story, *piccolina*?" Mars queried, and when he did, their monkey scurried out from under hair, over to Mars, where she tucked herself inside his shirt as if she was pulling the covers of a bed up to her neck.

And as the tiny creature did this, Mars did not twitch, as if the thing slept just like that, next to his heart, every night.

"I knew they fought. I knew it was over a woman. But this was not the story I read," Silence answered. "She was...well, not very romantically described."

"That's because you read the Airenzian version," Cassius told her. "If you find it in Firenze, it will be far closer to the truth."

"It does not have a happy ending," Jorie warned.

"Oh no," Silence whispered.

"They tore her apart," Cassius announced tersely.

The room went silent and everyone regarded Cass.

"Sweetheart," Elena murmured, curling her hand around his forearm.

"It is what you know, Silence," Cassius said gently. "All you know of how it is comes from Airen. What you do not know is *why* women are treated as such in this land. The second born son of the Fire King was always the Sky King. Brothers, for centuries, millennia, who ruled their dominions side by side, in accord, even bloody harmony. Upon coronation, they'd assume the magicks of their realms. Fire and Sky. Until her. Until neither man could get beyond their own passions and desires and pride."

He drained his glass, set it on a table by his side, and resumed speaking.

"And when they met to return her to the Green King so he could discover what *she* wanted, they clashed, magicks against magicks, with her in the middle. Some lore has them actually *physically* tearing her asunder, and their magicks exploded in grief and fury when they did, the Green King intervening in an effort to stop their power from destroying the earth. Other lore says that when the Green King saw what they were doing, saw his subject caught between these two powerful forces, he sent his magic to save her. The three magicks colliding disintegrated her on the spot.

However it happened, this magic drove deep into the earth and up to the heavens and scorched all around for miles. And it heralded war that lasted one hundred and fifty years before a stalemate was finally called, Firenze broke in two and Airen was born."

"I don't understand why this would be why women were so awfully treated here, Cass," Silence noted.

"Because they blamed her, love," he told her. "They couldn't assume the blame they'd earned, so they blamed her. They lost their magic, all of them, two of them because of pride and arrogance, and one, sadly, because of fairness and the desire to seek the truth. The Fire King went back to his land, demanded the greatest beauty of Firenze be brought to him, and he forced her to marry him. They eventually fell in love. The Sky King went back to his land and demanded *all* the greatest beauties of the realm be brought to him. He selected ten, married the lot, attempting to force them to mend his broken heart. None of them succeeded. Thus, he garroted them all, eventually, doing this personally. He had more brought forth, and died having had thirty-three wives, twenty-nine of them dead at his hand. But none of them were her."

He turned his head to look at Elena.

Farah clenched True's thigh.

"And that is my blood, darling," he finished.

"Well, it's good that your mother's blood is good and kind and won out in you, isn't it?" Elena retorted without a second's delay.

"Gods, nothing shakes it, does it?" Cassius muttered.

"No," Elena responded easily on a large smile.

It took a moment, but Cassius's lips quirked.

"You're the Sky King," Farah blurted.

True turned to her to see her gaze on Cass.

And thus, he only heard Cassius's reply, "In name only."

Farah looked to True. "And you're the Green King."

"Also, in name only, darling," he murmured.

She turned to Mars. "And you're the Fire King and you," she looked to Aramus, "are the Sea King."

"And you will note, *my* people didn't get caught up in that messy bloody business," Aramus stated.

True felt his own lips twitch.

"This is...we are..." she stammered but said no more.

"Farah?" Ha-Lah called.

"We are their power," Farah stated.

The room went silent again.

Someone cleared their throat, and all looked to the door.

A servant was there, his eyes on Elena.

"Your Grace, dinner is ready," he announced.

Before Elena could say anything, Bram appeared in the door, rounding the servant, and his eyes were locked on True.

"True, a word?" he asked.

At the look on his brother's face, True did not delay in murmuring his apologies, straightening from his seat, and following Bram out of the room.

Bram headed down the hall the opposite direction of the dining room.

He stopped nearly to the entry of the Citadel.

"I don't like the look on your face," True noted after he stopped with him.

"We've had ravens from Alfie. He says he's sending a messenger with the fullness of his report, including the evidence he has that supports what the ravens bear. That being, he believes it was The Rising who conspired to surface the Beast. And True...*fuck*."

"What?" True asked with dread.

"He thinks there's strong evidence that the Beast is risen."

True closed his eyes.

And whispered...

"*Fuck*."

136

THE ASSIGNMENTS

The Great Coven
Silbury Henge, Argyll Forest
AIREN

In the clearing of the forest, the first flash of light came before the first of the five standing stones.

The light was coral.

The witch Melisse of the Nadirii Sisterhood.

The next flash was green.

Rebecca of Wodell.

And at her side, arms linked, was Queen Farah.

The next light was crimson.

Nandra of Firenze.

And linked to her was Queen Silence.

Then there was marine-blue.

The witch Lena of Mar-el.

And with her came Queen Ha-Lah.

The last flash was bright white.

Fern of Airen.

At her side, with arms linked, was Queen Elena.

Without a word, they moved as one to the slab in the center of the stones.

Touching the stone with her fingertips, Lena stated clearly, "The moon."

Fern of the Airenzian touched it. "The star."

Nandra of the Firenz also put fingers to stone. "The blood."

Rebecca followed suit. "The dirt."

Melisse hesitated, closed her eyes, breathed deep, took a moment with love, respect and sorrow to remember her sister, her friend, and then said, "The sisterhood."

Instantly, Elena broke from Fern and declared, "You need to cease your activities in Dunlyn."

"It is too far gone for that, Your Grace," Fern replied.

"It is on orders from your Regent," Elena returned heatedly.

"We have weightier topics to discuss," Rebecca broke in.

And Nandra of Firenze did not hesitate in doing that.

"We would feel him, would we not?" she asked.

"We felt the disturbance in the veil," Lena remarked.

"But then...nothing?" Rebecca asked. "How could he ascend after these many millennia and then...*nothing*?"

"We must seek him in the now," Fern stated, leaning forward into both her palms on the stone before them. "We must discover if he has surfaced."

"And then what?" Nandra asked.

"Vanquish him," Fern replied, pushing back. She then indicated the queens amongst them with a sweep of her arm. "They are at their full powers."

"Elena must marry," Melisse stated. "She is the last. This union, their vows, must be felt by the veil. Only then will those prophesied be at their full powers."

There seemed a general agreement with that, but Melisse did not make verbal note of it.

She continued, "And Ha-Lah, Jorie and Silence must make alliances with the beasts of the seas."

"Do you think to drive him to the seas again?" Rebecca asked.

"I think we must consider all avenues, regardless if they are used," Melisse answered.

"But Silence hasn't even used her fin yet," Ha-Lah shared.

"Then teach her," Melisse replied. "And do it swiftly."

Ha-Lah glanced at Silence.

Silence nodded her head to Ha-Lah.

The Firenz Queen did not appear afraid.

She appeared excited.

"And you must bring peace in your realm," Melisse said to Fern, her gaze then shifted to Elena to finish making her point.

"You say this as if I could snap my fingers and it would be done," Fern stated irritably. "And if I could do that, it *would be done*."

"You cannot, I know this. But you have dragons," Melisse returned. "Use them."

"Melisse," Elena whispered, never having been at one with the idea of using the incalculably destructive powers of those creatures.

"It is not only castles and keeps you can reign fire upon, sister-daughter," Melisse told her. "There are fields of grape and groves of olives, mines of salt, and much more, the loss of which will be felt dearly."

"Cassius is bestowing the land to the people who work it," Elena replied. "If it is destroyed, now it is they who would feel it most."

"Right." Melisse considered this as she looked amongst the witches. She then came to a decision. "We have the power to come here. Lena, you and I will use it to go to Lord Felix's hall. We see to it that it's cleared. And then Frey can call his dragons."

"The stones strengthen us as we're here," Rebecca pointed out. "Such transport would be incredibly draining if it is not done to the stones. It would take months to replenish it. This is why we do not do it."

"And we are saving our magicks for what?" Melisse asked.

"To defeat the Beast," Rebecca answered.

"And what do you think I'm talking about?" Melisse pressed. "Cassius and Elena, and the rest of them for that matter, cannot have their minds divided. Nor their efforts. If this unrest is not quelled, the Allied Gentry could use Cassius's distraction with the Beast to press forward their interests."

"That would be foolhardy," Lena murmured.

"And these men are bastions of intelligence?" Melisse queried.

For the first time, the women amongst the stones quirked smiles.

"Should you be in the field on such a mission?" Nandra asked. "After what befell you from The Rising, are you at your full strength?"

"Does it matter when things need to get done?" Melisse asked back.

"Yes, if you were to fail in the mission," Nandra returned.

"I will not fail," Melisse declared in a manner that not another woman thought to press that particular subject.

"I will hasten to bring to fruition my mission in Dunlyn," Fern decreed.

"You should abandon it altogether," Elena advised.

"I do not intend to remain in the services of my Regent's forces after this is over, Elena," Fern replied quietly. "Thus, if he wishes to punish me for insurrection when all is said and done, I will accept whatever punishment he chooses. But the work of my women must reach completion in Dunlyn."

"Can you explain why?" Farah queried.

Fern looked to the Dellish Queen.

"Lord Felix is the only one who has come forth to share he is officially of this insurgence. Others were identified by their militias battling your forces in the Night Heights and at The Enchantments. We have strong reason to believe, however, that not all have come forward to state where their allegiance lies. We also have strong reason to believe that a council of *all* those united to depose Cassius, restore Gallienus to his throne, and resume the ways of Airen meets there to plan their war," Fern shared. "And we have reason to believe that orders are coming from the Bailey, direct from Gallienus himself."

Her voice dropped when she continued.

"You do not kill a weed by picking off its leaves. You must dig it out of the dirt. We must know who our enemy is, Farah. All of them."

Farah could not argue that point, so she didn't.

But Elena entered the conversation.

"Serena has become quite skilled at being a spy."

"She is very well known by this faction," Fern replied. "As such, it would be difficult for her to spy."

"She is very well known everywhere, but she still managed to strike a crippling blow to The Rising," Elena replied.

"I will consider this," Fern murmured.

"And consider using her lover, Chu," Elena added.

Fern's chin lifted. "We need no man."

"He taught Serena much of what she knows. And Serena has a crew. Two gnomes. And everyone knows that gnomes are exceptionally skilled at espionage."

Fern appeared most interested in this idea.

"Someone must volunteer to track down the Beast," Melisse noted at this juncture, her eyes on Rebecca and Nandra. "It will be dangerous, and Lena and I can join in the search when we've completed our assignment. But we cannot delay in searching to ascertain if he has, or has not, come to ground."

"I will do this," Nandra declared.

"As will I," Rebecca stated.

Melisse nodded and carried on.

"As it is, and as most of you know it is, our recent losses have caused great mourning," she stated softly. "But they have also released great amounts of magic. It goes without saying we, all of us, would wish the witches who bore that magic to be amongst us, using their gifts to fight our foes. They are not. Thus, we must endeavor to use what they have left for us. Use it in their honor and use it to ensure their lives on this earth, and their deaths for a righteous cause, were not in vain."

"I am uncertain if this is a good idea," Rebecca said worriedly.

"It might not be," Nandra replied. "But drawing down that amount of power would be useful."

"I don't understand what this means," Silence murmured.

"We must draw down Mum's, Jasmine's, Rose's and the magics of all the other Nadirii who fell," Elena explained.

"And it must be yours," Melisse told the prophesied. "The four of yours."

"I would include Serena," Elena said.

Melisse inclined her head.

Ha-Lah was glancing around before she asked, "Is this not normally done?"

"It is avoided, unless needed, such as in a time like this," Rebecca shared. "We, all of us, absorb magic naturally. It is not done to make maneuvers to take more than we can organically absorb. But beyond that, it is generally agreed it is not right to take more than our fair share. But mostly, too much magic is a burden to bear. It can get unwieldy. It can make your command of it unreliable. And unreliable magic is as you would expect, not good, especially for those who try to use it."

"As my command of it is already unreliable, is this wise?" Farah asked.

"Risks are never wise, but that doesn't mean they shouldn't be taken," Nandra answered.

"And I would assume, as you are the prophesied," Melisse put in, "that you would be able to wield much more than most."

Although this made sense, none of the women at the stones looked comfortable with that.

But none of them said a word against it.

"And thus, we have a plan," Melisse decreed.

All nodded.

"We understand our assignments?" Melisse pressed.
All nodded.
Melisse looked amongst them.
And then she whispered...
"So mote it be."

137

THE SHIMMERING

King Mars
Guest Bedchamber, Sky Citadel, Sky Bay
AIREN

"I do not like this," Mars growled to his wife who sat astride him in their bed as he rested his shoulders against the headboard.

She was wearing far too many clothes.

This being naught but a nightgown.

Though she was also wearing his marital chain, which soothed him.

But after she had shared what she had shared that she'd learned from the Great Coven, even his chain she wore so proudly, something he loved immensely, did not provide enough comfort.

"They think it's the right thing to do," Silence replied.

"You are admirable with your magic, *bellezza.* But it is new to you. Is it not important you have a firm grasp on what you have before you take in more?"

Silence put her hands on his chest and leaned down to get closer to him.

"I think that evidence suggests that the Beast has risen, Mars. And if he has, I think we need all the power we can get."

Mars looked beyond her, the feeling in his stomach not one he enjoyed, even if the words she said were right.

She tugged on the point of his beard and his gaze came back to her.

"We are prophesied," she reminded him.

"The prophecy is that we are the only ones who can fight this creature with any hope of victory. There is no guarantee of defeating it," he reminded her in return.

"We are formidable," she whispered, using his own words of months ago as to what he felt of their union.

And they were. He believed that to his bones.

In truth, his unease in that moment was not simply this information shared after she went with the other women to meet the Coven.

It was the news that the Beast was amongst them.

Men, he could and would fight, doing this at all times with great confidence he would prevail.

And he was learning his wife had skills and power, which she used deftly, and of which he was tremendously proud.

But Silence flinging balls of fire at sorcerers and Silence facing the Beast were two vastly different things.

"Mars," she called, and the focus on her he had lost, he again gained.

"I wish to make children with you," he said softly.

"I know," she replied in the same tone as her beautiful face grew gentle and her eyes turned quicksilver.

"I wish to watch you grow old," he continued, moving his hands from her hips to her waist and upward.

"And I the same with you. Both, my darling king."

He slid one hand up her spine to the back of her neck and around, to cup her jaw while he wound his other arm around her to pull her closer.

"It is a contradiction," he murmured. "For if this had not befallen us, this fate we share, I would not have met you. But now that it is here, I dread it with a power that is almost paralyzing."

"We will prevail," she assured him with a strength in her tone he wished he could find in his heart.

"I have never felt this feeling before," he admitted.

She cast him a playful grin. "Welcome to the world we all inhabit where we understand we are but human and not gods walking the earth."

He did not share her humor, but he gave her a smile regardless.

Silence read it was false.

"Mars," she said soothingly, moving one hand up to stroke along his collarbone.

"I do not mind the weight of Triton on my shoulders, Silence. I mind it on yours."

"We will prevail," she repeated, trailing the fingers of her other hand low, down his chest, his stomach and beyond.

"My love," he grunted when her little hand wrapped around his thickening cock.

She dropped closer, stroking him as she whispered against his lips. "We will prevail."

He surged into her hand.

Her eyes grew lazy.

He liked that look on his wife, always very much liked that particular look on his wife, so much so, he slid his fingers back into her hair and formed a fist in its silk.

His Silence positioned his hardness to her sex and impaled herself on him.

"Silence," he murmured against her mouth as she took him, her eyes open, staring into his.

She breathed against his mouth.

He traced his hand at her hip to a cheek of her arse and squeezed encouragingly.

Silence obliged.

"I love you, Mars," she said.

"And I you, my beautiful Silence."

She clamped her hand on his neck and moved faster.

"We will prevail," she gasped, beginning to move wildly atop him, his queen, always running so hot.

"We will prevail," he growled, assisting her by bucking up inside her.

"The formidables," she breathed.

"Yes," he grunted.

And then he felt her sex tighten around his cock, drawing his climax along with hers.

But right before they both gave over, Mars clutched his queen tight in both hands.

For he saw the silver in her eyes disappear completely when they blazed twin flames of fire.

≈

King Aramus
Guest Bedchamber, Sky Citadel, Sky Bay
AIREN

"THEY HAVE HAD experience of this. For fuck's sake, Elena is a bloody warrior," Aramus groused, pacing the floor before their bed in their bedchamber. "You have not."

"It was not unknown to us that we would reach this point, my husband," Ha-Lah pointed out, sitting atop their bed, her legs crossed under her, wearing a brief, surf-blue nightgown that he knew from seeing it right then, but also having seen it before that he liked on her.

Though he liked more taking it off.

She also had a webby, teal shawl wrapped around her arms to keep out the chill.

"It is not. It is also not unknown that I would not like it when we did."

She sunk her white teeth in her full lower lip.

This was always something he enjoyed watching her do, thinking of those lips under his, around his cock, or just watching them move with her words.

He did not like it in the now.

"Do you not think it's best you understand the powers you have when you must use them in times like these *before* you take on *more*?" he demanded.

"Yes," she said calmingly, "but I don't have that choice."

"Yes," he agreed. "And that's the part I do not bloody like."

His queen threw off her shawl, pushed up to her knees and then fell to her hands, whereupon she crawled to the edge of the bed, calling, "Aramus."

Due to their current circumstances—his queen travelling distances magically to meet with the Great Coven, learning she must draw in power that might be a burden, and most importantly, the bloody, sirens-damned Beast possibly having risen—the biting of her lip might not have had its regular effect on him.

But watching her crawl to him did.

He moved directly to the bed and stood before her as she again sat back to her arse and reached out to him with both hands, wrapping her fingers at the skin of his waist.

"You do know, this is why I was brought to you," she said softly.

He shook his head and said, not softly, "I know no such thing."

Her lips parted.

That, he also felt.

But he ignored it and carried on speaking.

"Why you were brought to me was to show me your love and allow me to give you mine. It was to open my eyes to the true understanding of what being the Sea King meant and delivering me to the place I would do something about it. It was to mitigate my temper so I would be a more patient ruler. It was to make children with me. It was to reign at my side. It was to leave Mar-el to our son stronger, showing him the way for any future is to be brave enough to make righteous change. It was so that we could argue and reconcile, debate and decide, make each other laugh and make each other climax."

He took her head in both hands, bent to her and finished.

"I refuse to believe the Beast had anything to do with us finding each other, Ha-Lah. What I believe is that you were destined to be mine and I was destined to be yours and that is the beginning and the end of it."

Her crystal eyes warm on him, she pushed up to her knees, skating her hands up his bare chest as she did so, and curling her fingers around his shoulder in the end.

"A love like that can defeat all evil," she whispered.

He wished he had that same conviction.

"You must trust in that, my darling," she pushed, one hand disengaging from his shoulder to glide down his chest. "And you must admit, there is a lot to trust in."

He definitely could admit that.

Though in the now, he did not for he made an unintelligible noise when she pressed her hand into his sleep pants and found his cock.

"Wife," he grunted.

"Trust in us. Trust in our friends," she urged, her fingers tightening, and he automatically thrust in her hand. "Trust in love."

"I trust in your love," he muttered.

Her eyes smiled. "That will work."

Then her body dropped, she released his shaft, pulled his sleep pants down and treated him to the vision of her beauty on her knees at the edge of the bed, working his cock with her mouth.

When her fingernails dug into his arse, he took her cue and thrust gently into her moist suckling, groaning when she began to suckle harder.

He was about to drop his head back and close his eyes to concentrate on it fully, when her gaze shifted up to his.

At what he saw, at what he had never seen before, but it was right there before him in that moment—the blue crystal of her gaze turning to the blue and white crash of the waves of the sea—Aramus suddenly withdrew.

He ignored Ha-Lah emitting a sound of protest at the loss of him as he took her under the arms, dragged her up the bed, then put a knee to the mattress that he'd hauled her into.

He came down atop her, disposed of her panties with a violent tug along with a ripping noise, and then he buried himself inside his queen.

"Darling," she breathed, wrapping her legs about his arse.

"Yes," he grunted, driving fast and deep into her tight wet.

"Aramus," she said urgently, lifting her hips to receive more from his thrusts.

He put his lips to hers, stared into the seas of her eyes, and rumbled, *"Yes, baby."*

"You...your...by Medusa, darling, your..." She clasped his head in both hands as his balls got tight, he lifted her hips even further to take his thrusts, and right before they both came, she cried...

"Eyes."

~

King True
Guest Bedchamber, Sky Citadel, Sky Bay
AIREN

"CARO," Farah said soothingly.

"I suppose it wouldn't matter if I said I didn't like it," he replied.

He was sitting at the end of the bed.

She was sitting with her legs curved under her on the rugs on floor before him, her thick, dark hair down about her shoulders, the silk of a rose-red nightgown peeking from the opening of her pine-green velvet dressing gown.

And she had just told him that she would need to attend a ritual with the other women, her Sisters of the Beast, to draw in more power.

Power she not only did not yet fully know how to wield, apparently, it wasn't the most sterling idea for her to hold that much at all.

"I know not what to say to make you feel better," she murmured miserably.

"And this is the crux of the matter," he replied gently. "Our lives are not our own."

She tipped her head to the side and curled her lips slightly up. "Is anyone's life truly their own, *bello*?"

"Not just anyone has to confront the Beast," he replied.

"This is troubling you," she muttered, causing him to blink very slowly.

"It doesn't trouble you?" he asked.

"My love, even if we were not prophesied to confront the Beast, we have no control over the lives we lead. You know that."

"I like to think I have *some* control," he grumbled.

At that, his wife grinned fully.

"Yes, well, you *are* king," she teased. "So, I suppose you have more control than most everyone else, outside of other kings, of course."

"Of course," he murmured, his own lips twitching.

The humor in her lovely topaz eyes changed to warmth when she shared, "I have faith."

This was True's issue.

The things he had seen. The things he had done. The things he had lost. All of this dogging his every moment, even following him into his dreams.

He lacked faith.

"True," Farah called.

He focused on his wife.

"We have different gods, no?" she asked.

"Yes," he answered.

"I do not know a great deal about your gods. Though I know they look after you. They give you wisdom and power and magic. My gods give energy and balance and clear-headedness. If we listen, if we *believe*, they guide us to where we need to be. They give us the gifts we need to see things through."

She pushed up to her knees and moved toward True in a manner he opened his legs, and she settled between them, her hands on his thighs up high, close to his groin.

"My gift is you," she whispered, her words taking his mind from her touch so close to his groin.

He took her jaw in both is hands and whispered in return, "Darling."

"I have to have faith in my gods that they did not guide me through my life...to *you*, only to take you away. But True?"

"Yes, my beloved," he murmured, his gaze dropping to her mouth not only to watch her speak, but because her hand had moved to cover what was stiffening between his legs.

"Even if we only have our now, what we have shared..." Her fingers moved to the string of his sleep pants and pulled it, diving in so he had her, skin-against-skin at his shaft. "I could not wake up in the morning, and I would have lived the life I needed, having fallen asleep at your side."

"Farah," he growled.

She surged up, pulled her dressing gown off her shoulders and let it fall, pooling at her feet.

She then lifted the long skirt of her nightgown to her hips and pushed down her panties, so they fell to her ankles.

She kept her nightgown up as she stepped out of her panties and climbed astride him, knees to the bed on either side of him.

He held his cock ready for her to lower upon, which she did, and when he had her, he groaned, a noise mingling seductively with her moan.

She touched each of his eyes with her lips before she rested her mouth against his, not to kiss, to be close to mingle her breath with his, her gaze with his as she curled her fingers around the sides of his neck and moved atop him.

"Does this not feel like it is the life we need?" she asked.

He curved his fingers in her bottom, digging the pads in, answering, "I will not argue that."

"Every minute with you is a treasure," she whispered.

At her words, automatically, his fingers dug in harder.

She started moving faster.

"I have earned you," she said fiercely, squeezing him with her sex, making him grunt and use her arse to urge her to go faster. "I fought in this life, and I won," she declared. "*You* are my victory. I have that and I will never lose it. No matter what happens."

"And you are mine," he replied, moving one hand to clasp her about the waist and take over, drawing her up and slamming her down.

"We have already won, True."

"Yes," he groaned, his balls contracting, his orgasm imminent. "We have won, my darling."

"Yes," she hissed against his mouth.

He was about to close his eyes with his climax, knowing with the way she tightened like a fist around his shaft, she was on the verge of hers…

When he caught the topaz of her eyes fading to vibrant leaf green.

And the instant she cried out her climax, he shot his seed inside his wife.

~

Prince Cassius
Bedchamber of the Prince Regent, Sky Citadel, Sky Bay
AIREN

"I DON'T SUPPOSE you'd be willing to collect Theodora and Aelia, board a ship, and sail for The Mystics at the break of dawn on the morrow?" Cassius suggested as Elena walked in from her dressing chamber wearing a pair of slouchy-knit socks and the long-sleeved undershirt he had worn that day.

This had become her habit.

When he took it off, if she was there, she took it up and changed into it.

If she wasn't there, she sought it out and *then* she changed into it.

She also appeared to be rubbing something into her hands as she came his way, a small smile flirting with her lips.

"And make our friends face the Beast by themselves?" she asked, coming to where he lay across the foot of the bed, with his head in his hand, his elbow to the bed, not hiding the fact he was in this position waiting so he could watch her walk to him wearing his shirt.

He did not hide it because he did this every night, if he didn't take her right to bed to make love to her the moment they found their chamber of an evening.

He reached out a hand, caught his shirt on his woman's body by the hem, and drew her to him, saying, "They can come with us."

He fell to his back as she put a knee to the bed by his hip, swung her other leg around, and settled astride him.

"And leave all of the rest of Triton to be devoured by pure evil?" she queried.

"I don't know all the rest of Triton," he told her. "How do I know I care about all the rest of Triton? They might be a continent of arseholes."

She placed her hands on his chest and smiled down at him.

He allowed her smile to settle deep into his stomach and then he whispered, "I am happy."

Her smile faltered as bright hit her eyes.

"Cass," she whispered in return.

"I am," he asserted. "I am happy, Ellie. We have lost ones we love. My country is at war. The Beast may have risen. But my daughter is asleep down the hall in her bed in a bedchamber that is no longer black and blue, but lavender and pink. My other daughter's chamber adjoins hers and I know they sneak into each other's rooms at night, to whisper and connive little-girl plots and share little-girl dreams. I have friends I care about close to drink and dine with. And last, I have you here, astride me, smiling down at me, washing me with your sun even in the middle of the night."

She dropped down as if she could not hold her torso up any longer, doing this as she covered his face with both of her hands so that he could smell her balm was made with aloe and lavender.

She slid her hands down to the sides of his head when her forehead hit his.

"I fear for my daughter," he whispered when all he could see was her amethyst eyes.

"I know," she also whispered.

"I fear for your daughter."

"I do as well."

"Our friends."

"Yes."

"Our realms."

Her voice was husky when she said his name, "Cassius."

"I do not want this happiness to end. And all I know of life is that any happiness that comes, comes to an end."

"Sweetheart, listen to me," she urged, putting mild pressure on either side of his head. "We charged down a mountain to face sure and imminent death, and here we are."

"Ellie."

"I am Nadirii and you are Airenzian and for nearly three hundred years, it was impossible to consider such a union amongst our royal lines. And here we are."

He drew her hair up at both sides of her head and held it at the back, but he made no reply.

"We have already beat the odds, Cassius. More than once. There is no stopping us now."

His fingers fisted and he growled, "I will not lose you."

"No, you will not," she stated fiercely.

"I will plant babies in you."

"Yes," she said breathlessly, tipping her chin down so her lips were against his.

"I will sleep beside you as the days pass and I will do so until your hair turns white. Until one of us wakes in the morn not breathing. And if it is you that goes first, I will close my eyes and the gods will know I have no further purpose on this earth, so they will know to take the last of my breaths so I can join you."

"Yes," she whispered, one of her hands leaving his head so it could reach between them.

And in a few deft moves, she was sliding onto his cock.

He lunged up inside her, forcing a breath from between her lips to caress his.

"And if it is you who is first lost, the goddess will take my breath and guide me to you," she panted.

"*Yes*," he grunted, bucking beneath her, meeting her strokes, holding her hair in his fingers so he could hold her lips close, and he stared into her eyes.

They moved as one, and when he felt it gathering in his sac, when he felt her breaths come faster, her pussy clutch his cock greedily, he stated ferociously, "You own my heart, Ellie."

And moments before they both came, he watched in distracted surprise, but surprise nevertheless, as she gasped, "And you own mine, Cass."

And her eyes became a starry-night sky.

~

Jellan

Cyrus, Town at the Northeast of the Argyll Forest, Forty-Five Miles from Silbury Henge

AIREN

IT WAS DONE FOR HIM.

He would take no more.

This he thought as he lay on his back in the bed in that little, squalid inn, his knees commanded to be bent, up and spread (and as commanded by Daemon, obviously, they were thus) as Marian brutally fingered his arse in a way he knew she intended him not to enjoy it (not that he would, it coming from *her*) and Daemon tugged on Jellan's cock while he was in the midst of fucking Jellan's mouth.

Through this, Daemon alternately watched Marian's ministrations, or by the sounds of it, kissed her.

It was revolting.

The lot of it.

Unfortunately, his body's chemistry was such his workings at his cock could not be ignored.

Though he did not get to finish, not that he'd wish to do that anyway with their hands upon him.

Daemon pulled out of his mouth, yanked Marian up Jellan's body, positioned her above Jellan's head, and Jellan received the most enjoyment he'd had that evening when Daemon shoved his spectacular member up her unsuspecting arsehole, and he heard her cry of pain.

She swallowed that cry, the bitch. The whore. The liar. The *cunt*.

And then she moaned falsely, as if she was enjoying it.

He closed his eyes against the sight.

Yes, he was done.

Finished.

No more.

He would never win Daemon.

He suspected even Marian didn't have her clutches in Daemon.

Thus, Jellan would get away. Escape. Find some way to get to Sky Bay. Then make his way straight to the Citadel.

They knew him. They trusted him. They would receive him.

And this civil war they'd learned of was most convenient for Jellan, for all the rulers were there.

At that moment.

In Airen.

And he'd have all their ears.

He'd tell them of the Beast. He'd share about Marian. He'd put the blame entirely on her shoulders that the creature most feared in Triton was on the surface. He'd advise on how they could fulfill the prophecy.

And they would be grateful.

They might shower him with treasure. And when he shared he had no stomach for the ways of the Go'Doan, not after the mess of The Rising, and he renounced his priesthood, they might even give him a manor (he'd pick southern Airen, it was rather temperate down there, perhaps a lovely vineyard all his own, he quite fancied making wine).

Daemon's grunts grew louder. The bed shook more powerfully. And Marian couldn't quite conceal the lilt of pain in her moans.

And Jellan closed his eyes tighter.

But even attempting to drown them out, he would have felt the shimmering.

It was not only in the veil; it was of the earth.

Of the earth.

The very bed he lay upon hummed with it.

Like a coo.

Even a cuddle.

Enfolding him in warmth.

He opened his eyes and by the true gods…

He could even see it glimmer *in the air*.

Marian's moans became high-pitched before Daemon shouted his release and Jellan turned his head to the side, not seeing their calves there.

Holding his breath.

Waiting.

Daemon shoved her off and she fell to the bed above Jellan's head.

"Now, you," Daemon decreed, and Jellan found his body also pushed up as Daemon positioned between his legs.

He held them high behind Jellan's knees as he used him, but Jellan didn't think on it.

He stroked his own cock, as Daemon liked, and brought forth a mediocre orgasm, something Daemon didn't know was mediocre, and even if he did, he probably would not care, but either way, he liked that too.

But this was all a distraction.

Because they had not felt it.

Going about their vile business, they *had not felt it.*

The prophesied lovers' power was growing, even beyond what Jellan could have imagined.

Yes, he had to get to the them.

He'd made his choice.

It was time.

And he would.

He would escape.

For he had power too.

138

THE INTERROGATION

King Noctorno
Interrogation Cell, Crittich Keep, Notting Thicket
WODELL

"Alfie should be here," Apollo murmured. "I feel he is about to break."

"Allow Bronagh time to do her work and Alfie time to get stronger. He will venture out," Tor replied.

Or Tor hoped so.

Eventually.

"He's getting around well in that chair that Maddie and Cora helped Bronagh design for him that he can wheel himself," Apollo said.

"He can hardly wheel his way across the city, my friend," Tor pointed out.

Apollo drummed the leather-covered fingers of his right hand on the table at which he sat.

Tor fought a smile.

Apollo hadn't even taken off his gloves.

He grew impatient with this G'Seph-Seph-Joseph (as Cora would say, *whatever*) cretin.

As did Tor.

They should be away to Sky Bay. They needed to join the others, not dither about denying aught to a prisoner with no leverage trying to convince them he had leverage.

The door opened and two Keep guards dragged Joseph to the seat opposite Apollo and forced him in it.

Then they left the room.

Tor fought a flinch at the sight of his arms ending at his wrists.

Tor had fought wars, lost battles, but thankfully won the wars, and he'd seen men with Joseph's injuries, as with Alfie's.

The true warriors, in his estimation, were the kind like Alfie.

It was clear Alfie had not simply put his injury behind him and moved along. He struggled. There were frequent moments of darkness that he was not able to hide.

But he was robust. Fit. It seemed daily, his upper body physically strengthened, and this was because he worked hard at it.

And he had found a calling. He had shifted the meaning that was always his life to the same meaning, just going about it a different way.

And he carried on.

This...

Joseph.

He had earned his injuries at the hands of his own, who had turned on him for the gods didn't know what reason, but any brotherhood that would take the hands of a brother was no brotherhood at all.

All of them locked in an undertaking that was wrong from the start.

It turned Tor's stomach.

"I will warn you," Apollo said, his eyes jade daggers aimed to the prisoner who had rested his stumps on the table between them, "if you waste our time again, there will no longer be anyone to listen to your blathers. This will be our last visit."

"I—" Joseph started.

Tor spoke from where he stood with his shoulders against the wall to the side of Apollo.

"Your Golden Thomas is dead."

Joseph lifted his gaze to Tor and blinked at him repeatedly, all the while his face paled.

"He was found in a clearing in the Lesser Thicket Forest not far from a pile of dead women," Tor went on. "His head had been crushed."

"By the true gods," Joseph whispered.

"Another one of your people," Apollo took up the narrative, gaining

Joseph's attention when he did, "identified as G'Fenn, or Fennley Trehurst of Wodell, was with him. He'd been decapitated."

Joseph's mouth dropped open.

"Do you know what this clearing is used for?" Tor asked.

Joseph wasted most of both the men's remaining store of patience, which admittedly was not much, in pulling himself together, straightening in his chair, at the same time obviously trying to work out how to twist this to his advantage, when Tor decided to end it.

"We know the Beast has ascended. We can put the dead women together with the fact some ritual was performed to make that happen, and we can deduce from the dead Rising priests in that location that they did not get what they bargained for when he arrived. Though, their bodies there offers irrefutable evidence your lost cause was behind it."

And the minute Tor spoke the words *the Beast*, all pretense dropped for Joseph.

"So they did it," he said.

"Apparently," Tor replied, pushing from the wall. "Which states, as of now, the level of your guilt rises with the level of atrocities your cause wished to unleash on this land. Not to mention the fact pertinent to this moment. You are useless."

"I didn't know!" he cried, lifting a stump toward Apollo as Apollo also shifted as if to rise.

"You haven't told us any of what you *do* know," Apollo reminded him. "However, at this juncture, whatever it is you know...or *knew*, has no meaning."

"What I mean to say is, they spoke of it. But I didn't know they were going forward with it," Joseph told them.

Apollo settled himself back in his chair and Tor again rested his shoulders against the wall as Apollo spoke.

"You didn't know they were going forward with what?"

"Working with the Society. Bringing forth the Beast," Joseph explained.

Apollo glanced at Tor.

Tor lifted his chin.

Apollo looked back to Joseph.

"What Society?" Apollo asked.

"I must have your assurances—" Joseph began.

"You have no assurances. You have nothing," Apollo stated impatiently. "Outside convincing us *you* had nothing to do with raising a creature we've even heard across a vast ocean about his last reign of terror. And that happened before man had thought to put pen to paper to record history, because pen nor paper had been invented yet. For I can assure you, as King True will be on the battle lines in fighting this thing, when he wins, he will not have a great deal of tolerance for anyone involved in the rising of it. And the last man he had little tolerance for endured a very prolonged, *very* public death."

Joseph's face twisted. "Then what is the point of saying anything? For if the Beast is indeed risen, we are all going to die."

"I don't intend to die," Tor said.

"I don't either," Apollo added.

"We have a friend who commands dragons and those dragons are here, on Triton," Tor informed him.

"And I command the wolves. Not to mention, our wives are witches." Apollo flung a hand Tor's way. "The wives of all the rulers of this continent are witches. And the King of the Mer, which are the people, it's my understanding, who defeated the creature the last time, has allied with all nations."

Joseph seemed shocked at all this information, most specifically the last.

"I don't know the ins and outs of the lore of this Beast, but I'd guess back then, this evil unknown, how to stop it most especially, the odds were stacked in his favor," Tor reflected. "Now, they most decidedly are not."

"And since we all intend to survive, though we know it will not be pretty," Apollo continued, "my reckoning is that we'll all be in very foul moods in regards to anyone involved in this villainy when it's over."

"It wasn't me," Joseph said in a small voice.

"Convince us," Tor demanded.

"It wasn't me!" Joseph cried.

"*Convince us!*" Apollo barked.

"The Society of the Beast has been trying to draw him to the surface for centuries," Joseph spat.

Finally.

Tor and Apollo settled in.

"Go on," Apollo invited.

"May I have some fresh water?" Joseph requested snidely.

"You may," Apollo agreed. "When you tell us something we give a shite about."

Joseph glared at him and then he sat back, crossing his arms on his chest.

"It is in the tomes. Of Go'Doan," he stated. "The Society of the Beast. I've read them myself and I thought it was ridiculous. Wicked men going about the wicked business of rape and murder and convincing themselves it had some higher power, some purpose, by telling themselves this was at the calling of the Beast. That in sacrificing virgins every fortnight, or whatever the schedule, the Beast would be roused, and he would ascend."

Neither Tor nor Apollo spoke a word, though the thickness of the air in that cold, cramped room spoke to their moods at hearing what they were hearing.

"It was G'Thom's idea," Joseph carried on. "To discover if they continued to do this, and if they did, seek them out and infiltrate their organization for the purpose of taking control of the Beast when it rose and using it to complete the work of The Rising should we need that assistance. He sent G'Jell on this mission, which, in my opinion, something I shared at the time, was a faulty decision. Jell cares for no one but Jell. And regardless, he only likes cock up his arse, so how is he going to rape anybody?"

"So G'Thom, who was the leader of your faction, sent another priest to join this Society," Apollo stated.

"Yes."

"However, you said you didn't know they did it, but here, you're stating you knew they sent a priest to do this," Apollo observed.

"I do not keep track of Jell. I did not *wish* to keep track of Jell. Thom deciding to assess the situation and sending Jell to do it is one thing. Jell actually *doing* it is another. Indeed, I didn't even know they had discovered there still *was* a Society. But truly, think on this. It's ludicrous. Bringing forth the Beast? If that insane idea could come to fruition, then thinking you could control it? I actually thought it a good errand for Jell in the end. Useless but it kept him out of the way."

Apollo looked up to Tor.

Tor dipped his chin.

Apollo then looked to Joseph. "It clearly wasn't as ludicrous as you thought, for they succeeded."

Joseph shrugged.

Tor felt himself sneer.

Gods, this man.

"Do you know where this Jell is?" Apollo queried.

"The last time I saw him was when the procession was travelling from Fire City to Notting Thicket for True and Farah's wedding. Then again, Fenn took my hands about that time and then pressed me into service for The

Rising in exchange that I would continue to be seen to by priests with advanced healing knowledge. Thus, I really wasn't paying much attention to anything but no longer having hands."

"So it is Fenn who maimed you," Apollo murmured.

"Yes," Joseph hissed. "And thus, I do not feel very badly to know his head was struck from his body by the Beast."

"And you were then 'pressed into service,' as you say," Apollo went on.

"Would you carry on for a cause who treated you thus?" he asked, uncrossing his arms and lifting his stubs for them to see.

"No, I wouldn't be in that place at all," Apollo shared. "But if I found I'd gone astray, after that happened, I would find the nearest constabulary and share about my mistake and help them put a stop to plans that would end in a good number of people suffering greatly."

"Of course you would. With hindsight, anyone would know all the best plays," Joseph muttered irritably.

"What I know is, you took none of them. And when the forces you helped to critically injure a high-ranking Nadirii warrior to bring down The Enchantments were defeated, you *still* did not seek a local constabulary. You were caught impersonating a Zee who had lost his tribe in order to escape."

Joseph's lips thinned and he again crossed his arms on his chest.

"Do you have any idea where this G'Jell might be?" Tor asked.

"None," Seph answered. "I'm just sorry not to hear the news that his body was found with the others."

"Do you know anything about who is in this Society or where they might be found?" Tor kept at him.

"No, for as I said, I didn't even know they were still in existence," Joseph answered.

"Is there anything further at all at this juncture you wish to share?" Tor pressed.

"What would be the point?" Joseph asked in return. "You won't even give me fresh water. The water they offer in the cells is fetid, at best."

"You look hearty enough to me," Tor muttered.

Joseph began glaring again, at Tor.

"We will share with Sir Alfie what you told us," Apollo told him, gaining his attention. "And perhaps that will mean nothing in the end. Or perhaps it will mean something. Though I wonder if it's a waste of words, what I'll tell you is that, just now, for once in this mess, you did the right thing."

"I can sleep better on my wafer-thin pallet with my holey blanket in the chill of a Dellish winter knowing this," Joseph sneered.

"I think with that, we will be done," Tor decided, pushing from the wall.

Apollo rose.

As they made their way to the door, Joseph's voice came at them, so they turned.

"It was for faith," he said dejectedly. "I thought I was serving the gods."

"When your gods tell you to rape and murder and bend people to your will," Tor began. "It is time to find new gods."

And with that, he and his friend walked out.

Sir Alfie Henriksson
The King's Informal Study, Birchlire Castle, Notting Thicket
WODELL

"I'LL DISPATCH trackers to find Jell immediately and send word to True," Alfie said on a sigh.

The sigh was of annoyance.

And relief.

This part was done.

The Rising dismantled.

Now it was just war in Airen.

And the Beast.

Weighty circumstances.

But at least one issue was settled.

"With this concluded," Tor started, "we should be away to Sky Bay."

Alfie nodded.

"Go knowing you will be missed," he said with feeling, for they would. Good men he considered friends. "And it is True who will decide how Wodell will thank you for your efforts. But knowing him, I will advise you, he is generous. So be certain to keep a hold empty on your ship, for he will fill it with wool and pewter for your return journey home."

"Personally, I was just glad for the adventure. Peace and harmony was getting boring," Tor muttered.

Alfie did not know if he jested, though he did see Apollo stare at his friend as if he were mad, so for both reasons, he did not attempt to stop his laugh.

Both men stood and said their goodbyes, these consisting of two variations of, "We shall see you at supper."

They then left.

Alfie did not waste time writing the orders, nor the message for the raven to True.

He then called his corporal to deal with these missives with haste.

After the corporal had left the study, he put his hands to the locks on the wheels of his new chair. He unlocked them, shifted it back, relocked it, reached for his sticks and took them up.

He pulled himself out of the chair and moved to another one, this by the fire.

He eased himself down, set his eyes to the blaze and stared at it.

He had no idea how long he sat there before he heard the knock with the immediate sound of the opening of the latch, thus he didn't bother even to begin to call out.

He heard the door open, close, and out of the corner of his eye, he saw Bronagh sit in the chair at an angle to the side of his.

She didn't say anything for long moments.

She broke their silence, stating, "It is getting late, Alfie."

He had not told her of his suspicions that The Rising had conspired, and succeeded, in raising the creature that forced Silence to Mars, Farah to True, Elena to Cassius as well as all the other events that occurred.

He did not want her frightened.

So he didn't speak of it then.

He kept his gaze to the fire and said, "Faith."

"Faith?" she asked softly, clearly having fallen into his mood.

"The prisoner Tor and Apollo have been interrogating said that he did what he did due to faith."

"Alfie," she whispered.

He looked to her. "What god would take my legs? What god would take my queen's life?"

"I do not know."

"You were right, Bronagh. Life is more than work. And it is tragedy that I learned that when my life was reduced to," he indicated his chair, "this."

"Your life is not that small," she replied.

"Really? When I leave this place, I will need to purchase a new house, for my home will need to be one story, with widened halls so I can negotiate it in my chair. I might be able to manage stairs, but in all frankness, although the ascent holds no concern for me, the idea of attempting a descent scares the shite out of me. I cannot sit astride a horse. I will not stand at an altar and take a woman to wife. I cannot—"

"We can have a transport created for you, so you can command a horse, but it will be low, so you can get yourself in it and out of it. Or, say, wheel your chair in it and lock it in place."

"Bronagh—"

"And you can stand fine, with your sticks, so if you were to take a wife, you could meet her at the altar upright, if that means so much to you. Though I don't know why you wouldn't just meet her in your chair. She would be marrying *you*, not your legs."

Marrying you, *not your legs.*

His chest started to warm.

"I—"

"I have seen injuries less than yours, I have seen injuries worse than yours, a good deal worse," she continued. "And far too many of them. So do not ask me what war means. What god or king causes man to do what man does to man for the sake of anything. All I know is it happens and forces all manner of men to do different, but no less heroic things. Those being, discover reasons to find ways to live their life to the fullest, no matter what became of their person. And then go about living life *to its fullest.*"

She stood after saying these words and came to Alfie's chair.

With no choice but to tip his head back when she arrived, she bent to him the instant he did.

Her face so close, *her* so close, he could smell her perfume.

Something he had scented often and something, from the beginning, he had adored.

She smelled of green grass and mossy woods and flowers.

Gods dammit.

His cock stirred.

"And now that you are asking these questions, my champion," she whispered, placing a hand on his chest. "I will stop pussyfooting about and tell it to you true. I want to be part of the new meaning to your life because I think you're marvelous. And I don't care one whit about your legs."

And with that, she pressed her lips to his.

Her there, her scent, her words, her spirit, the time spent in her company, the vision of her burned in his brain, on his heart, Alfie did not fight his hands reaching to her, his fingers sifting into her hair, holding her head to him, or the very ungentlemanly act of touching his tongue to her lips, insisting they open.

On a sweet mew, she gave him this, and if all had not been lost before—when he had to admit it was—it was lost then, *he* was lost, when he had her taste.

He was lost to anything but deepening the kiss, angling his head to do so, drinking more.

More of Bronagh.

More of her spirit and sweetness.

More of life.

When his body had responded to the point he'd desire to take the kiss somewhere else, he broke his mouth from hers and whispered against her lips, "We must stop."

"Hmm?" she hummed dazedly, and he felt her weight in her hand at his chest.

He grinned against her mouth and watched as her eyes slowly opened.

That was life too.

"I'll take dinner with you tonight, honey," he murmured. "And vol-au-vents filled with stew for lunch tomorrow."

She snapped into focus and gifted him with relief and excitement filling her eyes before they got wet.

He pressed his mouth to hers and pulled away, saying, "Now we must change for dinner."

She suddenly shot straight, he lost the feel of her hair, but she gained it as she smoothed it, then smoothed her skirts at her front, and said nonsensically, "Yes, quite."

"Yes, quite, what?" he asked, unable to remove the teasing thread of his tone.

"Yes, quite, I shall meet you at your chambers to go with you to dinner and...and arrange for us to go on an outing tomorrow."

"Please allow me," he murmured.

"Of course." She touched her throat and her eyes grew somewhat wild.

In turn, he grew concerned he'd been too forward.

"Have you not been kissed, Bronagh?" he asked gently.

"I, yes, well..." She smoothed her hair again. "Well, *yes*, but not like that."

He fought his grin.

"You're very pleased with yourself, Alfie Henriksson," she snapped when she saw his struggle.

"I am, indeed, very pleased, Bronagh."

She huffed.

He chuckled.

She stared.

He took her hand.

"Thank you," he said softly.

She grew adorably awkward again.

"My pleasure," she mumbled.

"I do not know how to—" he began.

Her hand twisted so she could hold his fingers in hers tightly. "We will find our way."

Alfie nodded. "Dinner, honey."

"Oh, right."

He smiled at her again, squeezed her hand and then let her go.

She hesitated, rubbing her lips together while gazing down at him, then nodded and began to move away.

When he lost sight of her, he looked to the fire.

"Alfie?" she called.

He twisted to look at her around his chair.

She was at the door, her hand on the latch.

"You've made me very happy," she said.

And then she rushed out the door.

Alfie stared at it for some time after it was shut.

He then turned and stared at the fire for more time.

Finally, he took his sticks, hefted himself up and made his way to his chair.

He set the sticks across his lap as he wheeled himself out of the room.

He had only one thought and it was the only thought on his mind since Bronagh's words were spoken before she left the room.

This thought was that he had it now.

Absolutely.

He had it.

You've made me very happy.

A new meaning to life.

139
THE DRAWING

Queen Ha-Lah
Riding through Sky Bay to Lowgate
AIREN

"I should not be here."

I was riding at Serena's side on the way to Lowgate, along with a grand procession of guards. A procession that included all of our husbands.

And in Serena's case, her lover, Chu.

As well as, considering he felt it imperative to make up for time lost and thus was frequently found close to his little sister, Jorie.

We were intent to perform the ritual that would draw down more power.

Elena had suggested that we should more than likely do this ritual amongst ourselves, only the Sisters of the Beast (and Serena, who we had all adopted, so really, we felt she was one too) in attendance, but the men would not hear of it.

Elena then shared that it would not hurt that they were there.

"It's just too bad it won't be just a sister thing," she had finished on a mumble.

I agreed.

However, my husband was on edge, and if being close to me assuaged that in any way, I would give him that.

"Elena thinks it important you are at your fullest power," I told her something Elena already had. "You leave to go to Dunlyn after the wedding. There is much danger for you there. I believe it will help her in her worry with you far away performing perilous deeds, that you are steeped in magic."

Serena appeared confused by this for a moment, and I did not understand her reaction.

I then harkened back to all the things I had heard of Serena of the Nadirii before I had come to know her and wondered if she might not understand how a loved one worrying would come about.

I allowed what I said to settle before I went on, "And I am glad you're here. It gives me the chance to tell you that your training has been very helpful these last days."

She turned her head from watching the lane we were on that traced the city to the side at the base of the incline to the cliffs that surrounded the Bay.

She looked at me, now appearing surprised.

I smiled at her. "We are no Nadirii warriors, but please trust in the fact it helps my state of mind having the skills you've taught me as we face what we might be facing. Thus, I must give you my gratitude for your time and sharing of expertise."

"I enjoy doing that, the training, so there is no need to express your gratitude," she replied.

"What you give is what you know. What I received is what I need," I returned. "Thus, I disagree. Gratitude should be expressed."

"Well," she shifted in her saddle, "you're welcome."

I looked away, smiling at the lane and enjoying the air, which was becoming saltier the closer we got to the sea.

"He wishes to make children with me."

Serena's words, sounding forcefully divulged, came to my ears, and I looked her way again.

"Pardon?" I asked.

She turned her eyes to me.

"Chu," she pushed out. "He says he wishes to make daughters with me."

I smiled tentatively at her. "Are you not...at that point in your mind with him?"

She cast her gaze forward. "I would give him a dozen children, if this was his wish."

I felt my brows go up.

"I am no longer me," she whispered.

"I am no longer the me of yesterday either," I shared, and her head whipped around to face me again. "This is best, if we are to learn and grow, that every day we wake up a new person, learning from the day past, going into the future smarter and stronger."

"This is wise," she stated, like she did, as well as didn't quite believe her words.

"Well, I hope so," I replied with humor.

"I wish sons. Or at least one son," she said.

"It's my understanding you can magick the sex in your womb, so have a son," I returned.

"He does not wish sons."

This surprised me. "Truly?"

"He has...family issues," she muttered, turning her face away.

I studied her profile.

Then I noted carefully, "You wish very much to have a boy child."

"It is not very Nadirii of me, but he is handsome. He has...has...well, he has a manner about him that is unique. I simply enjoy watching him walk or contemplating his face when he is thinking. I would give that to a son. Or I would watch Chu teach a son to be thus."

"And you worry because of his...*issues* he will refuse this."

She didn't reply.

"Tell him how badly you want it," I advised.

"There are reasons behind why this is not what he wants. Reasons that I cannot deny, especially for him."

"I am certain," I replied. "I still think, if this is something you want badly, Serena, that you should talk to him."

"I do not want..."

She didn't finish that.

"You do not want?" I prompted.

She still didn't share.

"If you don't wish to talk about it," I murmured.

Again, she gave me her gaze. "I almost lost him once for doing something he did not like. I do not want to lose him again."

Ah.

Understandable, but not recommendable.

"That is no union," I told her gently.

She stared at me.

"He cannot have all he wishes just because you desire greatly not to lose him," I told her. "You will lose too much of yourself in that and either become a shadow of what you once were, or your love for him will dim before it entirely fades away as you begin to hate him for the things you cannot have, for you have given so much to him."

Her gaze drifted down to the mane of her mount.

"Serena," I called, and watched as it took some effort, but she again looked to me. "I do not know Chu hardly at all," I said. "But from what I have seen, especially when he is with you, he strikes me as a man who not only would want to know your desires, but also would be willing to discuss them with you."

She thought on this a moment before she replied, "This likely matters not, depending on what might befall us as we fight the Beast."

"This is true, but trust me, my friend, it is in the now that you must establish how you will communicate with the one you love. I did not do that with Aramus, and we wasted months of our marriage to anger and frustration. And now, we face..."

"Ha-Lah," she murmured when I was unable to continue.

I lifted my chin. "I believe in my heart we will succeed. I must. There would be no point going on if I did not. But this does not mean I do not think about that not happening, and in doing so, regret the time I wasted having the man I loved and not talking to him."

She studied me a moment with thoughtful, but warm brown eyes before she nodded decisively and declared, "I will be forthcoming with Chu about my desires."

"Good," I murmured.

"And now I will express my gratitude to you for *your* training."

I started laughing, but through it said, "You are most welcome."

She again faced forward, remarking, "She has given me much I do not deserve."

"Who?" I asked.

"Elena."

I was perplexed. "What has she given you that you don't deserve?"

"You. Silence. Farah. Herself."

It was this time that I stared.

"Serena, she has not given you this," I told her.

She gave me her eyes.

"You earned it," I said.

A becoming pink tinged her cheeks that had nothing to do with the chill air coming off the sea.

And again, I lost her gaze.

But I left it at that, wishing her to think on it, and understand it, as we came upon a part of the lane that was, on one side, nothing but craggy black rock that inclined so steeply, no houses or building could be built upon it.

It did not take much time for us to reach Lowgate, which was named thus as it was at sea level. But the gate was not low, nor was it small. As was Highgate, Lowgate was most tall and it was very wide. It was made up of thick wood painted a glistening black, and it was elaborately ornate with wrought iron in a way that was both splendid to look at and forbidding.

Last, it was opened for us before our arrival.

We rode through, our grand procession, with the guards at the gate standing at attention and saluting Cassius as we did.

I noted often, my husband, some ways in front of me, riding next to True, looked back as if I might disappear into thin air.

Each time he did, I gave him a reassuring smile.

As for me, I took heart in the sea as we traversed the track beside it, feeling, and glorying in the mist striking the skin of my face as the waves struck the rocks at our sides.

As the road curved inland, the guards at the front of the procession took a narrower path that would keep us traversing alongside the sea.

And in some time, they guided their mounts up along the cliffs. Mars and Cassius were at the lead, Jorie and Chu behind them, my husband and True behind *them*, then Elena and Silence, Farah and Melisse, and myself and Serena broke off from them to ride low.

I saw the small outcropping, that formed a kind of bowl, which Melisse had referred to as "The Cauldron."

And when I saw it, a shiver stole through me.

This was where, in times gone by, the women of Airen would steal away to meet to discuss their plight and make plans to alleviate it, many of these being petitions to the king.

And this was where, to make his point brutally known, the king put the leader of this effort to death by hanging her from her neck.

Last, this was where her daughter, in lament, prayed to the land gods and the sea gods to give her strength and magic to avenge her mother and free her sisters.

In other words, this was where the Nadirii Sisterhood was formed from oppression, anger, heartbreak and hope.

The men directed their steeds off to the side, positioning them in a semi-circle to face The Cauldron.

And in turn, each woman rode to her man, situated her horse, dismounted and handed over the reins.

The wind was whipping my cloak and frock about me, my curls catching my lips and eyelashes, as we approached the bowl of black rock at the edge of the sea.

The waters smacked against the short cliff at our side, sending up spray, and I looked to Silence to see if she was feeling what I was feeling.

Her eyes were alive at the same time wistful, and I wondered if her desire was the same as mine.

That being to rush to the cliff and dive off.

Feeling my attention on her, hers came to me and a brightness came about her expression where I knew she did, indeed, feel precisely as I did.

I sent her a small smile before I began to pay attention to the matter at hand.

"The rocks are rough, but I bid you to sit on them, cross-legged, in a circle," Melisse instructed. "Knees touching, holding hands, gazes to each other, and nothing else. This is important, witches," she stated sternly. "No matter what happens during the drawing, concentrate on your sisters, and naught else."

These words did not fill me with delight.

However, I did as told, taking Serena's hand on one side, Farah's on the other. And Elena held Farah's other hand, and Silence's. Thus, Silence held Elena and Serena.

Once we made a circle, we held tight and all sat down, crossing our legs as we did, so that our knees were touching.

I felt the coarseness of the rock at my bottom, the cold of it, the damp, but I did not move and did not place my gaze anywhere but to one of my sisters.

Though, it sounded and even felt as if the sea close to us had begun to churn.

"Are you ready to begin?" Melisse asked.

Elena started the round of "Yes."

"You will not interrupt," Melisse ordered, and I was assuming this was to the men. "You are here as observers only. You keep your seats on your mounts and your distance. This is crucial. Am I heard?"

A masculine chorus of "Yes," sounded, but they did not sound as positive as the feminine version.

"We will begin," Melisse decreed.

I looked amongst all my sisters at once, feeling their expectation and restlessness along with my own.

"It is to Ophelia we call," Melisse intoned, and I turned my gaze to Elena to see hers holding direct to Serena's. "It is to Jasmine that we call," Melisse went on. "Rosehana. Tatiana. Eladora. Millicent. It is to Mary and Brianna and Bella and Kalla. We call to Nissa, June, Alicia, Emma. And we call to Audrey and Blythe, Dya and Magga, Abigail and Frieda. We call to Aileen and Coral, and we call to Fahla. We call to you. We call to our sisters who were lost on this land who have now joined the veil. We call to you for this drawing."

I could now not only sense but hear the sea was definitely churning.

And the sky was darkening.

Further, there was an odd warmth at my knees.

I shifted my gaze to Silence.

Melisse's voice rose, out of necessity to be heard above the noise of nature, but also as she fell deeper into the spell.

And now she was rounding us, walking close behind us. I could feel her cloak drift across my skin as she passed me, the material cracking like a whip in a now bitter wind.

"We call to you to fill your sisters," she chanted. "We call to you to lend your magic. We call to you to give your strength. We call to you to offer your power. We call to you to do what you did when your feet walked this earth. We call you to stand amongst the Sisterhood. To strengthen it. To protect it. To bring it glory."

As we were becoming wet through, I turned my gaze to Farah. The waters were slapping against the rocks, showering us with their spray.

And I was finding it hard to see her for not only did it seem the sun was disappearing from the sky, there was a thick mist, almost a fog, or maybe it was smoke, blowing up from the center of The Cauldron in the middle of us, at the same time the heat I was feeling grew more intense.

Farah's hand tightened in mine, mine in hers, as well as my other in Serena's, and Serena returned my grip as Melisse droned on.

"Cast them down!" she exclaimed. "Offer the blessing! Provide the gift! Give them power!"

The wind was fierce now, and the sea violent.

I could feel it against my skin, hear it in my ears.

And I could sense it, as if I could *see* the wind blowing, the sea rising up to crash against rock.

No, it wasn't seeing.

It was as if I was a part of it.

It was a part of *me* blowing.

It was a part of *me* rising against the shore.

I felt something touch me at my hip, another at my ankle, and I held the hands in mine even tighter as more crawled over my lower half, and I turned my eyes to Serena.

"Yes! For justice! For freedom! For victory! For safety! For peace in all Triton! Cast it down!" Melisse exclaimed and then she commanded, "*Draw it down, my sisters!*"

Even seated, I was finding it hard to keep my place. The wind had become a gale, I was wet through, finding it difficult to hold Serena's eyes through the smoky fog that had enveloped us, to hold the hands in mine as they grew slippery with wet.

I heard a shout I thought was Cassius and Melisse shrieked, "*Stay back!*"

"Patience, strength, sister," Serena encouraged, holding my hand fast.

"Draw it down! Draw it down!" Melisse yelled.

Whatever was slithering over me was snaking up my chest, my back.

And I was one with it.

And the sky beyond the smoke was night, the heat at our legs burning.

And I was one with that too.

I whipped my head around to Farah and then jumped in fear when I heard the terrible roar.

"We must abort!" I heard Jorie boom.

"*Stay back!*" Melisse screamed, and then to us urgently, "Draw it down! Draw it down, my sisters! Draw it down and *take it in you!*"

I lifted my hands and tensed my arms, and as I did, I slid across the stone and pulled my sisters closer. The others did the same, and we were all now sitting atop what felt like burning coals, but ones that did not scorch flesh.

Our circle growing tighter, we were almost in each other's laps.

Another roar, followed by a third and what sounded like the snapping together of gigantic jaws coming from the direction of the sea.

"We are the Sisters of the Beast!" Elena suddenly cried.

And I felt it like I had not before.

I was born thus.

I was born of them.

I was born of Ophelia and Jasmine and Rosehana and all the others.

And they were born of me.

I felt the mother of the Nadirii rise in me.

I felt *her* mother draw up in me.

I felt the mother of *all* mothers deep within me.

And I knew the others did too when Silence, Farah and I repeated, "*We are the Sisters of the Beast!*"

"I serve my sisters!" Serena yelled.

"We draw down the power of mighty witches!" Elena shouted.

"We draw down the power of mighty witches!" the rest of us exclaimed.

"We hold sacred the strength of women!" Elena yelled.

"We hold sacred the strength of women!" we shouted.

More roars, right on top of each other, so close, too close, almost upon us coming from the sea...one, two, three, *four*.

"*Cease this at once!*" Mars bellowed.

"*Do not disturb the spell!*" Melisse shrieked.

The things crawling on me made it to my neck, slinking around, the tentacles gliding up into my hair.

And they were of me.

I welcomed them.

"*We are Sisters of the Beast!*" Elena screamed.

"We are Sisters of the Beast!" the lot of us cried. "We are Sisters of the Beast! We are Sisters of the Beast!"

I felt a gust of heated breath above my head and then I heard my husband roar, "*Ha-Lah!*"

"*WE ARE SISTERS OF THE BEAST!*"

And with the might of the magic that descended, I was forced back, painfully hitting stone, my hands still clasped on each side, holding fast.

Holding strong.

Then, of a sudden, the warmth of sun shone down on me.

I blinked into the blue sky above me before I saw a leaf idly blow in the breeze at the corner of my eye.

Such was my surprise, I shifted my gaze to it and saw a vine of ivy retreating as I felt those that bound my body doing the same.

Serena gave my hand a tug and I sat up, pulling Farah up on my other side.

"You can look around now," Serena shared.

I turned my gaze to my lap, and I was correct.

Vast tangles of ivy vines were receding to the stone.

And the bowl in the middle of us was no longer billowing smoke. Instead, the embers of a dying fire were quickly disappearing.

I turned my head to the sea and gasped.

For I saw the colossally-long, scaly, eel-like forms of two double-headed *angmostros* slithering out to sea.

My body hummed. My skin felt alive.

No.

I felt alive.

More alive than I ever had.

I was of the earth.

I was of the sea.

The sky.

The fire.

These women.

The ones who had come before.

And my power would serve the ones born after.

"Can we bloody approach now?" Cassius bit off.

"Yes," Melisse allowed. "It is done."

In an instant, I was dragged off my arse, disconnected from my sisters, and pulled into Aramus's arms.

"*Fuck, shite,*" he spat over my head. "Bloody sirens-damned hell."

Well, apparently that was as intense to watch as it was to feel.

I curved my arms around him to show him I was all right, and to make him the same.

"You will not be doing that ever *fucking* again, *piccolina,*" I heard Mars decree.

"Boarding a ship bound for any-damned-place else is looking a bloody sight better right now, Ellie," Cassius clipped.

"True?" I heard Farah call hesitantly.

"We will talk later," True bit out.

"That was extraordinary," I heard Chu murmur.

"Wasn't it?" Serena asked.

I smiled against my husband's chest.

Chu would most definitely be at one with discussing Serena's desires.

Aramus pulled just enough away to scowl down at me.

"I do not know what there is to smile about, wife," he ground out. "A bloody *angmostros* almost bit your bloody head off."

"Really?" I queried.

"Really," he stated curtly. "Or at least one bloody head of one, the other head of it nearly took Silence."

"How remarkable," I muttered.

"It wasn't remarkable, Ha-Lah. It scared the shite out of me."

I pressed my lips together.

He carried on scowling.

"Can we get them back and dry and away from this gods-damned place?" Cassius demanded.

"Of course, the ritual is done, the spell complete. We can go now," Melisse stated calmly.

She had barely finished speaking before Aramus was guiding me toward our mounts.

I went with him, for he was in a state.

But I did so looking back, to Elena, who was similarly being "guided" (though it appeared more like she was being dragged) to her mount by Cassius.

To Silence, who was actually being carried by Mars.

Also, to Farah, who was tucked so closely to True's side, it was difficult to see where she ended and True started.

And last, to Serena, who was talking calmly with Chu, still at The Cauldron.

They were all casting glances around as well, we were catching eyes, catching smiles, sharing spirits.

The future was a complete unknown.

But in the present, I had this.

I had these people.

I had my sisters.

And we...were...

Magnificent.

140
THE REVELATION

Teddy
Office of the Head Constable, Crittich Keep, Notting Thicket
WODELL

"You'll wait here a moment, if you don't mind," the head constable murmured after one of his men put his head around the door.

"We don't mind," Teddy murmured back, though it was clear Faunus minded.

Sitting at one side of him, Teddy saw him shifting in his seat.

The constable rose from behind his desk and left the room.

"We should be finished soon," Teddy said to Faunus when the door closed behind the constable.

Faunus said nothing.

"He's keen to take you home," Moira declared from his other side.

Teddy looked her way.

"I am patient to do whatever Teddy feels needs done," Faunus decreed.

"You want to be done with Wodell in order to take him away," she retorted.

"Of course, I want to go home, and as it is also Teddy's home, take him with me," Faunus returned.

215

"Wodell is Teddy's home," she fired back.

"Firenze is Teddy's home," Faunus retorted.

"Look at him," she demanded, tossing a hand to Teddy. "Does he look Firenz to you?"

"He...is...*Firenz*," Faunus growled.

Teddy turned his gaze to the ceiling and then he looked to Saturn, who was standing behind Moira's chair.

It had been days of this bickering.

Faunus laying claim.

Moira laying hers in return.

He had gone his whole life, until recently, without anyone giving any real shite about him, and now two people he cared about deeply were constantly fighting over him.

And when he laid eyes on Saturn, he saw a muscle jump up his jaw, and Teddy read this as Saturn being angry, *at him*, for he thought Moira had feelings for him in a manner that she did not.

"I'm Dellish," he stated to Faunus then turned to Moira. "But my home is in Firenze. My family is in Firenze. My friends are in Firenze. And I'm sorry, love, but I'll be going back to Firenze once this business is done."

Her brows shot together. "Your family is in Firenze?"

"The one that matters," Faunus put in bitingly. "And they are *Firenz*."

Moira glared at Faunus.

Faunus scowled at Moira.

Teddy cast a look to Faunus that communicated he wished him to calm down and then he turned to Moira, reached out and took her hand.

And when he spoke, he did it gently.

"I fear you're feeling some unease now that we've made the Thicket. Now that we've made our report. And now that it is coming closer to me leaving."

"You don't know anything about what I'm feeling, Tedrey Swensson," she stated heatedly then jerked her hand away, cast her gaze to the top of the constable's desk and glared at it.

But Teddy was struck, by her words, her demeanor, the look on her face.

His eyes drifted up, to Saturn, who was studying Moira with not a small amount of attention, and then he turned to look at Faunus, who no longer appeared annoyed, and instead was also studying Moira contemplatively.

Teddy went back to Moira.

"Moira—"

"Fine," she snapped. "You're Firenz. I don't care."

"I think we need to—"

Her gaze cut to him. "You have missed that I am done talking."

She then again turned to the desk.

Teddy had little experience with women.

His mother left when he was young, not interested in a life with the husband she chose. So much so, she left her son behind in the leaving, Teddy suspected, because she had deduced that he was not the son she would wish to have.

Then there were his acolytes, but he had not spent much time getting to know them. He just told them what to do and in the now didn't like to think of them, for he had been vile.

And last there was Nyx, who could have moods, but these were usually explained by something Lorenz or Teddy did that annoyed her.

He had no idea how he'd annoyed Moira, he just knew he had.

"We will talk later, when we find our lodgings for the evening," he murmured.

Moira just made a noise, nothing more.

The feel of the room was uncomfortable for the surprisingly long time it took for the constable to return.

When he did, his manner had changed from attentive and efficient to deferential.

"You did not..." he began then nodded repeatedly as he seemed rather harried and awkward making his way to his desk, his gaze jumping from Faunus to Saturn and back again, but he did not sit. He remained standing. "I understand," he went on. "Incognito in a foreign land. Though, of course, you could have told me."

"I am sorry?" Faunus asked, watching the man closely, his big body suddenly tight with alertness in his chair.

"You do not wear the mantle of the Trusted Ones," the constable explained, again looking between Faunus and Saturn, this indication that he was speaking about them both.

"We do not," Faunus confirmed.

"Yes, well, I understand, of course, but I can assure you, I would have been appropriate in all ways. Regardless, of the now, Sir Alfie has requested when we are done that the two Trusted and their retinue move along to Birchlire Castle, where accommodation has been readied for you."

"The two...*Trusted*?" Teddy asked.

"Yes," he confirmed, nodding. "We just received word. From the castle.

It came from King True himself, speaking for King Mars. When his Trusted, Faunus and Saturn arrive…"

He stopped when not only Teddy shot straight in his chair, Faunus did too, and emotion was wafting from Saturn as well.

"I…was to…send you along…" the constable pushed out then asked, "Did I say something to offend you?"

"You are sure this was the message," Teddy pressed.

"Yes," the constable said. "Apparently, King Mars received a raven that you were coming to the Keep to report. And he returned that, once you are done, you were to hasten to Birchlire so they could receive you."

"And he said 'Trusted,'" Teddy pushed.

The constable looked confused. "It was made particular note of. 'They are members of the Trusted,' it said. 'Treat them as such.'"

Teddy felt the huge smile break out on his face as he turned to Faunus who was sitting, his handsome face stunned, staring at the constable.

"You do not have to hide your rank in Wodell," the constable shared. "We are allies now. Your Farah is our queen, and the Dellish rejoice. Our Silence is yours, and the Dellish take pride. No one would harm you."

"Well, thank you for that," Teddy said, his voice practically bouncing with elation. "It means much."

"Of course," the constable said. "And as we have your story and the names and descriptions of the men who participated in the massacre, and I can assure you they will be sought, thus, this information will be of great assistance to our colleagues in the east. You of course know the families of these women are searching for them, and I will personally send word they are found, in good health, and they can be collected forthwith from Birchlire Castle."

"*We* are invited to the castle too?" Moira asked.

The constable again appeared confused. "The entire party."

Slowly, she turned her head to Teddy.

Teddy grinned at her.

The constable spoke again before she could grin back.

"You and the other ladies will enjoy Queen Farah and King True's hospitality, although they are not here. They are fighting the righteous fight in Airen. But nonetheless, you will enjoy their hospitality until your families come to collect you," he shared.

But Teddy was watching Moira's face as he did so, and he saw it close off.

This was when Teddy's sense of elation wore off that Faunus and Saturn had clearly earned a promotion along their campaign to rescue him.

"The journey is not long to the castle, but do you need refreshments before you go?" the constable asked.

This was a commendably polite hint that he had things to do and they should be on their way.

Thus, Teddy stood.

"No, we're fine. We'll be on our way."

The constable nodded. "Thank you, again. There were many questions that needed answers with that sorry business out east and you provided them. Mixed tidings to those who lost, but soon, some families will rejoice."

Teddy nodded.

And then there was a good deal of hand shaking before they left the office, he collected his women, Faunus collected his men, and they rode to Birchlire Castle.

~

"I GO WITH YOU."

"Faunus."

"I go with you, Teddy."

They indeed had been *received* by the staff of Birchlire.

In fact, Sir Alfie Henriksson, True's captain and counsellor greeted them himself, stunning Teddy by looking in robust health and fine spirits while sitting in his chair.

There was a lovely woman at his side who had twinkling brown eyes, and both Sir Alfie and she, who went by the name of Bronagh, assured Teddy and his party all their needs would be met before asking them to join them for supper in the informal dining room.

They had accepted.

Teddy had seen to it his women were settled while Faunus had seen to it his men were.

And now, in their room, before they prepared for dinner, he needed to go speak with Moira.

"I hope it won't offend you, as I believe it won't surprise you, that you are not her favorite person. She has endured much. I do not know what the end of that means for her but clearly there is something troubling her and I would know it before we make our journey home."

"No, I am not her favorite person, for *you* are. To her, I am simply the man who will take you away," Faunus retorted. "But do not think she is not mine, for you are hers and this is something that gives me happiness."

Teddy liked his words so much, he didn't know what to say.

"And as such, I saw her reaction and I am concerned as well," he continued. "So, I will go with you to see to it she is all right."

Teddy considered this before he made a decision.

"Just keep quiet," he ordered.

"I will not keep quiet if I have something to say," Faunus returned.

"Well then, if you have something to say, make certain it is not something that will upset her."

Faunus sighed.

"All right, let us go," Teddy muttered.

He moved to the door, feeling Faunus move after him, but he stopped at it and looked up to his friend.

"We have not talked about you becoming a Trusted," he noted.

"No, we have not, but we must for I have not become a Trusted, not yet. And I must have your permission to do so."

Teddy blinked in bewilderment at this statement, and as he did, he did not have the opportunity to ask after what that meant for Faunus reached beyond him and opened the door himself.

He determined to understand Faunus's meaning later as they moved down the hall to where Moira's room was located.

One thing at a time.

Even Dellish, he'd never been to Notting Thicket, thus he'd never seen the castle.

He had heard it was grand and immense, but it was far grander and more immense than could be imagined.

They could host twice as many women and Firenz warriors and have room to spare.

And Teddy thought this was good, for after what they had endured, he quite liked them to be spoiled with a stay at King True's castle.

They both stood at the door, but it was Teddy who knocked.

Moira opened it, looked to Teddy, to Faunus, and said, "Oh, it's you."

"Poppet, let us in."

"I have to get ready for dinner. Bronagh sent us gowns to wear and—"

"Moira, please," he whispered.

She looked to the side, then again to him, to Faunus, and finally she stepped back, fully opening the door.

He and Faunus entered her chamber, but they did not take seats in the comfortable seating area by the cheerfully crackling fire.

They both turned to her.

"Now, tell me what's troubling you," he urged.

"Do *you* care? I mean, why are you even *here*?" she asked Faunus.

"Yes, he does care," Teddy said quickly before Faunus could reply. "He knows what you mean to me, what we've been through together, and what means something to me means something to him."

She was glaring again at Faunus.

"Moira," he called.

She kept glaring at Faunus, who stood there, holding her gaze, and silently taking it.

"Moira!" Teddy clipped.

Her eyes shot to Teddy.

"You will go, and you will be with him and you will...and I will...and the girls will go home, and I will..."

She swallowed.

"You will what?" he prompted gently.

"They were scared," she declared.

"Yes, we all were," he replied.

"Terrified."

"Yes," he agreed.

"But I was...I should have..."

When she stopped speaking, he told her, "Moira, with what we have been through, with what we have shared, you must know you've come to mean a great deal to me. Thus, love, I can assure you that you do not need to hold back. You can say anything to me."

She jerked her chin up like a stubborn mare and announced, "I did not encourage them to go back to their homes, or you to take them there, because I didn't want to go back to my own."

Teddy stood still, knowing instantly he would not like what came next.

Faunus did the same, likely knowing this too.

"My mother is dead, and my father likes his drink far more than he cares about his daughter," she stated. "He probably doesn't even know I've been gone. He probably didn't even know I was around *to* be gone."

"All right," he said quietly when she did not continue, though as suspected, he so did not like her words, he was uncertain he wished her to continue.

"I have, for a very long time, Teddy, taken care of myself *and* him, even though he does not care as he loses consciousness in front of the fire without putting the screen before it and thus it is a miracle our cottage has not burnt to the ground. Or he stumbles into the kitchen and breaks the crockery that I not only have to clean up, I have to find some way to make the coin to pay to replace it. Coin he steals to buy his grog. His whiskey. Whatever he can find to erase the loss of her and the existence of me, for I am *not* her, but would be a daily reminder of her if he allowed himself lucidity."

Yes, Teddy had been right.

If he would have known what was to come forth, he would not have wished her to continue.

Nevertheless, she carried on doing so.

"I wash his clothes that are always soaked with spirits and sometimes covered in his vomit. And it is..." She shook her head. "Too much. It's just," her voice dropped, "too much. And you...you...you took care of me. You...you...risked your life to save mine. And I have not had someone look after me, someone who cared about me in..."

She pulled her lips between her teeth and looked away.

He hated knowing this to the extent he wasn't able to form words before she spoke again.

"And I had purpose," she told the wall beside them. "A *good* purpose. I... what I did had meaning. They depended on you and me. They...you saved us, and then *we* kept them safe."

"Yes," he said softly.

"It was selfish," she whispered.

"It wasn't, love, they had a say. In all of it. And it was you that made that so. It was *you* who asked them what they wished to do and listened," he reminded her.

She took a deep, broken breath.

"And now you will be gone, and I will have to go back to him and that life and..." She again gave him her gaze. "It is just that, I will miss you."

"No, you will not," Faunus decreed.

Her body jerked, her eyes narrowed, and so did Teddy's as he swung them up to Faunus.

"Faunus," he hissed.

"She will not, for she's coming home with us."

Teddy again stood still.

Faunus cast his gaze Moira's way. "Saturn wishes you in his bed."

"Faunus!" Teddy bit.

Faunus looked down at him. "He does."

"Stop speaking," Teddy demanded.

He did not stop speaking.

He turned again to Moira and declared, "That is your decision, your desire to take him or not. He is randy and he is lusty, and I see this in you as well. If you were to accept him, you would be a good pairing. But if you do not, that is your choice and it does not affect our plans. You will come home. To Firenze. Where it is warm and where you will know affection and respect. You will be Teddy's sister. He will see to you. Through Teddy, you will be my sister, and I will see to you as well. And you will be Nyx's sister, most likely, for she has a bent to adopt the Dellish."

Slowly, Teddy turned to Moira to see she was gazing up at Faunus with her lips parted.

"It's true," he said, and her eyes skittered to him. "I do not have much. I am a teacher. I had not quite settled my life there, but I intend to find a dwelling, and if you come with us, I will just find one that has room for you."

"You would...you would..." she stammered.

"Of course I would," he said.

Tears sprang in her eyes.

"Oh, poppet, come here," he murmured.

She did, falling into his arms.

He closed them around her tightly.

She sobbed into his neck.

At that, Faunus's arms closed around both of them tightly.

She sobbed again.

"Hush," Teddy cooed to her. "There's nothing to cry about, love. Nothing's changed. We're doing what we've been doing since we met. We're off on another adventure."

"If Mama had b-been able to give me a b-b-brother, I'd want him to be just like you,' she said into his neck.

Teddy closed his eyes as the silk of that slid through him.

He opened them and teased, "I would not choose you as sister, for you're too bloody stubborn."

He heard her hiccup a laugh before she sobbed again.

He then met Faunus's gaze.

Faunus was staring at him with so much warmth in his eyes, Teddy knew he'd feel it for the rest of his life.

And that slid through him like silk too.

∼

Teddy moved from changing into borrowed sleep pants, splashing water on his face and washing his mouth out in the antechamber, to the bedchamber where Faunus was *not* wearing sleep pants, or anything, and lounging on top of the bed.

Teddy felt himself stir at the brilliance of the spectacle before him, but he did not give into that feeling.

He moved to stand at the foot of the bed, and he looked to his lover.

"Moira sorted, dinner at the royal castle with the King's Counsellor done, everyone bedded down under velvet and Dellish wool, now we must talk," he declared.

"Yes, it was my place to tell her she was coming with us because she belongs to you and you belong to me, so *she* belongs to me. No, you will not be finding a dwelling in which to live with her, for you will be living with me. She can live with Nyx and Lorenz, or Saturn, if he wishes this, and she takes him. Or we will find somewhere else she likes that is comfortable and close to us, for I know you and you will not let me fuck you like I like with her down the hall. Now, come to bed so I can fuck you like I like to fuck you."

Teddy didn't let that stir him either (though this was proving more difficult).

"That wasn't what I wanted to talk to you about, though now I wish to discuss all of that."

"There is nothing to discuss, it is done."

And again, he could not find an artist or a teacher or a spice vendor.

No, for him, it was a highhanded warrior.

Teddy chose where to start and did that.

"I'll be living with you?"

At his question, Faunus exited the bed and walked to their antechamber.

He was gone but moments before he returned.

And when he returned, he had something with him that Teddy had completely forgotten, but seeing it in the now made Teddy draw in a great deal of air.

And hold it.

His journal.

Faunus resumed his lounge in the bed, head and back to headboard, long legs sprawled, and tossed the book to the end, close to Teddy.

"You are in love with me," he announced.

By the gods.

"You read it?" Teddy whispered, aghast.

In the gift of the pages of the book that Lorenz had given him, he had written everything.

About his father and mother.

The first stable boy he took up his arse.

Fenn and the Go'Doan and how he had lost his way in The Rising, confusing lust with love, misinterpreting manipulation for affection.

How he had treated his acolytes.

How Lorenz and Nyx had found him, what they had offered him, how they had changed him and how deeply he felt for the both of them.

How Saturn amused him and enticed him and taught him the parts about what true friendship was that Nyx and Lorenz had not.

And how he had fallen in love with Faunus. His beauty. His strength. His loyalty. His humor. His affection. His protectiveness.

"I did," Faunus answered "It was found as we searched for you. Upon perusing, it was clear it was yours. I wondered if it would give us clues as to where you might be—"

"That isn't why you read it," Teddy accused.

Faunus shrugged. "Perhaps not the only reason, but it is one of them."

"Faunus, those are my most private thoughts."

His brows shot up. "Do you think your love for me should be private?"

"My feelings for you should be mine to share when I want to share them," Teddy retorted.

"And when would that be?"

"I don't know." Teddy threw up both of his hands. "Whenever I decided."

"To be a Trusted, I have to take the cock of every Trusted," he declared. "And I have to fuck them in return. Even Lorenz. This is why I am not yet a Trusted, Teddy. The invitation was extended. But until I go through the rituals, that being one of them, I will not get the mantle with the red and green."

"And?" Teddy asked.

"And?" Faunus parroted dangerously.

"Outside Lorenz's position, that is the highest rank a Firenz warrior can have," he told him something he already knew. "The Trusted Ones are revered in Firenze. Hell, they're revered *everywhere*."

"Yes, and the man I love, who loves me, and owns my cock, *not* incidentally, indeed, who owns *my entire body*, will not be invited to these rituals. Thus, it would be an infidelity unless you give me permission. And I will tell you right now, unless I am watching someone play with you, Teddy, or participating along with it, it will not happen."

Teddy was stunned.

"You...you want my...*permission* to be a Trusted?"

Faunus shook his head. "I don't want it. I must have it for you are mine and I am yours and that is the way of the Firenz."

It was?

He didn't ask that.

He asked, "And if I say no, you would not do it?"

"If you said no, I *could* not do it."

Teddy was no less stunned.

"And you would...that would...you would be all right with that?"

Faunus shook his head, but said, "I would wish to understand what is in you that does not trust me to go through the ritual understanding I am yours alone and am doing something I will enjoy physically but will mean little outside what it is supposed to build between me and my brothers. And after it is done, it will be done. But if there is something within you that cannot abide this without it coming between us, it is something I will come to terms with."

"I would not...*ever*...keep from you something you desire to have," Teddy whispered fiercely.

Faunus did not respond.

That wasn't true.

He did.

Or two parts of him did.

His eyes, which were burning into Teddy.

And his cock, which was stiffening.

"Do you love me?" Faunus finally whispered in return.

"Yes."

"When did you fall in love with me?"

"It began when you kissed me after you fucked Saturn that first time at Lorenz and Nyx's."

Faunus's face grew soft and his hand went to his cock to stroke.

"I am sorry, *mio amore*, but it took me longer," he replied gently. "I liked you very much and wanted more from you. But I knew it would go much deeper when you annoyed me greatly by demanding to put your life at risk to become a spy."

"Don't be sorry, I wasn't worthy of your love until then."

"You are wrong, but we will not discuss it in the now for you need to come to me and kiss me, then you need to suckle me, Teddy," Faunus growled.

Teddy did not delay.

He crawled into bed and did just that.

And their avowals of love were not sealed by making love, as Faunus had been doing to him since he saved Teddy and his women.

No.

It was rough and wild and domineering.

And when Faunus pulled Teddy up to his knees after Teddy had been taking his cock on all fours, and he seized his shaft and was stroking it savagely, Teddy would know why.

"Is this mine?" he demanded on a tug.

"Yes," Teddy breathed, riding the big cock up his arse.

"Is this yours?" Faunus asked, ramming up inside him.

"*Yes*," Teddy groaned.

"Yes," Faunus whispered, fucking him and milking him and *fucking him* and *milking him* until his lover, his love forced him to gush his seed up his chest right before he took Faunus's up his arse.

They were both breathing heavily, Teddy's head back on Faunus's shoulder, Faunus claiming him by filling him as well as at his cock and with an arm about his upper chest, his breaths whispering in Teddy's ear.

"You are mine," he said softly.

"And you are mine," Teddy returned.

"Yes, I am. But you are mine."

Teddy started to turn his head but stopped to grunt when Faunus pulsed up his arse.

"You are *mine*," he growled.

"Yes,' Teddy confirmed.

"That means we detour, *bello*."

He was not following.

"What?"

Suddenly, he was down, on his stomach, with Faunus still in him, and covering him.

And his mouth was still at Teddy's ear.

"We're going to visit your father."

Oh.

Shite.

141

THE ESCAPE

Jellan
Road Between Cyrus and Sky Bay
AIREN

Jellan was likely the only man on Triton who was pleased Airen was engaged in a civil war.

And in that moment, he was the only man perhaps in history who was pleased to be set upon by highwaymen.

He had not, since his decision to escape, found an opportunity to do that.

Until, hopefully now, as moonlight lit their path and the mount that Marian and Daemon were atop, bearing both their weight, had trouble racing away from the highwaymen chasing them.

Thus, once they caught them, Jellan felt he could get away.

In the fracas, he would magick a cloak about him so they could not see him, and he would ride off.

Maybe they would think his horse panicked, took flight, and he was lost.

Or perhaps they'd know he escaped.

Though, as he would be gone, it wouldn't matter what they thought.

But in case it didn't work, he had to make it look good.

It was late at night, they were in the middle of nowhere, nothing about them but fields and forest.

He had told them the last town they rode through, miles back, they should stop at the inn.

Did Marian and Daemon (mostly Marian) listen?

No, they did not.

She said press forward, complaining she didn't like the looks of that inn and, truth be told, she was correct. It appeared rank.

But would they be dashing down a road in the moonlight chased by highwaymen if they'd stopped?

No, they would not.

Did they ever listen to Jellan?

No, they did not.

But hopefully this would end well for Jellan.

Even if he suspected it would definitely not end well for the highwaymen.

Which was a shame.

They rode up alongside them, and Jellan surmised it was a band of five.

This he surmised for he could hear hooves pounding at their backs, they had a man either side of them, and one was taking the front.

In a well-established maneuver, they cut both horses off, making Jellan's rear, and he was forced to lean well forward to keep his seat.

He needed his steed to appear panicked.

But he couldn't have the animal throw him.

For, in the end, he'd just need his steed.

As a warning, one of the highwaymen cracked a whip.

And as Daemon and Marian's mount circled in place and whinnied, Jellan shushed his and patted its neck to soothe its dancing even as he squeezed it with his thighs, giving it mixed messages that he hoped would be confusing to the steed.

He then looked about the men.

All in dark clothing. All wearing large-brimmed, handsome hats adorned with wafting feathers with their hair flowing long from under them. All with dark scarves with holes at the eyes covering the top half of their faces.

He had never been set upon by highwaymen, though he'd heard the tales since he was a boy, and he'd never tired of listening to the telling of them.

In the now, seeing them, their sturdy bodies with their thick thighs on their glorious steeds washed in moonlight, he lamented his choice to become a Go'Doan priest and not a highwayman.

All those men in one city, it had been an enticement Jellan could not forego.

But a life beholden to no one and nothing...you had your merry band, preyed on the weak, enjoyed your takings, wore a handsome hat, and then you did it all again.

Oh, what a life that would have been.

Jellan had a decent seat on a horse. If he spent more time on one, he was sure it would get better.

And he'd be keen to learn his way about a whip.

"Stand and deliver!" one of the men shouted.

Ah, the romance.

"What do these words mean?" Daemon asked Marian, regarding the men with some interest, and surprisingly, or perhaps guilelessly, no ire.

"Let me handle this," Marian said by way of answer. Then, to the highwayman who spoke, she called, "It would be good you leave us be."

"It would be good you toss that purse, madam," the man replied. "And then we would be pleased to bid you goodnight and take our leave."

Of course, they had a purse. Or Daemon did, hanging at his belt.

This was because Marian proved deft at lifting them from unsuspecting citizens strolling the pavements.

She was a clever cunt, that Marian. Crafty. Skilled.

Jellan detested her.

"Truly, it's in your best interests to move along," Marian advised.

"I think not," the man said.

"I think so," Marian retorted.

Another crack of a whip, this from a different highwayman, and Jellan saw his chance.

He kicked his heels into his mount's sides, jerked the reins back, and with nowhere to go, as they were surrounded, his mount rose up, pawing the air with his front hooves.

When the highwaymen's steeds automatically drew back at the rearing horse, and Jellan's mount came down, he cut the reins again, cried out in false surprise, and dug his heels violently into his horse, who hunched his back haunches and burst forth, nearly bowling into one of the gentlemen robbers.

"Give chase!" he heard yelled, not by Marian or Daemon.

By a highwayman.

This was unexpected. He had no purse.

He had nothing.

And it was his understanding they took only coin, jewels worn by women, timepieces from men, thanked the travelers for their generosity (to the point a lady's hand was often kissed, to her swooning with desire), bid them good eve, then went about their way.

At least that was what the tales told.

Why would they give chase to him?

He bent over his steed's neck, slapping its reins, and cutting toward the trees, desperation driving him, for in truth, he knew he had no hope of outrunning a highwayman. They were legendary riders.

But if he could get into the shadows of the barren trees, and find the right turn to take, he could stop and be right there, but disappear, and his pursuer would ride right past him.

He heard shouting, his name bellowed by Daemon, and a commotion, but he kept speeding toward the trees.

He made them and raced into them, the lower branches whipping his face. He had to duck and sway this way and that to avoid stouter ones, but his lovely horse, to his delight, did most of the work.

And in no time, the gods shined fortune on him for he saw a rise, a tall mound that he hoped he could ride behind with enough time to gather a magical cloak to shield him.

He called upon his power, feeling it sing through him, gather in his balls, and oh...there it was. Unused for so long, it was mighty.

For the first time in a very long time, Jellan smiled.

Then he rode behind the mound and put his hand to his face, his fingers extended, before he drew it over his head, through his hair, to the back of his neck.

And he and his steed were hidden.

He rounded his horse, pulled it to a stop so the beating hooves of an apparently invisible animal would not sound in the dead leaves, or be seen thrashing them, and he threw his hand up, out and over himself, magically muting the noises of his and his mount's labored breathing.

Jellan then watched as the highwayman chasing him rounded the mound, rode the length of it and beyond, disappearing into the night.

He held steady and did not move.

He gave it time, listening to the faraway shouts of men, Marian's repeated screeching of Daemon's name, feeling morose that the fantasy of those highwaymen would be no more.

He then heard his name being called by both Marian and Daemon.

Gods.

It was done.

These calls echoed into the night and got farther and farther away until he could hear them no more.

Eventually, the one who gave chase after him rode back and Jellan had to fight calling out to warn him not to find Marian and her creature.

But in order to look after himself, something he was adept at doing, he won that fight, sat astride his horse and waited.

He was not wrong to wait.

For Jellan heard Marian and Daemon come back, still calling for him, and he held his breath, and his magical cloak, as they entered the forest.

Marian had magic and Daemon was...whatever Daemon was.

They might sense him. Even though he was concealing his magic as well, they might sense his power and that he was using it.

Not only sense him and find him.

But also realize he had tried to escape.

He held his breath as they came into view around the end of the mound and Jellan sat very still atop his horse. As such, he prayed to every god he knew that he would remain undiscovered.

"Where the fuck *is* that arsehole?" Marian groused as their horse picked its way through the trees not thirty feet away from him.

"Can you not use your magic to track him?" Daemon asked.

"It doesn't work like that," Marian snapped.

It absolutely did.

Or it could, if you knew how to do it.

Jellan stared as they wandered, looking this way and that.

She did not only not know how to read the veil.

She did not have a very good understanding of her power.

By the gods, he wished he'd known that before.

But in the now, he relaxed, kept himself cloaked and felt the sneer hit his lips as they rode past him.

His sneer faltered when he saw, to his astonishment, that it appeared Daemon had cuts that were bleeding through his shirt at his forearms and one along his neck.

Marian had none.

The lash of a highwayman.

Ever the chevalier, he would never strike out at a woman.

However, he would a man.

But...

Daemon let it get to that?

And...

Daemon *bled*?

He turned in his saddle to watch them ramble away, but that was all he did, and he remained where his was, how he was, for a good long time.

After that, he closed his eyes, cast his senses, and when he did not feel them near his vicinity, he cast his senses to something else.

Remaining masked, he clicked his teeth, touched his heels to his now-beloved steed, for the animal had served him well, and started to amble through the forest, following where his perceptions told him to go.

And he was surprised it did not lead him back to the road where they were confronted.

It led him deep into the forest.

It was a long ride, in the opposite direction he should be taking, but he eventually saw the merrily roaring campfire.

He cautiously approached it.

And to his shock, not only did it appear the highwaymen had rather a lovely bohemian outdoor abode tucked in a curvature of black stone amongst the forest. It included many thick rugs upon the ground, rich hides, tasseled, rolled pillows, sturdy awnings hung to hold back the elements, some low tables, logs that had been dragged in to serve as back rests or shields from the wind, and lanterns and candles scattered about to give it a cozy feeling.

They also had wenches who looked like a cross between a Zee and a doxy. These women wore low-cut, striped blouses under stiff Airenzian corsets that stretched along their midriffs and came to a point in the middle, beneath their breasts. With these they had skirts with deep ruffles at the edges, a few of them that included lace. The skirts fell to their heels at the back but were cut so high at the front, they *just* covered the pubis. Thus, legs were exposed with lace-topped stockings encasing upper thighs and boots that rode up to just under their knees.

But last...

There were ten of them.

Five women.

And all five men.

The men had all escaped.

But...

How?

"It wasn't right," one man said.

"It's done," another one replied wearily. "Let us cease talking about it."

"I swear to the gods, Nick, that man with the woman...at one point he had grown *fangs*," the first man said.

"Think not on it, for it is *done*," Nick replied.

"The one I chased disappeared into thin air," another said.

"A sorcerer?" one of the women asked.

"Had to be," the man who chased him answered.

"If he was a sorcerer, Leith, he would not run. He'd cast," another man said.

"He did cast, Angus, to *disappear*," Leith replied.

"And be glad of it," Nick advised. "For this night we rode up on evil, so intent on coin, we didn't feel it until it was almost too late, and now, we are all here, still breathing."

Yes, they were.

All there.

Still breathing.

But...

How?

"I'll take that bottle of gin, love," the first man who spoke said.

"Here you go, my Rory," a woman whispered, proffering a bottle.

He took it then pulled her down to her hip beside where he lounged on a thick rug against a rolled pillow up against a log.

"Kaden?" Nick called, apparently to the last man, who was at the edge of their encampment, staring into the night.

"We should report this," he said.

There was silence.

Eventually, Nick, who Jellan sensed was the leader, muttered, "Aye."

"Report what?" another of the women asked.

"I'm not sure we should report anything," Leith said.

Kaden turned to the gathering. "That...*thing* on Airenzian soil, our Regent finally sticking it to those arseholes, he does not need another bother. And where there is one, there might be others. He might even be at the call of the AG. Prince Cassius should know."

Jellan was shaken.

No one along their journey had sensed anything amiss with Daemon.

Indeed, many a woman had gazed on him with no small amount of admiration.

How had these men sensed what he was?

Or that he was...*other*.

They had mentioned fangs, but they had also all survived a run-in with the Beast.

And if he had fully transformed, there was no chance of that happening.

The only answer to this puzzle was that it was clear, for some reason, he had not.

He had let them get away.

And Jellan did not have to ponder the why of that.

Marian.

But now, these men lived to share their tale. Perhaps even with Prince Cassius.

Oh yes, the woman was a crafty, clever cunt.

And it should please Jellan they were both about the same business.

But he loathed her so much, it did not.

He would be the hero of this tale.

He would have the stories told about how he helped save Triton.

She would be forever remembered as the harridan who raised the Beast.

"We will think on it the night and vote on it on the morrow," Nick decreed. "Now I need whiskey and my wench," he stated, reaching out and jerking the arm of one of the women so she cried out *not* in protest and fell astride him with a husky laugh. "And all will be well," he finished.

It appeared the course of the evening had changed for this crew, something Jellan did not intend to witness, so he turned his mount and headed away.

He made certain he could no longer see the campfire before he relieved himself of his magical shroud.

And he rode on.

There was much to think on of that night.

He was also tired.

But he could not rest.

"You need a name, old boy, what should we call you?" he muttered to his steed to turn his thoughts to something that was not sleep.

The animal had naught to say.

"Chance," Jellan decided, gazing into the moonlit night.

Making his way through Airen.

On his way to Sky Bay.

142

THE RAINBOW

Prince Cassius
Divinity Boulevard, Sky Bay
AIREN

Cassius rode with Aelia tucked to his front, Theodora astride Caelus at his back, and he did this with his eyes to their surroundings, wondering why the bloody hell he'd allowed Ellie to convince him they should participate in this ridiculous affair.

But he had.

Thus, on his wedding day, he rode to the Combined Cathedral of the Gods in order to take his woman to wife.

And he did this with crowds on either side of the boulevard, held back by Airenzian soldiers, what seemed like the lot of them throwing coral, purple and sky-blue bloody confetti at him.

Lahn and Circe, Frey and Finnie led the way.

Apollo and Madeleine, Noctorno and Cora rode behind them.

True and Farah rode side by side next to Jorie just ahead of Cass and his girls.

Aramus and Ha-Lah rode to his left.

Mars and Silence to his right.

A guard of twenty paraded before Lahn, Circe, Frey and Finnie.

And a guard of twenty trotted to Cass's back.

Elena was somewhere even farther back, and the only argument he'd won in this hellish affair (notwithstanding him demanding their daughters rode with him, thus under his guard) was that Mac, Ian, Nero and Severus accompanied her, along with Hera, Serena and Chu.

When he'd married Liviana, they'd stolen inland, made their way to Abhainn Mouth, and married in a little chapel outside that port city.

The only people in attendance were Mac, Nero, Otho and Ian.

As well as Mars standing at his side.

And at Liv's side, as her father was not best pleased his beloved daughter was going to marry into Airenzian royalty, this because his father and Trajan cast long wretched shadows, stood Ares.

They had all gotten far too inebriated after the ceremony.

But he had not gotten so inebriated he could not consummate his marriage to his wife in the little cottage by the sea he'd hired for just that occasion when one celebration was done, and another one had started.

It had been perfect.

This was not.

"Golly! Isn't it pretty, Papa?" Aelia cried.

"Fairytale," Dora murmured behind him, her thin arms around his middle tightening, and he felt her lay her cheek to his back.

Right, the feel of her cheek there, the word she said that she felt, he might be able to put up with this day.

Perhaps.

"Allo there!" Aelia called and waved to a boy child her age who had gotten through the legs of the soldiers and was scampering beside them.

"Princess Aelia!" he yelled. "Will you marry me?"

Aelia giggled.

Cassius scowled down at the child.

The boy caught Cassius's look and fell back.

Mars chuckled.

Cassius turned his scowl to him.

"My brother, you marry today, and the Bay celebrates. This is no reason to appear dour, no?" Mars asked.

"I wish to be married. I do not wish for myself, or my daughters, to choke on confetti," Cassius returned, only for Mars to throw his head back and roar his laughter.

Silence, riding between he and Mars, smiled happily up to Cass.

"Have you seen her gown?" she asked Cassius.

"No," he grunted. "She has not allowed this."

"Oh, I cannot wait for you to see her gown," Silence replied while looking forward.

"Me either!" Aelia peeped.

"It's the perfect gown to wear to become a princess," Dora said.

Cass twisted his head around to catch her eyes. "Little bean, she's always been a princess and now she is queen."

She peered up at him and replied, "I know, Cass. But today, she *becomes* a princess."

He saw this had some meaning for her he did not understand.

But from the moment the knowledge he had a daughter cut through his grief at losing his wife, he knew there would be many things he would not understand, and he'd reconciled then to let that be.

So, in that moment, he let that be and simply smiled at his girl.

She pressed her cheek again to his back and Cassius looked forward to the looming Combined Cathedral that rose grandly at the top of the cliffs opposite the Sky Citadel, its five, high, black spires spiking into a clear, blue sky.

It was called thus, for unlike other temples that were sanctioned for a certain god, the cathedral was where those who went to worship could worship any Airenzian god they needed.

There were lesser ones, but most all worshipped the greater ones, some of them more than others, but at some point, everyone cast their prayers to all.

There was Jupiter, the sky god, Summanus, the thunder god, and Sol, the sun god.

There were also Lune, the god of moon and night and Aurorus, the god of the dawn.

But in olden times, Lune was Luna, a goddess, and Aurorus was Aurora, also a goddess.

However, since Airenzian men refused to worship female deities, they'd been changed.

Which meant their gods were a farce too, for if they were real, they wouldn't likely thrill to the idea of changing their gender.

Though, as Cassius thought it, this was why the female gods cast the pall Airen lived under, for such hubris and blasphemy from man deserved punishment.

Cass did not know of any Airenzian king that had been married at the cathedral.

This, too, was Ellie's idea, for Airenzian kings married in a small chapel at the Citadel, or in the throne room, such was their desire to share this event mattered little.

Though, he reckoned, with this spectacle occurring in the "New Airen," marriage ceremonies would enjoy a resurgence.

He sighed, held his daughter close, listened to the clop of many horses, the cheers of the crowd and watched the wisps of color drift through the air as the basilica came closer.

And through this he thought, she was his already, but after this day, she would be his officially.

Plus, their daughters would enjoy the day.

So indeed, yes.

He could put up with it.

And a bonus, they neared the cathedral, so it would be over soon.

As such, in little time they made the base of the wide set of steep steps that ran the length of the cathedral, and as they did, he saw the various personages that the steward had suggested, Elena had approved, then Cassius had approved, all milling about the steps.

There were a few lords who had sworn fealty to Cassius, though not many as most were at their homes in order to be there to defend them if need be, however, those members of the gentry had sent representatives.

There were also professors. Healers. Architects. Merchants. He saw Reginald, his chief of Slán Bailey standing with his wife, both of them smiling large.

And he saw a number of faces he recognized, for they were servants in the Citadel, but few he knew their names, and they were dressed at their best and also smiling large at the honor that Elena had bestowed on them.

As they were at his wedding, Cass determined to learn their names.

At some point.

Without any fanfare, he stopped Caelus and waited until Mars and Aramus dismounted, for he'd prearranged that Mars take hold of Aelia and put her to her feet while Aramus did the same for Dora.

When this happened, only then did he swing off his steed allowing a page to rush up and take the reins.

He saw Theodora round Caelus's rump as the horse walked away, this the big sister doing in order to get to Aelia and take her hand, whereupon

Aelia imparted on a loud whisper, "I want to marry a man just like Uncle Mars one day."

"Well, I want to marry a man just like Cassius," Dora replied.

At her words, Cass stood stock still, a burning warmth he did not mind sweeping through him.

Mars chuckled, Silence giggled and Ha-Lah laughed.

Aramus took affront.

"Do neither of you wish to marry the likes of me?"

Aelia's eyes became huge before she broke from her sister, rushed to him and threw her arms around his legs, crying, "Me! I do! I want a husband just like you too! It was just that you didn't help me off Papa's horse and I forgot!"

Aramus put his hand to her head and grinned down at her, teasing, "You wish two husbands?"

"Yes!" she cried.

"Greedy minnow," Aramus muttered on a laugh.

"Trust me, my lovely," Ha-Lah entered the conversation, taking hold of Aelia's hand and drawing her away from Aramus. "You'll find one is *more* than enough."

Mars boomed with laughter again, Silence giggled and Aramus took further affront.

"I'll show you more than enough," Aramus warned.

"Promise?" Ha-Lah asked on a cheeky smile.

"Absolutely," Aramus said low.

Good gods.

"Why the laughter?" Farah asked, arriving with True at her side, as well as Jorie, who approached Silence and Mars.

She was smiling brightly at them all.

"Aelia wants two husbands," Silence shared.

Farah's eyes grew large.

"And I do *not* take that reaction as a compliment," True jested.

Farah's expression melted to adoration as she turned her face to her king.

"I forgot, I want a husband like you too, Uncle True," Aelia declared.

"How about you grow up first, my beauty, and then see what you wish," True suggested.

"I don't need to grow up," she told him. "A boy asked me to marry him *on the way here*. I'll be married *in no time*."

"You will not," Cass decreed.

His daughter whirled on him. "Papa! I want to wear a gown *just like Ellie's.*"

"And you can," he allowed.

She beamed.

"In forty years," he finished.

She frowned.

He smiled at her.

She stopped frowning.

"Let us reach the top of the steps so we can watch Elena arriving," Ha-Lah proposed.

"Yes!" Aelia hopped up. "Let's!"

Still holding Ha-Lah's hand, they started up the steps.

Dora moved to follow.

But Cassius stopped her by touching her shoulder.

She looked up to him.

He offered his arm. "The groom needs an escort, little bean."

She looked to his arm, her cheeks got rosy, her eyes got wet, then she tucked her fingers in his elbow and shot him a trembling smile.

In turn, he moved to her and tucked her to his side before they began their stroll up the steps.

He almost immediately noticed Silvanus, and his clan of Zees, as they were dressed more audaciously than normally.

He tipped his chin to the man, who had his shirt undone all the way down to his navel, but at least his chest was partially covered by his copious, doubtlessly purloined necklaces.

In return, a broad, white smile on his lips, Silvanus tipped his hat.

As they ascended, there were well-wishes extended, bows and curtsies bobbed, and Cassius accepted these with dips of his chin.

But his attention was on his girl.

"I'm glad we have this time, for me it gives me the opportunity to thank you," he said.

"For what?" she asked.

"For much, my Dora," he answered, covering her gloved hand at his elbow with his. "For I had Aelia, and I had my brothers, but unless I was with them, and sometimes even when I was, I wasn't very happy." He cast his gaze down to her. "And then I met you and Ellie, and now, both Aelia and I have a family. So now, we are both happy. But being happy, and seeing Aelia happier, and making Ellie the same, and you, makes me *very* happy."

"We are. We're happy too," she assured him.

"I hope so, love."

"We are, Cass," she repeated. "Ellie especially. She loves you lots."

He smiled down at her. "And I love her lots."

"I know," she whispered, her eyes speaking words that made Cass take her fingers from his elbow as he bent so he could touch his lips to them.

He then tucked them back and finished ascending the stairs with his daughter at his side in order to stand at the top with his friends and await his bride.

"My, but the wind is chill up here," Aelia murmured, breaking from Ha-Lah to come to her papa.

She wrapped her arms around his thigh.

He pulled the hood of her cloak over her head and then wrapped his mantle about her back and held it there.

Dora moved in at his other side and curved her arms about his middle.

He wrapped her in his mantle too.

And as such, suddenly content with the day, he looked down at his city, the bastion of his kingdom, and noted for the first time that the guests milling about the steps wore not black or gray or brown but had donned all the colors of the rainbow.

He blinked slowly at this site and then gazed beyond, where tufts of confetti drifted in the air and the cheers of Bayzians called as the second half of the procession began to be seen.

And he shook his head when he saw her, flanked on all sides by his guard, hers, Hera to her right, Serena to her left, and Nadirii warriors in battle dress with their pennants flying from the tops of their staffs all around.

But this was not why he shook his head.

He shook his head because she wore a voluminous, dove-gray velvet cloak with the hood pulled over the sunshine of her hair, the nap of the velvet so rich, it shone in the sun.

However, she rode Diana side saddle.

And the whole of what she wore covered her horse so all he could see of the beast was head, neck, chest and legs.

Last, at an opening of her cape he saw a froth of pink.

They made the bottom of the steps.

She dismounted.

And a trainee Nadirii warrior rushed forward.

This because Elena's hand went to the frogs at her throat.

The hood fell back exposing her hair pulled away from her face to form a cluster of curls at the nape of her neck.

And with a flourish, the cape was gone, the trainee was scurrying away with it, and a gasp scored through the crowd as she stood resplendent at the foot of the grand sweep wearing a gown no Airenzian bride in centuries would ever consider.

But the ones of the future would.

The skirt was wide. So wide, a being could lie beneath it stretched out with arms over their head and be concealed. It was made of delicate pink organza and ended in a deep, thick layer of organza rosettes.

The boned bodice was of the same color, but made of silk, and it fit her slender waist and ribs like a smooth glove.

And at her neckline, which was far off the shoulder, was another line of rosettes, doubled at her breasts, single where they rounded her arms.

She wore something brilliant as studs at her ears.

Other than that, there was no further adornment.

Just that...

Bloody...

Huge...

Frothy pink...

Magnificent.

Gown.

And thus, Prince Cassius, the Regent of Airen, the Liberator of Women, the Equalizer of all Peoples, stood at the top of the sweep to the Combined Cathedral of the Gods in Sky Bay of Airen, the thunder of his laughter pouring down, as an honor guard of his men and her women surrounded her, and Queen Elena of the Nadirii lifted her resplendent skirt and ascended the steps in order to go about the business of marrying her prince.

❧

Queen Elena
Combined Cathedral of the Gods, Sky Bay
AIREN

THERE WAS MUCH I found odd about the Airenzian.

Including the fact that a bride and her groom led the guests of their wedding into the sanctuary, rather than them being seated and waiting for the bride and groom to appear, as happened in Wodell and Firenze, and it was my understanding (for sadly I'd missed Aramus and Ha-Lah's nuptials), Mar-el.

Thus, when I met a still-laughing Cassius at the top of the ridiculously long flight of steps (for negotiating my skirts was far from easy just walking —climbing, it was a nightmare), he took my face in both his hands, kissed me soundly (still laughing), let me go, then tucked my hand in his elbow.

He then offered his other elbow to Dora, which she took. I clasped Aelia's hand. And we walked in with everyone filing in behind us.

Once inside, Cassius's waning laughter waxed, reverberating around the sanctuary so loudly, I almost didn't hear Aelia's, "*Golly.*"

Hmm.

All right, so perhaps I'd gone a bit mad with the plethora of pink roses, orchids, lilies, hydrangeas, carnations and astilbe.

They were everywhere.

Indeed, tall poles shafted up from both ends of every single pew atop of which was a gargantuan floral display with blooms floating down and even larger sprays of these decorated the altar.

Heavily.

And that did not get into the bunting.

Maybe it was too much.

But a queen only became a princess once in her life.

"Papa, I want a wedding *just like this,*" Aelia declared.

"Now you've done it," Cassius muttered.

"Gads, but Ellie's gone pink mad," Dora said.

"That she has, bean." Cassius didn't mutter that time.

"I like pink!" Aelia stated, and I looked down at her.

"So do I."

"*I know!*" she breathed. "I can *tell,*" she continued breathing.

It was then, I started giggling.

Aelia giggled with me.

Then Dora chimed in.

And that was when I felt it.

We were almost to the altar, and I looked to my right, and up, to see Cassius gazing down at me.

His eyes were a starry night.

"I love you," I whispered.

"Yes, and every day, I thank the gods," he whispered in return.

My heart melted.

And in mere seconds we stopped in front of the pink-strewn altar, Cassius and I, our girls with us, as the guests filed in.

They found their seats.

The priest in his black robes with his satin sash in colors of blue and silver dangling from about his neck came out.

And our wedding began.

~

Combined Cathedral of the Gods, Sky Bay
AIREN

IT HAPPENED after the priest declared Elena, Queen of the Nadirii, to be Princess Regent of Airen and wife to Cassius, and proclaimed him, Prince Regent of Airen, her husband.

It happened after Aelia clapped, King Mars let out a roaring boom, coming up from his seat, his big hands striking each other making a thundering noise, King Aramus coming up with him much the same, King True, their queens, Princess Serena, Cassius's men, her remaining lieutenant, and the visiting royalty from across the Green Sea.

And amongst the pews, the Zees whooped, and at the back, the Nadirii warriors lent their battle cry.

It was when Elena arched into Cassius, Cassius cupped her jaw in one hand and rounded her waist with the other.

It was when she rested both of her hands on his wide chest.

It was when he dropped his head and hers tipped well back.

His long legs all but disappeared in her bounteous skirts.

His upper body curved around hers, and her torso all but vanished behind the wall of his broad back.

And unlike any Airenzian royal wedding ceremony for centuries, for such an event was *never* sealed with a kiss, their lips met in front of the eyes of men and women and under the eyes of the gods.

That was when it happened.

When the air inside the Combined Cathedral of the Gods shot with color.

Red. Orange. Yellow. Green. Blue. Indigo. And violet.

These colors deluged every inch with such brilliance, the dust mites floating in the air became glitter.

They shafted out the windows and up through the roof.

Snaking the city, the countryside, and reaching to the heavens.

It would become lore, that rainbow that shone from two lovers.

It would be talked about all the way to The Mystics and the Northlands and Southlands.

The power of the prophecy was fulfilled.

The fate of Triton was in their hands.

Jellan
Road to Sky Bay
AIREN

JELLAN WAS FAR AWAY, but he saw it.

He stopped Chance and stared at the rainbow streaking straight up into the sky on the horizon.

"Haste," he whispered.

Then he dug his heels into his mount.

"*Fly, Chance! Fly!*" he encouraged.

And they galloped toward Sky Bay.

Marian
Road to Seemingly Nowhere
AIREN

DAEMON STOPPED THE HORSE, and as she was gazing glumly down at the ground going by beneath them, in her mind cursing Jellan for making good his escape and leaving her with this *creature*, this *thing*, leaving it *all to her* to find a way to stop it, the selfish *sop*, she had no idea why Daemon suddenly did that.

Thus, she looked up, to him, to see him gazing at the distance with an expression on his deceptively handsome face that did not make her feel like rejoicing.

"What is it?" she asked.

"This is my query," he said as answer.

She turned in the direction of where he was staring and blinked.

"It's a rainbow," she said.

Though she could not be certain it was. She'd never seen the likes of it.

It seemed to go straight up into the sky without an arch.

And the sky was cloudless, so it was not that it was just very tall, and it disappeared in white.

"It is not thus," Daemon stated.

She turned her attention back to him. "Then what is it?"

"It is not thus," he repeated.

"Then what is it?" she demanded snappishly.

And then she jerked away, fear choking her, as his eyes bulged, his head sunk into his neck, his mouth widened, and he snapped at her with teeth gone ghastly.

"I tire of your tone," his voice rumbled, animal and primal.

"I-I'm..." She swallowed. "I'm sorry. I was simply asking a question."

"We need to make the stones," he declared.

"The...what?"

He snapped at her again, literally, with dreadful teeth.

"We must make *the stones*," he decreed, bent to her, and she again reared away.

But he was only preparing to dig his heels into their horse and start galloping.

Something he did.

Toward what, she did not know.

To where, she had no idea.

But clearly, he sought the stones, whatever they were.

One thing she knew they were...

They were important.

Thus, she hoped to the goddess, along the way, she was able to discover how to stop him.

⌤

Queen Elena

Bedchamber of the Prince and Princess Regent, Sky Citadel, Sky Bay
AIREN

WITH MY TONGUE, I traced my mark on Cassius that adorned the skin above his handsome cock.

"Please tell me I did not make a mistake with this and my wife pays it all her attention and does not give it where it is needed," Cassius growled.

I lifted my eyes to him, wrapped my fingers around the member in need, then licked it from root to tip.

His eyes went midnight.

"Come here," he murmured.

"I'm doing something," I told him, then kept licking.

"My queen, come here."

That made me go there.

I crawled up his body, but before he could speak, I put my fingers to his lips.

"I am not your queen," I whispered. "I am your princess. Even when you are king and I _am_ your queen, please, Cass, don't call me that anymore. Since we started, I've been your princess, and you my prince."

Another growl emitted from him, his arms locked around me, and he rolled us over clouds of pink organza (for, in divesting me of my dress, there was so much of it, tossing it aside didn't get it very far).

He did this negotiating his hips between my legs along the way and entering me splendidly when he had me to my back.

His thrusts were not languid.

"Yes, sweetheart," I whispered my encouragement, my eyes drifting closed, my body jolting in taking his drives.

"Look at me," he grunted. "I want to see my night in your eyes."

His new obsession, giving the night to me.

As well as mine.

"Yes," I breathed, giving him what he desired and opening my eyes.

"My princess," he ground out.

"My prince," I gasped.

"My wife," he bit.

"My husband," I said.

"There it is," he whispered, staring into my eyes, his expression shifting from fierce to soft.

Then he kissed me.

And then he made love to me.

Under an Airenzian moon.

That shone from the ceiling of our bedchamber.

143
THE DISCUSSION

Princess Serena
Outskirts of Dunlyn
AIREN

The whipping about ended, and her feet struck ground walking as she formed, Chu's arms about her face-to-face meant he formed too, walking backward.

And as Brix was on Chu's back and Gal was on hers, they formed too.

They stopped, Chu standing strong, Serena not the same, and both gnomes immediately jumped to the ground.

But Serena swayed.

"*That* was bloody humiliating," Brix groused.

"Mouse," Chu murmured, dipping his face down to hers.

"We could hardly make hundreds of miles in a trice if we hadn't done it," Gal retorted to Brix.

"Serena," Chu whispered.

"If you tell anyone I climbed aboard a man's back and rode the magical plane, I will gut you," Brix threatened Gal.

Chu cupped Serena's face in both hands and clipped, "*My love.*"

"Who am I going to tell? I rode *a woman,*" Gal retorted. "And not in the manner I prefer."

Chu took her by the shoulders and shook her.

"*Serena!*" he barked in her face.

"I need a minute," she whispered, staring, unseeing at his chin.

Chu put pressure on her shoulders until she was on her arse on the ground.

He then crouched before her, pulled her cloak about her, undid and swung off his mantle, and he tossed that about her as well, pulling it close under her chin.

"Too much?" he asked.

She nodded.

"What's happening?" Gal queried, coming to stand to one side of Serena.

"She's used too much magic," Chu said, staring into her eyes. "That's it. Keep looking at me."

"I'm fine, Chu, I just need a minute," she muttered.

"Take it, but do it looking at me," he ordered.

Overprotective and overbearing.

She did not make note of that.

She did as asked and took her minute looking at him.

Brix was at her other side, where he queried, "I thought she drew down a bunch to top herself up?"

"She just transported four bodies halfway across Airen, you fool," Gal bit out, his words aimed at Brix, his worried gaze on Serena.

For once, Brix ignored Gal, and he did so in order to state to Chu, "That's it. She's out. So are you. You'll take care of her and Gal and I'll take care of that situation."

And with that, he jerked a thumb toward Dunlyn.

"I'm not out," Serena said.

"You can't even stand, missy," Brix retorted.

She turned her head to him and said slowly. "I. Am. *Not.* Out."

"You are," he retorted, and when she opened her mouth, he lifted a hand her way and shook his head. "For now. Hunker down here. Chant to your goddess to fill the well, or whatever it is you witches do. You'll do the mission no good going in not at your best. We'll head in, make contact with the others, get the lay of the land, come back and report."

"I just need a minute," she repeated.

"You need to take care," Brix said low. "Because I'm not going in there worried about you. Are you hearing me?"

Serena straightened her shoulders.

Then she nodded.

Brix looked to Chu. "We'll go in, see if we can procure some supplies. Rendezvous with Fern's women. Get some blankets at least. Food. We'll be back and then we'll get stuck in."

Chu nodded.

Brix jerked up his chin to Gal, gave Serena a stern look which stated she was to look after herself, then turned and stomped away.

Gal put his hand on Serena's shoulder.

She looked to him.

"He's a horse's arse, but he's right," he said. He turned his attention to Chu. "Take care. We'll return. If you recover and decide to go in, we all know the checkpoint."

Chu didn't nod again.

He went from crouching in front of Serena to twisting to sit his arse beside her.

Gal watched this before he took off after Brix.

"This is not making me happy," Chu said to her.

"It's just that I've never cast that spell before. I was unprepared for how much energy it took to hold the three of you with me."

"We need your magic for our disguises, my princess," he reminded her.

She did need her magic.

They had decided. She would magic him to appear Airenzian—a shift of the eyes, a different cast to his skin—and somewhat the same for her—dark, straight hair, olive skin.

She was already wearing Airenzian garb. It was just, when they were in the city, she wouldn't wear her weapons as she was then.

She blew out a breath, shook her head sharply and turned to him.

"I have an enormous amount of power inside me, Chu. If we had attempted to make that jump with my normal powers, we would have been lost on the magical plane, I am certain. But in the now, I have more than enough for that with much to spare. It was fine when it was stored untapped. But I tapped it. I simply need to order it and we can proceed."

He studied her face for a lie.

And when he assessed she wasn't giving him one, he asked, "Can you walk?"

"Of course, I can bloody walk," she muttered.

He grinned at her, pushed to his feet and reached a hand down to her. "We are in the open, princess. And exposed. Let us find cover."

She considered smacking his hand away and taking her feet on her own power, but she decided against that, grasped his hand and allowed him to pull her up.

He did not take her far, in amongst some evergreen trees.

The chill was fierce, and she worried about the smell of the air.

She scented snow.

She knew Chu scented it too, when they made haste and together, they worked, gathering some pine boughs, some fallen branches to use as supports and combing the floor of dead needles, and in no time erected a small shelter of boughs, and under it, a thick blanket of needles to sit upon to protect them from the cold earth.

Serena stood before it as Chu unsheathed his sword, tossed it under the boughs, and settled into it.

She swung his mantle off, stating, "Take your standard."

"Keep it," he muttered.

"Chu—"

She said no more as, quick as the strike of a snake, he reached out, clasped her hand and yanked her under the shelter, onto his lap. He then pulled his mantle from her hands, whipped it about them, and cocooned them both in it.

She did not wish this to be a warm and comfortable position.

But she could not deny it was.

"Does this suit, my princess?" he teased.

Instead of deigning to answer, she huffed out a sound and turned her gaze to scan the beyond.

He wrapped his arms and the ends of his mantle around her.

"If you relax, it'll be more comfortable," he suggested.

She tried to relax.

She did not succeed.

"Rena," he murmured. "What's the matter?"

Ha-Lah said they must learn to talk.

And she was right, they must learn to talk.

Or she must.

Chu seemed to know how.

And now they had nothing to do but sit, stare at nature...

And talk.

"Is it your wish to...?"

She could not finish.

"Is it my wish to...?" he prompted.

She drew in an unsteady breath.

"Serena," he growled, giving her a squeeze of his arms. "*Talk to me.*"

She turned to face him.

"Do you wish to marry?"

His head jerked.

She understood *that* with no words.

And she suddenly needed to get away.

His arms kept her where she was.

"If you do not wish it, I would understand," she said quickly, again facing the beyond.

"You *would* understand?"

She did not understand the emphasis.

She also didn't ask him to explain.

"Yes," she forced out.

"Rena—"

"I am...we could just—"

"Be quiet, warrior, and look at me."

Slowly, she turned her head to look at him.

"Do *you* wish to get married?" he asked.

Absolutely not.

But...

She pulled her bottom lip between her teeth.

"Gods, you do," he whispered, staring at her mouth.

"It is not very Nadi—"

His eyes jumped to hers. "My sweet mouse, you are Nadirii, but that is not *all* you are."

She stared at him.

"You are so much more."

She continued to stare at him.

"Your sister is Nadirii, and she married."

"Yes, I know. It was yesterday, Chu, and we sat side by side watching it. But that marriage was arranged."

"And you wish me to believe Elena, Queen of the Nadirii, wouldn't ride to the under-realm battling demons all the way to wed Cassius Laird?"

Her sister would do just that and more.

Chu didn't make her confirm that.

He asked, "Is she the only Nadirii ever wed?"

"No."

"Then?"

She watched him closely while she stated, "So, you *do* wish to get married."

He grinned wickedly. "Are you asking?"

She made a much greater attempt to launch herself from his lap.

But she found herself on her back atop a bed of pine needles with her Trusted atop her, his face close to hers, his expression very serious, his maneuver deft, for she had not unscabbarded her sword and neither of them had been impaled upon it.

"I want only to be free to do whatever makes us happy," he said. "Without the strictures of the Nadirii or what you feel is your duty as a Nadirii princess standing in our way."

"I have something to tell you that is important to me that I fear you will not like."

His face closed down.

Damn it.

She knew it.

"You feel your duty is to your queen and thus you must stay at her side," he said tonelessly.

She did not know what he was on about.

"What?" she asked.

"And my duty is to my king and I have vowed to remain at his side to see him and his family safe."

She now knew what he was on about and in the knowing, she grew solid beneath him.

"And thus, we reach a stalemate after this is all done," he concluded. "For you will not leave your queen and I cannot leave my king."

This was not the issue.

Or it hadn't *been* the issue.

Though it was now partially the issue since it was clear he'd thought much on it and the thoughts he'd had were not cheerful.

She began to broach that with him when he said, "But I will."

She had thought she'd grown solid before.

But now it felt like all the muscles in her body had atrophied.

"You...*will?*" she pushed out between stiff lips.

"Although I do not relish waiting for Elena to leave The Enchantments, and you to follow her, so that I can see you, for I cannot live with you in them, I will wait for my times with you and Mars will understand when I take them. It is not only he, but he was taught by his father, family is most important. This is why Guard is not with us. He has a new child. Mars is more likely to cut off his own arm than take Guard from his wife and daughter when she is that wee and Zosime needs him. And I know this because times are this rife, and Guard is not here. He's with his family. When it is our times to share, Mars will arrange something for me."

"After this, I am free to do as I wish," she told him quietly. "Elena might want me at her side, yes, but she would prefer me to do what makes me happy."

His eyes lit.

"It is that I wish a son."

These words rushed out before she could stop them.

"Rena—"

"I know it is not what you wish but," she raised her hands to frame his face, "you are beautiful, and you are a good man, and I want to raise a son with you. I do not know what kind of mother I would be. I never thought I would wish to be a mother. Now, having you, I do."

His eyes warmed.

But she was not finished.

"What I know is, men like you, and women who can teach their sons to respect the sisterhood, *should* be the ones making sons. I have thought on this long, and I feel the Nadirii got it wrong. I see it through what I know I could have with you. We should have been making girls *and* boys. Our ancestors should have taken their sons with them and built a *true* army. The kind that fought at the Heights. The kind that stood, side by side, and it did not matter who was what. What country. What sex. Just fighting for right. I...I..."

She realized she'd descended into a giving speech and finished it quickly.

"I just wish for you to consider giving me a son."

"Then I will say I have considered this, and when the time comes, I will give you one."

She felt her brows shoot up.

"Though, if you agree, he will be second born so he knows humility," he carried on.

"I...well, yes. I...er, that would be, I would agree," she stammered, her stomach warming, the area around her heart feeling light.

He grinned.

"So, marriage and Firenze and a son," he decreed.

"I would not wear a pink dress," she stated firmly.

"It would not look good with your hair." His head dipped close and his tone dipped low. "The purple of Nadirii. Or the green of Firenze."

"Maybe," she muttered.

If it was a tunic and leg casings.

Though, she would consider a fancy tunic.

He was grinning again.

And then he wasn't when his head shot up and turned, as if he was listening.

But she heard it then too.

They were both out of their shelter, back to back, Chu had his sword in hand, and she had her fingers about the hilt of the weapon on her belt.

They turned in a circle, keeping the other at their backs, and scanning the area.

"Which way did you hear it?" she whispered.

"North," he said.

"Yes," she agreed.

"I'm high. You're low. You're on tracks, warrior," he ordered, turned and then he moved up the hill behind their shelter.

Stealthily, gazing about and opening her senses, she moved in the direction where she heard the noise.

It had been soft. Needles rustling.

She thought this sound came through an approach.

Thus, she often cast her eyes to the ground to check for tracks.

But she saw nothing.

She'd searched a relatively thorough area before she heard, "Zsst."

Her head turned and she moved up the incline to Chu.

"Nothing," she said. "Maybe an animal?"

He pointed.

She turned in the direction he indicated and only saw some evergreens.

"I don't—"

"The trees, Rena."

She looked closer.

Disturbed needles.

Bent boughs.

"Gnomes," she said.

"Hmm," he hummed.

She looked to him. "How did they get bloody gnomes on their side? The gnomes hate Airen as it was, almost as much as the Nadirii."

Chu simply continued regarding the disturbed trees.

"Chu?" she called.

"Before I left my birth country, I had just started training in the Mystics."

"Sorry?" she asked.

"Not the continent." He looked to her. "The arts."

Oh.

The Mystics.

Her gaze slid back to the trees as a chill slithered up her spine.

"I can harness my momentum to propel me to do a number of things many cannot. But I did not train long enough to ascend to the art of weightlessness."

She again gave him her attention. "Do you think they have Mystics?"

"I think a gnome would disturb the needles, but he would not break boughs."

Serena fully turned to study the area.

The vantage was good for their cover.

"They were spying on us," she deduced.

"Yes."

"We need to go into Dunlyn."

"Yes."

She gave him her eyes. "Disguises?"

"Pull up the hood of your cloak," he ordered. "I shall take my chances. You are not changing us here."

She nodded.

"Let us go," he murmured.

She nodded again and led.

Chu followed.

144

THE DEEP

Queen Silence
Aboard The Finnie, *Seil Sea*
Off the Coast of Airen

I stood at the railing of the handsome galleon, staring down into the waters, a bitter, stiff wind blowing my hair about my face.

The waters were somewhat choppy.

Ha-Lah, Aramus, Jorie, Frey and Finnie were just down the deck from me.

And my husband stood before me.

The vein in his temple was pulsing.

"This is natural for me," I said soothingly.

"It is cold," he replied.

"And Ha-Lah and Jorie have assured us that I will not feel that," I reminded him.

"A being can die swiftly in this cold," he said, as if I had not spoken.

"A being could, if they were not mermaid."

He cast his gaze down to the water.

I lifted my hand and pressed it to his cheek.

He gave his beautiful eyes to me.

"I will be fine," I promised.

"I find suddenly I would wish for a wife who was less dauntless and bold," he muttered.

I started giggling.

He, too, put his hands to my face, both of them, before his head descended, and he took my mouth in relentless kiss.

I was clinging to him when it ended.

"Now go," he murmured. "Before I commandeer this ship and take us back to Sky Bay."

I nodded, his hands still on my face moving as I did.

Mars removed them but wrapped his fingers around one of mine and led me down to the others.

Jorie watched me the entirety of this short journey.

"You are ready, little sister?" he asked when we arrived.

I nodded to him too.

His gaze went to Mars's.

"I will be with her every length," he stated. "And Ha-Lah will be with us."

"Do not keep her down there long," Mars grunted.

For a moment, Jorie didn't say anything.

Until finally, he spoke and did this solemnly.

"My brother, you can trust me."

They locked eyes, and I waited.

I was glad it didn't take my husband long before he jerked up his chin, gave my fingers a squeeze and let me go.

"Right. Ladies, for your convenience," Frey murmured.

He then unlatched and swung open a gate in the railing which was where they put the gangplank.

Ha-Lah and I moved the few feet to that as Jorie called from behind us, "Do not turn around."

Regardless of his words, I began to do that, but Ha-Lah grabbed my arm and whispered, "He's disrobing."

Faith.

I nodded to her earnestly and absolutely did not turn around.

I was wearing a heavy dressing gown over a light shift that ended just over my bottom, slippers on my feet.

Ha-Lah was in much the same.

We heard a splash, and I peered over the railing to the waters and watched until Jorie's head surfaced, his dark hair slicked back.

He smiled encouragingly up at me.

I drew in a deep breath.

"Now remember," Ha-Lah started, remaining close. "We are in The Deep. It will happen nearly instantly when you hit the water. A knitting. You won't be able to control it. Don't panic. It is natural. Just relax into it and let it happen. Jorie and I will be right there. Yes?"

"What if it doesn't happen?" I asked.

"It'll happen," she assured.

"But what if it doesn't," I pressed. "What if, in the joining of a human and a Mer, the human wins out?"

"That has never happened, Silence, and you will not be the first. Trust me." Ha-Lah took my hand then demanded, "Tell me you don't feel it."

I drew in another deep breath.

"Tell me it doesn't call to you," she continued.

I could not do that for just being in Sky Bay, all the way up at the Citadel, I was still close to the sea.

And it called to me.

"It calls to me," I whispered.

And standing on the deck of that ship, the water but steps away, I realized it had been doing so all my life.

A yearning I'd grown used to denying, for I didn't know what it was, thus had no idea how to assuage it.

She tipped her head to mine, resting her forehead to my own.

And there, she smiled happily.

"You're about to go home, my sister," she whispered.

Then she stepped back, undid the tie on her dressing grown, dropped it to the deck (and yes, she was wearing the same as me, a small shift, hers marine blue). She flipped off her slippers, and with taking but the time it took to aim a smile at Aramus, she dashed to the opening in the railing and executed a graceful dive into the sea.

I moved to the opening, stood there and watched the waters until she surfaced.

She did so beaming.

Home.

I looked up to Mars.

He nodded his head.

I *so* loved my husband.

I then took several paces back, divested myself of dressing gown and slippers, stood in the cold for a moment in my red shift, drew in one more very deep breath.

Then I raced to the opening and dove in.

I sluiced through the waters and the panic came instantly, for I felt the cold.

And it was *so cold*.

Relax, Ha-Lah had instructed.

A knitting, she had told me.

Even in reminding myself of these, automatically, I arced up, wishing the surface, when Ha-Lah's words were proved true.

I felt a knitting.

All sense of cold vanished when it started at my waist, the feeling, so strange, like something was pressing through my skin, I could do nothing but float in the water and experience it.

But once it started, it went fast, speeding about my hips.

And then my thighs were forced together.

I looked down, opening my eyes for the first time under the water, and was surprised at the clarity I could see through the wet.

And thus, I looked to my lower half and saw the scales push out and form over my knees, my calves, ankles...

My feet reflexively pointed, and as my toes disappeared, a glorious, filmy caudal tail sprung forth, scalloping down the sides and drifting well off the point at the end.

The scales of my fin gleamed silver and lagoon blue, with glimmers that appeared like aquamarines, the translucent caudal at the end was a lovely silvery lilac.

As I drifted under the surface, staring in wonder at my tail, I saw a long, winding fin the same colors as my own, with some aqua as well (but the caudal was not translucent or filmy, it was strong and spined), coil and drift about me.

I turned my head to the left to see my brother there.

Faith, but his tail was very long.

And his chest was very defined.

Further, upon perusal, I saw he had extra fins. Dorsal ones at his hips, and others farther down, on either side, where, if he still had his legs, his thighs would meet his knees.

I smiled at him.

He spoke, and it was deep, rumbling, and only slightly bubbly when he ordered, "Strike for the surface, little sister. Your husband will want to see you're all right."

I nodded, and started to kick, but as I didn't have legs, the movement I made forced me down.

"Watch," Jorie instructed and lifted his chin up to something beyond me.

I turned my head and saw Ha-Lah there.

Her fin was a dark teal, her caudal a lovely carnation pink, and her scales glistened *like diamonds*.

She was smiling merrily at me as she rippled her fin and swum gracefully before me.

Jorie was doing somewhat the same, but as his tail was at least three times longer than Ha-Lah's, and mine was Ha-lah's length, I watched her far more closely.

Once I felt I understood her movements, and could mimic them, I emulated her, and it felt both natural and unnatural, as I made my way to the surface.

I broke it, experienced an odd sensation at my neck, but ignored it to seek my husband.

I found I had my back to the ship. Thus, I twirled around and saw him, his fingers curved over the railing as if he was preparing to jump it, and he was glowering over the side.

When he caught sight of me, relief swept through his expression.

I lifted my arm and waved as I heard Jorie and Ha-Lah surface either side of me.

"You are well?" Mars boomed.

"I am, husband!" I called back, still waving.

It took but a moment before he grinned indulgently and shouted, "Have fun, *bellezza*."

Oh, but I *loved* my husband.

I blew him a kiss, looked to Ha-Lah, Jorie, and Jorie said, "Let's go swimming, little sister."

Then he surged up, and down, the entirety of his big, powerful body, including his glorious fin breaking the surface, the powerful caudal striking up on a spray of sea before he disappeared into The Deep.

Ha-Lah grabbed my hand, I turned to her, and she pulled us both up with the strength of her tail.

I tucked my head as she did...

And we were under.

We held hands as we undulated our fins, and I felt it that time, as I was not experiencing my tail forming, thus that taking the whole of my attention.

There was a sensation on either side of my neck, like the scratch of a kitten.

Ha-Lah must have read my thoughts for she said, "Gills. This is why you can breathe."

That hadn't even occurred to me, that I could breathe.

But I could.

I could breathe underwater!

I nodded, more than likely smiling like a fool, and I asked a question, the answer being obvious, as we were doing it, "We can talk underwater?"

"We can, and we can understand one another. But when I guided Aramus from Amphite to home, I spoke to him and he said it came out as gibberish. I asked Jorie about this, for I didn't know of it, and he said this is why we understand the beasts of the sea, something the Mer are as well, for we have the ability to listen and understand underwater."

This was important to know.

And I wondered, if this hearing underwater had something to do with why I could hear so well out of it.

"Silence," she called.

"Yes," I answered, I thought unnecessarily, as I was right there.

"My friend..." she let me go, "*swim*."

For a moment, I was suspended. Uncertain.

Then I looked around.

The water was very blue.

The depths below seemed very gray.

And I saw a vast school of tiny, shimmering, silvery fish swimming some distance away.

This was before I felt a whisper of something against my fin, another, and I flipped it automatically as all about me another school of glistening fish swept by me, causing what felt like an all-over tickle.

I laughed and pushed after them, feeling Jorie and Ha-Lah swimming at my sides, but behind me, and I looked over my shoulders in turn to send them grins.

A sentiment they both reciprocated.

The school as one suddenly darted to the left, and I missed the turn, going wide, but I watched as Ha-lah looped her head, dipped a shoulder, and spiraled into her turn in an elegant manner I made mental note to try myself.

We followed the school for some time, striking ever deeper, though it was probably only me doing it in wonder.

I could see fish, floating bits of detached seaweed.

But mostly, I sensed the vastness around me.

It went so far down, and so wide in all directions, it felt like I could swim for years and years and then keep swimming.

However, this was not overwhelming.

No.

Instead, I felt...

Free.

Of a sudden, Jorie powered ahead of us, before he swam in front of me, cutting me off, helixing up, and Ha-Lah and I followed him.

And when Ha-Lah passed me, smiling back my way, she did this exclaiming, "Oh, Silence! You're in for a treat!"

We both chased after Jorie's powerful tail, me doing so pleased that I had found my pacing with my fin, and it wasn't long before I saw them.

And *begorrah*.

What marvel!

I kicked my fin faster as Ha-Lah and Jorie pursued them.

This was when I felt a tickle in my throat, the emotion sting my eyes, as I watched Jorie, then Ha-Lah, join a large pod of dolphins.

There had to be thirty of them, maybe forty, even babies!

They were *glorious*.

Jorie's big body and long fin curled around one, then another, and they began to butt him with their bottle noses, and I would swear to the gods, they were smiling at him.

Come play.

When these words came to me, I stopped swimming abruptly.

Jorie, Ha-Lah and the dolphins were swirling on, distance forming between us, but three dolphins at the end of the school broke off, swum to me, beyond me...

They then turned, surged up all about me, causing the waters to churn and bubble and propel me with them, and I heard it again.

Come play.

By the gods!

Just as Ha-Lah said!

They could speak to me!

I kicked and struck out with my arms as one dashed over the top of me from one side to the other, one doing the same below, and then another over me, then one raced in front of me.

I liked this "play."

I liked it very much.

Thus, I laughed, joined in and swam with the dolphins.

Jorie made his way back, curved around, took position beside me and guided me deeper into the pod.

Some of the dolphins rose up, breaking the surface, only to dive back down, causing effervescent white foam and bubbles to form around us that tingled as you swam through them and just felt...

Happy.

My brother and I swam side by side, skimming through it.

"How do you feel, my little sister?" Jorie asked.

I turned my head to my handsome brother.

And answered with complete honesty, "Like I've finally come home."

His smile could light up the sea.

Then we both struck forward.

And we played with the dolphins.

I HELD the rope tight in my hands as they heaved me up.

When I made the deck, Mars caught me in his arms in the cocoon of a large sheet of toweling and pulled me aboard, dropping to his behind on the deck and holding me against the warmth of his chest.

My tail flipped and flopped on the wood as I looked up at my husband to see his eyes locked on my fin.

"But of course, it's beautiful," he muttered.

I started to smile at his words, and then I winced.

"Steady, angelfish," Jorie's voice could be heard above me. "We talked about this. Just breathe through it, Silence."

We *had* talked about it.

But *faith*, the pain of the split was blinding, and each scale reentering my skin felt like thousands of little cuts.

"I do not like this," Mars stated on a rumble, and I knew I was not hiding the unpleasantness of the sensations.

"It will be over in moments, and eventually she'll get so used to it, she'll barely feel it," Jorie assured.

"She's feeling it now," Mars noted in a threatening tone.

I had been.

But suddenly, I wasn't.

I looked down to my legs which looked like naught but my legs. No marks from where the scales had pushed through. Not even a whisper of my lovely caudal left.

I missed it, and I cuddled closer to the warmth of Mars, for I didn't feel the cold in The Deep, but I felt it on the deck.

I looked up to my brother.

"Can we do that again soon?" I requested.

He burst with laughter.

I decided, and was delighted, that meant yes.

"And this weariness?" I heard Mars ask as I rode before him, in his arms, atop Hephaestus, on our way back to the Citadel.

And I did it with my eyelids drooping.

"She has had much activity. It doesn't seem thus, for in the doing, it seems easy. But in truth, swimming requires the use of your whole body at all times you're doing it, and she is not accustomed to this. She will become so, my brother, and this weariness after a swim will fade," Jorie explained.

As I was, indeed, weary, I did not take issue with my husband and brother speaking about me when I was right there.

Instead, I peeked through my flagging eyes and noted with great relief that we'd made the bottom of the lane to the Citadel. I was gladdened by the seeing of it, for all I wished to do was find our bed, crawl into it and take a nap that would last until supper.

I was so tired, along the way, I hadn't even glanced around to enjoy the cheerful hustle and bustle of Sky Bay that always so heartened me when we rode through it.

Indeed, I nearly fell asleep riding the long lane up to the Citadel.

We were almost there when I heard Jorie say, "If I did not like him so, his overprotection would be irksome."

"His sister is my wife and his wife is my sister. This is the man you would wish for both, no?" Mars replied, and I knew they were talking about True.

Thus, suddenly excited to share with my cousin about my day, I forced my eyes open, raised my head, looked forward and saw True striding purposefully around the large fire that rose in the courtyard in front of the Citadel.

It was then I found that my adventure had been so delightful, my desire to share about it beat back the fatigue and I aimed a beaming smile to my cousin.

"True, it was glorious!" I called.

His return smile was oddly tight as Mars reined in Hephaestus close to True.

"This makes me happy for you," he replied.

Then his gaze went direct to Mars.

Oh no.

"What is it?" Mars clipped, noting what I had noted.

True was not greeting us upon our return from my first swim as a mermaid, keen to know how it went.

Something was amiss.

His jaw hardened, his gaze bore into Mars's, then it came to me and it softened.

"Silence," he said like he was trying not to talk through his teeth, "your mother is here."

I shot straight in my husband's arms.

"Fuck," I heard Jorie mutter.

"Where is she?" Mars bit off.

"I demanded she remain behind in the red room so that she did not surprise Silence with her appearance as she did me," True told him.

"Thank you," I said, cutting into their conversation. "Now, if I could ask you to have the servants delay for fifteen minutes so I can see to my state and make my way to the throne room. After that time, they can escort her there, and I will grant her an audience."

True's brows rose at my words and my tone in saying them

My husband's arm tightened about me, and he called, "Silence."

I looked up to Mars.

"I am not her queen, but I am a queen, and when you wish to speak to a queen, and that wish is granted, she provides you an audience, which shortly, I will do," I stated. "Now, will you let me down, husband?"

He gazed at my face and murmured, "My love, a queen can also refuse an audience."

"Why would I do that?" I asked. "For I wish to hear what she has to say."

Mars did not, at once, acquiesce to my earlier request.

But then, he hefted me down into True's waiting hands before he dismounted behind me.

Jorie was at our side in a flash.

"I would attend this audience," he stated.

I looked up at my brother.

"I would have it no other way than have both my kings," I glanced at True, "*all* my kings with me, should that be their wish."

"I shall be there," True said, before turning stiffly on his boot and sauntering away.

I headed toward the door.

Mars was at my side, querying, "Would you like me to call for Tril?"

"No, for I will hold my patience, and she might not," I answered.

"Silence," he called as we entered the doors.

"I will be all right," I said to the spray of coral and purple gladiolus on the table in the center of the entryway.

"*Piccolina.*"

I stopped and looked up at my husband, who stopped with me, as did my brother who was right there.

Always right there, Jorie.

Making up for time lost.

Making up for nearly twenty-four years of having a sister.

And not having her.

Because of my mother.

"My love," I said to Mars. "*I will be fine.*"

He didn't seem convinced.

I didn't have the energy to convince him.

And what energy I did have, I had to conserve.

I divested myself of gloves and cloak, tossing them over a chair before I found the small antechamber off the Great Hall that had a privy and a basin with a faucet that looked like the face of an angry god blowing wind from his mouth and out of that wind came (hot and cold, depending on the dial you turned) water.

During the return sail into Twilight Harbor, Finnie had helped Ha-Lah and I wash the salt from our skin and rinse it from our hair and I had donned a lovely gown.

But for this meeting, I would have wished something a might grander and perhaps my hair arranged, not simply pulled back at the nape.

I wanted this meeting done.

Therefore, I would not get this wish.

I splashed water on my face, toweled it off, looked in the mirror before me and whispered, "I shall have to do."

I left the antechamber to find my husband and brother loitering outside it.

And in the seeing, it struck me.

These tall, handsome, powerful men were *my* tall, handsome, powerful men.

I had earned one through love and the other through blood.

But now they were *mine*.

And neither had anything to do with *him*.

Or her.

My life no longer had anything to do with *him*.

Or *her*.

And this bolstered me.

They said nothing as we made our way to the stairs to seek the throne room.

Cassius had had a wedding gift made for his bride, of which we had witnessed the giving, something that made Elena trill with laughter and kiss him deeply, even if she finished the kiss by saying, "You didn't have to and I mean that truly. I'll lose my vantage, but I suppose I'll be more comfortable."

And thus, a room that had had very little furniture—a throne on the dais at the front, two sofas set before it—now had one added piece.

An almost identical throne set next to Cassius's.

However, his had silver-painted wood and sky-blue cushions.

But Elena's was a rich mahogany and the material that upholstered it was a golden velvet.

For of course, the sky must have its sun.

It was only in seeing them, I hesitated.

I looked up to Mars. "Do you think they would—?"

"No," he answered shortly.

I pressed my lips together and made my way to the podium.

My husband remained standing while I seated myself in Elena's throne before he took his own seat in Cassius's.

Jorie positioned himself to my right.

"We could delay, call your sisters here," Mars suggested.

"I am fine."

"I would think Tril would wish to be close," Mars remarked.

"She would. She would also be unpredictable," I told him.

Tril had become a devotee of Jorie's, almost as much as she was of Mars.

This, for she loved anyone who loved me.

My mother and not-father and their shenanigans?

Not in the slightest.

"Wife."

I turned my head to him. "Husband."

"I am uneasy, for I cannot read you," he said quietly, studying me intently.

"All my life, she lied to me," I declared. "All my life, she chose him over me. All my life I had a family that, it may have been unwitting, but it cannot be argued, due to her silence, she kept them from me. And I will have her answer to all of that."

His eyes fired.

Jorie muttered, "Absolutely."

I drew in a very deep breath for the umpteenth time that day.

And faced forward.

"A queen does not sit at the edge of her throne," Mars noted gently.

This was good counsel.

I was shifting back, resting my forearms on the arms of the chair, when True strode in, an openly irked Farah at his side, and my mother was trailing them.

I saw she had lost weight. Not to mention, in the time since I'd seen her, which wasn't very long, she looked like she'd aged years.

And her eyes were anxious on me.

I realized then that she was always anxious.

Always worried.

Always fretting.

The only times she didn't seem as such were when she was at her embroidery, at her knitting, or staring vacantly out a window.

Her step stuttered when she noted Jorie.

"Vanka," True said. "Allow me to present you to Jorie, King of the Mer and Silence's brother."

She'd come to a halt between the two sofas before us, her attention fixed on my brother, her expression a mask of shock.

"My...you look...you...*King of the Mer?*" she stammered. Jorie said nothing, but I assumed he indicated his affirmation of this, for Mother said, "You look just like—"

"My father?" he asked.

It took noticeable effort for her to pull herself together, and she didn't completely accomplish it, before she asked, "He is well?"

"As I am king, obviously, he is passed," Jorie stated curtly. "Doing this not knowing he had a daughter."

Her face grew red.

"He would have wished to know this, and he would have wished it very much," Jorie continued.

She straightened her shoulders. "And I would have wished to know he was King of the Mer."

"And how is that important?" Jorie asked.

"How...?" Mother shook her head. "I knew not my daughter was a princess."

"And my father knew not that he had relations with a woman who was intent to use him to impregnate herself to give her sterile husband a child, so perhaps we can call that a draw, hmm?" Jorie suggested.

With that, her gaze shot to me. "Silence—"

"Why?" I asked.

To this, she gave little short shakes of her head. "Why what?"

"This is a pertinent question, for there are many *whys* I could ask," I replied. "Why did you do as he asked? Why did you allow him to treat me the way he did? Why didn't you tell me he wasn't my father so I would understand why he had no use for me? So that maybe I could seek my true father and find, not only him, but also that I had a brother? So that maybe I could know my father before he was gone? So that maybe I could find some love in my life?"

"I loved you," she said meekly.

"You loved him," I returned.

"I loved you." She leaned toward me, "Silence, you must know I loved you."

I did.

Though the love she had for me was not enough.

"Why are you here?" I asked.

"Because you're here," she answered.

"Why are you here without him?"

She looked uncomfortable and did not reply immediately.

But True did.

Lounging on a sofa with his ankle atop his opposite knee, his arm about Farah seated beside him, he said false casually, "She's sued for dissolution of the household, due to adultery, which I've granted. I have as well levied recompense at an amount that would break Bower Manor if your father wasn't in a position to have to hand over his holdings, which he has, and his land and title, which he's done. This latter punishment I imposed considering he committed treason. His title will be held, unrepresented, until your second child is born to which you, continuing as Countess of the Arbor, can bestow on him as Lord of the Arbor, or Lady, if it is a girl."

My head slowly turned to look at Mars.

He was tapping a bored tattoo on the arm of his chair, his eyes on True.

"That was deftly maneuvered," I murmured.

His gaze shifted to me. "Hmm?"

I rolled my eyes and turned my attention again to Mother.

"None of this really explains why you're here," I noted.

"Because you're my daughter."

"And?"

"And I love you and I wished to say how very sorry I am."

"For what?"

This appeared to stymy her.

"I'm tiring of this," Mars growled.

Truth be told, I was as well.

"She is a mighty witch, indeed, my little sister," Jorie proclaimed.

I tipped my head back to look at him to see his silver gaze pinned to my mother.

He carried on.

"In your shame, you cursed her with her name."

My attention jumped back to Mother.

The red was again in her face.

"But she broke your curse, did she not?" Jorie asked. "She made something weak into something strong. She took something void and made it into something beautiful. But this is often the way of things, is it not? A parent, so intent to make a child suffer for their own sins, certain in their hubris that these transfer to the next generation, and when the child doesn't break under their parents' guilt, in my estimation, that is mighty magic, indeed."

Mother tore her gaze from Jorie and looked to me. "I did what your father—"

"You are not Airenzian," Mars cut in. "You had a choice."

"And if I made a different choice, you would not have the woman you so clearly love," she retorted.

"And every time I have been around you, this surprises you," Mars returned coldly. "That I love your daughter. I have always thought it was because you did not think the mindless, rutting Firenz could feel such emotion. But I must wonder if your surprise stemmed from the fact you wondered how your daughter earned it."

Mother gasped.

Mars ignored it.

"Some time ago, Johan and I had a vexing conversation," Mars went on. "I pointed out to him how he had not been a good father. This angered him to the point of action. I see now this was a mistake on my part. It earned me an enemy unworthy of me, which was a bother I did not need in having to deal with his mischiefs. I should have simply ignored him, and he would have gone away. This is what I will advise my wife to do with you."

Mother's head moved as if she'd been slapped.

"Mars," I murmured.

"But *my* wife," Mars continued, now ignoring *me*, "has her own mind. She knows that mind. She voices it. I listen to her. And I accede to her wishes, when they will not cause her harm. And this, I will do with what she decides about you."

The room fell silent.

Mother had her eyes downcast and was looking beaten.

And my anger and grief at the loss of what I should have had but didn't dissipated.

This did not negate the fact that I suffered a loss of what I should have had...

But didn't.

"I went swimming today," I said softly.

Mother lifted her gaze.

"It was so beautiful, swimming with Jorie. Being in The Deep, transformed. Inhabiting a part of me I lived my life never knowing was of me," I shared. "But I always wondered. About so many things that were me."

"I didn't know either, Silence."

"I know," I replied.

Hope filled her face.

"Since he has known me, he has barely left my side," I told her.

"I have noticed your husband's devotion, and am glad for it," she said earnestly.

"I wasn't talking about Mars. I was talking about Jorie," I shared.

She flinched.

"A brother. A *father*," I said.

"I did not know," she stated miserably. "I thought he was naught but a Zee."

"Well, Mother, I have, of late, had the occasion to meet many Zees here in Airen. They fought alongside Cassius and Elena in the Battle of the Heights. They lost people they loved in a cause that is just. They are also amusing and full of life. They are not 'naught but Zees.' But regardless, if they had been of him, they would have been my family."

"You know your father can be—"

"He is not my father."

She shook that off with an actual physical shake of her body.

"I have made some poor decisions," she admitted.

"Do you think?" Jorie murmured.

I threw a look at him over my shoulder.

His expression, when he caught my look, returned a silent "What?"

"But I've always loved you," she persevered.

I turned back to her and brought us full circle.

"Why did you come here, to Airen, to me? From what True says, you are now Mistress of the Arbor, not simply its Lady. And you are this until Mars and I make our second child and he or she is old enough to assume their title. You have means. You have freedom. This land is at war."

"You are here," she repeated.

"And you cannot be alone," I said quietly. "You cannot fend for yourself. You cannot make decisions or keep your own company. You were willing to do anything to keep him so you would not have to do any of this. And now that he is gone, you need me."

I shook my head, feeling many things I did not wish to feel.

Pity for my mother, which was something a child should not have unless that emotion was earned by something that was beyond their parent's control.

Anger that I felt this pity.

And frustration, that she had come here, when all that was happening was happening, and in the midst of it, we could at any time have to face the Beast.

And she had come here so she could deliver the burden of herself on me.

"You are just like Uncle Wilmer," I declared. "You need your life simple and you need someone else to make the decisions and take the responsibility."

She lifted her chin. "My brother is a good man."

"Maybe so," I replied. "And some men might be good, but they should not be kings. And some women might be decent, but they should not be mothers."

"Silence." My name gusted out in a shocked breath.

"You will always have me, Mother. I will always have affection for you, and love. But I am a queen. I have a husband. He will, I hope, give me many children. I will always have responsibilities. You have a place in my life and my home. But I must warn you, you must understand your place. I cannot have the care of you. For you taught me one thing about which I agree. My husband comes first. But Mars taught me something far more important. For he will always come first, and when we make it, so will our family."

With that, I stood and felt Jorie move and Mars unfold out of his chair beside me.

"I think with that, we should be done," I proclaimed. "I will call to a servant to be certain a room is prepared for you. Then I will see you at dinner."

And with a glance to True, who had also stood and was studying me proudly, and Farah, who was smiling encouragingly at me, I wrapped my fingers around my husband's offered arm, and he walked me from the room.

Jorie followed us.

When we had exited, I stopped us and turned to my brother.

"Jorie, I can't—"

He didn't make me finish.

He bent low and kissed my cheek.

When he straightened, he said, "Well done, little sister. I'll see you at dinner."

I nodded.

He gave me a soft smile, turned and walked away.

Without a word, my husband led us to our bedchamber.

I disengaged from him when we were behind closed doors.

He stopped in the middle of the room and crossed his arms on his chest.

I went to the window and stared out at the grazing fields beneath the sheer cliffs outside Sky Bay.

"Silence?" Mars called.

"Was I too cold?" I inquired of the field. "Or should I ask? Should I think on it? Should I question a decision I made? An action I took? A word I uttered? I am queen. I should be decisive."

"If you do not question and consider matters of import, before the doing of them, *mio amore*, as well as after, you will be a very bad queen."

I looked to him, but I did not see him for my eyes were swimming.

And then I was in his arms.

I did not sob.

But I wept.

Mars allowed this for a bit, before he said into the top of my hair.

"You will forgive her, and we will look after her, Silence. All will be well."

I nodded, my cheek brushing against his chest as I did.

"And I understand your struggle," he murmured. "Is it a folly, to point out weaknesses to the weak who are thus, because the effort is futile as they'll never understand? Especially if doing such does harm to ourselves? Or does one persevere in hopes that perhaps they'll one day understand?"

He understood completely.

"Do you know the answer to that?" I asked.

"No. Except you must act on instinct. Which you did. That situation would never be right for her as well as for you. It could be you making it right for her, at the sacrifice of it doing any good for you. You decided not to sacrifice. And that, *mia bellezza*, I believe firmly was the right thing to do."

Of course he would believe that.

He carried on.

"And now my instincts are telling me that my queen must rest, and as such, we will eat abed tonight, this after you nap."

I tipped my head back to look up at him. "Mars—"

He shook his head, knowing what I would say. "She can have a meal with whatever others join her without you providing interference for her to make it easier, or she can call for a tray for herself. Tonight, I'm seeing to my wife in our chambers."

As far as I could tell, his instincts were always right.

And now was no different.

"Thank you, my husband."

"You are welcome, my wife."

I sent him a shaky grin.

He replied by touching his lips to mine.

He guided me to bed.

I flipped off my slippers and entered it.

Mars threw a warm rug over me.

I curled up under it.

And it was my king who went to the cord, called a servant, had my mother seen to, and ordered a tray for later.

As for me.

I was exhausted.

Thus, I fell asleep.

145

THE DRAGONS

Melisse
Riverburn Castle, Seat of Lord Felix Edgar, Gairn Plain
AIREN

The twisting stopped and their feet were on the ground.

She instantly felt that the bitter winter winds that swept up from the sea and whistled through Sky Bay were gone, and the cold here was merely chill.

Melisse looked up to Jorie, who was pulling his trident out of the dirt.

He then glanced about at the four other mermales who were doing the same.

When they all had their staffs in hand, and had jerked their chins up to their king, his eyes came to her.

"We will return," he stated, turned, let fly his javelin, and he disappeared in a whirl about it.

She looked to Lena.

Lena, who another of the mermales had carried from the Bay on two magical throws of their tridents, also looked to her.

In the distance, they heard grunts and a number of thuds, a truncated shout, and in naught but ten minutes, five tridents embedded themselves in the dirt about them, and Jorie and his males had returned.

"The outer guard has been dealt with. I will give watch out here. You have but half an hour," he warned them. "If you do not meet me right here," he pointed with the elaborately—and fearsomely—fashioned end of his pronged staff to the ground, "you will learn what else this can do."

He finished his statement bringing the "this" in front of him—his trident—and circling it twice before he leaned into it, staff end to the earth.

They nodded and quickly stole across the deserted bailey, each witch with a guard of two mermales.

Having made their plan before they left, they knew what they were about.

Thus, after Melisse swung her hand in front of her and they heard the locks open and the bolt slide across on the inside, these to the studded double doors to the castle, they made them, and two of the Mer pushed them open.

They entered.

Without hesitation, Melisse went up the hall.

Lena down it.

She had to magic three guards they encountered to sleep before they arrived at the door of the bedchamber they sought.

It, too, was locked.

She made swift work of opening it, entering, and moving directly to the bed, her guard at her back.

Without hesitation, she swept aside the curtains that held the draughts at bay.

The woman in the bed shot to sitting as if she'd been awake.

For a woman who lived her life, Melisse suspected sleep was rarely easy.

In these times, she doubted the woman enjoyed much of it at all.

"Who are you?" the lady of the manor asked.

Melisse didn't answer.

She asked her own question.

"You have children, yes?"

"I—"

"You have twenty minutes to get dressed, get them dressed, pack anything of importance to you, and make way to the town square. Your dungeons are of the now being emptied of the hostages your husband's men took. I will rouse your servants. Anything, and *anyone*, left in this castle will not exist in an hour."

"The Regent sends the dragons," she whispered in horror.

Melisse opened her mouth to answer to this, but she got not a word out.

The bedclothes flew.

And then the woman flew.

Melisse left the room.

She found the servant's quarters and emptied them by delivering the same message.

She was pleased to note that she did not have to waste precious time convincing anyone.

Some even had bags packed.

By the time she and the two Mer with her had cleared their part of the castle and sauntered out to where Jorie was standing, the exodus had begun.

She noted even the lady of the manor was carrying a rather hefty bag that, in racing after two young boys and dragging a little girl, all clothed warmly, she could not have had time to pack.

Melisse stopped next to Jorie and watched the procession.

Lena was not far behind in joining them.

"Is it empty?" Jorie asked.

She cast her senses through the space.

She then answered, "Nine guards. All unconscious."

"Do we go and wake them?" Lena queried.

"No," Jorie answered. "Come," he grunted.

He then turned and strolled toward the guardhouse.

Melisse and Lena shared a glance before they followed him.

They moved through the guardhouse and across the drawbridge to the other side.

They then walked the short trek into the town.

Hearing the commotion, shutters were open with heads poked out, and doors were ajar with people standing on stoops to watch.

Jorie stopped in the town's square, Melisse and Lena joined him, and the lady of the manor made haste to their position.

"I have conducted a rollcall. All are here, save, my husband's, erm..."

Indeed, they had prepared for this.

It was smart.

And it gave Melisse relief.

"They should have chosen more wisely. Now they are casualties of war," Jorie declared.

"You killed them?" she peeped.

"No," he replied, turned, slammed the shaft of his trident into the turf and then touched it to his forehead before, holding it about three feet from the upper points, he swung it out and up.

A gasp sounded all around as a bright, white-blue burst shot forth from the middle spike and arced high into the night sky, soaring through it.

And soaring, soaring and soaring…

Until the sky swallowed it from sight.

Their signal.

A beacon.

It would reach Sky Bay many miles away.

And then the dragons would come.

"You are Mer," the lady of the manor (Melisse felt certain she'd heard her name was Ellen) whispered in awe.

"No," Jorie replied, turning again to her and looking down his nose at her. "I am King of the Mer."

Her eyes nearly burst from her head.

"The Regent has allied with the King of the Mer?" she wheezed.

"You landed are finally sorting yourselves out," Jorie told her. He then smiled, which made the woman blink, caught in an altogether different form of amazement. "We are back."

"It is not just the landed who have that reaction," Lena leaned into Melisse to mutter. "The mermaids slip all over themselves to gain his attention."

"Why is he not taken?" Melisse asked.

"I am right here, and I can assure you Mer hearing is exceptional," Jorie said.

"Why haven't you found your queen?" Melisse asked him directly.

He raised his brows. "And this is your business because…?"

"I'm simply making conversation until the dragons annihilate the castle," she replied.

He shrugged. "I do not know what I want."

"I am surprised, for you seem altogether decisive to me," Melisse returned.

"Spoken by a Nadirii," he said. "Those who do not wish one wouldn't know. Those who have found them do. This being, in finding a mate, it is not about deciding what you want and then searching for someone who fits it. It is finding her, and realizing she is what you always wanted."

Lena again leaned into Melisse. "He is also known to be exceptionally wise."

Melisse watched as Jorie smiled very slowly.

"Can I touch your trident?"

They all looked down to see a bold little boy of about six years on the earth standing there, staring up at Jorie with a mixture of bravado and terror.

"Who is your true ruler?" Jorie asked.

"The Prince Regent, Cassius of Airen," he replied.

"Do you say this because it is what you think I wish to hear?" Jorie pressed.

The boy looked confused. "No. It's because mama says, thanks be to the gods, the Prince Regent, Cassius of Airen is now our ruler."

"Yes," Jorie tipped his trident slightly out, "you may touch it."

The boy pulled his hand back twice before he struck up the nerve to set his fingertips to the staff.

The instant he did, it glowed a blue-white so bright, Melisse blinked against it as the light filled the square.

The boy jerked his hand back and the glow ceded.

But Melisse knew Jorie was teasing him with the way his mouth was twitching.

"Do I have magic?" the boy asked in wonder.

"Everyone has magic," Jorie answered. "Tomorrow, make your mother laugh. And when you do, watch her do it. Then you will see you have magic."

"Vitus! Come over here!" a woman yelled.

The boy whipped his head around, then whipped it back to Jorie, and said, "I want to be Mer when I grow up."

Jorie smiled and replied, "How about just being a good son for now?"

The child nodded, and it took a second for him to understand Jorie's meaning, and when he did, he raced across the square to his mother.

It was then Melisse saw the area around them had filled and all were gazing to the skies.

She sensed no threat.

None at all.

"It appears you were rather thorough in clearing the guard," she noted.

"A job is not worth doing if the doing of it isn't done well."

"Ah, would that my daughter were a Mer," Lena sighed.

Melisse found to her surprise that she was grinning.

It would take some time, but not much of it, for in preparation, The Drakkar had moved them close, when there was a murmur waving through the crowd.

And then the flapping could be heard in the distance.

But the noise grew eerie, sinister, threatening, as it got closer.

And closer.

Suddenly, she could see.

Frey had sent three, and seeing their huge, dark shapes, webbed wings, long necks and tails, and spiking scales flying through the night sky sent a chill down Melisse's spine.

But when they opened their mouths and rained fire on the castle, she winced and turned her head against the blinding brightness of the orange-red blaze.

The heat wafted toward them so strong, it blew back her hair and made her brace her feet to stay standing.

She heard the calls and shouts of shock and fear all about her.

These along with what sounded like suffocated explosions, as if they began and ended in the blink of an eye.

When the heat ceased as quickly as it came, she opened her eyes to see the dragons rounding in the air to fly back to where they came.

And the village raced to Riverburn Castle.

Much more slowly, Melisse, Lena, Jorie and his males followed them.

Jorie and his trident got them through the crowd to the front.

Indeed, Jorie, with his trident, the crowd parted for them.

And they stood, staring at the three, long, wide, deep craters of scorched earth with their still-glowing embers that used to be Riverburn, but now not even a stone of it remained.

"It is time to return," Jorie decreed.

Lena moved to one of his males and latched onto him.

Melisse took hold of Jorie.

When he had his arm about her waist, Jorie heaved his trident through the air.

And in a whirl, they went with it.

146
THE VISIT

Teddy
The Town of Trevor's Gorge
WODELL

"We will come back to this country, and often, when it is cold, so that we can enjoy drinking this." Faunus lifted his earthenware mug filled with thick liquid chocolate cream. "And eat these." He indicated the pile of pastries in the middle of the table that were laced with white icing, the flaky dough folded over thick, sweet cheese.

He turned a contented, but heating gaze to Teddy.

"And so we can curl up under heavy rugs in the chill of night with needs be to keep as close as possible in order to stay warm."

Teddy enjoyed Faunus's look, but he then shook his head at Saturn in a teasing way that he hoped would take Saturn out of his mood.

It failed.

Saturn scowled at Teddy and reached to the pile of pastries. And although Teddy wasn't counting, he believed that would be Saturn's fifth.

"After you deal with Teddy's arse of a father," Moira put in, munching her own pastry, oblivious to Saturn's mood, and her being the cause of it (that said, it was important to note that she was not oblivious to Saturn by any stretch of the imagination). "We will go to the shops and buy the goat's cheese of this region and some red onion marmalade with some fresh-baked Dellish loaves. Mum, before she died, would splurge on the cheese of Trevor's Gorge for Nippenlas. And because of it, that was always my favorite holiday. We will sup on that and think we've reached the heavens."

Her eyes skittered over Saturn, and she went on to ask him, but in a manner it seemed as if she was asking them all.

"Do you like goat's cheese?"

Faunus and Teddy replied in the affirmative.

Saturn merely grunted.

Moira looked to the table.

Although he did not like seeing his friend downcast and wished to shake by the shoulders his other friend who was making her downcast, this was, to Teddy's way of thinking, an excellent segue.

"And speaking of my father—" he began.

"Yes, speaking of his father, when we see him, can I cave his head in?" Saturn requested of Faunus.

Moira lifted her head and stared at Saturn with wide eyes.

She did this as Teddy beat back the urge to kick him under the table, for he was making no headway in winning her (the reason for his constant scowl) and expressing a tendency toward violence would not aid in this mission.

"I have not decided what we shall do," Faunus decreed. "This is why we sit and drink thick goodness and eat pastries that will make our bellies round instead of going to his farm."

"I would like to state at this point that visiting the Gorge has been a pleasant sojourn," Teddy began. "But I do not think there is any need to see my father before we resume our journey home."

And, in truth, to his surprise, it had been a pleasant sojourn.

He had found that he'd missed this town. The place where he had grown up. Especially the Gorge, somewhere he had gone often, for its beauty gave him succor.

The high, sheer, rugged brown rock covered mostly in fluffy moss leading down to the meandering green of the river, no matter how many times he had done so, it was always breathtaking to see.

And the town they were now in, at the western tip of the gorge, he had always liked, with its thatched buildings and plethora of shops selling all manner of things.

It was not as exciting or sprawling as the Thicket or as popular as The Lights.

But many a Dellish would journey there to see the gorge and then buy their wives filigreed silver-pewter earrings and pendants or purchase rounds of Trevor cheese, while eating in the cafés or sitting in the bakeries and noshing on the pastries.

Teddy found, with his friends around him, it felt nice to come home (of a sort).

But now that he had, he was ready to leave.

"I disagree," Faunus stated flatly.

Teddy opened his mouth to speak again.

But Moira did so before he could, partly to take them off the subject Teddy had introduced, partly for other reasons altogether.

"Tonight, we dine on the delicacies of the Gorge. But when we're in Firenz, I will cook for you," she decreed. And although she appeared anxious when stating her next words, she offered them a shaky, but cheeky grin, her eyes not *quite* falling on Saturn as she did so. "I'm rather good at it, even though I am the only judge I have. The gravy in my stews..."

She broke off only to roll her eyes in ecstasy.

This, as he watched it, causing Saturn to growl low.

And when he did, her startled gaze went to him.

But now, he was glowering at Faunus. "Let us go to deal with Teddy's father and then be away from this place."

"Don't you like it here, Saturn?" Moira asked quietly.

He turned his fierce glower to her and grunted, "No."

"You would not wish to come back for chocolate cream and...and...to erm, cuddle under a rug to beat back the cold?" she pressed.

Saturn repeated his grunt of, "No."

She sat back in her seat, appearing utterly crestfallen.

Oh yes, Teddy wished to shake his very stupid, very blind and seeming very *deaf* friend.

Gods dammit.

"We can journey to Teddy's father," Faunus said slowly, studying Saturn closely.

"Excellent," Saturn bit off.

"I will...I will just..." Moira touched her hair, seeming not to know where to cast her gaze, and then she took up the plate of pastries and said,

"Have them wrap these and send them to our inn. We will eat them for dessert tonight. And then I will freshen up."

She rose from her chair and scurried to the counter.

"What is the matter with you?" Faunus hissed at Saturn when Moira disappeared down a back hall to find the cloakroom.

"I know you are each other's chosen," his gaze pinned Teddy, "but I would request a session this eve where you allow Faunus to fuck me and do this hard and also *repeatedly*."

Faunus leaned into the table toward Saturn.

"You do not need me to fuck you, you need to do a better job at winning," he lifted a hand and jabbed a finger toward where Moira disappeared and finished, "*her*."

"She barely knows I exist."

"She is skittish as a doe around you," Faunus retorted. "You terrify her, and yet she's so desirous of falling on your cock, she can barely function. She nearly fell into the gorge, for watching how you would react to seeing it, she so hoped you'd like it. She does not wish to cook for *Teddy and me*, she wishes to cook for *you* and for *you* to think she does well at it. And she is Dellish and this is Dellish," he swung his hand out, "and she wishes you to like this for liking *this*, and the bloody cheese she enjoys so damned much that her mother bought for their festival, is akin to liking *her*. But are you indicating any of this, *amico*? Fuck...*no*."

Saturn appeared thunderstruck.

"He is right," Teddy put in a lot less irately, and Saturn looked to him. "Faunus told her you fancied her. And although that conversation was rife with a number of other things, since then, a woman I have not known long, but in the time I've known her, she is rarely unsure of herself, has been oftentimes awkward. Other times jumpy as a cat. And others, so hesitant in her manner, it is difficult to witness."

"Why is she these things if she wants my cock?" Saturn asked.

Teddy stared at him.

Faunus answered.

"She is not a bold Firenz female who is raised to understand her desires...and communicate them. She is Dellish, Saturn. And not long ago, she witnessed woman after woman violated before they were put to death. But look about you," he urged. "In all our time here, have you seen a single man as tall as you, or as built, save me?"

Saturn looked about him, even though it was the middle of the day, and there were not many around to look at.

Teddy still felt certain he'd take Faunus's point.

"You are handsome, or I would not fuck you," Faunus went on. "Nyx would not enjoy watching you get fucked. And all the varied males and females you take would not relish the same. But *Moira* might actually be virgin. And as the act she witnessed has naught to do with the beauty shared in intimacy, she might now be confused about it and in turn terrified of you, at the same time attracted to you, and along with your manner, you are causing her confusion and shaking her assurance."

"I knew this, this was why, at first, I kept my distance," Saturn stated. "But she is most affectionate, in her playful way with Teddy, and now also you, but not me."

"This is because she wants Teddy and my affection, but she wants that *and more* from you," Faunus returned.

Saturn slowly sat back in his chair.

"You do know," Teddy told him, "that if you are just you, loyal and good-natured, amusing and protective, she would have no option but to fall deep for you. She has seen the worst in men, and you are the opposite. But you aren't giving her that."

"She approaches," Faunus muttered.

Teddy stopped talking.

Saturn's head tipped back to look up at her when she came to stand by their table.

"Shall we go?" she suggested.

"You are most beautiful," Saturn declared.

Teddy sat stunned.

Moira's eyes jumped to him.

"You have perfect skin that I want my hands and mouth and tongue on," Saturn continued. "*Everywhere.*"

Oh gods.

"Fucking hell," Faunus whispered.

"And the smell of your hair makes my cock hard," Saturn carried on.

"Saturn," Teddy murmured urgently.

Saturn did not heed him.

"And I could listen to the sound of your voice all day. It fills me with pride, as we journey, and you try to learn my tongue from Teddy and Faunus, so you can speak to my people when you arrive in your new home."

Well, that was better.

For good, or worse, Saturn wasn't finished.

"In saying this, what I wish you to know is that you do not have to fear me, *tata*. Not only would I never harm you, I would kill a man a thousand times who tried, and I desire you greatly. You are not only beautiful to look at, you have spirit and fire and affection, and when we make love, I will make you explode for me again and again and again."

The table was deathly silent when Saturn stopped speaking.

But it was only Saturn who did not seem to have taken in the feel of it.

He stood, scraping back his chair, and Teddy nearly shot out of his seat to stop him when he seized Moira's hand, twisted their arms up so she was forced to press herself to his side, her head tilted far back to continue to hold his eyes, through all this her lips remained parted.

And he went on.

"We will wait until you are ready to lie with me. Though I would hope, in the waiting, you would allow me to kiss you and touch you and make you climax with my fingers or my mouth so you would be aware of all I will give to you when you finally have my cock. Until then *I* will teach you your new tongue. And Faunus and Teddy have impressed upon me that it is important to you to know that I very much like goat's cheese, and I very much look forward to eating it with you tonight."

After delivering that, he turned his attention to Teddy.

"Now we go deal with your father so we can have that unpleasantness done, eat cheese and on the morrow, journey home."

And with no further ado, pulling Moira with him, they walked to the door.

As they did, Moira looked back with an expression on her face that was a mixture of dumbfounded, afraid...

And excited.

"I don't know whether to laugh or charge after them and save her from Saturn's version of courting," Teddy told the door they'd disappeared through at which he was still looking over his shoulder.

"You told him to be him, *bello*," Faunus reminded him, and Teddy swung his head around to look at his lover. "He is being him. If she does not like it, she will either tell us, or we will sense it, and one of us will intervene. But she did not fight at all, the walking out of this place on his arm." He grinned. "So, I am thinking good thoughts."

Teddy was thinking good thoughts too.

Thus, he smiled.

"Now," Faunus began to push out of his seat, "we go deal with your father."

. . .

AND AT THAT, he was no longer thinking good thoughts.

Thus, he frowned.

~

TEDDY HAD LEARNED MUCH LIVING with Lorenz and Nyx.

One of the things he had learned was that, when you loved someone, and it was clear they were intent to do something they felt they needed to do, even if you didn't want them to do it, you let them.

And all right, there were occasions when Nyx did not do this with a great deal of grace.

But this was only about things she very much disagreed, like Teddy putting his life on the line to become a spy.

Other than that, if there was something in Lorenz that needed it, she gave it.

And Lorenz did the same.

He and Faunus had hardly begun to become what they were becoming when Faunus had declared he would do what he was now intent to do in the event of that becoming.

And as they rode ever closer to the farm where his father raised some sheep, and some goats, and alternated the fields over the years to grow wheat that was milled in town, seeing familiar landmarks he had not seen in years, and had thought he would never see again, he did what he had seen Nyx do. And Lorenz.

He kept his mouth shut and let the man he loved go about doing what he needed to do.

The day was growing late, the sun having begun its descent from the sky, and as Teddy knew from helping his father in his work, the day started early, in the dark, and ended early, when the darkness came again. Especially in the winters.

And then in you went for a hearty meal to begin to rejuvenate the vast amounts of energy you expended in the day. Then shortly after, you slept so you could finish that effort.

Thus, not long after they rode up the lane and dismounted, hanging about in wait, Teddy caught his father approaching from the north field.

His sire did not look happy to have visitors, but then he had never been a jovial man.

Life was toil, the earning of money from that, an occasional evening trip to visit the pub in town and listen to music, if it was on offer, while you drank your ale.

And not much else.

Thinking on this, Teddy found he was like his father in that respect.

He wanted a simple life.

He had had adventures, not entirely of his choice.

They were, until very recently, not enjoyable.

Thus, once he returned to Firenze, he wished naught but to embrace Nyx and Lorenz, settle Moira, settle himself with Faunus, teach his children at the school and spoil the ones Lorenz eventually gave to Nyx.

His father's step faltered, and his expression grew astonished when he noted Teddy in the midst of his party.

And then Teddy watched his face grow hard.

He waited until he was close before he called, "In the company of Firenz warriors after alliance. What's the poof done now?"

The instant fury seething from Faunus (and Saturn, not to mention Moira), made Teddy whisper, "Calm."

"I am Faunus, of the Trusted of the King of Firenze," Faunus decreed.

His father's chin shot back into his neck as he came to a stop a few feet away from them.

"And this is Saturn of the Trusted," he went on, indicating Saturn.

Saturn didn't move. Just stared at Teddy's father.

"And we escort Moira, of the Lesser Thicket, unblooded sister to your son," he stated.

Moira wore an openly contemptuous expression.

Teddy's father's head ticked as he glanced at her before he returned his attention to Faunus.

"We are here to inform you we return to Firenze, taking your son with us," Faunus continued.

"Like I said, what's he done now?" Hans Swensson asked.

"We are in Wodell on the mission of saving him after he was abducted by leaders of The Rising. This after Tedrey acted valiantly and was instrumental in the bringing down of the radicals," Faunus declared.

His father's eyes grew large.

"Unfortunately, we were unable to find him before the men who had taken him also abducted a large number of women. If you have not yet heard of it," Faunus said, "I have no doubt you eventually will. They were massacred up north. Only seven survived. And those seven survived because your son was able to free himself of his bonds, and at great peril to himself, he saved them all."

Hans turned his astonished gaze to Teddy.

"He returns to Firenze a hero of Firenze, a hero of Wodell, and as such, before we began our journey to here, he was King True and Queen Farah's guest at Birchlire Castle," Faunus carried on.

"By the gods," his father murmured.

"This is the man your son became," Faunus declared. "Thus, you have the gratitude of two nations."

At that, in surprise, all eyes shot to Faunus, even Teddy's.

Faunus did not take his attention from Hans.

"For if you had not turned him out due to the flaw in your soul," Faunus continued. "A flaw no man should have, and certainly no father, he would have been here, at work with you in your fields, unable to do the deeds he did to bring peace and save lives. Fortunately, he was not and the peoples of two realms, and specifically seven very grateful women and their families, are indebted to him."

Faunus then bowed low toward Hans.

"Tedrey," his father whispered, and Teddy looked to him.

Hans's skin had slightly paled, but his eyes were brightening with pride.

Faunus's voice sounded, regaining both a son and his father's attention.

"You should know, as Tedrey is a particular friend to the Captain of the Trusted and his wife, and they have grown to know him very well, that Mars, King of the Firenze, and your King True, are aware of your betrayal of your flesh. And although your son has great humility, and will probably have some difficulty in accepting the praise of kings and the rewards they will wish to bestow on him, it will be made clear to them that you had naught to do with this outside causing him to learn how to be extraordinary by surviving your cruelty."

Hans's body jolted.

"I—" his father began.

But he stopped when Faunus's hand came up.

"Your words are uninvited, but even if you spoke them, they would mean nothing. As you mean nothing. You are incidental in a man's learning to be a survivor. I am here as the one who loves him. I am here as the man who has given him my heart, to share with you the depth of your profound mistake, so you can think on that until you rest on your pyre."

Clearly finished, Faunus turned, his mantle swinging about his shoulders, and his gaze came to Tedrey.

"Now, we can go home."

And with that, he strode to his horse.

Teddy didn't follow him for Moira's voice took his attention to where she stood, Saturn close to her back, within inches of his father.

"I am one of those women he saved," she declared.

Tedrey jumped and his father flinched and took a step away as she spat in his face.

Directly, she moved away, Saturn following her.

He watched as his father slowly lifted a hand to swipe the spittle from his face, and Moira and Saturn came up beside him, Moira taking Teddy's hand.

"Let us go, Teddy," she urged.

He just stood there, staring at his sire.

"Teddy," Faunus called from where they had left their horses.

Father and son looked into each other's eyes.

His father opened his mouth to speak.

But he didn't, for Teddy said, "How odd. I feel nothing."

The man looked struck.

Moira tugged on his hand. "Good. Then let us go."

He turned to her.

Saturn was correct.

She had lovely skin.

And her voice was beautiful.

He curled his fingers around hers and allowed her to guide him to his horse.

Faunus was already mounted.

Teddy didn't hesitate to swing up in the saddle.

Saturn assisted Moira then he swung up in his own.

Faunus was the first to put his heels to his steed and the horse raced down the lane with Teddy following him, Moira following Teddy, and Saturn taking the rear.

They made the road and headed toward Trevor's Gorge.

Not a one of them looked back.

147

THE RECKONING

Jellan
Sky Citadel, Sky Bay
AIREN

Jellan was taken aback.

He thought it would be much more difficult, especially in a time of war, to gain access to the Citadel and an audience with the Regent.

But he had given his name at the guardhouse at the bottom of the lane, the guard had looked at him, allowed him into the structure to sit by their small fire (for which he was thankful, northern Airen by the sea was shockingly chill), and asked him to wait.

Another guard had cantered up the lane on his horse, only to canter back down in what could be naught but half an hour.

To which he had spoken quietly with the man who was in the guard-house with Jellan.

That guard came to him, and he said, "His Grace awaits you at the Citadel. Please remount your horse. The corporal will guide you there."

And now, there he was.

The guard who had guided him to the Regent's palace was sweeping open the grand doors to the Citadel, and Jellan was walking through.

Easy as that.

He nearly smiled to himself, and would have, if he did not have to assume an air of urgency in heroically escaping the Beast and sharing with them the creature walked amongst them.

But it was difficult to force it down.

He had sat a number of diplomatic tables, and he was a well-known Go'En of the Go'Doan.

But truly, he did not expect this quick reception.

The door barely closed behind him, and he was blinking in some shock at the massive spray of colorful gladiolus atop a handsome table that adorned the always severe, and even grim (to Jellan's opinion on the décor) entryway of the Sky Citadel, when he heard the quick staccato clip of boots hitting stone.

He looked in that direction to see Macrinus, Cassius's closest lieutenant, approaching, alongside him Hera, Elena's captain.

Dismissing Hera and watching Macrinus, Jellan thought, *Ah, but it is good to again be amongst the Airenzian.*

His dead lover Rupert had been Airenzian, with his tall, muscular body and his thick cock.

Airenzian, like the Firenz and Go'Doan, had little problem with male on male lovers. Though they were quieter about it than the Firenz.

It was female on female lovers that had been outlawed many years ago.

Jellan wondered, without much interest, in the sweeping change that the Regent was making that they'd heard much news of in their meanderings, if Cassius had put a stop to that law as well.

He then ceased wondering this as he noticed Hera move her arm out then in, to rest her hand on her stomach, just as he felt an odd chill, as if he was under a warm blanket, and someone had tugged it off.

"G'Jell," Macrinus greeted shortly, and the hall might no longer look severe and grim, but Macrinus's expression was.

Hera appeared even less inviting.

He shook the curious feeling he'd had aside as naught but a draught and focused on Cassius's man.

"Macrinus," he replied. "I am most grateful for a swift audience with the Regent. I have come from a—"

"You'll have your say," Macrinus cut him off to state oddly. "For the now, come with me, be quiet, and your turn will come where you will be heard."

It was with some surprise that Jellan abruptly found himself staring at

Macrinus's and Hera's backs after they'd turned and prowled away, and he had to hop to in order to follow them.

If he was correct with the direction they were taking, the two lieutenants were leading him to the throne room.

An odd choice for Cassius, though it wouldn't have been for Gallienus.

Gallienus was all about pomposity.

Jellan had thought Cassius would be far more informal.

However, as he approached, he saw the doors to the throne room were open, and he could hear some business was being discussed within.

This must be the reason why Cassius was there.

Still walking, Hera twisted to him before they arrived at the doors and ordered, "When you enter, you will remain at the back. You'll be called forward when it's your time to speak."

He looked from her to the man with her who was also gazing back at him.

"Macrinus, my journey has been long and arduous. If I could—" he began to ask after refreshments, which frankly should have been offered without being asked.

But Macrinus turned away from him, disappeared into the throne room, Hera with him, leaving Jellan to enter alone, with no fanfare, no announcement of his presence, nothing.

Odd, disrespectful and peeving.

He did not know Macrinus that well, or Hera at all (she was very quiet and circumspect, unlike her fellow captain, who was bawdy and oftentimes annoying), but it had been Jellan's impression Macrinus was always rather irreverent, something Cassius not only put up with, he was much that way himself.

And Jellan considered, if these men weren't so pleasing to look upon, it would have been irritating.

Fortunately for them, they were pleasing to look upon.

This thought swept from his head as he entered the room, took in its occupants, and came to a swaying halt at experiencing at once all he surveyed.

For on the podium in the front, sitting in thrones side by side, were Cassius and Elena.

But also, to Cassius' left, sat Mars and Silence.

To their left, sat True and Farah, though in between True and Silence sat a large, striking man with black hair that Jellan had never seen before.

And to Elena's right, sat Aramus and Ha-Lah.

Through the people standing about the room, Jellan could just see Princess Serena seated at the step up to the podium, close to her sister's feet.

Serena had one foot to the floor, leg bent, one foot to the dais, that leg bent as well, her forearm resting atop that knee, and her eyes, as well as the attention of all the others, was on the man standing on the floor before the thronal platform.

As he had their backs, Jellan couldn't tell if he knew many of the people in the room, however he had been in that room before, and he was again stunned at the change of it with its carpets and pennants—and everywhere you looked—*color*.

However, as great a change as this was, it barely registered on him for Gallienus, in a tatty, loose, ill-fitting, and not all that clean outfit of matching pants and tunic of nondescript color was apparently in full bluster.

"Stop," Cassius demanded of his father before Jellan had heard a word the ill-kempt king was saying. "You committed multiple acts of treason against your own realm."

Jellan blinked rapidly.

"And naught you're saying is giving me reason not to take your head," Cassius finished.

Take his head?

By the gods.

Cassius turned his attention to someone else standing before him that Jellan could not see.

"Your castle is gone," he stated. His gaze went to someone else Jellan couldn't see. "Your manor is gone." Another shift from Cassius. "And your keep. I'll not have any universities or hospitals if things keep going at this rate. My peoples are in awe of the show of the dragons, but really, I tire of it. It is time to move on. But if we must, you've seen the list. The guards who were assisting you at the Bailey have been apprehended and now grace their own cells. We know the name of every lord who sat council in Dunlyn against me. The dragons will fly, but I'll also be forced to send word to the executioner to sharpen his blade."

"You have my capitulation," one of the men Jellan could not see at the front called.

"That's all well and good, Lord Jordy, but in the now you have no home, you have no militia, and you are but one of twenty-seven names on that list." Cassius's gaze swept the front of the assembly. "I want a surrender signed by all of you, as well as every man on that list, with every member of your armies denouncing their lords and swearing fealty to me, and then I will accept capitulation."

"And after that we face Slán Bailey for life, and for our sons...what?" Another man from the front asked. "You've obliterated my home. Taken my land. I leave him nothing. That keep your dragons eradicated had been in my family for twelve generations."

"Well, then I hope your son has acquired some skill, or does so in future, so he can feed himself," Cassius replied.

"Is it *that* difficult to consider instituting your changes in a lengthier manner to allow all, gentry and laborer alike, to become used to one in order to be better prepared for the next?" another man asked.

"This is wise advice," Cassius relented, to a feeling of not a small amount of relief sweeping from the front of the room.

Sadly for them, Cassius hadn't finished speaking.

"The issue I have with it is twofold, for I have gentry who are not at odds with this and have offered coin to the crown to keep their holdings as well as extended all manner of employment to their vassals, for which they will now pay them a fair wage. They do understand that their lives will change, but they're bloody fucking wealthy, couldn't eat through the coin they have in five generations, unless they suffer grave amounts of stupidity, and are keen for the challenge in discovering different ways to keep their coffers topped up."

When no one had a response to this, Cassius carried on.

"Secondly, for laborer or merchant, soldier or sailor, nothing changes. Laborers will simply keep the coin they earn from their endeavors, rather than paying much of it to a lord who owns the land they work who thinks it's their due. So, really, it is a small minority of my citizenry who has to grow accustomed to a new way of doing things. And as what I ask is not very difficult to come to grips with, I don't see any reason to draw it out."

"We are simply asking for the concession of keeping our own bloody holdings and *homes*," another man spat. "And frankly, this is beyond a fair concession to request."

Cassius's entire demeanor changed when he retorted harshly, "It would have been, if you hadn't killed Jasmine. If Antonius had not fallen to your men's swords. If in the night, Rosehana still warmed her lover's bed. If I did not return Otho's body to his family for burial after it was desecrated and decayed, and I had to speak to his father to be certain his mother didn't unbind him to witness what had become of his remains. I could utter many a name of one who was lost, one who was loved, one who is mourned, and this blame, I assign where it is due. On *you*."

Well then, this must be why Macrinus and Hera appeared so dour.

Jasmine, Otho and Antonius had fallen.

And if he was not wrong, Hera's lover's name was Rosehana.

Grave loss for the Regent.

And shockingly stupid of the gentry.

Truly, with the way Cassius Laird had mourned the loss of his first wife, how could they not know they should not earn this manner of his ire?

"Now," Cassius continued, "I'll have your full capitulation, or I'll not only have your homes and holdings, I'll have your heads. Speak to your fellow conspirators. Given the flight of a raven and back, you have five days. If you do not offer your surrender then, I...will...*take it*."

Jellan then watched as the Regent turned his head to the side and spoke on.

"Get them out of my sight," he said to a guard. "And as for my father, after the ravens fly, he sees no one, he speaks to no one. Windowless cell. Malcontent's rations."

"I will not hesitate to take *your* head!" Gallienus stormed as a guard came forth to take hold on him and drag him out.

"You are beaten, fool," Cassius retorted. "And you were before you even began."

"We shall see!" Gallienus yelled as, wrists and ankles in chains dragging the carpets, chains that Jellan did not see with Gallienus's back to him, the fallen king was hauled unceremoniously from the room.

Jellan stood where he was and observed, as the others, dressed the same as Gallienus, chained the same, were escorted out as well.

He then saw Macrinus approach Cassius and bend to speak into his ear.

Cassius nodded and called, "G'Jell, you may come forward."

Instantly, Jellan moved down a center aisle that was kept clear, apparently for comings and goings, and as he walked swiftly toward the dais, he cast his gaze about, and saw no one he knew.

No Go'Doan priests.

No gentry.

Though there were a number of Zees, which was unexpected.

Indeed, it appeared most of them were Zees.

Most unexpected.

He could not wonder about this.

He was hungry. He needed food. A bath. A good sleep.

And then...regroup.

"Your Grace, Prince Cassius," he greeted as he came to stand between two sofas, both of them vacant, and dipped his chin into his neck. He lifted his head and caught the prince's eyes. "I am most grateful to be here. I am also *most* grateful to you for welcoming me into your home so swiftly. For I have just survived a daunting adventure regarding which I needs make haste in reporting to you."

"Indeed, I am all ears," Cassius replied.

Excellent.

"It has been some days since I've eaten, thus, before I begin, could I trouble you to order up some food?" he requested.

"I thought you needed to make haste in reporting?" Cassius asked.

"Well, I...yes, of course, however..." He gestured to the sofa beside him. "My journey was arduous. May I sit?"

"No."

Jellan's spine straightened, and of a sudden, he paid much closer attention to Cassius, and the people who sat amongst him.

They were not friends of Jellan's, but they were allies, and he had thought he had their regard.

He was a priest of the Go'Doan.

He was called upon to...

Ah.

"I am not of The Rising," he assured them.

"This is a lie," Cassius replied.

Jellan blinked.

"Are we to wait long for the story of your adventure?" Cassius prompted when Jellan lost his voice. "For the lot of us have things to do, and if you wish to draw this out, I'm in the position to tell you that you will fail. We'll just deal with you and carry on."

"Deal with me?" he asked softly.

Cassius's head tipped to the side. "Did you or did you not kill Sofia Magos of the Firenz with the intent to kill Farah Magos of the Firenz, now Farah, Queen of Wodell?" Cassius queried, and Jellan's heart started to beat a quick tattoo as his attention cut to Farah.

She was regarding him with hatred in her eyes.

But worse, when his gaze shifted to King True...

By the gods...

He had never...

Not ever...

Seen the like.

True's eyes on Jellan were *green*.

Not the green they normally were.

Overtaken with the color, no white to be seen.

Jellan took a step back, ran into something, and jerked his head about to look over his shoulder.

A wall of men stood behind him consisting, he noted with a sinking stomach, of lieutenants from three separate realms.

That sinking stomach clutched, and his throat closed.

He turned back to Cassius.

"I-I'm sorry," he forced out. "I do not know what you mean."

"All right. I'll ask another question," Cassius said. "Did you, or did you not, infiltrate a group known as the Society of the Beast, participate in the seizure, rape and murder of countless women over several decades, doing this conspiring to surface the Beast in order to control it for the purposes of The Rising?"

Oh gods.

Jellan leaned toward the Regent, his mind racing.

"This is...this is what you must know. It was not me. It was a woman named Marian. But the Beast is risen. He is amongst us."

Jellan would have said more but Cassius's gaze shifted to the side, and he said, "I know."

Jellan looked in that direction and stood solid when he saw five men had moved to the front of the crowd at that side.

The highwaymen.

He pointed at them.

"Those men set upon me to steal my purse!" he cried. "They are highwaymen!"

"I must admit, I had my suspicions, but as I have no evidence..." Cassius muttered, sounding amused.

Jellan's attention whipped back to him.

"You must listen to me," he begged.

"Do you deny any of this?" he asked.

"Yes!" Jellan shouted. "All of it! I must tell you of Marian."

"Marian? G'Ry's acolyte who's gone missing?"

This question came from Farah.

"Yes, my queen." He nodded repeatedly, not knowing if this was true, but willing to say anything to sound important to them. "It is *vital* you listen to what I have to say. The Beast—"

"Has great claws that can sever a man's head and great strength that he can crush one. He can also transform from looking like simply a man, a fair-haired, blue-eyed one, to his real incarnation."

It was Mars that spoke this.

How did they know so very much?

The priests and those girls who had gotten away.

They must have discovered them.

"Yes." Jellan nodded fervently. "He is fearsome and conniving. He can act guileless, but he is not. It is falsity. He...he...also *bleeds*," he shared, turning to the highwaymen. "When they set upon us, they used their whips." He looked back to the podium. "They made him bleed."

"And now he wanders about the countryside of Airen with a woman," Aramus remarked.

"Yes." Jellan continued nodding. "She is...not to be trusted. And he is, I do not know. I think he searches for something."

"But you know not what?" Aramus asked.

Jellan did not wish to, but he shook his head.

And then his mind tripped upon an idea.

"But I think he is...he has some *affection* for her. As well as...as well as..." He swallowed. "*Me*. They think I am lost. A fright my horse took when we were set upon by the highwaymen. This I maneuvered in order to escape. I took a grave risk in order to come to you and warn you that the quakes were as we suspected. That it is good the prophesied are at full strength. And...p-perhaps, I-I could be used to...to lure him, to...to...bring him to you so that maybe you can use these dragons of which you speak—"

"Rest assured, G'Jell, we will be utilizing everything we have to eradicate this creature from Triton," Cassius told him.

Jellan nodded again.

"Except you," Cassius finished.

Jellan stood frozen before them.

He also felt his bladder begin to loosen when Cassius's eyes became what True's were.

Except black.

"How many women was it, in the end?" he asked softly. "Do you even know?"

"It was not the Society who roused the Beast!" Jellan exclaimed. "It was Marian! The sacrifices...the terrible things they did to those girls...it was not that. It was *her*."

"So, you know of the sacrifices?" Cassius asked.

Gods damn it!

If this did not get better, he might have to expose his magic to get him out of this place.

"I read it in a tome," he only partly lied, but went on to fully do just that. "When...when we journeyed to Wodell for King True's wedding, I remembered the reading of them. I had an idea. I went to inspect. Came upon them performing their ghastly ritual—"

"You are aware that lying will not change matters for you, no?" Mars asked.

"I do not lie!" he cried. "And I am here to help. I know what he looks like. I know where they wander."

"As do they," Mars pointed out, indicating the highwaymen.

Gods damn it!

He started to call upon his magic, just in case.

"They don't know where they wander," he pushed.

"They are good trackers. They will find out," Cassius said.

His eyes were back to normal, as were True's.

But even so, Jellan did not get the sense this indicated good things for him.

"I am a priest of the Go'Doan," he stated.

"You are a priest of The Rising," Cassius stated in return. "A priest who murdered countless women, one of them the mother of a queen, and conspired to subjugate citizens of four realms to your beliefs."

"I cared naught about *The Rising*," he spat.

After all he'd witnessed, all he'd endured, being repeatedly raped, watching the deaths, experiencing the fear, the maltreatment, something inside him snapped, and he could not control his words or emotion, even if he had tried.

But he no longer had it in him to try.

He drew upon his magic as he asked, "What man needs religion when he controls omnipotence?"

"So, it is solely for you, you sought to rise him," Queen Ha-Lah spoke for the first time.

"I go about the unpleasant business of bringing him forth, why would I hand him over to others?" he asked snidely. "Especially for them to use it to force people to serve their paltry gods. If you have that power, you *are* a god."

"And Marian?" Elena also entered the conversation. "Does she desire to control omnipotence?"

"The bloody *fool*, a half-trained witch who convinced herself she's powerful when she doesn't even know how to read *the veil*," he snapped. "She simply wanted the rituals to stop. But he liked her, so he took her and now he'll use her as he sees fit before he destroys the lot *of you*."

This was met with silence.

Jellan found himself breathing heavily.

And as he did, he realized he'd been calling on his magic, but...

It wasn't there.

"You might wish to know at this juncture, Hera bound you when she met you downstairs," Cassius said.

Jellan blinked and tried to pull up his power again.

He could not access it.

Her movement, with her arm.

The chill he felt.

His stomach clutched so violently, he feared he'd be ill.

He then watched as Cassius slouched in his chair, stretched his long legs before him, and crossed them at ankles.

The Regent then linked his fingers over his flat stomach.

"There is a man," he began, as if he were settling in to tell a story. "Most odd. Here in Sky Bay."

Jellan glared at him.

"When Mars's men's reports started coming in, I remembered talk of him," Cassius shared.

"If you are to jail me, jail me," Jellan ordered tersely. "At least if you did that, I'd be closer to a meal."

"He collects snakes."

Jellan froze, his mind doing the same, to the point he did not feel the warm trickle running down his leg.

Cassius's gaze dropped to the floor, and his lip curled before it came back to Jellan's face.

"True's men have made inquiries, just in case," Cassius told him. "Just in case we were to find you, or you were to seek us. This man, he has never seen his pets at work. He was quite keen to be of service, if he were called."

The room filled with the noises of the air rapidly going in and out of Jellan's nose.

"It might not be of interest to you, but Mars wishes to keep you alive," Cassius informed him.

Jellan's gaze jumped to Mars before returning to Cassius when he spoke again.

"He felt, if we were to lose anyone else who had meaning to us, that you should be breathing so we could share with you the fullness of our ire. True, however, disagrees. And although you committed at least one crime on Firenz soil, you committed incalculable on Dellish. Thus, we've decided True gets to do what he wishes to you," Cassius concluded.

Cassius then turned his head in True's direction.

"True?" he prompted.

"Is there somewhere he can start digging his own pit?" True asked.

"I'm sure we can figure something out," Cassius muttered.

"Then let us do that without delay," True decreed.

Jellan closed his eyes.

There seemed a great rustling and he again opened them to see all about him shifting.

"He can clean up his piss before you take him to the dungeon," Cassius said to someone behind him. "I won't have Elena's carpets sullied."

"Right," he heard a man grunt.

Then he was pushed to his hands and knees, the puddle on the rug right in front of his face.

"Don't move. We'll get you soap and a brush."

He heard footfalls on the rugs all around him. Murmurings of conversation.

But in the end, he was left in the room, on his hands and knees, staring at a puddle of his own piss, with a guard standing over him, chatting casually with each other.

This before he was scrubbing up that piss.

And this was before he was tossed, without a bath, or a meal, into a cell without a pillow or pallet, in the dungeon of the Sky Citadel.

AND THIS WAS BEFORE, quite some time later, indeed, late the next day, under a light fall of snow, Jellan stood at the bottom of a deep pit he'd spent hours digging himself.

When they started raining on him, he vaguely noted they were not all emerald oil asps.

But several of them were.

He felt the pain of the bites, the poison searing through his system.

But the last three thoughts he had before he died was that he wished they were not gazing down on him from above.

It was humiliating.

Though at the very least, in the end, he was the manner of a man who endured such under the eyes of four kings.

He further wished they'd only selected venomous ones.

For the serpent squeezing him about his neck was utterly terrifying.

148

THE TWIST

Marian
Argyll Forest
AIREN

Marian felt the buzzing.

And she knew.

They were getting close.

It had snowed in the night.

Thus, when he woke her and forced her from under their warm rug and made her move her limbs that had frozen stiff while she slept in order to make her climb atop their steed in the pre-dawn morning, the light dusting of snow that had fallen several days before and had not gone away in this cold had become a thick blanket.

She had not appreciated this at all, for after their encounter with the highwaymen, they no longer sought the warmth of inns of an evening. Nor hot meals.

Thus, she had also woken with a chilled-numb nose, fingers and toes.

And gone to bed after eating a rabbit he'd killed for her that she'd roasted over their fire.

She had grown to become glad for the rabbits, for at times it had been but rats.

For his meals, Daemon did not wait for her to go through the painstaking process of roasting the meat.

He ate what he killed raw.

But she knew now, she did not have the luxury to lament her plight.

And she had long since ceased complaining, and not because it fell on deaf ears, but because the creature who was her companion terrified her to her core.

Neither of these mattered any longer, however.

For she felt the buzz.

His quickening.

And she was not prepared.

She had not come up with a plan to stop him.

And if she did not, all would be lost.

$\sim$

Chu of the Trusted
Guest Bedchamber, Sky Citadel, Sky Bay
Airen

Chu woke her with a kiss on her neck.

He'd lit a lamp low on the other side of the bed so the light would not hurt her eyes, but he could watch them flutter as she gained consciousness.

Mm, those copper eyelashes.

Watching them, his hand went from where it was shaking her hip, down and *in*.

He toyed with her clit and she arched her neck.

"Chu," she whispered sleepily.

"They amass," he shared.

And he felt his lips curl as her head immediately turned, all business.

"My master teases," she griped.

"My mouse walks, talks, breathes and *sleeps* a tease," he returned.

Her eyes did a roll.

He removed his finger from her nub and leant in to touch his lips to hers.

When he pulled away, he ordered, "Up. We must position."
She nodded.
Chu exited the bed one way.
His princess went the other.

Reginald, Royal Warden
Slán Bailey, Sky Bay
Airen

His, as well as six other pairs of boots, echoed on the stone steps as they jogged down the stairs.

Reginald made the lower hall, turned right and saw them loitering about outside the open door to a cell.

All the men except one, who was on his arse on the floor, his back to the wall beside the open door, holding a bloodied cloth to his head, rivulets of red that had not been wiped up marring the ink he had chosen to tell his story on the left side of his face.

Reginald walked swiftly toward them and the guards milling about stepped away from the door, and in doing such, none of them met his eyes.

He said nothing as he went to the doorway of the cell.

There he stopped.

Looked.

And then drew in a deep breath.

King Gallienus lay motionless on his blood-soaked pallet, his throat an open maw.

Reginald followed the trail of the crimson which had dripped to the floor and run across it, nearly reaching the door.

He looked down and left.

The guard on his arse was struggling to take his feet.

"Stay seated," Reginald grunted before he turned. The first man he saw, he ordered, "Get him to the bloody infirmary."

That guard nodded and moved.

Reginald then caught the eyes of the next man. "She was found in the room?"

"She was not. She was sitting in the hall with our man, holding a kerchief to his head. The bloody blade at her side," the man answered.

"Where is she now?"

"She is above. In...in..." the guard stammered.

"Spit it out, man," Reginald said between his teeth.

"In the visitor's lounge."

Of course she was.

He made a move to leave and kept doing it even when another guard called, "Should we send a messenger to the Regent?"

"I will report this to him myself," Reginald answered, not looking forward to that and turning to the steps, alighting them, and not wasting time on his way to the visitor's lounge.

There were two guards outside it, both of whom stood straighter and dipped their chins when Reginald came to the door.

He opened it and entered.

Inside the room, a table sat, bolted to the floor, iron loops in it as well as in the stone of the floor on which to lock chains. There were also four chairs, one on one side, three far more comfortable ones on the other.

And in the one on the one side sat Horatia, a Lady Royal, one of the wives of a now-dead king.

She was facing the door.

She was not chained.

Behind her stood a single guard.

On the table in front of her was a pot of bloody tea and a cup with saucer.

She was still wearing her cloak, regardless that a fire had been lit in the small fireplace and the room was cozy warm.

And across the chest of her gown and cloak was a spray of blood.

Crikey.

Reginald came to stand opposite her.

"Lady Royal," he greeted.

"Warden," she returned.

"It seems you made some friends during your brief stay here," he noted.

Her head only slightly tipped to the side.

But at first, she said nothing.

Then she asked, "Is the guard I struck going to be all right?"

She, personally, struck no guard.

Not delivering the power behind the clout he'd seen.

"He's being taken to the infirmary," he told her.

"I lamented that part of the proceedings. Please extend my apologies."

There were, he knew, many things that made a lady.

Now, he knew one of them was a lady remaining a lady even after she committed murder.

He moved to the three chairs opposite her, pulled out the middle, and sat in it.

"It's my understanding Prince Cassius provided you with a lovely manor to the south," he remarked.

"I had occasion to return," she murmured.

"Mm," he hummed.

"I suppose I'll occupy a different cell now," she said.

"This is for the Regent, uh, that is to say...the king to decide."

She inclined her head, but he did not fail to note a flash of gladness in her eyes when he had called Cassius their king.

Reginald sighed before he queried gently, "Do I need to ask why?"

"Moran died at the Battle of the Heights."

Reginald was confused.

"Moran?"

She tapped a finger on the table, then stopped herself doing that.

And she spoke. "I had a love once, Master Reginald. He was a good man. But he could not have me, for I caught the eye of the king. But that did not mean his life ended. He married. They made two daughters, but their first-born was a son. A son who became a soldier with the ambition of earning the coveted position as lieutenant to a prince he admired. Cassius Laird."

Reginald's heart lurched as he whispered, "Milady."

"So of course, although he was still quite young, he had just finished his training and was proudly an endorsed soldier. Thus, when the prince called for his most loyal to fight the just fight, Moran was one of the first to volunteer. Thus, he was there," she continued.

Reginald had nothing to say.

She had one hand in her lap, one hand close to her cup of tea.

The hand by the tea flipped out as she said, "And he was behind it, you see."

Yes, the dead king was behind a great many terrible things.

Including that.

"I see," Reginald replied.

"Coram had lost enough at his hands. I am an Airenzian woman, and you know, Master Reginald, we are made of rather stern stuff. We are this, for we are born to lose. I was born in this land knowing I would have nothing but what a man allowed me to have, and I would give everything a man chose to take. But Coram?" she shook her head. "He had already suffered at the king's hand. His losing Moran, well, really...it could not be abided."

"I understand," Reginald said, and he did.

However, as it was his duty, he was forced to continue.

"I don't suppose you'll share with me who assisted you in gaining entry to the Bailey and access to the man who once was king."

"You are right," she replied. "I will not share that with you."

"This will mean a full inquiry of all my guards and all others who are employed here," he informed her.

"Yes," she said, and the next she spoke with all sincerity. "And please accept my apologies for the time it will take you to do that. However, I feel safe in the knowledge they will not be discovered, but if they are, I request that you deal with them with a kind heart. They wished nothing but to right a wrong, and I'm afraid I was rather clever in disguising how a wrong would be committed in order to do that."

She then spoke no more.

So be it.

He nodded and said, "I will petition the king to do his best to make you comfortable again in your stay with us, as I suspect it will be rather long."

She nodded in return, took up her tea, and sipped a dainty sip.

However, her hand was slightly shaking.

"It is good to know," he started gently as she set her cup back in its saucer and her gaze came to his, "that love does not die."

Her nostrils flared before she looked away.

Reginald stood and turned his attention to the guard in the room.

"Find her a clean, warm gown, bag the one she wears, and then escort her to her previous quarters," he commanded.

"Yes, sir," the guard said.

"Milady," he murmured to her.

"Master Reginald," she murmured back.

With that, Reginald exited the room.

~

King True
Guest Bedchamber, Sky Citadel, Sky Bay
Aɪʀᴇɴ

"Dᴀʀʟɪɴɢ, ʟᴏᴏᴋ ᴀᴛ ᴍᴇ," True demanded.

Farah, concerning herself greatly with the clasp of his mantle at the base of his throat, lifted her gaze and looked into his eyes.

"It is soon to be done," he said.

"What if there's some trick?" she asked.

"Then it would be a foolhardy trick," he answered.

"Yes, but that doesn't mean more lives won't be lost."

He took her chin against the crook of his finger and his thumb.

"This will be done," he stated firmly. "And then we will seek and dispatch the Beast. After that, we will return home, be coronated, and then set about the arduous work of making a family."

Her lips quirked.

He fully grinned and asked, "Can I take that as indication you are at one with my plan?"

"Can I request a single amendment? That we go about the practicing of the making of a family for, oh, say, six or seven months before we actually get busy with the work of doing it?"

His grin widened. "I can grant that amendment."

She smiled up at him.

He bent his head and kissed it on her lips.

When he lifted away, he said, "Today will be a New Airen."

"Praise the gods."

He touched his mouth to hers again, took his fingers from her chin only to stroke her cheek, and then he left her in their chamber.

~

Teddy
Sheep's Head Inn, Gulliver, A Town Seventy-Five Miles from the Firenz Border
WODELL

TEDDY WAS INTERRUPTED in what he was doing when the noises came through the wall.

He was certain to close his lips tight at the tip and keep his hold about the base strong as he released his mouth from Faunus's cock and looked up to his warrior.

Faunus had his fingers wrapped tenderly around the back of Teddy's neck, and even though he had been watching Teddy's work, his head was now turned to the side, his gaze to the wall.

Feeling Teddy's eyes, he looked down.

And smiled.

A knock sounded at the door.

Both men shifted their attention to it.

"Stay where you are," Faunus ordered on a growl, before he threw one of his long legs over Teddy's head in order to leave the bed.

Teddy rolled to his side and watched his warrior walk to the door, snatching up a sheet of toweling as he went and casually wrapping it about his hips.

Although it wasn't yet dawn, and Teddy did not like a pre-dawn knock at the door, he could not stop his smile as he watched Faunus open the door, fully erect, hidden by nothing but some toweling.

It was so very...

Firenz.

They should be home in a little over a week.

And he couldn't wait.

"Yes?" Faunus asked.

"A bird for you, sir," the innkeeper's voice could be heard.

Then something else could be heard that was unmistakable, and while he watched Faunus take the missive, he also saw Faunus's head turn to the wall.

His love then returned his attention to the innkeeper, muttered, "My gratitude," stepped back, closed and locked the door.

He let the toweling fall to the ground and Teddy enjoyed the view as he walked back to the bed.

He then did not protest, indeed he adjusted his position to accommodate it, when Faunus entered the bed and rested his considerable weight atop Teddy.

"I wonder if he used his fingers or his mouth to teach her to explode," Faunus said on a grin, referring to the earlier unmistakable noise.

Teddy grinned back, but did it shifting his hand to something else he wished to make explode.

Faunus made a sound like a purr and gently thrust into Teddy's hand as he used his own fingers to unroll the narrow scroll of parchment and cast his eyes to it.

Faunus's movements stopped and his brows drew together, so Teddy's ministrations also stopped.

"What is it?" Teddy asked.

Faunus did not immediately reply. He simply stared at the strip.

Teddy squeezed his cock, thus earned his attention.

"What is it?" he repeated.

"My king orders Saturn and I to make haste to Sky Bay."

But...

They were so close to home.

"No," Teddy whispered.

"Yes, *bello*," Faunus whispered back. He began thrusting again, at the same time commanding. "You will take Moira to Nyx and Lorenz." He then switched to assuring, "And you will do so safe on your journey, Teddy."

"We'll go with you," Teddy returned.

"You will not. This," he lifted the parchment, "is an order to a warrior from my king as my commander. This is not a summons from my king as a subject."

"We still will go with you," Teddy retorted.

Faunus shook his head. "Airen is at war."

"And I will not leave you, and Moira will not leave me, or, I suspect, in the now," he tipped his head to the wall, "Saturn."

"You do not take your mates to war."

There it was again.

War.

Teddy released his still-plunging shaft.

"Teddy," he growled.

"I'm not leaving you."

"You, nor our sister, is going with us."

"I feel safe with you and she feels safe only with *us*."

"Our countries are now allies. You will have no issue getting home."

"Faunus."

"Teddy."

They had reached a stalemate.

Teddy was the first to attempt to break it.

"What if something happens to you?" Teddy asked.

"It won't," Faunus stated swiftly.

"So, you would have me, and *our sister*, journey home in the same state of mind you were in the entire time you searched for me?"

This caused Faunus to keep his silence.

Teddy took heart.

"We will not be a bother and we will not slow you down," he said hastily.

"I do not want you near danger," Faunus bit off.

"I do not want you near danger either, but I have no choice, and I'll add, *tato*, neither do you," Teddy stated firmly. "You cannot simply tell me to go home and expect that to happen. If you leave, I am free to follow you. And this I will do."

Faunus's face grew dark, and seeing it, Teddy had to fight against grabbing hold of his cock again.

"Right," he rumbled. "Then if you will not slow me down, you better hurry up."

Teddy smiled victoriously.

"This is not hurrying up," Faunus warned.

Teddy wasted not a moment hurrying up.

~

Queen Ha-Lah
Guest Bedchamber, Sky Citadel, Sky Bay
AIREN

"HOW MANY?" my husband asked.

"Three," I mumbled, beyond sated, practically stupefied from his lovemaking.

"I only counted two."

I studied his arrogant grin before I lifted my gaze to his and declared, "It is unbecoming of a king to seek compliments."

Aramus started chuckling and dipped his head as if to take my mouth, but I pushed further into the pillows behind me and he stopped.

"You are sure that all is in order to thwart what they intend to do?" I whispered.

"I am sure."

"If it is not?" I asked.

The question had excellent timing, for above us could be heard a great flapping.

My king's eyes had gone vague in the listening to it, but they again focused on me.

"Cass is rather proud of the architecture of Sky Bay and as such is rather intent on keeping it just the way it is," he stated.

It was then, my eyes went vague.

"My queen," he murmured.

I pushed up to sitting in the bed, and as he had been leaning over me, held up by a hand in the bed to one side of me, he came up as well.

But I grasped his head behind either ear to keep him close.

"I do not have a good feeling about today," I admitted.

"It will be well."

"Something is very wrong," I told him.

"If you are right, then we will see it through."

"Darling—"

"Ha-Lah, I want to be home. I want to spend long lengths of time in my castle with my wife. And then I want a great number of other things, but as those are most important, I wish to start with that and do it without a great delay. I am not alone in wishing to be amongst my own, in peace, with the woman I love, guiding my realm to prosperity. Thus, we will *see it through*."

I nodded.

He kissed me, pulled away and said, "I shall join you for a late breakfast."

At his optimism that what was about to happen would not take very long, I shook my head, but did it smiling.

Yes, my king was arrogant.

And truly, though I would never tell him this, I wouldn't have it any other way.

He grinned at me, lifted to kiss my forehead then pushed from the bed.

He had his hand on the door when I called, "I love you, my king."

Aramus looked back. "And I you, with the depth and breadth of the sea."

And with that, he was gone.

~

Marian
Argyll Forest
AIREN

I SAW THEM, but not before he.

I could feel his elation.

And I could sense the power coming from there.

It was a hum so strong, it was a vibration.

And not from the veil that the priest spoke about.

From that place in the trees.

Five stones standing around what appeared to be a slab.

Those stones were not of nature, but they were so large, I could not imagine how they had gotten there.

Except, perhaps, very mighty magic.

"Finally," he whispered jubilantly.

And then he kicked his heels into our steed.

~

Princess Serena
Lowgate, Sky Bay
AIREN

THEIR FOUR HORSES galloped through the gate, and the guards there did not delay in rushing it closed behind them.

They took the sea path only shortly, before they cut onto the track that would guide them to the top of the cliffs.

It was a grueling climb for their steeds, but they made it and galloped over the top and down into the forested mountains on the other side.

Brix broke off first when his Fell, Baldrick and their mounted squad of gnomes came into view.

Brix joined his people and they immediately rode to their positions.

Gal broke off next when Fern and her women came into view.

Gal joined them and they rode to their positions.

They made a turn and passed Silvanus.

Serena lifted her staff, and the Zees, on foot, turned and stole through the trees.

She felt it before they joined the final battalion, and when she did, her gaze jerked up to the tips of the trees.

"Ride on," Chu clipped, and she realized she'd lost speed.

She loosened her grip on the reins and again drew abreast of him.

"You feel it?" she asked.

"Ride on," he grunted.

"Chu, do you feel it?" she pushed.

He turned to her and slightly lifted his chin.

He felt it.

Then he faced forward and they both rode on.

When they met them, they headed straight to the front.

Darma, Genia and Heloise were there.

Serena and Chu rounded them and turned their mounts to come to a halt facing them.

"All are in position?" Serena asked.

"Yes," Heloise answered, and Serena noted her lieutenant did not look at Chu.

"One squadron will have to take orders from a Trusted, is this going to be an issue?" she demanded.

"No, Serena," Darma stated firmly.

Serena stared hard at her mentor.

She then did the same with both of her friends.

It was Heloise who spoke.

"A new Airen. A new era."

With that, her heart grew light.

These words had a double meaning.

One of them was that, they would try.

That was all that could be asked.

Serena nodded once, sharply.

She then ordered, "To your posts."

Instantly, they broke off.

Serena looked to Chu, and before she could speak, he did.

"They will lay down their arms."

She opened her mouth.

"My love," he said quietly, "they will lay down their arms."

She didn't care about that.

She knew that.

She cared about what might come before that.

"You are my love too," she stated.

"Pardon?"

"You are my love too. I am in love with you, Chu."

He smiled. "I know."

She frowned. "I know you know, but it needed the saying."

"Yes," he whispered. "It did."

He then shifted his horse so it was right alongside hers, grasped her about the neck with his hand, and pulled her to him for a wet, thorough kiss.

Chu released her mouth, but not her neck, when he declared a gruff, "And I love you."

Only then did he let her go, pull his reins to the right and ride off to head his squadron of Nadirii.

She watched him until she could see him no more through the trees.

She then turned to the warriors that sat atop their horses amongst the forest.

Her gaze moved through them.

"Fortitude, sisters," she whispered. "For if the goddess is with us, we will not lose a one of us today."

And then she shifted her mount to face the direction of the grazing plain.

～

Queen Silence
Antechamber, Guest Bedchamber, Sky Citadel, Sky Bay
AIREN

AS WAS MARS'S WONT, he had already given me mine, so I held on tight with limbs and other parts of me as I enjoyed the velvet violence of his thrusts as he sought his.

"You're…a gods-damned…minx," he grunted, his fingers digging into the curves of my behind where he held me aloft against the wall.

I grinned.

"I should be atop Hephaestus," he growled.

"Then hurry," I whispered, pulled his head down and kissed him.

My bottom slammed repeatedly into stone, and my throat welcomed his groan, as he gave me his seed.

He pulled his mouth from mine, his torso back, but kept his neck bent so he could watch himself glide in and out of me through his aftermath.

Mars finally sunk deep and I sighed in contentment at the feel.

And his eyes came to mine.

"Brazen," he muttered on a false complaint.

"You may thank me later," I told him.

His mouth twitched before he pulled me off his shaft and set me on the ground.

My husband made certain I was steady before he moved away, tucked himself in and began to do up his pants.

He looked so handsome in his leathers and mantle, his sword scabbarded at his back.

Which was why, upon seeing him, I had instigated what had just happened.

Then again, he always looked handsome.

He was almost to the door when I called, "Should I wait for you to have breakfast?"

His eyes came to mine.

"Yes."

I smiled brightly at him.

His face softened.

And then he was gone.

~

Prince Cassius
Outside Highgate, Sky Bay
AIREN

MARS MOVED into position next to Elena.

When he was there, Cassius leaned forward and said, "Good of you to show up."

"My queen was in a mood," Mars muttered.

"So was his," Elena stated, jerking her head toward Cass. "So we got started early."

"We did as well," Mars retorted. "She just wanted seconds."

Elena burst out laughing.

He could hear True at his other side groaning about such words uttered regarding his cousin.

But Aramus was on the other side of Mars, and he was chuckling.

Cassius clenched his teeth.

He then looked down to the plain which was covered in snow.

And lines of battle-ready AG soldiers.

He turned his gaze right, looking beyond True, to where the entirety of the road up to Highgate was lined with Airenzian, Nadirii, Firenz and Dellish soldiers.

His eyes went up, and there he saw two of Frey's dragons.

One was seated on an outcropping halfway up the cliffs, tail stirring, tongue lolling. The other lay regal across a back balcony of the Citadel, its neck arced tall, wings at rest high at its back, clawed front arms crossed at its breast, tail curled about its flank, red eyes aimed at the plain.

The silhouette of Frey stood on the railing next to it.

Cassius's head turned left.

Beyond Ellie, Mars, to Aramus, Tor, Lahn...

Apollo.

As if sensing his attention, Apollo leaned well forward.

"I would not lose another woman or man," Cassius called.

Apollo said not a word.

He wheeled his horse and rode back through the Highgate.

Watching him go, Cassius raised his gaze to the cliffs beyond the gate that had, for centuries, been the first bastion of defense for the all-important Bay.

Along it stood manned cannons.

And amongst them, ordinary citizens.

Some who had come to watch.

Some who held bows in their hands and quivers of arrows at their backs who had come to help if it was needed.

It would not be needed.

"They will lay down their arms."

Ellie saying this brought his attention to her.

"They will not lay down their arms," he replied.

"They will lay down their arms."

"My darling, they're not going to lay down their arms."

Her gaze swung to the plain. "We are not outnumbered this time."

They would not lay down their arms.

He did not repeat himself.

He ordered, "You do not leave this position."

Her eyes jumped again to him.

"We agreed," he reminded her. "We do not leave this position. The rulers of all realms, including the Princess Regent of this one, stands still, watching their defeat, gaining it not having to lift a finger. Yes?"

She didn't reply.

"It'll be over soon," he muttered, his eyes drifting back to the plain.

"They must know this is futile. Why won't they lay down their arms?" she asked.

"I don't know the answer to that question," he told her, not taking his attention from the thousands of men lined before him. "For, honest to the gods, I do not know why they're taken up in the first place."

His wife shuffled her horse closer to his.

He remained steady on Caelus.

They sat their steeds.

And waited.

~

Marian
Silbury Henge, Argyll Forest
Airen

"What is this place?" Marian asked carefully as she watched him move from stone to stone, touching each with a reverence she had never seen of him.

Nor would have ever expected.

He did not answer at first.

"Daemon, I do not get a good feeling about this place," she warned, when he was standing at the last, great stone that protruded from the ground.

It was one that had part of it shorn by time or other earthly element, the great slab that had fallen away embedded in the earth beside it.

And he was glaring at it with distaste.

He turned to her, his expression changing, and she absolutely did not get a good feeling about that new look on his face.

She started backing up.

"You should not run, for you know I will catch you," he said.

She continued backing up.

He shrugged, the apology all over his expression screaming in her face even if he was fifteen feet away.

"I needed your magic, of course," he said.

"You cannot have it," she replied.

He nodded his head, slowly moving her way.

She started backing up much faster.

"I know," he told her. "Thus, I shall have to take it. It is too bad he escaped. I could have perhaps..._eased_ things for you if I had his magic too. It was rather strong. Not as strong as he liked to think. But it was strong. Indeed, I hope yours is enough. I would hate to have to delay, having to find another witch."

That fucking, _fucking priest._

"Daemon, what do you intend to do?" she asked, still backing away.

"Free them," he answered.

That surprised her, so much, it nearly caused her to stop.

But only nearly.

"Free who?"

He smiled.

It was horrible.

And thus, no other thought entered her head.

Instead, she turned to race away.

Frey Drakkar
Back Balcony, Sky Citadel, Sky Bay
AIREN

THE CRY of the captain at the front who raised his sword carried all the way up to him where he stood on the balcony.

"Seriously?" he heard his wife ask behind him.

She'd heard it too.

"I'd rather you be inside," he said, *again*.

"Compromise, husband," she reminded him. "I'm back here, so no stray arrows or whatever, come near me, you're there, like you're immune to stray arrows, but we won't get into that. And you tell me what's happening."

"Loud enough we can hear too!" Cora called from her place at an opened window where all the women had gathered.

Gods save him from parallel-world women.

Or any of them, for that matter, since the queens of this realm were back there too.

"Fuck," he bit, as he watched and saw the first lines break into a charge at the lane.

"It's beginning," Finnie said.

"They're charging," he announced.

"Balls," he heard Silence say.

And then they came as whirling *zing* noises.

The strike of them against rock came as loud cracks.

The company of mermales formed from their tridents imbedded at random intervals all over the sides of the cliffs.

They took their tridents up.

And on a call from Jorie, who had formed amongst them, they let fly.

The tridents soared through the air, puncturing all the soldiers charging at the front of the line, bringing it down.

Those long staffs with their wide, cruel, triple prongs did not cause a wound from which a soldier could arise.

The weapons winged their bloodied journey back to their owners just as wolves raced, barking loud, from the forest, to stop at the edges of the plain, surrounding the troops.

The lines became wavy as surprise at being confronted by mermales and wolves rippled through the standing.

"Is it done?" Finnie called.

Frey watched.

Another call from another captain and another line broke off to press forward.

"What are they thinking?" Finnie asked.

He did not know, for they'd have to climb over the dying bodies of their own only to face a zigzag phalanx of soldiers at better vantages than they.

"They're making a point," he said.

"A stupid one," she replied.

He could not argue that.

More disarray was occurring through the rest as the Nadirii battle cry could be heard and all around them, Nadirii warriors came charging out of the forest, except to their left flank. That was fortified by Zees, gnomes and female Airenzian.

They simply came out, surrounding them, lining up behind the wolves, cutting off any means of escape.

The charging squad at the front was easily picked off one by one by archers higher up the road to the Bay.

Gods, he hoped this didn't last much longer.

Frey looked down to where Cass sat astride his horse, watching, just as another AG captain set two squads to charging the road.

He watched Cass turn his head and look up.

The Regent nodded.

Frey looked to the beast at his right.

"Go, boy," he murmured, jumped from the railing to the balcony and stood at it, the wind from the dragon's wings whipping his hair about his head and his mantle about his body.

The male went straight up from where he had rested.

And up.

The female, down the cliff, rose with him.

He felt his ice princess come up on one side.

He then felt someone else come to his other side.

And they lined up at the railing, not only Finnie and Cora, but Circe, Maddie, Silence, Ha-Lah and Farah.

Frey did not protest.

It was now done.

One way or another.

He just hoped he didn't have to give the order to affect one of those ways.

A great noise came from behind them and they all twisted to look.

The sun in the sky was weak.

Still, it was blotted out when the entirety of his dragons soared overhead.

They created a stiff breeze that floated down on them, mussing his hair, as Frey turned around.

The dragons halted above the standing in the plain, pulling back their heads and chests, their wings flapping, clawed legs stretched out, but long necks arched up with heads down, hovering over the enemy, ready to strike.

No, it was *now*, one way or another, it would be done.

He just hoped it would be the right way.

Frey held, and they held.

Everyone held.

It started at the right flank.

Soldiers setting their weapons to the snow and taking their knees.

The long moments it took from the first squad to ripple to the next felt like an hour.

But then the next laid down their arms.

And the next.

The one before it.

The one behind it.

Right to left.

Back to front.

The wolves slunk back.

The mermales launched their tridents and disappeared in a whirl.

The warriors surrounding them and the ones that lined the lane rode in to process the surrender.

And it was done.

A New Airen.

~

Marian
Silbury Henge, Argyll Forest
AIREN

"*Noooo!*" Marian shrieked, fighting him as he carried her back to the circle. "You cannot! You cannot *do this to me*! I helped you get free!"

"And now you serve a further purpose, my witch," he said.

She bucked, scratched, bit.

"*Noooo!*" she screeched. "Let me *gooooo!*"

He slammed her to her back on the slab in the center of the circle with such strength, her head cracked against it, her eyelids drooped, and her limbs grew weak.

"I lament you will not see what it is you helped to bring about," he whispered, his face close to hers.

All she saw was the gray seeping in at the sides of her eyes.

She had to fight it.

She had to stay conscious.

Get focus.

She was a witch.

She had forgotten in her fright, she had magic.

She had to *get her focus* and *use it*.

In the meantime, she needed to try to reach him another way.

"*Me brutum*," she said desperately.

"*Patrona*," he moaned.

That moan gave her hope.

With effort, she blinked away the gray and focused.

"We could do so many wondrous things, you and I," she told him.

"I find I will miss you," he said morosely.

Oh gods.

Miss her?

Fear took her in its clutch.

"Then...do not...do what it is...you intend...to do," she pushed out.

"Oh no." He shook his head. "This was the mistake I made last time, my witch. And I shan't make it again."

Marian had just managed to start the tingle she felt at the small of her back...

When there was nothing she could do but *scream*.

Gods.

Agony.

"*Yes*," he breathed, his voice animal, her eyelids fluttering.

Still, through them, she saw *the Beast*.

His beauty gone, his breath fetid, his claws embedded in her gut.

Her entire body jerked, pain blistering throughout her frame as he pulled them out, drew back his arm, and she saw his long talons dripping with her blood before she cried out again, this much weaker, as he struck down.

Automatically, she shut her eyes tight as his claws scored into the stone of the slab beside her head and a great light rose out.

"*Yes!*" he bellowed, and she tightened her eyes tight, for even closed, that light burned them.

She felt his presence leave her, the light dimmed, and her head fell to the side as she again opened her eyes.

"Come, brother!" he shouted, and she watched him from behind as he again drew back his arm and embedded his claws into one of the standing stones.

Bright light poured out and she flinched against it before she saw a figure fall out of the light, out of the stone, into the snow before it.

By the gods.

He had...

The time before, he had emerged from that broken stone.

"Up, brother," the Beast urged, moving to the next stone, in which he rooted his claws, crying, "Come, sister!"

With effort, Marian turned to the side, thinking vaguely of escape, feeling in her movement another rush of her blood over the slab under her.

And she watched as the creature freed from the stone pressed up to its hands and knees in the snow.

"Come, brother!" the Beast exclaimed and there was another shaft of light.

She reached to the edge of the slab, curled her fingers around it, tried to pull her weight toward it, and felt another gush of blood come from her.

She stilled and her eyelids drooped.

"Come, sister!" the Beast called on another flash of light.

She had failed.

She had failed dearly.

For there was not one of them.

There were *five*.

Her eyes were almost closed when the light in the circle changed.

She saw colored streaks and heard an almighty squawk of pain that was so grotesque, it scored at her ears, and with the last of her strength, she could do naught but lift her hands and cover them.

The circle filled with a flash of green.

"Four!" she heard a woman shout.

"No!" A flash of red and another woman's shout. "*Five!*"

There was then a flare of blue.

And a roar of fury.

"Nandra! Lena! That one! Concentrate on the one still down in the snow!"

Another gods-awful screech and a flash of coral.

A flare of it scored over her.

"Melisse! Return! Give warning!"

Another pained, hideous screech.

Marian curled into herself.

"*Sister!*" the Beast thundered.

The circle filled with an explosion that was a mix of blue, coral, green and red light.

The green blinked out.

"Rebecca!"

"No!"

"Return! Return! Return!"

"Nandra, *go!*"

Her body was jolted as another went careening over her and Marian saw over the edge of the slab the dark hair of a Firenz woman fanned out on the snow.

It did not move.

"Give...it...*all!*"

Bright coral and intense blue suffused the circle and then a boom exploded so mighty, her frame jerked with it.

"We can do no more! Go!"

A flash of blue.

One of coral.

And...

Silence.

Marian noted vaguely it was snowing again.

Not snow.

No.

A heavy downfall of black ash.

As her vision faded, she watched the Beast in the form of a beast drop to his knees into the snow, murmuring, "Sister."

Her eyes closed.

They opened on hearing him snarl and the hair of the Firenz woman was dragged from sight. She heard a terrible ripping noise, saw a spurt of crimson desecrate the white.

And her eyes did not close again.

But they could see no longer.

~

King Cassius
Upper Hall, Sky Citadel, Sky Bay
Airen

He stood, ignoring the boom of fireworks above, the sounds of celebrations that rose up from the bottom gate, and stared at Reginald standing before him.

"I have situated her in the room she had before, but she shall be moved at your direction, if this is your requirement. As ever, your orders will be carried out to the letter," Reginald said.

Cassius said nothing.

When he did not, Reginald did.

"If you wish my bars, sire, I will give them to you," he declared. "My watch. My responsibility. And as I've failed it, not only with this, but also not knowing communications were getting through my guard, if you intend to relieve me of it, this is something I will not argue."

Cassius continued to say nothing.

"I am sorry, my king, that my failure in my duties has put a pall on such a triumphant day," Reginald muttered. "I am also sorry for your loss."

"What did you say?" Cassius asked.

Reginald studied him a moment before asking, "Which part?"

"What did you call me?"

"Um...my king?" Reginald queried, as if Cassius's confirmation was needed to state he did, or did not, call him that.

"Fuck, I am," Cassius said.

"Sorry, sire?"

Cassius snapped into the conversation.

"Your king," he said. "I'm your king."

"Well, yes, uh, since, you see, the other one is rather...um...*dead*," Reginald replied.

Cass studied his uncomfortable warden.

Then he made his decision.

"We have spoken of the other," Cassius began. "I understand feeling responsible for the entirety of your men. I would have no man in your position who didn't. But no one is all-knowing and all-seeing. The men who are responsible have been identified and dealt with. And that is all that needs said about that."

Reginald inclined his head.

"And he ordered today's nonsense through his council, Reginald," Cassius told the man. "One hundred and fifty-seven Airenzian men are dead today because of him. A stand they should not have taken that could never have been won, ordered by a king who was no longer in the position to put his people in the path of harm. I would have had to take his head, Reginald. Through sheer obstinacy, he is responsible for what befell my citizens today. For even if they stood against the changes I've made, they're still Airenzian. So, it's rather fortunate that Horatia saved me from needing to order the execution of my father."

"Well, I suppose, if you're looking for a bright side," Reginald mumbled.

"He was a terrible king, a dreadful father and a hideous husband. He will be missed by few, and those would do as such, in the doing, do not matter," Cassius said.

Reginald nodded. "And what do you wish for her Lady Royal?"

"Perform an investigation," Cass commanded. "We obviously can't have guard or staff at the Bailey circumventing justice. If you discover her conspirator, we'll deal with him, or her, then. Horatia will serve, in her current quarters, the sentence of a seditious soldier who defies the orders of a commanding officer. This is six months confinement then dismissal from service. As she's not a member of my army, when she's done with her confinement, she'll simply be returned to her manor in the south. Done."

Reginald dipped his chin. "Yes, my king."

"Reg?"

"Yes, my king?"

"Bloody call me Cass, would you?"

Reginald smiled. "Yes…Cass."

"Go home and celebrate," he ordered.

"Righty ho."

Reginald affected a cocky salute, turned and walked away.

Cass watched him, then he too turned, but he did not take that first step.

This was because Ellie was coming out of the red room.

She exited it only enough to step to the side of the door and lean her back there.

"I'm sorry, sweetheart," she whispered.

She'd heard.

No.

She'd been listening.

"He will not be mourned," he told her something he knew she knew.

"I'm not sorry for his loss, for he was horrid. I'm sorry you did not have a good father. I'm sorry his last command acted out on this earth proved that beyond all doubt. And I'm sorry because I know you, you'll draw that in and allow it to harm you until me and Aelia and Dora can dig it out from where it never should be, for he is no part of you. You left him behind long, long ago."

Cassius did nothing and said nothing but expel a deep breath.

"And her legacy is complete," she said softly.

His gut burned as he stared at her.

"She is standing beside my mother and they are very proud of you, my king."

"We agreed not to call each other such," he growled.

"Just this once," she whispered.

And he was upon her, pressing her against the wall of *his* bloody Citadel, in *his* bloody capital, *in his bloody realm.*

Kissing her.

Deeply.

The sound of Macrinus calling, "Fuck, Cass. *Cass!*" was the only reason he broke the embrace.

Both he and Elena looked down to the mouth of the hall where Mac was standing.

"Now…come…*now!*" Mac shouted, then he was away.

They hesitated long enough to glance at each other before they both jogged that way.

The entryway was vacant, but voices could be heard in the Great Hall, thus, they moved there.

A handsome, dark-skinned Mar-el woman lay back on a couch, gasping for air and appearing in pain.

Melisse sat on her arse on the floor as if she'd collapsed there, knees up, head and back bowed, forearms on her knees, deep breathing into her lap.

Fern was standing above the woman on the couch, her eyes closed, her hands hovering over her, her lips moving in silent wording.

True and Farah were already there, and Aramus and Ha-Lah ran in moments after Cassius and Elena had arrived.

Elena dropped down to a knee beside Melisse, one hand on her friend's back, bending to her.

"What's happened?" she asked.

Cassius stood close to them but looked to his right to see Mars jog in, holding Silence's hand, (though, Silence wasn't jogging, she was on the trot to keep up with him).

"What's the urgency?" Mars demanded, his gaze snapping about the room, taking it in.

"Melisse, what's happened?" Elena asked.

Everyone drew in close as Melisse tipped her head back.

"Rebecca. Nandra," she said.

But then said no more.

"Rebecca?" True asked.

"What of Nandra?" Mars bit off.

"We...we killed one. It...she...it had not quite recovered from its emergence, I think. Vulnerable. They...my sisters, my sisters are gone, but before they were lost to us, they made it so *it* is also gone," Melisse said.

"It? What it?" Elena asked.

Cassius watched as Melisse looked into Elena's eyes before her gaze moved all around.

She finished, however, back on her sister-daughter.

"There is not but one beast," she whispered.

The air in the room stood still.

"There are four."

149

THE EXAMINATION

Silbury Henge, Argyll Forest
AIREN

The zinging stopped and mists of snow and ash bloomed up when the tridents struck it all around the slab in the center of the circle.

Immediately, there formed ten men, two to each trident.

They stood in the circle, motionless, alert, hands on their weapons.

When they heard nothing, they glanced about.

The clearing all around was mostly covered in black soot, with some disturbances, indications of the movements of beings.

The origin of the ash, it was clear, was the area in front of one of the stones, where there was crater in the earth, the frozen dirt that was exposed oozing with some form of black sludge.

King Cassius Laird was the first to move, his boots crunching in the snow.

He went to the crater and crouched beside it, staring into it in contemplation.

King True Axelsson of Wodell shifted next, going to the slab in the center upon which, covered in fallen ash, there was the corpse of a woman who, through the dark powder that covered her features, he noted had been quite pretty.

But now the skin of her face he could see through the dust was ashen, except about her lips and eyes, where it was blue.

The lifeblood that had flowed from her onto the slab was a muddy red-black color, as it had dried or frozen, but before doing so, had soaked up the ash. Though he could see it was fully crimson where it had seeped over the side into the snow.

King Aramus Nereus of Mar-el moved next, going to squat beside another lifeless body.

She was a woman in Dellish clothes with light-brown hair. She lay face-down in the snow. One arm was cast above her, her wool skirts covered her legs, her cloak was fanned out beside her as if someone had lifted it to let it catch the air and fall in order to spread it artfully.

Blood soaked the soot-covered snow in a pool all about her.

The next to move was King Mars Laches of Firenze.

His boots crunched through the black and white and a vein beat in his temple as he cast his eyes along the length of the slaughter.

He noted immediately there were body parts missing.

Thus, his gaze followed some red droplets, and in the not far distance, he saw her head and her pelvis.

He closed his eyes.

His captains began to shift about outside the stones, keeping alert, tridents at the ready, as King Jorie of the Mer moved from stone to stone, examining the large impressions in the snow before them. The disturbances of nature's blanket on the ground.

And the footfalls, or what looked like hoof falls that led away from this place.

One of his males came to him and asked low, "Do you wish us to follow them?"

"No," he grunted, watching True reach out with a gloved hand to close the eyes of the dead woman on the slab.

He then turned to watch as Aramus gently rolled the woman in the snow to her back, and Jorie drew in a deep breath at the gore that had been made of her, from her face all the way down to her sex.

Cassius straightened from his crouch at the crater, his eyes to the body Aramus had turned, and his words came as a rumble.

"They did not die in vain," he stated. "Four is worse than one, but five is worse than four."

True moved to stand by Aramus, looking down at the witch from his realm, his expression an oddly affecting mixture of gentle and enraged.

"These stones imprisoned them," Aramus noted. "One of them somehow freed himself. The one of lore." He indicated the broken stone that had no impression in the snow before it. "The others have been here, perhaps since time began."

Mars also moved close to Aramus and True, indicating a stone with a jerk of his head, stating, "This is the work of the gods."

Cassius and Jorie joined them, Cassius glancing at a stone embedded in the earth, agreeing, "It has to be."

"We must come back, with men, follow those tracks, discover where they went," True said.

"Look upon them," Aramus said quietly, indicating the woman at their feet and then with a slight lift of his other hand, the one in parts across the circle. "This was done with bare hands. Men who track these creatures must do it with witches. Powerful ones."

"Melisse and Lena are completely depleted," Cassius said. "And our wives are getting nowhere bloody near this mess until we have a better handle on what we're dealing with."

"We return to Sky Bay," Mars grunted. "Now. We send men to collect these bodies, take them to their realms where they will join the veil. And then we plan at the Citadel."

"Mars—" True started.

Mars locked his gaze with his friend. "I do not like to leave them here as they are either, True. But the longer we are away, the more afeared our queens will become. I will not be here any longer than I must before I return to my Silence to show her I am all right. We will send men to take care of them. Now let us leave this...*fucking*...*place*."

Jorie jerked up his chin to his men.

They approached.

Arms were linked.

Tridents were thrown.

And they embedded themselves in the courtyard of the Sky Citadel.

~

The Mouth of Triton, Fifteen Miles Down the Coast from Nautilus
MAR-EL

HIS ORBS WERE GLOWING SO BRIGHTLY, their light had to reach the top of the vortex.

He remembered the creation of this vortex.

In his fury, he had cast her to the depths of the sea, and when she did not emerge, his grief was so strong, he had driven himself into the earth.

And he did this not knowing he would never climb out of this hole.

He lifted his hand to the orbs, seeing his fingers gnarled, his knuckles grotesquely swollen, his nail a long claw, the bed of it black with dirt.

Ah, so much lost.

And not simply the glory of what he once was.

He touched the orbs and closed his eyes.

"Our children," he whispered. "Our naughty children, my love. They are awake."

Her voice was weak when it came to him, not weak as in she was not strong, weak because she was very far away.

But he heard it.

He heard it for the first time in over four thousand years.

I told you the stone would not hold.

He could not stop his smile, even if these decisions he had made—the one to create them, and the one to banish them—were the ones that drove them apart.

Drove him to flinging her to her cave.

Drove him to his hole.

And the mistakes he had made, the loss of her had slowly drained his power over millennia.

"I should have listened to you."

I know you were proud of them. I know you felt their work was needed. But we lost control so quickly. And they were so very destructive, my darling.

"Yes," he murmured. He opened his eyes and looked at his orbs. "And you were right, we should have eliminated them before our powers grew too weak."

She did not reply, and he worried he had lost her again and the wait to hear her beloved voice would be another four thousand years.

But then she spoke, and when she did, his heart grew light for the orbs glowed even brighter.

Take heart, my darling. We have new children now.

150

THE TOMES

Princess Serena
Parade Grounds, Outside the Soldier's Barracks, Sky Bay
AIREN

At the call, she made haste from where she was drilling Fern's female Airenzian soldiers who wished to remain in service to their realm alongside Luther, Wallace and Nero, Darma, Genia and Heloise, to the Citadel.

Her timing was exceptional for she saw her sister striding purposefully through the entryway as she arrived.

And her sister's husband was not with her.

It was not that Serena did not wish Cassius to know.

It was that Serena did not know if Chu wished *anyone* to know.

"Elena," she called.

Elena stopped, looked to Serena and smiled a small, tight smile.

There were not many bright smiles this last two weeks since Cassius won the war, but they lost Rebecca and Nandra and the threat of the Beast quadrupled.

"The Go'Doan priest G'Ry has arrived," Elena informed her. "He has brought the tomes."

"Excellent, but can I have a word?" Serena asked, arriving at her sister and stopping.

"I'm keen to know what he reports, Rena," Elena said carefully.

"I am too, Ellie," Serena said quietly. "But I have something to report as well. I have for some time, and thus, I feel perhaps it is now beyond time to report it."

She watched her sister brace as she asked, "What?"

"There is a presence about the Bay. It has naught to do with Beasts or even this realm. And it follows Chu."

And with that, she had Elena's full attention.

"Chu?" Elena queried.

Serena nodded.

"Do you know what it is and why it follows him?" Elena asked.

Serena shook her head. "He is aware of it as well. He knows I am. He refuses to discuss it."

"Do you have a guess?"

"Yes," Serena stated flatly. "It is, or they are, Mystics. Those who practice the *art*, not simply those who come from that land."

"Bloody hell," Elena muttered, as she would, for she knew about the Mystic Arts. The learning of them took much time, much patience, much skill, much talent, but mostly, acquiring the grasp of tremendous amounts of spiritualism. And because of this, the mastery of them, only few achieved. "Did he leave trouble behind when he left that empire?"

Serena hesitated, studying her sister.

"Rena," Elena prompted impatiently.

"He did, of a sort," she confided. "For he did so fleeing the assassins his mother had set upon him and two of his brothers to assure the stability of the future rule of his elder brother, the firstborn prince."

Elena blinked. "Chu is a prince?"

Serena again nodded.

"And his mother tried to have him killed?"

Serena continued to nod.

"Good goddess," Ellie whispered.

And then Serena confided again, not hiding the thread of fear in her tone.

"They must know he survived, Ellie, and they come to kill him."

Concern suffused her features as Elena moved closer and took her hand. "Are you sure?"

"I can think of no other reason they are here. I move about, even outside the Citadel, I don't sense them. Not ever. But if I am with Chu, anywhere outside the Citadel, in the Bay, by the sea, in the forest, they are always there."

"Is Chu a master of the Mystic Arts?"

Serena shook her head. "He began his study, but he didn't finish before he was forced to escape."

"When did you first sense them?"

"Before we moved into Dunlyn."

Elena's head twitched. "That was weeks ago, Rena."

"Yes," Serena confirmed.

"If they wish to do as you think, would they not have done it?"

This question gave Serena pause.

"What do you wish to do?" Elena asked.

"Cast for them."

Elena's hand spasmed around hers.

"Rena," she whispered. "That would take great magic. And we must build. We must conserve."

"Yes, but I have much left from our ritual at The Cauldron. Even with my activities in Dunlyn, Ellie," Serena replied.

"They slaughtered five entire families, sister," Ellie reminded her. "They've stolen clothes. As such, we are led to believe they've taken human shape. And we have lost their trail. We have no idea where they are, what they look like, save one. Nor what they intend to do. Melisse and Lena are depleted. It will take months for them to cast a spell, even if they cast to form naught but a butterfly. We've lost the magic of Rebecca and Nandra. We need all the power we can get, my sister."

"And if some unknown was following Cassius, with the possible intent to do him harm, what would you do?" Serena asked.

Serena should not have been surprised, but she was when happiness flooded Elena's eyes.

"It is love between the two of you?"

"Yes," Serena forced out.

She jumped when Elena pulled her in a tight embrace.

And in her ear, her sister whispered, "Then you must cast." She pulled slightly away, though did not take her arms from about Serena, to ask, "Would you like some help?"

"I only wish to bring one forward. Talk to him. And when I do so, I would request Hera and Mac."

Elena let her go then, querying, "Hera and Mac?"

"Mac, for he is gifted with a sword. I have not seen reflexes like his in any warrior. Hera, for I would wish her skills and magic at my side."

"Not Heloise? Genia? Darma?"

"They are trying, but I feel those who understand what it is like to love will be more...*committed* to the effort."

"This is wise," Elena murmured before she queried, "Do you wish me to talk to them?"

"Would you?"

Elena smiled at her. "Of course."

"You have my thanks," Serena muttered.

Elena took hold of her, linking their arms and starting them down the hall that would lead them to Cassius's study.

She did this inquiring, "Do I need to plan another wedding?"

Her mind filled with visions of Elena's wedding.

"Oh goddess, please no," Serena replied.

Elena chuckled through her promise of, "I will not use so much pink."

Serena made a choking noise and Elena's laughter grew.

"When that time comes, we will wed where he desires in his home. Firenze," she informed her sister.

Elena's arm in hers contracted.

"I will look forward to this with great relish," she whispered.

Surprisingly, Serena felt the same.

They entered Cass's study to have all eyes turn to them.

Serena's gaze went direct to Chu, who was openly pleased to see the two sisters arriving in such a manner.

Thus, he shot her an audacious grin.

She purposefully ignored it and held her sister strong for a moment before she let her go and turned her attention to the large table that occupied the space opposite Cassius's desk, at the same time she did a quick inventory of the room.

The players were all there.

Aramus and Ha-Lah. True and Farah. Mars and Silence. Cass. Melisse. Fern. Lena. The couples from across the Green Sea. Mac. Hera. Bram. Tint.

And of course, Chu.

Also, for some reason, her mother's physician, Liam.

And last, an elderly man Serena had never seen before wearing Go'Doan robes and appearing struck with melancholy.

He stood at the table, beside Cass.

A table covered in, upon quick calculations, approximately fifteen large and small—but all old, and some dusty—tomes.

"Elena, Serena," Liam called. "Greetings."

"Liam," Serena murmured as she moved to stand by Chu where he was close to the table, Elena offering her own greeting.

"This is G'Ry," True introduced. "A Go'Nix of the Go'Doan."

The elderly gentleman dipped his chin to the both of them.

Go'Nix were priests who recorded history.

And no doubt they were very busy as of late.

"Shall we start?" Mars inquired impatiently, his words a barely veiled order to do just that.

"Yes," G'Ry said. He then cleared his throat. "Of course." He moved to the table and put his hand atop a stack of books. "And I shall do so by stating I am honored to be here today, in service to you in this most troubling time."

"We are most sorry, Ry, for the loss of your Marian," Farah said gently.

"I am too, I am...we are..." Ry glanced at Liam.

"There is much discussion in the Dome City regarding acolytes," Liam reported. "The situation with Marian is both sad at the same time it's disconcerting, for it seems clear she consorted with the Beast, perhaps even played a part in rising him. However, her loss is having some measure of an optimistic affect. For our own have been in deep discussions about a variety of topics, as I'm sure does not surprise you. And there is a sway toward rather significant changes. Including with the acolytes. And Marian..." He hesitated, glancing at Ry before he went on, "going astray has only strengthened the argument of those who wish the role of our women to be more...inclusive."

Serena exchanged a glance with Elena, but neither said a word.

"I do believe my Marian would wish this," Ry said quietly, then he shook his shoulders and glanced about. "But in the now, far more pertinent matters need discussing. For, since news came of what occurred at the henge, all of our Go'Nix and Go'Tec have been scouring the tomes. I am here to report our findings and bring those to you that have notations of these creatures."

Go'Tec were their scholars.

Serena never had any use for those in the Dome City, but it could not be argued the Go'Tec, to earn that distinction, were rather learned men.

Finally, these priests were serving at least one of the purposes that had started that religion.

"It is pieced together," Ry went on. "And there has been much discussion about what actually was, and what is fable. I myself have read all the notations, repeatedly, and should any of you wish a thorough briefing, I would be at your service. However, I feel at the moment, that which we all could agree on is where we should start."

"Then do it," Mars prompted.

Serena caught Silence brushing the backs of her fingers against those of her husband, an indication that he might wish to be more patient, or perhaps less rude.

His expression as he scowled at Ry, however, did not change.

Then again, Mars had never had any use for these priests, and one had murdered his father.

Ry clearly took no offense, for he nodded and began.

"It is agreed they are creations direct of the gods," he stated. "It is agreed they have powers that are awesome and terrible. It is agreed that they abused these powers and the gods then banished them to the stones. It is agreed one found his way free, and wrought havoc and destruction on the land before he was captured and contained by the Mer. Thus, now, it is agreed he has risen, and in doing so, he sought and freed his siblings."

"We figured this much out ourselves," Aramus told him.

Ry nodded. "We are also agreed they have a name. They are demons."

"Fuck," Cass bit off.

Serena agreed with Cass's sentiment, for they had all heard of the evil of demons, beings who were of the earth so long ago, they were not even lore. They were myth.

Or, obviously, not.

They were creatures of the gods run amuck. And why not? When your makers gave you extraordinary powers and made you nearly impossible to kill.

"I have good news," Ry shared.

"Then tell us that," Mars demanded.

"It is clear from the tomes there were only five. Now, with the heroic efforts of the Great Coven, there are only four. Thus, they are not seeking others to be released," Ry said.

This was good news for they had all wondered, and worried, in the time between their release, and now, when not much had happened, that they were about the business of just that.

"We know they have the power to transform," Ry continued. "And we know they have great might. We also know they are not mindless. They are not but animals who act on instinct, for survival or dominion or their pack. They have reason. And last, in also closely studying the lore after the Beast freed himself previously, we feel confident in sharing this is all they are."

"All?" Farah asked.

Ry tipped his chin to her.

"All. Poison spewing from their mouths that could freeze a being?" He shook his head. "We feel that is myth. We do not know for certain the ability of their quickness, but in examining the time it took for them to leave the stones and find the homesteads in proximity to them in order to commit the atrocities against those five families, it would seem their speed is not beyond a normal human. These we feel, albeit strongly, were exaggerations. Manifestations of the lore passing along the centuries, heightened for the teller to keep the hearer in their grip."

"You *feel* this, but you do not *know* this," Aramus pressed.

Ry nodded.

No one spoke.

Thus, Ry continued.

"There is, I'm afraid, some bad news."

"We're used to that," Ha-Lah murmured.

"What is it?" Cass asked.

Ry looked to Liam who returned a nonverbal indication he should spit it out.

And he did.

"We feel it is not coincidence, that Rebecca and Nandra were lost."

That earned the attention of all.

"We feel," Ry carried on, "it was foretold, that the power of the Great Coven, created after the last time the Beast walked the earth, would rise up to do exactly what it did. Eradicate one of them. And do it at the henge, where the Coven met, and where a witch could garner more power."

It took a moment for him to speak on, and it did this for it seemed like he wished not to do such, and then he did.

"And we feel there is a reason there are four," he stated. "Four Beasts. Four couples prophesied. We feel, the way forward, is not that you act as one. We feel it is likely they will not move as a pack. We believe that each prophesied couple will need to strike out on their own to..."

He hesitated.

Everyone listened closely.

And then he finished.

"*Hunt.*"

Well...
Shite.

❧

Queen Elena
Red Room, Sky Citadel, Sky Bay
Airen

"I don't give a fuck what he suggests," my husband declared. "It's lunacy for us to separate."

I had to agree.

"I do not know," True murmured.

"True, it took the four mightiest witches in our realms to kill one of them, and it was vulnerable when they did, and two of them perished in the doing of it," Cassius reminded him.

"I'm aware of that, Cass," True said patiently.

"And you wish to separate?" Cass asked.

"I wish to divide and conquer," True answered. "But to do so, I feel we must not be hunters."

"And how do you suggest doing this? For I do not wish to be following in their path, ten steps behind as they slaughter more families, entire villages, leaving panic, mayhem and anarchy in their wake," Mars put in.

"I feel we should become the hunted," True declared.

No one spoke.

"What is the most magical place on Triton?" True queried.

"The Enchantments, of course, True, but obviously, although I don't want them anywhere, I have grave issue leading them *there*," I said.

"If we could take them to the place where the Green King and the Sky King and the Fire King drove their magic into the earth, the sky?" True inquired. "Break them from each other, make them chase us. Not realizing their brethren are being led to the same place. And when we get them there, surround them and do...whatever it is we're meant to do."

"I don't like it," I said.

"I don't either," Serena said.

"This is not the most magical place in Triton," Aramus said.

Everyone looked to him.

"We must drive them to Mar-el," he declared.

"Husband," Ha-Lah said softly.

"Why?" Mars asked.

Aramus looked to Jorie and stated, "I know how the Mer captured him."

"Aramus," Jorie rumbled warningly.

"I see there's something going on between you two," Cass remarked. "But I feel it's important to note we don't want to capture them. We want to *kill them*."

"I do not know much about this, but isn't what's important, in the now, that we first *find them*?" Farah asked.

"We need to speak," Jorie said to Aramus.

"Perhaps we can go to The Cauldron?" Silence suggested, her gaze moving between her sisters. "To, maybe, perform another ritual, seek where they are?"

General discussion broke out, no one agreeing on a way to move forward, everyone becoming more frustrated as we talked.

This followed us into dinner.

After dinner.

And the only reason it broke off was when everyone headed to their bedchambers.

Cassius entered ours, jerking at the buttons of his shirt.

"Sweetheart—" I began.

"This is not right," he hissed, turning to me. "There is something wrong. It's been weeks, and I do not diminish the loss of those families, but *four* demons created by fucking *gods* walk my land and...that's it?"

"I think we should be glad of it," I said carefully.

"Of course, Ellie, but what are they bloody waiting for?" he asked. "Or more to the point, all this time they've had, what are they *doing*?"

I did not know the answer to either of those questions, and I did not have the opportunity to tell him I didn't.

A knock came at the door.

I turned to look at it as Cassius called out, "Enter!"

I expected a servant.

Not Mars.

Our friend did not lead into it.

He announced, "They've separated."

I stood solid.

Cassius came to stand beside me.

"The demons?" Cass asked.

"Yes," Mars said. "I've had a bird from Faunus. They've found one and they're following him."

"Dear goddess," I whispered. "How do they know it's a demon?"

"They saw it transform."

"Bloody hell."

Mars looked to Cassius, and when they locked eyes, they did not break the contact.

"Whatever we're going to do, my brother, the time is now," Mars said.

"Bloody right," my husband replied.

Thus, in but an hour, dressed warm, packed light, astride our horses, the lot of us galloped behind Star and Sky.

To meet our destinies.

151
THE FEINT

King Mars
Lesser Thicket Forest
Wodell

Mars rode Hephaestus, Silence on Epona at his left flank.

They were bending, leaning, ducking, as their mounts weaved through the dead trees, their hooves pounding into the snow.

He did this by reflex and instinct.

His wife, an exceptional horsewoman, did it the same.

Mostly he kept his gaze on the golden hair that shone in the moonlight of the woman on the horse who was attempting to escape pursuit.

He cut his reins to round a tree, Silence followed, and they drew closer to her.

"Now?" Silence yelled.

"No!" he shouted.

Opposite them, Elena was moving abreast of the human-like creature.

And it was then Cassius rode straight in front of her.

Her horse reared.

"*Now!*" Mars roared.

Silence's balls of flame soared through the air.

And hit nothing.

The woman with the golden hair had leaped into the trees. Then, abandoning her steed, she swung from limb to limb with a speed that made her blur from focus.

True and Aramus started to give chase but realized quickly there was no hope.

They wheeled their horses around and galloped back, reining in where the rest of them sat atop their steeds, breaths coming heavy, forming vapor as they hit the cold air.

"Well, I think we can say the Go'Doan were wrong about their exceptional speed," Ha-Lah drawled.

"And agility," Farah muttered.

"Regardless that I run the risk of us entering another five-hour, fruitless discussion, I must point out we're reacting, when we all bloody know that's the most foolish thing we can do," True said.

"And you suggest?" Elena asked.

"I suggest we're right where they want us to be because they led us here, and they're somewhere else altogether doing something we don't want them to be doing," True told her.

"How close is the Dome City from here?" Farah asked.

Everyone looked at everyone else.

But on these words, Mars rounded his horse and dug his heels in, shouting, "*Yah!*"

The rest all followed.

Dawn was touching the horizon when Star and Sky led them out of the purple onto the bleached cobbles of the Dome City.

Those amongst them who had never been had at first gazed around in awe at the tall white buildings built one right against the other, with their golden domes in the middle of which, striking toward the heavens, were spiking finials.

There were lanes, avenues, paths, elevated walkways, but Mars knew from past visits any green they had was in carefully cultivated gardens on the outskirts of the city or courtyards that could not be seen from the streets.

The pristine, whitewashed edifices with their priceless domes were all the creators of this place, and those who lived there, wished you to see.

It was striking upon first sight, how sleek and seamless and clean it all was.

It took some time to realize it had no character, no color, no depth, no emotion.

And the outside hid what happened within.

However, that had been some hours ago.

Now they had lost patience with the ambassadors who were summoned to speak to them, the sun was in the sky, not a one of them had had any sleep, and Mars and Cass were leading their band across the snow-white cobbles at Elena's direction.

She'd studied there. She could guide them.

This was good.

For the priests were being exceedingly unhelpful.

Case in point, the one who had lifted his white robes at the front of him and was jogging to keep up at Mars and Cassius's sides.

Doing this speaking breathlessly.

"As you were told, back in our Communion Hall, it would take no time at all to discuss this amongst the Go'En and garner approval for you to enter the Narration Hall."

"We do not need approval," Mars countered, still striding.

"I understand that things are quite...*unresolved* between our peoples, but no one enters the Narration Hall without prior approval of the Go'En," the priest said. "We were caught unawares by your visit, and—"

"Turn left up ahead," Elena instructed.

"Really, this is...*gulk!*"

Mars held him aloft by his throat.

"You are trying me," he growled.

"My darling," he heard his wife say.

He tossed the priest aside, ignoring the man's cry, and the thud his body made when he hit a wall, and Mars continued striding.

They turned left as Ellie had said, and all saw it up ahead.

It couldn't be missed.

The ornamentation was spartan, but regardless, the colossal circular building was grand.

And they went right to it.

They pushed through the double doors, but they barely took five steps in before they all stopped.

Not because what lay before them, in a round, was spectacular.

The acres of curved shelves at the outer walls that rose stories and stories up high and were filled with books. The ornately carved, white-washed desks scattered about with the long feathery, white plums of the quills drifting in the air, stuck at an angle in their beds beside ornate ink pots made of white porcelain. The white marble floors with veins of gold.

No.

They did so because they all felt it.

Farah spoke first and it was tremulous.

"True."

Mars looked to her as True demanded, "Take the women outside."

"They stay with us," Aramus decreed.

"Then cover their eyes," True shot back.

But it was too late.

He heard his wife gasp.

Gods bloody damn it.

He walked that way and saw another piece of lore that it was clear was passed through the generations as successfully notated information.

The demons drank from the necks of their victims.

Three mauled corpses lay behind a short shelving unit, heads torn from bodies, pools of blood forming from the separation.

The heads were not close to their remains. They lay some ways away. There was gore at the neck, but no blood had leaked out onto the floor.

"They might still be here," Cass said low.

"Then we all must stay close," Aramus decreed.

"Fuck, fuck, *shite*," Mars bit, not wanting his Silence anywhere near this madness, but taking hold of his wife and pulling her to his back.

Pushing aside his mantle, she curled her fingers around the waist of his trousers.

When she had a hold on him, he lifted his hand behind his neck, grasped the hilt of his sword and released it from its scabbard.

He heard the other men do the same.

They advanced together, Cassius with Elena and Aramus with Ha-Lah at the lead, Mars and Silence fanned to their left, True and Farah to their right.

In this manner, they walked down the center aisle to the middle of the spherical building.

"*By Chas!*" they heard exclaimed.

The priest had caught up.

None of them slowed.

They found more carnage amongst the desks and shelves and stacks.

And more.

The center of the great building had a circular railing, and peering over it, they could see the structure led into the earth. The shelves that rose above them were accessed by ladders of varying lengths that rolled along the walls.

The shelves and floors below were accessed by a spiral of stairs.

They headed down it

The epicenter of activity, they found on a floor two down from the ground level.

And it was not of carnage.

It was what appeared to be a great frenzy of books pulled from shelves, opened, pages torn or smeared with blood.

"They've found what they wanted, and they're gone," Mars murmured.

The men scabbarded their swords.

Elena and Silence bent by the pile of books.

"*This is a desecration!*" the priest shrieked, and Mars watched as he indicated his words did not share his feelings about the gruesome deaths of his brethren when he threw himself down to the volumes close to Elena, holding his hands above them as if afraid to touch them. "The word! The art! The history!"

"You passed at least fifteen of your brothers, torn to bits on your way to this location," True pointed out, and the man whipped his head around and back to glare up at True.

"There is *nothing* more important than *the tomes*," he snapped.

"What are these particular tomes about?" Mars asked.

The priest looked down at them, but was apparently so beside himself, he couldn't answer.

Thus, he didn't.

"They are, many of them, in the old or ancient tongue," Silence said.

"They should not be *touched* unless your fingers are *protected*. They *are* old *and* ancient for they are of the Collected," the priest stated.

"The Collected?" Ha-Lah asked.

"They are not ours, of the Go'Doan. We did not write them. They were written before the true gods were worshipped. We *saved* them from the other realms and keep them protected here," the priest answered.

"Shite," Cassius muttered.

"Have they been translated?" Silence asked.

The man reared back in offense. "*All* the Collected were *painstakingly* translated."

"Get us those," Mars ordered.

"You still do not even have approval to *be here*," the man spat.

Mars was about to move, but True did it before him.

Thus, the man scuttled back on his hands and feet, True in pursuit. The priest eventually smacked his head into the leg of a desk and stopped before True leaned deeply over him to come face to face.

"He said," True whispered. "Get...us...*those*."

"I love it when he gets like that," Farah said breathily, and at a glance, Mars saw it was to Ha-Lah.

Ha-Lah was eyes to True and grinning.

"True, calm," Elena called, straightening. "I'll go to the catalogue, discover what these were about and locate the translations."

She then walked right to and up the winding staircase with Cassius dogging her heels.

"Isn't there someone you should report the massacre of your brothers to?" Aramus asked the priest.

"I can't leave you *alone* with *the tomes*," he retorted in horror.

Aramus looked to Mars.

Mars shrugged.

It was not long before they heard a loud whistle.

Mars moved to the center railing and looked up.

Cass was peering down.

"We've been had," he called.

"What?" Mars asked.

"She was leading us away," Cassius shouted as Mars felt the others join him at the railing. "Those volumes are about the prophecy. If they did not before, they know about us now."

"Fuck," Mars clipped.

"Is that all?" True called.

"Ellie's checking."

Silence pressed in front of him, her head down, but her voice loud when she yelled, "Tell her two-one point five-seven. Two-one point five-nine. Two-one point six-three. And two-two point naught-one."

She was reading from numbers she'd commandeered a quill and inked on the palm of her hand.

"Louder!" Ellie's disembodied voice could be heard from above.

Silence started shouting but Mars pulled his queen to his front, took her wrist, and boomed a repeat of the numbers.

"Right!" Elena called.

Mars kept his wife close even as he released her wrist and looked to True. "Do you feel like a bloody fucking fool, standing in a library amongst a slew of dead bodies, accompanied by an ignoramus, shouting at each other?"

"Yes," True answered.

Silence giggled.

Mars did not find anything amusing.

He felt this less so when he sensed movement above, looked up, saw Elena was nearly hanging over the railing, her honeyed hair swaying about her face, and her voice was urgent when she called, "Aramus? Do you know what the 'Mouth of Triton' is?"

Aramus looked to True. To Mars.

Then he raced up the stairs.

They all raced up after him.

152

THE PURSUIT

Teddy
Aboard the Passenger Galleon, the Pentacle
Strait of Medusa

"I never *in my life* thought I'd go to *Mar-el*," Moira, standing in the curve of Saturn's arm at the railing of the ship, breathed as they saw land come into view. "This is *so exciting*."

Saturn looked over her head to Faunus.

He did not share in his woman's excitement.

"I love seafood," she declared. "We never had it, except once, when I was a little girl, and we went for a holiday in Seil Haven. So that's why I know I love it."

Saturn grunted.

She twisted her head to look up at him. "You don't like seafood?"

"I have no idea, *gioia*," Saturn murmured. "I have never tasted it."

Her eyes got large. "Truly?"

His face softened a tad. "Truly."

"We must go to an eatery the minute we disembark," she decreed. "Get you some white fish fried in batter. It's *delicious*."

"You do know," Saturn began carefully, "we are not here to holiday."

"Yes," she mumbled, now not looking at any of them, "of course."

She turned back to face the sea.

Her excitement had deflated, and Teddy knew precisely what she was feeling, but he loved her all the more for trying to make this into a delightful adventure.

Saturn again looked to Faunus, to Teddy, then he visibly pulled her deeper into his body with his arms about her chest and bent to her ear.

"But we will take time before we leave to have this fish in batter," he promised.

"All right," she whispered.

Faunus brushed his arm and Teddy looked up to him.

He then followed him down the deck.

When they were out of earshot of their friends, Faunus stopped and turned back to Teddy.

"I wish to review the plan," Faunus said.

"I know the plan," Teddy sighed.

"You do not deviate from it," Faunus decreed.

Teddy pressed his lips tightly together.

"You wanted to come, your job is to keep her safe," Faunus reminded him, jerking his head back to Moira.

And your and Saturn's job is to keep Mars and his queen and their fellow rulers safe. So, who's going to keep you *safe?* he thought but he did not ask.

"We were in agreement with this, Teddy," Faunus said.

That wasn't entirely true. Faunus decreed it and Teddy had tired of arguing about it.

"I am a trained warrior, *bello,*" Faunus said quietly. "And you are not."

"Neither is Queen Silence, and she will fight these things," Teddy pointed out.

"Yes, but she is a witch."

Stymied.

"Do not make me worry about you," Faunus warned.

"I won't," he decreed, relatively certain he told the truth. "Though we reach Nautilus with you knowing that there are five beings on this planet who have ever, *ever,* Faunus, held a place in my heart. Nyx, Lorenz, Saturn, Moira, and most especially, *you.* So, you stand right there and promise me you will keep *you* safe."

"I will come back to you, Teddy," Faunus whispered, moving closer to him and taking him by the side of the neck, bending to look into his eyes. "I promise."

"You have my love," Teddy mumbled.

Faunus grinned. "And you have mine."

"You have my devotion," Teddy went on.

"And you have mine," Faunus repeated.

"And adoration."

"You can be quiet now," Faunus said, his words trembling with amusement.

Teddy thought that was a good idea, and thus, he did as told.

Faunus gave his neck a squeeze, let him go and they moved to the railing, standing there and doing this close.

"Have you had fish in batter?" Faunus asked.

"Never," Teddy answered.

"Something to look forward to," Faunus murmured.

He hoped so.

By the gods, he hoped so.

~

Chu of the Trusted
Aboard the Passenger Galleon, the Constant
STRAIT OF MEDUSA

"YOU WILL NOT PERFORM THIS RITUAL," Chu growled.

"Chu, they're aboard this very vessel," Serena returned. "I can sense them."

"You will leave them be."

"I will draw one to me and ask why they follow you."

"You will do no such thing."

"I will know why they follow you!"

"I do not care why they follow me, Rena."

"Well, I do!"

They glared at each other across their cabin.

He watched her get a hold on herself, something she did much faster than he.

"I fear you're in danger," she said far more quietly.

"If they wished me dead, I would have met that fate outside Dunlyn."

She was now confused. "Then why are they here?"

"I do not know, and as I said, I do not care. I won't be drawn into whatever is happening across the Triton Sea. It is not my life. My world. My home. And it never again will be."

"Do you think they'll just go away?"

"I think, when they wish their presence to be known, and their message to be delivered, they will do it."

"But they don't wish you harm." She made a statement that was a question.

"Harm comes in many forms, my warrior," he replied. "And whatever their business, them coming from *there* will cause me harm."

"Chu," she whispered.

"I survived assassins, mouse, I'll survive whatever this is."

She did not look convinced, but she didn't say more.

"Have you ever fucked aboard a ship?" he asked.

Her face changed, and not to what it normally did when he would utter such words.

To obstinacy.

His woman was anxious.

"We are nearly there," she remarked.

"And?" he asked.

She shook her head, "It won't work, Chu, you will not turn my mind from my worries."

"Care to wager?"

She studied him.

He moved to her.

She did not wager.

Which was well and good.

For she would have lost.

~

Queen Ha-Lah
Queen's Study, Keel Castle, Nautilus
Mar-el

"You feel sure of this," Farah asked Ry where they all sat about, pouring over the tomes they had confiscated from Go'Doan, as well as the ones Ry had brought to Sky Bay, all of which covered the makeshift table that Tint, Bond, Ore and Nis had set up in my study.

"Before they were captured in the stones, they cursed the gods who created them, and..." Ry lifted the armless spectacles to his eyes, but even so, he squinted over the volume before him and read from it, "*and vowed vengeance with no mercy that they would wreak destruction across the lands and to the peoples the gods had also created, before they sought the gods and consumed them, taking their all-powerfulness within themselves and replacing the makers so all would worship them or know tyranny.*"

"And you are certain the gods who created them are Triton and Medusa?" I queried.

Ry shoved aside the book in front of him and reached for another beyond that, which was opened to a pertinent page.

I had earlier read from that book myself.

It was entitled, *The Creators: Triton and his Queen.*

He bent over it and read, "*To the sirens, as demi-gods, they gave them their dominion as was their wont, fearsome power to play with those on the seas, so the sailors would revere them and pray to them. To the Mer, their chosen, the ones that sprang forth from their love, they gave the bounty of The Deep. To the beings, they gave them land to sow and reap and make plenty. To the charmed, they gave magic, to hold and protect. To the demons, they gave havoc, in order that all their creatures would know adversity, and how to draw together to overcome it.*"

Ry pushed that tome away, pulled another out from under one to his left, opened it at a marked page, and read.

"*But the demons did not lose their purpose. And when the land was locked in turmoil, the Beasts would sleep. But when the land sought serenity, the Beasts would awaken. And those proclaimed would face the challenge. In victory, this homage to the goodness of the gods would make them rise. In defeat, the demons would kill the gods to become gods themselves and the realm of Triton would grow dark for eternity.*"

He turned to another marked page.

"*For the proclaimed would be born holding the power of the gods. And they would wield it. But the god would call his sacrifice. And he would have it. And then the power would be unleashed.*"

"What sacrifice?" Farah whispered.

"You have all sacrificed along this journey, have you not?" Ry, catching her mood, said soothingly.

I sat, struck.

"Yes," Farah answered.

"No," I said.

They both looked at me.

"You…" Farah began, but she didn't go on, for it was true. I hadn't. Not like the rest of them. Then she said, "Aramus lost his man in Fire City."

"Aramus did, but I barely knew him."

I said these words at the same time I felt my blood run cold.

Farah reached a hand to me and murmured, "Ha-Lah."

"Is there more about this sacrifice?" I asked G'Ry.

He shook his head. "That is the only mention of it, my dear."

"You barely knew Aramus when you married," Farah tried. "You didn't get along."

My eyes drifted to the window.

"You might not have known Aramus's man, but your husband mourned his loss and he is a part of you," Farah continued. "You definitely knew Jasmine. You—"

"Triton will require of me," I whispered.

"Ha-Lah," Farah curled her fingers around my forearm, "don't say that."

"I have not sacrificed for the prophecy," I said tonelessly.

"There is but one note about it, my queen. We have already learned some of the words were written in error. Perhaps it means nothing," Ry suggested.

I looked to him. "There is nothing in all of this that means *nothing*. We've righted wrongs. We've brought peace. And in doing so, brought forth the demons. To keep what we earned, we must sacrifice. And everyone has sacrificed, *except me*."

Ry looked deep into my eyes and stated, "You know this is untrue."

"I—"

"You are not your true self, even now. You do not live your whole life in hiding without sacrifice," he declared.

"She knows I'm Mer," I told him, referring to Farah.

"Well they," he threw his arm to the window, "do not. Not yet. You will find victory, my queen, all of you will. And you will be written in the tomes as the Protectors. You and *your people*. You have helped them to rise again from the depths. To be known and *seen*. And I do not believe you did this without sacrifice." He patted the table with his hand and finished, "Think not of this any longer. You need your wits about you."

He was so very right.

I nodded.

I then glanced at Farah.

She squeezed my arm.

"The plan is set," Ry stated, his voice firm. "We must drive them to Triton."

"We must drive them to Triton," Farah agreed.

I looked to the window.

And wondered where my husband was.

King Cassius

The Abyss, Fifteen Miles Down the Coast from Nautilus

MAR-EL

"IF I WAS A GOD, this is not where I'd be," Cassius muttered, staring down into the dark maw.

"The gnomes have reported?" Aramus asked him.

He looked to his friend, surprised at this abrupt question.

"They have. They track them. And the creatures are here," he confirmed. "We simply await everyone's arrival before we enact the plan."

"And we have all, so far, successfully made Mar-el without them knowing we have sailed the sea?" Aramus pressed.

"As far as I know," Cassius said, glancing at Ellie, who was patrolling the wide edge of the abyss along the sea, gazing into the hole, before turning fully to him. "My brother—"

"He is not at his full strength. I do not know what power he has, if any, that can help," Aramus said. "And I have broken a vow every king of this realm has kept sacred that you even know he exists."

"I've known Triton exists since I had conscious thought," Cassius told him reassuringly. "Granted, I didn't know where he *dwelt*, but I knew he existed."

"He's lonely," Aramus murmured.

"We're working on that," Cassius said.

"They could come for him before we have our plan in place," Aramus stated.

Cassius felt Elena's gaze and looked to her.

She lifted her chin then moved away from the abyss, seeing to their mission there, which was to check the lay of the land, tighten their approach, understand what they had to work with before they had to work with it.

He watched her move farther away before he again gave his attention to Aramus.

"Would you like to tell me precisely what has you so uneasy?" he demanded low.

"He is a god and gods do not do something for nothing."

"We have no choice but to move forward," Cassius pointed out.

Aramus opened his mouth.

But Cassius spoke first.

"The sprites and pixies fly, and Lahn rides with True and Farah as they drive their demons here," Cassius bit. "The gnomes and Tor ride with Elena and I as we drive ours here. The Mer ride with you and Ha-Lah as you drive yours here. And the fairies fly, and Apollo rides with Mars and Silence as they drive theirs here. All our captains will already be here to offer might and magic. Frey uses the dragons to keep them here. We unleash all hell on them with the Mer in the depths at the ready to force them into that underground cavern if we fail to do nothing but shove them over the edge. At the least, in the end, they will be contained. This is our plan. It's a shite plan, but it's a plan. We chuck everything we've got at the bastards and hope like fuck it works."

Cassius moved closer to his friend.

And he spoke on.

"I'm uneasy too. Everyone I love, save my daughters, will be here." He pointed to the rock beneath their feet. "I don't wish to lose a single one of you. I definitely don't want to lose all of you. And I for one am going to fight like hell to make sure none of that happens."

Aramus's stare was intent.

He then grinned.

"Just to note, I love you too."

"Always a pain in my arse," Cass muttered, looking away.

Aramus clapped him on the shoulder and held.

Therefore, Cass looked back.

"If there's loss, if the good we accomplished in our realms remains despite that loss, it was worth it," his friend said quietly.

Cassius drew in a deep breath, shifted his eyes to the side, and saw his wife standing, staring out at sea, hands on hips, the sunshine of her hair blowing in the sea breeze.

And he determined he wasn't going to lose shite.

Regardless, he looked to Aramus.

And said, "Absolutely."

~

King True

The Beach, Keel Castle, Nautilus

MAR-EL

"SHE'LL BE FINE," True assured.

Mars scowled at the lapping water that, not long ago, Silence and Jorie waded into.

And then disappeared.

"She's with Jorie," True reminded him. "She'll come back, pink in her cheeks, delighted with her adventure."

Mars looked into the horizon. "Two years ago today, you and I faced each other on a battlefield."

True's body locked.

Gods, he was right.

"And now you are my brother," Mars went on.

True said nothing.

"They will not take her from me," he told the horizon.

"No," True replied.

Slowly, Mars turned his head and locked eyes with True.

"They will not take *you* from me."

True drew breath into his nose.

And he repeated, "No."

"I know she will be all right, True. But when she is away from me, I will always, *always* worry."

"All right, my friend," True whispered.

"Worry with me," Mars invited on a murmur, then he bent his knees and fell to his arse in the sand.

True followed him.

They sat, wrists to their knees, and stared at the sea.

Two men who loved a woman.

Waiting for her return.

~

Queen Silence
The Deep

THE SWIM WAS LONG, and this was good, for it took me quite some time to get used to the many, *many* Mer that swam at our backs, not all males, there were a good many females.

And they all carried tridents.

There were a great number of us.

My people.

With me.

I loved that.

However, the swim was long, and I worried, for Mars would worry after me.

These were my thoughts when I saw it.

A warm, blue glow that rose out of the depths.

Jorie, beside me, struck lower, swimming toward it, and as he had instructed, I remained close to his side.

But I could not stop myself from rearing back when, from where the glow emanated—what looked like the mouth of a cave—the beasts formed out of the shadows on either side of it.

Angmostros.

Two of them.

I had never seen one.

They were colossal.

And *terrifying*.

Jorie stopped with me and drifted close, his long tail coiling about mine.

This felt like a hug, a mermaid embrace, and it was a thing of beauty.

"Steady, my little sister," he murmured, also winding his arms around me. "We are of royal blood. She will make them let us pass."

"The others...the...the others won't be coming with us?" I asked, ignoring my hair floating about my face, running along my neck, under my jaw.

He shook his head. "They have swum with us solely in case the Beasts that have risen on land could get to mischief in the depths."

I nodded.

"I have gone to her," he said comfortingly. "Our father has gone to her. His father before him. She is our benefactress. She is a friend to all Mer. But others could seek her for reasons she does not wish. So she guards herself. Regardless, you need not fear the beasts of the sea."

I nodded slowly.

"Except sharks, but only because they're rabble-rousers," he muttered.

And this made me grin.

He grinned back, pressed a kiss to my forehead, and unwound himself from around me.

And then, my big brother, my Jorie, gave me one last, long look to ascertain I was all right, and I showed him that I was.

He then nodded and struck out toward the mouth of the cave.

I swam beside him.

The long, *long* necks and flat, jagged heads of the *angmostros* coasted in the water, their mouths agape, out of the dark depths of which spiked pointed tongues, those dread mouths were further lined with sharp teeth, and the gleaming pinpoints of their blue eyes followed us as we swam to the opening of the cave.

Jorie was right.

They allowed us to pass.

We entered its light, and instantly, I felt a contented warmth from within.

And with a few kicks of my fin, gazing in wonder all about me, all I could think was...

I wished I could take Mars here.

153
THE RISING

Magnus Reardon
Aboard the Pirate Ship, Medusa's Navel, *Outside Bloody Boy Cove, Twenty Miles North of Nautilus*
STRAIT OF MEDUSA

"Captain!" Bellamy shouted, and Magnus looked down from the helm to watch his man's swift approach. "You need to see!"

Just looking at Bellamy's face, he knew it.

He knew there was a reason he'd turned back from delivering their load to Fleuridia in the Northlands.

He jerked up his chin to Tallis beside him and Tallis took the wheel as Magnus made his way to the stairs, down to the main deck and all the way to the bow.

When he saw what he saw in Bloody Boy Cove, he grunted, "Spyglass," to Bellamy.

Bellamy handed him his telescope.

Magnus elongated it and held it to his eye.

Sirens damn it.

He turned on his boot and ordered, "Birds. Now. We need to get word to Aramus. Mar-el is being invaded."

"But...by whom. And...why?" Bellamy asked, the gods not granting the man much stature, thus he was running to keep up with the long strides of his captain.

The answer to his question was, by the looks of it, everyone. Airenzian. Dellish. He even caught sight of some Nadirii.

He did not share that with Bellamy.

He stopped short, turned to look down to his man and repeated, *"Birds. Now."*

He then made haste to the helm in order to come about and head to Nautilus.

Nick Walsh
Hayloft, Public Stable, Nautilus
MAR-EL

"THE FEMALE HAS SEPARATED from the pack," Angus reported.

He'd seen this from his vantage, studying the inn.

She'd gone out the back.

He'd also seen the gnomes go after her.

"Follow her," Nick ordered.

Angus immediately ran to the stairs.

"I will repeat, I do not know why we're here," Rory said.

Nick did not take his eyes from the inn as he asked, "Do you wish to go on thieving?"

"Of course," Rory replied.

Slowly, he turned his head to look at his friend. "If you wish there to be an Airen, and Airenzian, to charm out of their baubles, we have work to do. *Here.*"

"Nick, mate, one of the males has gone," Leith stated.

Bloody hell.

They were initiating.

Nick did not break contact with Rory's eyes as he commanded Leith, "Go after him."

He heard Leith's boots on the boards.

"Highwaymen, helping to save all realms," Rory muttered in disgust.

"That's about it," Nick confirmed.

"If I get dead in gods-damned Mar-el, trying to save all realms, I'm dragging you to the under-realm with me," Rory declared.

Nick grinned at him.

Then he looked back out from the loft to see another of the creatures in human form steal away.

"I've got that one," Kaden called.

"That means we're on the last," Nick murmured.

"Fantastic," Rory replied.

Nick grinned again.

Even if his stomach felt sour.

This did not stop him from saying, "Let us move."

And this, they did.

~

Galbdor and Welbrix
Nautilus
Mar-el

They made the roof and raced across it.

Gal made the leap to the next roof, and Brix jumped after him.

Gal then took a turn, dropped down, caught a finial, swung around it, launched himself across the alley, and landed on his feet on the roof opposite.

He did not wait until Brix had landed solid with him.

He kept running.

Though he was glad to hear his friend's boots hit tile.

They made many jumps, swings and heaves before, thanks be to their Green god, they made the roof they sought.

Gal dropped to shimmy down a drainpipe. He then swung to the window ledge and did not hesitate a moment before he kicked the window in with his boots.

He landed on the floor inside amongst a sprinkle of glass, only to face Serena and Chu, both of whom, in the commotion, had drawn their arms and were at the ready to attack.

Brix landed beside him as Gal said, "The priests were wrong. They have venom. You need to gather the others. They need to ride. *Now.*"

"Venom? They can freeze people with their poison?" Serena asked in a grim tone.

"No," Brix answered. "They can *turn them.*"

"Turn them?" Chu queried.

"There's no time to explain. They are not only here," Gal began. "They have created an army."

"By the goddess," Serena breathed.

"That's what they've been doing," Chu bit.

But no one said another word.

They all raced out.

~

Teddy
Smuggler's Den Inn, Nautilus
MAR-EL

FAUNUS HAD BARELY DROPPED his bag in their room when he turned to Teddy and declared, "We need to report we've arrived."

Teddy nodded and said, "But you'll be back."

Faunus came to him. "I'll be back. Tonight, I stay with you. Tomorrow…"

He didn't finish this, but he didn't need to, for Teddy already knew what would happen on the morrow.

Or what they all *hoped* would happen.

They both tensed when they heard a faraway scream.

Faunus moved swiftly to the window and looked out.

Teddy quickly joined him, and as he was taking these strides, another scream could be heard.

There also seemed a muted commotion from belowstairs.

"I don't—" Teddy began to say he didn't see anything amiss, as he gazed out the window at the meandering lane very close to which attractive, very seaside-city-looking (to his estimation, though this was the only seaside city he'd visited) buildings were built.

The view they could see from their vantage point at the back of the inn.

There were pedestrians, not quite going about their business, for they'd all turned their attention in the direction of the screams.

Teddy startled and stopped speaking, and Faunus shifted to stand before him, when they heard a thump belowstairs.

Faunus then moved directly to his bags, unbuckled them, and pulled out his two long kris blades.

"Faunus," Teddy murmured as they heard fast steps ascending the stairs down the hall from their room.

Because of this, and more screams from outside, when Faunus handed him the blades and unsheathed his sword from his back, Teddy did not demur in taking them.

He barely had a handle on them when the door was kicked open.

Faunus prepared to attack but did not for Moira came careening into the room because Saturn had hurled her inside.

Faunus caught her one-armed and tossed her to Teddy, who carefully, seeing as he had two daggers in his hands, shunted her behind him just as what looked like three Airenzian males came storming into the room behind Saturn.

They were armed.

And they did not hesitate to attack.

By the gods.

What was happening?

"Give me one of those!" Moira shouted, wresting the dagger from his left hand as sounds of steel striking steel filled the room.

"*Get to the other side of the bed!*" Faunus roared as he held a sword from striking him from above with his own at the same time, he plunged a dagger into the gut of one of the males and dragged it upwards.

Teddy grabbed Moira and hauled her toward the bed.

They jumped it and made the other side, Teddy shoving Moira in the corner and standing strong in front of her, his weapon raised, just in time to watch Saturn swinging his sword low and cutting another of the males off at his knees.

Gruesomely, the man toppled to the ground.

The one Faunus had injured was also down.

The last man was rounding the bed to get to Teddy and Moira, but he didn't make it as, in a gods-awful spray of blood, Faunus took his head.

They heard more screams, shouts, and noises of panic outside as they all stood frozen inside, everyone's eyes to the door.

It was Saturn who moved to shut it, but as he'd broken it to enter, it did not latch.

He thus simply set it to and walked back to the legless man on the floor.

He lifted his weapon and cut off the fallen man's sword arm at the elbow.

Teddy's lip automatically curled.

Moira groaned.

Hearing it, Teddy turned to her and pulled her into his arms, putting a hand to the back of her head and tucking her face to his chest.

Saturn kicked the man's weapon away (indeed, he kicked his entire forearm away) and straightened, still staring down at him.

"He is not dead," he stated.

Faunus did not move from his position of barring the path to Moira and Teddy.

But he did ask, "What?"

"He is legless and has lost an arm, but he is not dead, and yet he does not moan," Saturn pointed out.

Teddy let Moira go, jumped the bed, and hastened to Saturn on Faunus's growled, "*Tedrey*."

His whole name.

Tedrey.

Gods, save him from overprotective warriors.

He ignored his warrior's warning, squatted beside the Airenzian and studied him, feeling cold enter his chest as he did.

"Moira, *stellina*," Faunus murmured as Teddy heard Moira jump on and over the bed.

He loved it when Faunus called her *stellina*.

His little star.

He let that love settle, as it always did, but he could not think much on it.

"This man is gone," he stated, staring into eyes that were open, alive, but there was nothing there.

No pain. No emotion.

Vacant.

There were noises from the room beside them as it occurred to him.

"The venom," he whispered.

"We must leave this place," Faunus declared.

Teddy straightened and pulled Moira away, turning her into him again as he instructed Saturn, "Put him out of his misery."

Saturn did not delay.

Moira pressed close as her warrior moved to perform what was now an act of mercy.

Teddy looked to Faunus.

"The legends of the Beast said he could freeze humans," he said. "That was always the worst part. That you could be there, alive, paralyzed, helpless to help yourself, and you would just waste away."

There were more screams, more commotion outside the window, and thus Faunus grew visibly more impatient.

"I know the lore, *amore*," he growled.

"What if it's the same, of a sort, but actually worse?" Teddy whispered and indicated the men on the floor with a dip of his head.

After hearing Teddy's words, Faunus moved to the man he'd gutted.

He was still alive, lying on his stomach, staring blankly at the floor.

Faunus studied him a moment before he crouched, pulled the man's head back and drew his blade across his neck.

Blood poured forth, and Faunus straightened and stepped away from it.

"We must leave here, *amico*," Saturn warned.

"We go to the Mouth," Teddy said quietly.

Faunus's gaze jumped to him. "No."

"It will be the safest place," Teddy said.

"The rulers will know this happens and they will drive them there," Faunus retorted.

"And they will be there to stop them. It's the safest place, Faunus." He indicated the window with a jerk of his head. "Listen to it out there."

Faunus had excellent hearing, but you didn't need it to know something was very amiss in Nautilus.

Faunus's mouth tightened.

He looked to Saturn.

Teddy looked to Saturn.

His mouth was tight too.

"Let us go see if we can find our horses," Faunus muttered, but moved to the men on the floor.

He took their weapons, disbursed them between their crew, and unsurprisingly, he then took the lead as he carefully guided them into what sounded like pandemonium.

~

Queen Farah
Queen's Study, Keel Castle, Nautilus
MAR-EL

IT STARTED as the sound of running feet.

Then the door burst open and Nav was there.

We all slowly stood from our seats around the table even as he spoke.

"Lock this behind me and do not leave this room."

"What's happening?" Ha-Lah asked.

He didn't answer.

He slammed the door.

Ha-Lah rushed to it.

I rushed to the window.

"Do you see anything?" Ha-Lah called.

I did not, except for the lovely grounds of Keel Castle and the back of Medusa's Gate at the end of the lane.

Thus, I answered, "No."

But I whipped around when more running feet could be heard as well as some shouts.

"We have no weapons," Ha-Lah hissed, standing several feet back, but staring at the door.

The screech of steel against steel could be heard, and I turned my head toward the fireplace.

Ry stood there holding the fire poker. "Yes, we do."

Ha-Lah and I rushed to him.

He gave Ha-Lah the poker, me the shovel, and he took the tongs.

Even less optimistic noises came from beyond the door.

We all took hold of our makeshift weapons, steadied our stances, and kept our gazes alert on the door.

～

King Mars
The Beach, Keel Castle, Nautilus
MAR-EL

"TRUE! *TRUE!*"

Both men turned from their study of the sea, only to see Florian sprinting their way.

They were on their feet in less than a breath and tearing through the sand to him.

When they met, Florian did not delay.

"They attack."

"The Beasts?" True asked.

"No, their army," Florian answered.

True recoiled.

"*What army?*" Mars barked.

Florian looked to him. "I don't know what army. But they have a gods-damned, bloody, fucking *army*."

"We must instigate the plan," True declared. "Immediately."

Mars looked back to the sea.

"Mars, Farah is in that castle!" True bit out.

He looked to his friend. "Silence."

"Warn her and let us go!"

But True did not wait.

He and Florian raced back to the castle.

Mars raced back down the sand.

Quickly, with his boot, he gouged out one word.

Only when he was done did he sprint to the seat of the King of Mar-el.

Leaving behind a message that couldn't be misread.

DANGER.

~

Queen Ha-Lah
Queen's Study, Keel Castle, Nautilus
MAR-EL

THE FIGHTING COULD BE HEARD outside the door.

However, it didn't last long before the door burst open with the force of five men rolling through it.

One was Nav, one was Xi, one was Wallace, and two were men I did not know, but I could see one was Dellish and one was Airenzian.

But several more of the last barreled through the door, plus a few Mar-el, walking right over them as if they were floor, not men.

Ry scuttled forward, raising his long tongs, and striking the first man to approach us with a hearty clout upside his head.

He staggered to the side.

Only for another to take his place.

More were coming through the door, and Farah and I as one engaged, because we should, but also because we had to.

My poker was not my first choice in weapons, but at least it was strong, a good defense, but within blocking three strikes, my arms were humming with the effort of deflecting the blows.

I was not quick enough for his recovery, and made to duck to escape his next attempt, when the point of a sword came through his chest from the back.

It was swiftly pulled out, the man fell, exposing Wallace behind him.

He did not even meet my eyes.

He whirled to become my defense, and I was heartened to see Ore and Luther had joined the fight in the room.

But there were so many of them.

Why were the Airenzian, Dellish and *Mar-el* fighting kings' men in a king's castle?

With no way to find an answer to that in the now, I squatted to pull the weapon out of the hand of the man that Wallace had wounded, chilled when I saw from his face that he had not died, but even so, in a manner, he looked like he had.

Alive.

But gone.

I could also not think on that.

I took his weapon from his hand and stood just as Farah shrieked, *"Ry!"*

My eyes went to our friend to see him reeling from a blow.

This, right before he took a mortal strike to the side of his neck.

He collapsed to his hip and a hand.

I screamed in fury and charged the man who had taken him, swinging well right with the hefty weapon (we should have asked Serena to teach us swordplay, too late now).

Before he could recover from the blow he dealt Ry, I swiped him across his gut.

His innards spilled forth as he fell to his back.

I then found my arm in a clench, and I was being dragged.

I began to fight but saw Bram had hold on me.

"We make the stables!" he shouted, not to me.

He did this just as True's green filled the room and he stormed in behind it.

Only for red to wash through it in waves and Mars roared in.

Bram shoved me against the wall, Ore tossing Farah to it beside me, they stood in front of us as True and Mars turned a gruesome scene grisly.

I sensed it was done at the same time as Farah, and thus we both dashed around our protectors.

Straight to Ry.

"We must go," Mars grunted.

We both hunkered down beside him.

He was on his side, blinking, his neck covered in blood where it wasn't opened flesh.

"Ry," Farah whispered.

"I..." he pushed out.

"Darling," True said to his wife between gritted teeth.

"Believe," Ry whispered.

We did not stay with him in order to be with him as he met his end.

For we were taken hold of and hauled from the room.

❀

Nick Walsh
Outside Nautilus
Mar-el

They reined in as one.

"Bloody hell," Rory whispered.

Nick clenched his teeth.

Before them, over the rock of Mar-el, the army of the Beasts was obliterating the fighting charmed folk.

Gods, he had seen many ugly things in his life.

But he'd never seen anything as ugly as a dead pixie.

"We must stop this. They're going to decimate them," Rory bit out.

They couldn't stop this.

But they could try to ride through it and assist what was left of them in beating their retreat.

Both men drew their blades and hunched over their steeds in preparation to launch forth when both men sensed it and wheeled their horses to face a new threat.

Immediately, Nick had to drop his reins to catch the thing flying at him.

He also had to snap his head back so the edge of it didn't hit him and render him unconscious.

When he'd adjusted the long, curved, rectangular, wooden shield and held it by the leather strap attached at the back, he looked at the sea of Zees on horseback before him.

"You'll need that," a man he did not know was named Silvanus advised. And then that man shouted, "_Heeyah._"

And Nick, nor Rory, had any choice but to join them as a sea of Zees charged a battlefield.

〜

Princess Serena
On the Road to Keel Castle
Mar-el

They were going to be overcome.

She hacked at one, screeching, "*Goddess damn it!*"

He fell away only for another to take his place.

The enemy was so thick, their horses couldn't get through.

They'd never make the castle.

Goddess, she was going to die on a road in bloody Mar-el with the man she loved at her side and the two best friends she'd ever had riding point.

She hacked at another one.

"*Gal!*" Brix yelled from his place astride his horse in front of them.

She hastened a glance forward just in time to see Gal pulled from his mount.

"*No!*" she shrieked, rage boiling through her, using her blade at random, slashing and hacking and...

A fierce wind blew her hair back at the same time she felt the impossible.

A wisp of invisible fabric slid across her face, and in astonishment, she froze and watched as necks were broken, throats were slit, intestines oozed forth, and bodies dropped all about them.

Suddenly, there was nothing but stillness and the only living creature standing on the ground was Gal.

And then, six flashes of lightning struck the road before them, these happening on a blustery, but clear and sunny day.

From these strikes formed four men and two women.

On their chests, they had metal shields that sparkled in the sun. Layered leather armor cupping their shoulders and going down their upper arms. Aprons flowing out from under their heavy weapons belts. These were red with yellow and orange markings on them: a face with hair that was flame around which curved a dragon. Plated forearm shields. Extremely long-bladed, bloodied swords in hands and double quivers filled with arrows at their backs. Thick scarves were bunched and coiled about their necks. Their black hair swept back from widows' peaks and fell long past their shoulders.

And their red trimmed in orange mantles were drifting lazily in the breeze.

As one, they planted the points of their swords in the dirt of the road, hands one folded atop the other at the crest of ornate silver hilts.

And each fell to a knee with bowed heads.

After but a moment, one of the women lifted her head, her eyes pinned to Chu.

"My king," she said.

Oh dear, I thought.

"What the hell?" Brix demanded.

"Shite," Chu whispered.

~

King Aramus

Mar-el

They had received Magnus's bird.

The raven had come direct to him with the dire message.

And if Aramus lived beyond that day, he vowed never to tell a soul, except (perhaps) her, that when he sighted his queen galloping toward him, his relief was so great, he nearly fell off his horse.

"What the fuck is happening?" Cassius demanded, reining in Caelus so tightly, his mount's head arced to the side, his front hooves came up from the earth, and his hind end shunted around to accommodate his body's movements.

"They have an army," Mars reported.

"How do they have a gods-damned bloody army?" Cassius asked. "And who the fuck are they?" he went on, jerking his head toward a cadre of the party they'd greeted.

"They're Mystics," Serena answered, explaining the four men and two women on steeds adorned with scalloped red bunting along their reins and long blankets over their rumps, the flesh of the horses so elegant, Aramus would be sending ships to that continent to procure some.

If, again, he lived beyond that day.

"I can see they're Mystics," Cass bit out.

"They're *Mystics*?" Elena asked, her emphasis drawing Aramus and Cass's attention.

"You know about this?" Cass asked her.

"It doesn't matter about this, they're Chu's," Serena stated. "What matters is, the priests were wrong. The Beasts have venom. And it *does* freeze a being. But only their conscious inside them. Their bodies become instruments of the Beasts."

Well…

Fuck.

"Nautilus has been besieged by their army," Ha-Lah said, shuffling her horse closer to his. "It is very bad, Aramus," she finished on a horrified whisper.

He looked down at her, wasted precious time doing what he considered a priority, thus taking her by the neck, pulling her to him, and pressing his lips to hers.

He let her go, and she whispered, "I am all right."

None of them were all right.

Thus, he simply grunted.

"Our women," Lahn barked, regaining Aramus's attention to their populace huddle.

"Your men, all of them," Nav began, "remain behind guarding them. And the women have erected a magical barrier, rendering their hiding place invisible."

This apparently sufficed for Lahn for he said no more, his large body visibly relaxing.

"Do we know anything else?" Elena asked.

True was gazing up as he said, "We hunt."

"We hunt?" Cassius asked.

"It's time to institute the plan," True stated.

And then they heard them and all either looked up or twisted in order to do the same.

There, in the sky, they saw the dragons.

"*Yah!*" he heard, turned back around and saw Mars charging, followed by Apollo, Basil and Kyril.

"*Heeya!*" True shouted, and off went True with Farah, Lahn, Wallace, Luther, Bram and Florian.

Chu wheeled around, set off, and Serena, the gnomes, and the Mystics rode after him.

"Fortune shine on you, my brother," Cassius stated gutturally, and then he set his heels into Caelus and burst forth, Elena at his side, Tor, Mac, Hera, Nero, Rus and Ian going with them.

"Let's go, darling," Hal-Lah urged softly.

He looked down to his wife, who had weapons at her belt, his men, all of them bloodied, but fortunately, none of them wounded.

"Where is Silence?" he asked.

He felt instant hatred of the look that came over her face.

"I do not know," she whispered.

And he drew in breath.

"*Jah!*" he yelled, digging his heels in his horse.

And they rode.

∽

King True
MAR-EL

HE WINCED as the stream of fire raged down from the sky, the heat wafting from it feeling like it singed his flesh.

But when the dragon's flame receded, the horse and rider racing before them could still be seen, and he and all the riders behind had to avoid the crater.

Frey had warned that the elves in his realm had shared the Beast would be immune to the blaze of a dragon.

But his horse?

Another stream of fire shot down and True rode carefully in order not to cross it.

Then, almost not making the jump, he and Majesty nearly ran into the charred remains of a horse.

Right then, the horse was not immune to dragonfire.

The last had been a mishit.

An almighty shriek could be heard from above.

They looked up, and True immediately shouted, "*Evade!*" as the great dragon started to spiral through the air toward the earth.

He, Farah and Lahn scattered, and the ground trembled when the dragon crashed to the earth.

And, riding on, but looking back, True got his first glimpse of a Beast as creature, not in the form of a man, ludicrously tall, head sunk into a matted ruff at its broad neck, long, shocking claws raised, standing on his back hooves atop the regal, powerful body of the flailing dragon.

"I thought they were indestructible!" Farah cried in distress.

Dragons were.

Unless, apparently, they came up against a demon of the gods.

Bloody fabulous.

Another awesome and terrible shriek sounded behind them just as another dragon flapped forth and rained fire on the Beast and the dragon's fallen brethren.

"*Round and re-engage!*" True roared, not liking the knowledge the Beasts could leap great heights and bring down dragons.

He pulled his reins left and Farah and Lahn followed him.

"He goes to the Mouth!" Lahn yelled. "We do not have to give chase! We can follow him!"

"We know that!" True yelled in return. "But he does not know that."

Lahn either saw the wisdom of keeping the Beast on the run and getting the damned thing where they wanted him without delay or decided not to waste energy arguing about it as they made their round only to cut it tighter when the fallen dragon righted itself.

It took hold of the Beast in its jaws, shook it and then let fly, sending it careening across the black rock of Mar-el.

"Thank the gods," Farah called in relief.

He had a wife who worried for dragons.

He'd rejoice about that later, seeing as, in the now, after taking that brutal roll, the Beast simply jumped to its cloven feet and raced away.

And it did this *fast*.

He bent over Majesty's neck and whispered, "Fly."

As ever, his righteous steed gave all he could give to his master.

And as they rode, hell bent for the Mouth of Triton, above them soared two dragons.

~

Teddy
Just Outside the Abyss
MAR-EL

THE GREAT DRAGONS circling in the air, the sea beyond the gaping hole in the earth churning wildly, they came.

Nineteen lieutenants of four rulers (and six Mystics, wherever the bloody hell *they* came from) stood against the onslaught as what seemed like thousands of armed, expressionless, Airenzian, Dellish, Mar-el and even Nadirii living wraiths charged toward the abyss.

"They'll be slaughtered," Moira whispered.

"You stay with them, I go," Faunus ordered Saturn.

Teddy opened his mouth to shout *No!* but Saturn covered it with his hand and pulled him back down behind the outcropping of rock where they hid.

And the love of his life charged forward.

~

Chu of the Trusted
Just Above the Abyss
MAR-EL

THE MYSTICS WERE LEGENDARY.

But even they could not bring down what Chu estimated were at least five hundred men and women with weapons, no thought, no free will and no sense of pain.

And Serena was using battle magic to attempt to gain them the upper hand.

Thus, because of it, she was flagging.

"Fight, not cast!" he grunted, staving off two blows, one with sword, one with dagger.

His warrior did not reply.

He fought on and did it knowing, if a miracle did not occur, and soon, he would die by the sea fighting beside the woman he loved and men he respected.

He came to terms with that in naught but a second.

But he did so determining that his end would not come until she was no more.

So yes.

He fought on.

And even when the first Beast burst forth and the dragons pulled back, for Frey would not send down their fire if it might strike an ally, and True, Farah and Lahn on their horses exploded into the clearing, he did not feel hope.

Until he witnessed Dax Lahn of the Korwahk whirl on his arse in his saddle, jumping over the rump and landing stoutly on his big, booted feet.

"What's that man doing?" Serena yelled.

Chu was otherwise engaged.

He could not answer, and he could not fully watch.

But that did not mean he did not catch the king of the Korwahk stand strong and dispatch a stream of challengers, most coming more than one at once, and he did this without moving either foot.

Just wielding his sword.

Even when he had to fight at his back, he simply twisted at the waist, as skilled with his blade at his rear flank as he was faced forward.

Chu had never seen the like of it.

But in that moment, he was glad as fuck for it.

Elena, Cassius and Tor rode in, chasing their own creature, and they entered the fight.

And then Aramus and Ha-Lah.

Not long after, the regiments that the realms had brought with them finally made it from where they'd gathered in hiding, and they entered the fray.

Only then did Chu take heart.

Until a new wave of the enemy came racing up the coast.

They were chasing fairies, pixies, sprites and gnomes.

But they were being chased by Zees carrying broad, curved shields, and they were accompanied by...

Bloody hell.

Highwaymen.

~

King Cassius
Just Above the Abyss
Mar-el

The Beasts had engaged.

It was bedlam, he had no idea who was winning, or who was losing, or when they came into the fight.

First, they spat their venom.

But Elena and Serena had prepared for that, doing this finding high ground, and casting magical shields for those who didn't have them (for the Zees, always smart, had shown and played it just that way).

So, then the Beasts fought.

And as the bloody fucking fates would have it, Mac was the closest to one.

Emotion roared through Cass as he saw Mac's body fly through the air.

He landed on the stone and skidded on his leathers, his limbs uncontrolled, his friend obviously unconscious (or gods forbid, dead), toward the end of a cliff.

"_No!_" Cass roared as Hera chased after him with such intent, when he rolled over the edge...

She went with him.

Of a sudden, Cassius stood stock still.

He raised his face to the heavens.

"_NO!_" he thundered.

And the day was banished.

And all about them there was night.

~

Teddy
Just Outside the Abyss
Mar-el

"They're losing," Saturn whispered, watching a battlefield that was now impossibly being fought in the night, a battle that was lit coral by Nadirii magic.

A sprite came flying their way, and they all ducked, then they all flinched when they heard the moist noise of it hitting a rock behind them.

"Teddy, take her and go," Saturn ordered. "Get her to safety. Just *go.*"

Teddy looked to his friend.

He was warrior.

He could no longer hide behind a rock in a time like this than he could fly.

"Go," Teddy forced out, his voice thick.

"No," Moira whimpered.

Saturn took her mouth in a fierce kiss.

Then he rose, leapt the rock, and raced to the fray.

Teddy put his arm about his friend and pulled her closer.

"I'm not running," she stated.

Teddy stared at what was happening before them.

All the rulers were there. Their lieutenants. Rulers from across an ocean. Gnomes. Fairies. Pixies. Sprites. Zees. Soldiers. Dragons were raining fire on the outskirts, incinerating men and stone. People were falling into the hole in the middle that they were all fighting around.

And day had become night.

But there was more.

Vines were breaking up from the rocks, snaking swiftly across the stone, wrapping around the legs of the enemy and pulling them back, dragging bodies across the grit and hurling them into the distance or over the edge of the cliff.

Great waves were crashing against the rocks, rising high, the water falling what seemed like with aim, washing away members of the army with blank faces, taking them over the side into the sea.

And still, that mindless army, hacking and hewing, killing or falling in droves...

And those Beasts, with their slashing claws and ridiculous speed...

This is what hell looks like, Teddy thought.

"I'm not running either," he whispered to Moira, tightening his hold on her.

They both jumped when, suddenly, they heard a boom from a cannon.

The earth shook and a great mass of the side of the cliff fell away, taking down enemy, as well as some gnomes, who fairies and pixies dashed to grab and heft back up to land, all this because a cannonball had slammed into it.

Another boom.

And that cannonball tore through some of the enemy, and into the belly of one of the Beasts, who took it then zoomed across the stone.

Yet another boom that hit the side of the cliff and made the earth shake.

"Good aim," Moira whispered.

"The gods are with us," Teddy said by rote.

"I disagree," she retorted furiously.

With what was happening, he could not argue that.

"What...?" Moira asked, her question having more words, but she could not utter them.

But Teddy knew what it was.

For the dark sky shafted with coral light had now filled with waves of green light, and every swing True took, the earth exploded under his enemy, at the least taking the enemy combatant off balance, but for some, these detonations blasted away legs.

And then the sky took on surges of red.

And the blade of Mars's sword struck fire with each blow, thus every enemy it touched caught alight and toppled away, racing about meanderingly to burn to death unconsciously.

And then shafts of blue could be seen through the dark, and every swathe of Aramus's sickle sent a great sluice, a miniature tidal, the powerful gusts of water driving his enemy back to topple into the hole.

Last, beams of white slithered through the sky, and Cassius's sword struck... actual... *lightning*.

"Their eyes, Teddy, look at their *eyes*," Moira breathed.

Teddy did.

Cassius Laird's.

Pure black.

True Axelsson's.

Pure green.

Mars Laches's.

Pure fire.

Aramus Nereus's.

Sea blue.

"Maybe the gods *are* with us," Moira whispered.

Teddy searched for and found Faunus and then Saturn.

They both were up, uninjured, and they remained fighting.

Only seeing that did he silently agree.

The Beast thrown back by the cannonball careened again into the fray, bursting forth by digging his claws into the rock to propel him just as, of a sudden, whizzing zooms could be heard all around.

Dozens of tridents came from nowhere, embedding themselves into the rock, from which instantly spun men who yanked the tridents out.

In order to use them.

And streams of flame came from the hands of petite, black-haired woman with a purposeful look on her face wearing nothing but a wet nightgown and striding barefoot and fearless over jagged rock.

Silence Laches, Queen of the Firenze.

Shafts of electric blue shot from the ends of the tridents, striking the enemy. And any enemy it touched immediately fell.

Other tridents soared through the air, and through bodies, and when their mission was accomplished, they returned to their owners only to fly again.

Teddy gasped as it looked like the Firenz queen became a target of one of the Beasts.

But then Teddy gasped again when, right before it made a slash with its claws, the queen disappeared into thin air.

And suddenly, emanating some ways away from where Silence had been before, a stream of fire came from nothing, but shot all around, creating a wide circle of flame around the pit.

Those within the circle of fire, including the rulers and the Beasts, were stuck there.

But those without it were kept out.

"*We have Silence! Concentrate on one!*" True bellowed.

The men and women (gnomes, fairies, pixies and sprites) of the rulers dealt with the remaining enemy within the circle of fire as Mars fought his way to his queen.

She reappeared as he hefted her up with one arm so she sat atop his shoulders. She curled her legs under his arms, tucking the tops of her feet against his back.

True drew up Farah in the same manner.

Cassius raced to Elena and hauled her up on his shoulders.

Aramus hefted up Ha-Lah.

And...

Teddy's heart jumped when...

They...

Let...

Fly!

Teddy nearly stood to watch as fire soared from both of Silence's palms, at the same time one of the Beasts was swept up in a whirlwind it seemed was created by Farah who was twirling a hand around. And his body elongated grotesquely as Elena held her arms out, hands palm down, anchoring its feet to the stone.

It writhed in agony and Teddy's stomach clutched as its brethren roared in camaraderie and started to make their way to their sibling.

As swift as they were, they were too late.

Of a sudden, Ha-Lah raised an arm and an *angmostros* reared up over the cliff, one of its heads rising high, then bowing low, its monstrous mouth open.

It clamped down, not fully having the thing in its gullet, and as its lethal teeth pierced flesh, black ooze shot from its middle before its bottom half exploded in a burst of the same.

A cacophony of hideous shrieks filled the air from the remaining Beasts.

The *angmostros* head slithered away, jaws dripping ooze, gullet rippling with its swallow, as all the prophesied turned on the advancing brethren.

Silence held one back by fire.

Farah one by wind.

While Ha-Lah called a wave and took one off its feet.

It slipped along the rock and fell over the side of the cliff.

Silence resurrected the fire the wave had doused and then hurled a ball of flame that struck her Beast in its face and threw the creature back.

The one to its left suddenly shrieked and batted at what appeared to be nothing as the fur covering its body opened up seemingly on its own, blood flowing out.

"The Mystics are keeping it occupied! Concentrate!" Princess Serena screamed.

Fire, wind and the return of the sea creature commenced.

The Beast that flew over the side climbed back up it, made the top and raced through the circle of flame toward its stretching sibling.

But the *angmostros* clamped down and black ooze blasted out.

A mauled body that seemed to come from thin air flew across the rock and landed with a sickening thud on its back.

Teddy saw it was a man from The Mystics.

His gaze jumped back as the Beast being opened up by imperceptible blades caught another of its invisible tormentors in his huge clawed hand, making him visible.

Without delay, the creature rushed the hole and tossed the man inside.

"Retreat!" Mars's Trusted from The Mystics shouted.

"Oh, gods," Moira whimpered.

That Beast turned, like his remaining brother, to the prophesied.

"The one to the left!" Cassius shouted just as Mars yelled, "Focus on the right!"

The blue streams of the tridents struck the one to the right.

He bellowed, and then in a flash of fur and cries and grunts of men, the blue streams of the Mer stopped, and that Beast came to halt beside his brother, his claws wrapped around the staffs of a collection of tridents.

And with a squeeze and a crunch, they broke with a spray of blue sparks and the halves fell to the rock.

On no.

One of them began to walk toward the prophesied.

But he stopped when a stream of fire hit the stone before him, coming from Silence.

"Not a fucking step closer," Mars growled.

The thing's head seemed to descend more into its neck before it popped out, the fur withdrew, the claws receded.

And suddenly, before them stood a remarkably handsome, fit, naked blond man.

The man Teddy had seen back in that horrid glade in the forest of Wodell.

"Gads," Moira whispered, before she sneered, "That's a nifty damned trick."

"I am Daemon," the Beast man said.

No one spoke.

Daemon didn't mind.

"We admire you," he told them, lifting a hand to the other Beast, who Teddy's eyes went to and he saw not a Beast and not a man, but an attractive blonde woman, though her body was cut in many places and oozing blood. "Let us have the god and then we will rule beside you."

The thing calling himself Daemon took another step forward.

Both heads of the hovering *angmostros* dipped closer.

Dragons flew in from all sides and flapped, suspended in the air, red eyes aimed to the Beasts standing on stone.

"Not another sirens-damned step," Aramus warned.

"As we admire you, we do not wish to destroy you. And thus, you should know, we are holding back," Daemon warned in return.

"If that's the case, your brothers probably should have given it their all," Cassius drawled.

Teddy and Moira pressed closer when Daemon's head whipped to Cassius and he flashed awful teeth his way.

"Touchy," Mars said.

"Do not play with us for we are finished playing with you," Daemon threatened.

"Care to wager?" True asked.

"I will kill you last," Daemon promised.

"But we'll kill her first," True said.

And then another inhuman shriek as the female fell facedown to the rock with a sword sticking out of her back.

Cassius's and Elena's lieutenants stood beyond her, the man called Mac clearly being the one who hurled his sword, for he was still bent forward with the effort of doing so.

Instantly, fire blasted at Daemon while wind took the she-creature up and Elena reached behind her to snatch up her bow.

And one after another after another, with a swiftness that was impossible to believe, she strung it and let fly, each arrow that embedded itself in the female Beast making her body jump with the impacts before small coral and purple explosions burst from each wound.

But this time, Ha-Lah did not call her creature.

A wave rose up over the cliff, arched down in a pointed gush, sucked the body into its torrential wet, and then it fell to the rock with a crash, water mixed with black sludge shooting out where it landed.

With the end of the third Beast, there was no pithy repartee.

The prophesied immediately turned their powers on the final one.

But Daemon raced away, one step, and then two, and he was back to Beast, darting this way and that.

The men put their women to their feet, and the instant they had them on land, the witches hurled their magic at him.

The skies grew light, such were the streaks of blue, red, green and white as wind, fire, water and magic flooded the space, coming so quickly, Teddy couldn't keep track of it.

The *angmostros* heads descended and snapped wherever the flash of the Beast could be seen.

The dragons sent ruptures of flame.

"They have to get him, they have to get him, theyhavetogethim," Moira chanted.

And suddenly he took form.

As his human self.

Right at the edge to the abyss.

And when he did, the magic being hurled by the queens stopped immediately.

And Teddy's blood froze in his veins.

"Does one of you care about this one?" Daemon called.

And he held Faunus aloft by the throat.

"No," Teddy whispered.

"*Let him go!*" Mars roared.

Moira's arms came around Teddy.

And Teddy's eyes grew scratchy, he stared so hard at his warrior in a demon's clutch.

And memories of words said in the past surged into his head.

You have my love.

And you have mine.

You have my devotion.

And you have mine.

And adoration.

You can be quiet now.

"No," Teddy whispered again.

Moira held him tighter.

You will come home. To Firenze. Where it is warm and where you will know affection and respect. You will be Teddy's sister. He will see to you. Through Teddy, you will be my sister, and I will see to you as well.

Teddy watched as Faunus turned his head as best he could in a grip he was fighting against, both of his big, strong hands wrapped around Daemon's forearm.

And he looked Teddy's way.

Do you love me?

Yes.

When did you fall in love with me?

It began when you kissed me after you fucked Saturn that first time at Lorenz and Nyx's.

I am sorry, mio amore, *but it took me longer. I liked you very much and wanted more from you. But I knew it would go much deeper when you annoyed me greatly by demanding to put your life at risk to become a spy.*

Faunus's eyes found Teddy's.

I am here as the one who loves him. I am here as the man who has given him my heart, to share with you the depth of your profound mistake, so you can think on that until you rest on your pyre.

Still held by the Beast, Faunus's beautiful black eyes looked right into Teddy's.

This look was not a call for help.

Most handsome. I could keep you full of me for days. You'll be beautiful shooting before me with me moving deep inside.

Faunus's look was a call to hold.

I have a vast and beautiful family, Tedrey.

If we live them right, our whole lives are filled with family and that means you will one day be uncle to my children. Does that feel insignificant?

Daemon lifted Faunus up higher and Teddy saw him begin to transform into the Beast.

Those claws, when they came out, would take his warrior's head.

"*NOOOOOOOOOOOO!!!!*" he bellowed, rose up, and tore over the rock.

"*TEDDY!*" Moira shrieked.

"*TEDDY!*" he heard Saturn roar.

But Teddy raced.

Daemon's head turned to him and Teddy saw his surprise.

He then saw his lips begin to curl up.

And when Teddy didn't stop, he watched the thing's eyes get wide.

Faunus kicked him in the stomach.

Daemon lost hold.

Faunus's boots hit the ground.

He was free.

But he was too close.

Teddy would make him safe.

He hit an unsuspecting Daemon in the chest.

And Teddy and the demon toppled over the side.

Into the Mouth of Triton.

∾

"NOOOOOOOOO!"
Falling, Teddy heard Faunus's shout.
Alive.
Teddy closed his eyes.
And smiled.
Right before his head struck rock and his neck broke.

King Mars
At the Edge of the Mouth of Triton
Mar-el

"NOOOOOOOOO!" Faunus boomed.
Mars raced forward and caught his man about the chest and ribs before Faunus threw himself over the side.
They struggled.
But both suddenly stopped when a great shaft of light burst out of the mouth straight into the heavens.
Mars's gut dropped.
Fuck.
"No," Faunus whispered, head tipped back, staring into the sky.
Mars kept hold, but now not for fear he'd go after his lover.
They both knew his lover was gone.
Now, as his father would do, as any good king would do, he held his man in order to hold him up.
The light gleaming out of the hole stopped.
And they again stood in a day that was night.
"You would have defeated him," Faunus said dully.
They would have.
Mars didn't verbally confirm.
And he did not, for they would have, but it was without a doubt Faunus would have been lost to the fight.
And his Teddy knew this.
So, he took his place.
"Fucking Teddy, he always has to be the gods-damned hero," Faunus bit.

Mars had nothing to say to that either.

But from what he knew of the man, this seemed to be his bent.

They were attacked from the side by a brunette.

Only then did Mars let go, for Faunus now had someone to hold up.

She grasped his man's arms as she peered over the mouth and screamed, "*Teddy!*"

"Moira," Faunus murmured.

"*Teddy!*" she shrieked.

Pain for another shredded Mars's insides.

Fortunately, as this occurred, Mars felt Silence slide her arms about his middle.

He guided one of his around her shoulders and held her close.

Saturn approached them and sandwiched the woman between the two warriors, his eyes cast down into the mouth.

Mars felt his friends gather at his and Silence's sides.

"T-Teddy," she sobbed and then collapsed to her knees.

Faunus and Saturn went down with her.

The rays of the sun pierced through the night as another *angmostros* appeared over the side of the cliff.

Atop one of the heads was a stunning, redheaded woman with a mermaid's tail glittering brilliantly in the increasing daylight.

"He was always one to make the most of an entrance," she called.

Right before something shot out of the hole.

It darted into the air, then speeded down like a javelin, before it twisted, arse aiming down, and landed on the head of the other *angmostros*, which dipped slightly on impact, but mostly held strong.

And there sat a man who looked a lot like Aramus, except he had a head of short, tight, curly black hair and a much longer black beard.

Not to mention, the lengthy, winding tail of a Mer king.

"It is done!" he pronounced grandly.

"You took love!" Aramus shouted in fury.

"I did not take it, Sea King, it is love!" the mermale shouted back. "It gave itself!"

"You're a sirens-damned son of a bitch!" Aramus raged.

"And I made your many-greats grandfather king so I could get to *you*," the mermale returned.

Aramus had no retort to that.

The redhead smiled benevolently down at them through all of this.

The mermale tugged on a spike of the head of the beast he sat atop, and it swung toward her.

The instant they got close, he reached for her and took her into a hearty embrace.

"Erm, am I watching Triton and Medusa have a snog?" Silence asked.

"Yes," Mars answered.

"*Faith*," she breathed.

Dragons floated down to the stone all about them and Silence broke away from him to approach the trio holding onto each other at the edge of the mouth.

She crouched, knees together, legs to the side, and murmured, "Let us get you to the castle."

"I-I-m not l-l-leaving him," the woman called Moira declared. "N-not yet. He never left me. Not ever. *Not ever*. So I need to stay with him." There came a sniffle before she finished, "For a while."

"All right, love," Silence said soothingly. "Then we'll all stay for a while."

She received no response to that, but Mars heard a sob come, stifled against Faunus's throat.

Faunus dropped to his arse on the rock and Saturn shifted with him. They arranged the woman so she was somehow seated in both their laps, with their arms all about each other.

The men stared into the abyss.

The woman kept her face tucked into their bodies.

And Silence rose to stand behind them.

Mars joined her, pulling his mantle from his shoulders, wrapping it around hers, this before taking his wife in his arms.

Elena and Cassius came up on his right side.

Aramus and Ha-Lah to their right.

True and Farah to Silence's left.

Serena and Chu to their left.

Lahn, Tor, Apollo and Frey gathered around.

Jorie came to stand behind his sister.

The lieutenants walked (or limped) to join them.

Cassius gave Mac and Hera a look.

Mac, one side of his face bloodied and scraped, that side of his leathers jagged and torn, gave Cassius a shrug.

Gnomes pushed to the front.

Pixies drifted.

Sprites zinged.

Zees walked forward boldly, as was their wont, and sat at the edge of the mouth, feet dangling.

If Mars was correct, there were five Airenzian highwaymen amongst them.

The *angmostros* carrying risen gods shifted from the cliffs then slunk under the sea and swam away.

"Bloody hell, Aramus," he heard a man say. "What the fuck happened here?"

"I'll tell you later, Magnus," Aramus muttered.

Mars sighed.

In the horizon, the sun was journeying to The Mystics.

Mars heard Faunus's murmured words floating up to him, and he knew Silence did too with the way her hold on him strengthened.

"How do I live in a world without him?"

"You do it knowing he refused for there to be a world without you," Saturn replied.

Mars closed his eyes.

He opened them when Silvanus shouted, "He will always be remembered!"

"*He will always be remembered!*" the Zees cried.

"*To Our Brother Golden Hair!*" Silvanus yelled.

"*To Our Brother Golden Hair!*" the rest of them bellowed.

And it was then, Elena put her fingers to her lips, floated them out, her lips pursed like she was blowing a kiss.

And a rainbow shot out of the Mouth of Triton shafting all the way into forever.

154
THE AFTERMATH

The People of Mar-el
Nautilus
Mar-el

It was solemn when true night fell, the heralds rode, the call of victory proclaimed, and the citizens of Nautilus who had survived the Battle of the Beasts came out of hiding and made their way to the Great Beach.

Over time, it would become known great sacrifices had been made of the rulers of Triton to save them from the fall of the dark times.

But many felt it was Queen Ha-Lah who had to do the worst.

For even after the demons were dispatched, their venom continued to infect the ones it had touched, and they wandered, imprisoned by their own minds, mindlessly harming themselves...and others.

All the kings and all the kings' men rounded them up and gathered them on the beach.

And the fire of the dragons kept them there.

And the people understood why the decision was made that their ash would not mingle with the sand of shore.

They understood why it was decided they'd nurture the beasts of the sea.

And thus, the people of Nautilus watched as their queen, their Ha-Lah stood beside her husband and the other rulers atop a cliff to the south, and she raised her arms.

To a great gasp from her onlookers, she then caused the tidal that swept the poor, lost souls to peace in the depths of the sea.

But Ha-Lah did not feel peace in the doing.

She turned and collapsed in her king's arms.

IT WAS after they were all gone, when slowly, the peoples made their way, under the blanket of night sky and stars, to the sand.

Those who lived deeper into the rocks, hearing as word swept swiftly across the land, journeyed to Nautilus and walked the empty streets, gravitating toward the gathering, joining their brethren and sistren on the beach.

Wood was brought to build fires.

And the people of Mar-el sat about them on their shore, their eyes to the sea.

No one knew who first started the hum of mourning.

But all joined in, gazing into the waters, contemplating what was lost, what was gained, their fortune that they were still living, and their vows to continue to do it and do that well.

The hum rose up the cliffs to the rulers, who stayed amongst them, watching.

It rose up farther, to the heavens.

There wasn't a great amount of surprise when, well out to sea, the mighty beasts broke the waves.

One, two, five, three dozen, the whales rising up and crashing back into the sea, sharing the lament, the dolphins joining them, bursting from the waves and arcing back in, in a watery dance of grief.

But even with the spectacle, the humming did not stop.

As the people of the sea and the sea beasts shared their sorrow.

EVEN IN VICTORY, their king proclaimed that day forever to be the Day of Great Mourning for all who were taken from Airen, Wodell, the Nadirii, and on their own shores. For the gnomes, the pixies, the sprites, the Zees and the Mystics who were lost in the fight.

And for a man named Tedrey.

It was not only Aramus, but Cassius, Elena, True and Mars who proclaimed in their lands that day would be a day never forgotten.

There would never be a time, for centuries, millennia, when the day Triton rose again and was reunited with his Medusa, that day where so much was lost to cement what had been gained, when mothers and fathers, grandmothers and grandfathers, teachers and storytellers did not share the tale behind why there was a Day of Great Mourning.

Why, on that day, no one in any land of Triton toiled.

Why, on that day, all remembered the ones who were lost.

Or their own lost mothers.

Or fathers.

Aunts.

And uncles.

Brothers.

Or sisters.

Friends.

And lovers.

~

AND ONWARD FROM THAT HORRIBLE, victorious day, the people of Mar-el were glad to welcome the people of Airen. Of Firenze. Of Wodell. The Nadirii. The Zees. The charmed folk. Even the Go'Doan.

All of them, welcome to their shores.

For they all had fought as one.

They all had died as one.

And now they all lived as one.

Different countries.

Different borders.

Different gods.

Different cultures.

But brothers and sisters.

All.

I55

THE EPILOGUE

Faunus
The Cod's Eye Chippy, Nautilus
Mar-el

The tables outside the place that smelt heavy were rickety, the chairs as well.

Thus, when Faunus sat in one with his hand curled around his curious meal, he did not think the thing could bear his weight.

He didn't care.

The food was wrapped in naught but parchment, which was odd.

He didn't care about that either.

The outside of the fish was crunchy, the inside flaky, and the chipped, fried potatoes that were seasoned with salt and vinegar that came with it were interesting.

He didn't taste a thing.

When they were all done, as one, they stood and wandered to a bench by the sea.

Faunus sat.

Saturn sat close to him.

And Moira climbed in Faunus's lap, lifted her legs to Saturn's, and rested her head on Faunus's shoulder.

The breeze blew her hair against his nose and lips.

It was very soft and smelled of roses and the sea.

"How lucky are we?" she whispered.

Faunus did not understand, nor appreciate, the question.

"To be loved like that. To be loved..." her breath hitched, and she had to force out a husky, "*like that?*" to finish.

He wrapped his arms around her and bent his head, shoving his face in her neck.

His shoulders heaved.

He felt Saturn's hand wrap around the back of his neck.

And his Moira...

His *stellina*...

She did what she was very good at doing.

She held on tight.

～

Lorenz Chronis
Manor of the Captain of the Trusted, Fire City
Firenze

After he told her, Nyx burst out the back door.

And he followed.

She dashed to the side of their home.

"*Mia gazella,*" he called.

She stopped, practically immersed in the honeysuckle that grew so plentifully there, her back to him, and his chest burned, his heart squeezed, for her loss.

And for his.

"It is my fault," he said thickly. "I should not have let him spy. I should have kept him safe. I should not have listened to him. You were right. I was wrong. I should have kept our friend in our home. Under our roof. Safe under my protection."

She whirled, one hand going to her slightly rounded belly.

"It is *not* your fault," she hissed.

He moved direct to her.

She lifted both hands to his face.

And he smelled honeysuckle against her skin.

Her cheeks were wet, her eyes swimming.

"He would do what he would do. You know our Teddy," she reminded him.

He did.

"*Mio amore*," he said hoarsely.

"I just wish...wish..." She swallowed visibly painfully and finished on a whisper, "The last time he saw me..." She shook her head. "I just wish I could have said goodbye."

Lorenz pulled his wife into his arms.

She sobbed into his chest.

And he put his cheek to the top of her head as he felt the wet fall from his eyes.

A breeze blew through the bright pink and yellow and cream blooms behind her, their scent enveloping the couple in its embrace.

And their Teddy said goodbye.

~

Queen Elena
Port of Nautilus, Nautilus
Mar-el

I looked to the ship, then back to my sister.

"All right, well, I just want to be on record stating I don't want you to go. And that's not a jealousy thing, seeing as, if you two best this situation and Chu wrests control from his evil cousin who killed his brother to take his throne and now rules with tyranny, then he marries you, you'll be a queen like me. But because *you go to fight his evil, tyrannical cousin.*"

My sister quirked a grin at me.

Always up for a fight, my Serena.

"Serena—" I began.

"The Dragon's Breath are going to train me in the Arts," she stated.

I glanced at the four remaining Mystics, their faction known as the

Dragon's Breath, all of them standing at the railing of the ship, gazing transcendentally down at us, and this did not make me feel any better.

I looked back at my sister. "You know it takes great amounts of spiritualism to advance in the Arts."

"I'm spiritual," she completely lied.

"When was the last time you meditated?"

She searched the sky with her eyeballs.

I burst out laughing.

I stopped of a sudden when she tugged me violently in her arms.

"I will return," she said fiercely in my ear. "I will want my sons and daughters to meet their cousins."

And then she let me go, turned so quickly, her cloak whipped my body, and she made her way up the gangplank.

Chu came to stand in front of me.

"*I'll* be assassinating a king if anything happens to her," I decreed.

He shot me an audacious grin, bent in, touched my cheek with his lips then looked beyond me and jerked up his chin.

And then he was off up the gangplank.

Two arms circled me about my chest from behind.

"Are we going to stand here until we can't see them in the horizon?" Cassius asked over my head.

"Yes," I answered.

He chuckled.

The captain called out to push away.

He was a man I'd met whose name was Magnus, and who I knew was a lunatic, for he'd taken on this endeavor of delivering my sister and the man she loved to a place that, according to the Dragon's Breath, wasn't altogether stable.

As men rushed about the deck and the sails unfurled, Serena and Chu came to the railing.

And Gal and Brix walked down the pier as the galleon caught wind and started to make its way to the sea.

"You'll wish you had taken us with you!" Brix shouted irately.

"Go home! Find women! Make many daughters!" Serena shouted back. "And name them all Serena!"

I shook my head, smiling, and closing my eyes.

I swiftly opened them so I would not lose sight of her too soon.

"Be smart!" Gal yelled. "Send word if you need us!"

"Yes!" Cassius boomed from behind me. "Send word if you need us!"

The ship had cleared the pier and was sailing away, but I did not think that was why my sister made no reply other than to lift her arm and wave at us.

I watched and watched, and she did not leave that railing.

And Chu did not leave her side.

Gal and Brix left the end of the pier to come and stand with Cass and me.

"She is a powerful witch and a mighty warrior," Cass reminded me when the great galleon was naught but a dot on the horizon.

"She's a pain in the arse," Brix groused.

I burst out laughing.

I did it because that was funny (and true).

I also did it so I would not start crying.

King Mars
THE DEEP

IT WASN'T THE SWIMMING.

Mars was Firenz.

Water was revered in Firenze.

If they could, and they were not nomad, everyone in Firenze had at least a small pool in which to frolic and bathe.

And even the nomads sought water, and not just to drink.

It was also not that they were in The Deep.

Silence had tight hold on his hand, and he would admit, it seemed odd his lungs still worked the longer they were under and the deeper they went.

It was not even the amount of merfolk who swam after them.

He was glad to know they were a people of plenty, for his wife, as well as for all lands to know their goodness when they had a mind to journey to them.

And it wasn't the schools of fish and pods of dolphins that accompanied them as they swam behind Jorie, who held Elena by one hand, Cassius by the other. True and Farah were attached to another mermale. Aramus had his Ha-lah.

No, it was when the stingrays joined their party and waved about them.

And the bloody enormous whales arrived and undulated at their sides, filling the depths with their ethereal song.

Not to mention the damned sharks.

Though, as they approached the glowing-blue cave, Silence had warned him about the *angmostros*, thank the gods.

Jorie, Cassius and Elena entered first.

Silence took him in next.

Aramus and Ha-Lah followed and True and Farah were escorted in after.

And he found his wife was right.

The water in that tunnel glowed blue as well, and with it came a heartening feeling of goodness and light.

Not too far into it, the tunnel led them up and they broke the surface to breathe air.

The Mer who were escorting True and Farah retreated.

Mars's feet found sand and he held his wife close as her fin turned to legs.

The wet dripping from him, his eyes took in everything.

The cavern about them was shaped as a shell, the pearlescent surface glowing blue, green and pink.

Many globes all about laced with twine hung suspended by nothing in midair and they shone with the same colors.

The sand that led up to the island in the middle of the space was an immaculate white, and so fine, it was almost dust and soft as velvet under his feet.

And sitting two spectacular thrones on that island were Triton and Medusa.

Her throne was made of shell and pearls and tufted at the feet with floating anemone.

His was made of branches and rivulets and shelves of coral.

Mars studied the gods.

They had not worn their crowns when he had last seen them.

They wore them now.

At the front of Medusa's head, through her red hair, sprang a tiara made of spiraled shells and starfish, lengths of pearls and sprays of diamonds, a star of those last coasting onto her forehead, and ropes of both falling down the sides of her face.

Triton's crown of gold and shells surrounded his head, out of the inside of which sprung meandering spikes of coral.

And this time, instead of fins, they both had legs.

The lot of them walked up the sand and stood before the two gods as Triton studied them expressionlessly and Medusa smiled in welcome.

"It is good that you came," she stated.

"And thank you for the welcome," Jorie replied, dropping to a knee and bending his head to her.

Silence gave his hand a tug, and Mars was not feeling much like bending a knee to two gods he did not worship and who put him, his wife, his friends, and countless others through hell.

But he did it all the same.

As the others did beside him.

"Rise, my kings and queens," Medusa invited.

He stood as did Silence at his side as well as the others.

Medusa's face grew grave. "We wish you to know, we do understand how much was lost."

No one said anything.

Though, Mars doubted they did.

"And we know there is nothing that can salve the hurt or take away the pain," she went on.

Again, no one spoke.

But Mars knew that was the sad, bloody truth.

"But we shall try," she whispered, turned her head and prompted, "Beloved?"

Triton grunted.

Then he flicked a disinterested hand.

And before each of them gleamed a golden trident with three intricately forged spikes at the ends.

"Take hold, my kings and queens," Medusa instructed. "These are yours, for I sense you have grown close, and would like, with a toss of your trident, to be in the realm of another to commune and make merry."

Mars glanced down at his wife, who was reaching out to her trident, and as her fingers wrapped around, she looked up at him in happy wonder.

Gods, his Silence.

He grinned down at her and took hold of his own trident.

"This will also," Medusa went on, "if you have hold of it, allow you to visit Jorie. And perhaps," she lifted both hands, palms cupped and facing up in front of her before spreading them out, "*us.*"

Triton grunted again.

Medusa leaned forward and said conspiratorially, "He is used to his own company. We will have to work on his hospitality."

"You have our gratitude," True spoke for them all.

She tipped her head to the side and asked, "For all you did, all you lost, all you gave, do you think this is all we will give you to show our gratitude?"

A golden magical trident that made travel between realms happen in seconds and gave him the opportunity to visit his brother-in-law when Silence went to see him, Mars was content.

What further form a god might consider to show gratitude made Mars brace.

The goddess did not make them wait.

Medusa threw her arm out before her, cast it left, toward Aramus and Ha-Lah at the end, and brought it right, where Mars and Silence were at the other end.

From her fingers, shimmering glitter flew.

Gathered.

Multiplied.

Separated.

Formed.

And in front of Aramus formed his man Cat.

And in front of Farah formed Sofia.

In front of True formed Mercy.

In front of Elena formed Jasmine.

In front of Cassius formed a woman that Mars had never seen, but he knew was Cass's mother.

But he did not study her.

For in front of him formed...

His father.

Ares.

Blue-white glimmers shimmered around him, and he heard the others murmuring but he paid no mind to that.

He whispered, "Papa?"

Silence pressed herself to his side.

His father's head bent as he looked down to Silence.

"Papa," he called.

Ares looked to his son and he smiled greatly.

"I knew you would love her," Mars said softly, and Silence pressed closer to his side.

"I am sorry, you must say your farewells," Medusa warned.

"I am happy," Mars told his sire.

And then he watched his father's handsome face grow soft with love and pride.

This, before his form shimmered and disappeared to nothing.

Mars closed his eyes and tucked his chin in his neck.

"He's almost as handsome as you," he heard Silence whisper.

He opened his eyes and cupped her cheek with his hand, settling into the gift he'd just received that his father had seen his wife.

And could share that Mars had earned his pride.

She smiled tremulously up at him.

"Aramus," Medusa called. "Mars. One more thing. Please approach."

He dropped his hand from Silence and looked to the goddess.

He then moved her way as Aramus came from the other end to do the same.

Medusa stood.

Triton sighed with what sounded like displeasure.

Medusa shot him a look that was definitely displeasure.

She then turned her beatific gaze to the two kings.

"You love mermaids," she stated.

"Indeed," Aramus replied.

"Yes," Mars stated.

"Very much," Medusa said quietly, watching them closely.

"Indeed," Aramus replied.

"Yes," Mars stated.

"So be it," she said, then swept her hand in a line up her front before she regained her seat.

But she did this as Mars felt an odd sensation occurring under his jaw on either side of his neck.

"You will not transform," Medusa informed them. "You love a Mer, but you are not Mer. But you do not have to hold your tridents or another Mer to join your loves as they swim in The Deep."

Mars's body locked.

If this was true, when she frolicked in her (other) home, he would not have to wait for Silence's return.

And he would not have to worry.

"We can breathe on our own under the sea?" he asked.

"Yes," she answered. "And please, my Fire King, take her to see her brother often. They will miss each other if you don't."

"This I will do," he rumbled.

"You can go back to your wives," she murmured.

When he turned, he saw Silence was beaming.

He grinned at her as he moved over the sand.

She flung herself in his arms the instant he got close.

He wrapped his arms about her and lifted her off her feet.

"Can we be done with this now?" Triton's voice boomed low, and bored.

"*I* wasn't threatening and forbidding, making my kings and queens, princes and princess avoid keeping *me* company," Medusa returned as Mars set Silence on her feet and they returned their attention to the gods, Mars now holding his wife's hand. "I enjoy visitors," she finished.

"You always did," he muttered.

"Yes, I always did," she snapped.

"Perhaps we can argue *without* an audience," Triton suggested.

"And you make this suggestion to *rid us* of our audience," she retorted.

Triton sighed.

Medusa shifted her gaze about the women, declaring, "Marriage is difficult, my queens. Stay hearty."

Mars heard female laughter along with Silence's giggle.

He, however, was not thinking good thoughts about quarreling gods.

They'd learned that lesson surely enough.

"And I suppose you should go. We are grateful for your visit, even if one of us is very bad at showing it and..." Medusa's voice dropped, "I hope you now see we are most grateful for other things besides."

With this, Jorie, who was standing off to the side, jerked his chin up to them and led the way back down the velvety beach.

He entered the water.

His mighty tail formed.

Silence and Mars entered the water behind him.

Her beautiful tail formed.

But, holding tight to his trident in one hand, Silence's hand in his other, as Mars ducked under and kicked toward the tunnel, he felt the difference.

Before, it was as if his breath was suspended.

Now, however it occurred, after an odd ripple at his neck, he breathed freely.

He felt Silence's attention and turned his head toward her.

Through the water he saw her smiling happily.

And thus, Mars swum toward the depths at his wife's side.

Doing this contentedly.

~

Johan Mattson, Former Lord of the Arbor
The Shanty, Notting Thicket
WODELL

"I WUZ…" he slurred, "I wuz landed and my _daughter_ is a _queen._"

The man shoved at his head which made Johan tumble from his chair.

"Bugger off, arsehole," he said, pushing his own chair back, walking away, and in the doing, kicking Johan's face, accidentally, or on purpose, Johan did not know.

And as he forgot it happened but moments after it did, it did not matter.

"I wuz landed," he drunkenly told the floor. "And my _daughter_ is a _queen._"

No one heard because no one was listening.

Johan didn't say it again.

Because he'd passed out.

Eventually, the pub owner, checking his pockets and finding nothing in them, even if the man had totted up a hefty tab at the bar, took his boots and cloak as payment, and tossed him out the back.

By morning, in an alley in the Shanty, Johan of the Arbor had frozen to death.

One of the city guard who did the pickup in the Shanty that now, at King True's order, sent the mugs to the city morgue whereupon their descriptions were printed in the paper for three days before they were given a pauper's pyre, if they went unclaimed, recognized the dead man.

He'd seen him outside the Temple of Wohden on his great king's wedding day, all dressed up in a lord's finery.

He informed Birchlire Castle of his finding.

Who informed Sir Alfie Henriksson.

Who had the body collected, and at the behest of True, burned on a not-so-pauper's pyre.

No one but Alfie and Bronagh attended, and they only did it because it was the right thing to do.

Vanka didn't, because she refused.

Silence and True didn't, because they were still in Mar-el, in attendance at a celebration with the kings and queens from the Northlands and South-lands prior to their friends departing to journey home.

But also...

They simply just couldn't be bothered.

Sir Alfie Henriksson, King's Counsellor
Crittich Keep, Notting Thicket
WODELL

WHEN ALFIE ARRIVED at the Keep, he wound his reins around the hook in front of him, tossed the rug from his legs, bent to the side and unsnapped his wheel from the floor of the chariot.

He then bent to the other side to undo that one.

He pushed the lever which tipped the wain back, then twisted at the waist, and freed the lock on the back door, which swung open.

He then wrapped a gloved hand around one wheel as he unlocked the other, and vice versa.

His exit set, Alfie backed out, wheeled to the Keep, and nodded to the guards who opened the door for him.

One followed as he entered.

"Where are they?" Alfie asked.

"You asked for them all, sir, and seeing as there are a number of them fucks, 'scuse my language, milord, but no other way to describe 'em, we've set 'em in the Council Chambers," the man answered.

Alfie nodded.

He then turned right at the end of the entry hall and wheeled himself to the Council Chambers.

There were two guards on either side of the chambers' door.

One moved to open it.

Alfie wheeled in.

The men were standing against the back wall. They looked sunken and haggard and as if they were what they'd been for some time now.

On the run or incarcerated.

They had wrists chained in front of them connected to further chains that ran up to their throats and down to their ankles as well as being chained together.

Regardless, there were two guards on either side of the door on the interior, and three lining each side of the room.

Alfie wheeled in and instructed, "You can keep the door open. I won't be long."

"Sir," a guard murmured his assent.

Alfie looked down the lot of them, and as he had better things to do, he didn't delay.

"You've each been identified by one or more of the surviving women you abducted. And it's been reported you were also instrumental in the kidnapping of Tedrey Swensson, Our Brother Golden Hair, the hero of the Battle of the Beasts. As is your right on the soil of Wodell, you will stand tribunal. However, I've received a raven from our king, and he advises no pleas of mercy will be heard. Thus, when you're found guilty, you will be hung by the neck publicly, in the Lawn of this Keep. Due to the heinousness of your crimes, your families will be disallowed to collect your bodies. You will be burned on a communal pyre. Thus, if you have any family, I would advise you get word to them. You will each be allowed a single visit in order to say your goodbyes."

He looked to the side and up to a guard.

"That is all, you can take them back to their cells," he finished.

And not having removed his hands from his wheels, he began to make his turn to exit the room.

"It wasn't our idea!" one called out.

Alfie looked in the direction of the voice.

"It was...we were under orders," he stated. "You understand. We were at war."

"You were at war with forty-one women?" Alfie asked.

"They were...they were...that was..." the man stammered, shook his head. "I do not know what that was. I was not in my normal mind. None of us were. It was like a...a...frenzy. We'd all gone quite mad."

"To that, I'll agree," Alfie replied.

And before the man could say another word, he turned and wheeled away.

～

IT WAS UNSURPRISING WHEN, one month hence, Alfie sat in his chair on the Lawn at Crittich Keep and watched all the men who had been in chains in that room as they were hung by the neck until they were dead.

He did not allow his stubborn woman to accompany him.

And as a first, she did not argue.

~

Hans Swensson
Trevor's Gorge
WODELL

IT HAD BEEN a herald in royal livery who had stood at attention at his door and handed him the missive.

A missive with the green wax seal on the back.

The seal of the king.

News of late was much, it came swift, and it was weighty.

The treachery of that bloody Rising.

Servitude abolished in Mar-el.

Civil War fought and won by King Cassius in Airen.

The massacre of those poor girls in the Lesser Thicket, though he'd been pleased to hear them Rising arseholes who did those deeds were now good and dead.

And the Battle of the Beasts in Mar-el across the sea.

There were some who even said gods rose from that nonsense, which was ridiculous, but many people believed it.

Considering the visit he'd had from his son and his son's...*people*, Hans was not terribly surprised when he received a message with the royal seal.

But his system seemed to stop as he read it, as written, not by some aide or the King's Counsellor.

By the hand of the bloody *king*.

> Hans Swensson ~
> It is my sad duty to inform you that your son, Tedrey Swensson, was lost in the Battle of the Beasts.
> Tedrey's sacrifice was bold and courageous. He saved a

number of lives in his time on this earth, including one that day.

His actions were instrumental to the end of that grave, arduous battle, and without them, it is unknown if The Rising that occurred would have graced our company.

As such, I send this missive not only to share the sorrowful news that your son, understood by all who knew him as honorable and brave, is lost. But also to share that, due to his selfless act that terrible day, there will be a memorial erected in his honor~Tedrey Swensson, Our Brother Golden Hair~in the capital of his native land, Wodell, as well as one in the capital of his adopted land, Fire City in Firenze.

I would request that, when these memorials are unveiled, you would not attend either ceremony.

Yours,

~True

King of Wodell

I would request that, when these memorials are unveiled, you would not attend either ceremony.

Hans read those words again and again.

As well as the words, *understood by all who knew him as honorable and brave.*

And the ones, *Tedrey Swensson, was lost in the Battle of the Beasts.*

Only after all of these words were imprinted on his brain did he drop the hand holding the parchment and look out the window to his fields.

His boy worked those fields with him. He did not complain. He got up early, he worked hard, he fell in bed tired.

He did not complain when his mother left them.

He did not complain when Hans beat him and sent him away.

Hans's seed had made a solid man who became a hero.

And none of that glory was Hans's.

On this thought, he wept.

Not for glory he could not claim.

For the loss of a son he would never know.

Queen Elena
Royal Palace
THE ENCHANTMENTS

"*AELIA!*" Cassius boomed.

My head came up from reading the letter from Farah and I looked out the window to where my husband was standing on the balcony.

"Aelia, I swear to the gods, if you're astride a horse, you'll find it difficult to sit on *anything*!" he shouted.

I pressed my lips together to stop myself from laughing.

"Dora, is she on a horse?" he suddenly asked, and I saw him looking down to the ground at, obviously, our eldest girl.

"No, Cass," she answered.

"Are you lying to me?" Cass pushed.

I pressed my lips together harder.

Dora didn't answer at first.

This meant yes, she was lying.

"*Theodora*," Cassius growled.

Oh dear.

Her full name.

"All right!" she exploded. "It wasn't my idea. It was Aelia's!"

When I noted Cassius made to move, Dora went on speaking quickly.

"But she's fine, Cassius. Promise! She's with Mac and Hera!"

For a moment, Cassius didn't speak.

And when he did, his words were lethally measured.

"If you will, go tell my bloody captain, and Ellie's bloody captain, that I wish to see them. *Immediately*."

"All right, Cass," Dora agreed.

I envisioned her racing off.

My husband prowled into the room.

"I was riding at six," I, possibly foolishly, informed him.

"We're not having another child," he declared.

I blinked up at him.

"I survived an attack on a palace," he went on. "I survived a bombardment of arrows in a bloody temple, for fuck's sake. I survived the Battle of the Heights. The Battle of the Veil. The Battle of the bloody fucking *Beasts*. And my daughters are going to kill me."

It was actually beginning to hurt, holding back the laughter.

When I managed to do that, I said, "You know Mac and Hera will not allow anything to happen to her."

"She's too young," he gritted.

"She's smart, she's sure of her limbs, she loves animals so she can read one, and again, Mac and Hera would never allow anything to happen to her."

"I told her she could learn to ride in a couple of years, Ellie," he bit out.

"Yes, and she should have to endure your anger and disappointment that she disobeyed you," I said softly. "But Cass, you cannot protect us all, in all ways, in everything *against* everything."

"Yes, I can, for I must, it is why I'm breathing," he retorted.

Which, in turn, made me stop breathing.

"Though, I understand your point," he muttered.

"Good," I forced out.

With that, Domitia stormed in, doing this walking backwards.

And shouting.

"It's only *a little* magic, Ian!"

"You do not practice alone. You practice with your mentor," he growled in return, following her in. "Melisse was nowhere near you when you nearly singed your eyebrows off."

And I again found myself in the endeavor of having to stop myself from laughing.

"But I didn't!" she snapped.

"But you almost did," he retorted.

She brought her hands up in fists at her sides and shrieked, "*You're impossible!*"

"And you're a gods-damned menace," he fired back.

She made a huffing noise, turned and raced up the stairs that wound around the trunk of the tree.

Ian scowled after her.

Cassius decided to wade in as advisor.

"You really need to fuck her, mate."

Ian transferred his scowl to Cassius before he turned on his boot and stalked out the door.

"You do know, it was very rare people shouted at each other before men were allowed in The Enchantments," I remarked.

Cass looked down at me.

And then I received my treat for the day.

I was able to watch my husband throw back his handsome head and burst into laughter.

~

Queen Silence
Queen's Study, East Corridor, Catrame Palace, Fire City
FIRENZE

A GOOD QUEEN did not get bored.

A good queen did not get bored.

A good queen did not get bored.

I told myself this repeatedly as my eyes slid to Elpis, who was staring out the windows with an expression on her face that shared vividly she'd rather be anywhere else, say, perchance, having her fingernails torn out by their roots.

"And as such, we would behoove you, our beloved Queen Silence," one of the women sitting in front of me beseeched, "to take this matter to our king."

Oh, balls.

I'd already forgotten what matter they were behooving me about.

"Of course, I'll speak to my king," I only somewhat lied.

I felt Elpis's regard.

I ignored it and smiled benignly at the women before me as they rose, repeatedly expressing their gratitude.

I nodded and circled my hand in what I hoped was a royal way, and my secretary ushered them out.

"I'm not certain Mars would concern himself much with their plight, *mia figlia*," Elpis warned when the door closed behind them.

"I'll figure something out," I murmured.

"Is this all of our appointments for today?" she asked.

I grinned at her. "Yes."

She grinned in return. "Good, then shall we retire to a bath with some smoke?"

I could think of nothing better.

I did not have the opportunity to tell her this, for Angelo, my secretary, stuck his head in and said, "His Grace is between appointments and he asks if you'd join him in his study before his next arrives."

I turned to Elpis. "Shall I meet you there in a while?"

Her face softened. "Of course, *cara*."

We both left my office together, Elpis heading down the hall, me going across it to my husband's study.

I knocked and walked in to see him bent over his desk, scratching something with his pen on parchment.

My, but I loved his thick long hair.

He straightened, dropped his pen and sat back in his chair as I shut the door and started walking his way.

"There seems to be a grave issue about a plinth built in the seat of a particular clan, which you gave royal funding," I said as I moved to him, "that appears to have been erected much smaller than *another* plinth that was built in the seat of a clan they don't very much like."

I had made it around his desk by the time I was finished speaking.

And my husband did not reply until he grasped my hips on both sides, pushed his chair back, and pulled me to standing in front of him.

He kept his hands where they were, but his black eyes lifted to mine.

"Indeed?" he asked.

"Yes," I answered. "Though it also might be an urn."

He started chuckling.

"Elpis shared you would not very much care, but I promised them I would inform you of their concerns," I told him.

"You are a good queen, seeing to the needs of your people, even if they're absurd," he murmured.

"I must admit, husband, I, too, think they are absurd."

"Because they are," he stated, then hefted me up so I was seated in front of him on his desk.

He then scooted his chair closer.

"Mars," I whispered.

"Mm?" he asked, for I had lost his attention.

He was watching his hands as they performed the act of gliding the silk of the skirt of my gown up my thighs.

"About that urn," I teased.

He was not in the mood to tease.

I knew this when he told me, "You should really design to wear gowns that are much less attractive, wife."

"Why would I do such as that?"

He did not answer.

He looked up at me and ordered, "Lie back."

"Mars," I breathed.

His fingers slipped between my legs.

My head fell back.

Then *I* fell back.

Mars pushed the material up to my hips, opened my legs, and his head came down.

And then my king made it so I did not need smoke to make me hazy.

Though, after he was done with me, I spent the afternoon with my mother-in-law all the same.

~

Queen Ha-Lah
Aboard Her Majesty's Beauty
Green Sea

"It'd be nice if you didn't upstage me once in a while," my husband groused.

"You just like to shoot your cannons," I retorted.

"I do, indeed," he said irately, and suggestively.

Sirens save me from bawdy pirates.

"It was just a *small* wave," I told him.

"Ha-Lah, we'll be fishing their men out of the sea for an hour."

I shrugged.

"Cap, we've identified their captain," Tint said from beside us.

"Excellent," Aramus muttered, turned on his boot and stomped to the gangplank that led from our galleon to the one we'd just captured.

Due to *my* wave.

All right, so I nearly capsized the bloody thing.

I also managed to stop that drattedly *loud* cannon fire.

I followed after him.

When we made the deck of the other ship, I saw there were a great number of men on their knees and they were soggy.

This made me happy, and perhaps a little smug, but I didn't show that last.

Aramus followed Tintagel to a man whose clothing veritably *screamed* buccaneer.

But he wasn't.

He was a killer.

Aramus stopped before him.

I came up to my king's side.

"Do we have identification on them?" Aramus asked Ore, who was standing over the man at the man's back.

"Not yet," Ore answered.

"Their stores?" Aramus inquired.

"So far, they've been unsuccessful," Ore informed him. "They're empty."

I released a breath of relief.

Aramus studied the defeated captain and stated the obvious, "He's not Mar-el. He looks Dellish or from the Northlands. Where are you from, captain?"

"The Vale," the man spat.

"Merchant and passenger lanes have been open for some months," Aramus noted. "And as such, I'm certain you've received much news from Triton."

The man said nothing.

"And as King Noctorno is a particular friend of mine, I am aware that, at my urging, he made some proclamations of his own, which I would assume, him being a king, spread very widely," Aramus said.

The man stretched out his neck.

But no words came from his mouth.

"Including," Aramus continued, "that it is a punishable act to hunt whale in any of the waters around our continent."

The man remained silent.

"And yet, we came upon you, hunting whale," Aramus carried on. "Or, fortunately, *attempting* it, though not successful. As yet."

The man still said no words.

So Aramus did.

"Now, ignorance of the law is no excuse," he shared. "But as you took none of my wife's beloved beasts, I'm feeling generous."

Oreti looked to Aramus.

Tintagel looked to Aramus.

I looked to Aramus.

We all did this for, thus far, in matters such as these, Aramus had not felt generous.

Ever.

Aramus turned to Tint.

"Each of his men receive twenty lashes, he gets thirty. Take them to Nautilus. He's stockaded for a week. His men serve a term of nine months. Him a year. When they're released, they're given sailor's clothing and crewed on a ship bound to The Mystics. There, they'll be dropped. They can find their way home from that land."

Well then.

My husband wasn't feeling generous.

He was just playing.

"That's generous?" the captain demanded, not feeling very playful.

Aramus suddenly bent to him. "I'd have your blood draining from your throat while you hang from a yardarm if you'd taken one of my creatures. I am the King of the Sea, arsehole. And I will make it known the waters are safe for my beasts, and anyone who thinks differently will learn how adamantly I disagree."

And after delivering that, he turned and strode away.

I looked to Tint.

"Save us all from a convert," he muttered.

I was smiling when I followed my husband.

He was on the port side of our ship when I found him.

He was also leaning over the railings, saying, "You have to wait for her. I've no idea what you're talking about."

I came to stand by his side, looked over the railing, and saw the snouts of three dolphins, all of them chattering up at him.

"They say there are smugglers hiding booty on an island south of here that is officially in the waters of Triton," I told him.

Aramus grinned down at the glistening, gray noses.

"My beautiful spies," he cooed.

I rolled my eyes to the heavens.

The dolphins squealed their delight.

My husband turned.

"Bond!" he shouted. "You and Tint take some men and sail that ship to Nautilus. Impound it. Then set it for auction. We sail south."

"Aye," Bond replied.

"Sorry?" I asked.

Aramus looked down at me. "There's booty to be had."

"Husband, *you're king*. You're wealthy. You live in a castle. You have the ear of the gods. You don't *need* booty."

He then grasped me with an arm about my waist and pulled me tight to his body, dipping his face to mine.

"My Ha-Lah, I'm a *pirate* and pirates always need booty."

I experienced a lovely tingle.

It was as if Aramus sensed it for his eyes then dropped to my mouth and he muttered, "Now to shoot my cannon."

I really should have been exasperated.

But instead, I let my husband drag his wench to his cabin.

And I did it laughing.

Queen Farah
Guest Cell, Reception Hall
Dome City

"Why are we here again?" True asked, making a mess of his neckcloth.

This was unsurprising, for he detested wearing them, and as he did, he did not do so very often.

Thus, I moved to my husband, batted his hands away, took over and reminded him, "Mostly to see Ellie and Cass and the girls."

"Right," he muttered.

"And, say, because you are king of a great realm and history is being made that you've been invited to witness. Not to mention, these are your friends."

"Mars and Silence didn't come," True pointed out.

"Nyx is close to having her baby. Silence doesn't want to be far from her and Mars doesn't wish to be far from Lorenz," I told him something he knew.

"Aramus and Ha-Lah aren't here," he went on.

"Because they're visiting a Mer colony down in the Fotía and they couldn't get here in time."

He sighed.

I finished with his neckcloth.

"I bet Cass isn't wearing a neckcloth," he muttered.

This complaint drew my attention.

And my concern.

For it wasn't like my True to be grumpy.

So I pressed my hands to his chest in order to get his attention, this in order to get to the meat of the matter.

"What truly troubles you, *caro?*"

He held my gaze before he said, "You were visiting with Ellie when they came."

"Who came?"

"Not who. What."

I lifted my brows to share that this did not answer my question.

He wrapped his fingers around one of my hands, took it from his chest, and the other one naturally fell away when he guided me into the sitting room outside our bedchamber in the spacious, well-appointed cell we'd been given by the Go'Doan.

Definitely a different reception we'd had over the first time I was there.

Then again, much had changed for the Go'Doan.

And what was happening that day, and the lovely memorial plaque they'd mounted to G'Ry, were only two of a great many.

True took me to a bureau and pulled out a drawer.

Only then did he let me go as he reached in and took out two books.

He set them on the top of the bureau.

They were both handsomely leather bound.

One was maroon, the leather elegantly embossed, the very long title set in gold.

It said, *The Battle of the Beasts.*

And it had a subtitle, *The Rise of the Power of the Female.*

Which had a subtitle of, *And The Return of the Fire King, the Sea King, the Sky King & the Green King.*

The other book had a rich, green leather, embossed with leaves, acorns and trees.

And the title was set in pewter.

It said, *True, the Green King, & Farah, the Green Queen.*

"Oh my," I whispered.

"These are copies. They're sending the first to all the kingdoms. And they're keeping the originals of both in their Narration Hall."

"Of course," I said, for this was what the Go'Doan did.

And this was good, for if they hadn't done just so over the years, recording history, and protecting books that did the same, as well as books as a whole, we would not have learned so much about the Beasts.

"The other is unfinished, but presented as such as a gift to us," he went on.

"I see," I said in a way I shared I still did not understand why he was upset.

"We have our own fucking tome, darling," he stated, reached to it, flipped it open and then shuffled pages aside until it was lying flat, pages to either side half and half.

One side held carefully calligraphied words, the first letter in each paragraph much larger than the rest, surrounded by a square, in which, around the letter, lovely vines had been painted.

"That's rather beautiful," I murmured.

"We've got a tome, Farah," he mostly repeated.

I looked to him. "This troubles you because...?"

"It troubles me because it isn't just about you and me," he declared.

I stared up at him.

"Men died. Pixies died. Fairies died. Gnomes died. Alfie lost his legs. My mother lost her life. If a book has green leather, it should be about Wodell, not about—"

He stopped speaking when I put my fingers to his lips.

And then I spoke.

"There are so many words written in so many books in their library that share about vile things. And tragic things. And unpleasant things. And unjust things. Give them this, True. Give Triton this. Give us a book about nothing but good...nothing but good...and *true*." I slid my fingers across his cheek, into his soft, thick hair, to wrap them around the back of his head. "And help me fill the rest of that book with the same so our children can read it. And their children. And onward forever."

He looked down at the book.

"Though I don't have to ask you to do that," I said, and he looked back to me. "You'd do it anyway."

That was when he kissed me.

It became heated, as such between us was wont to do, and thus it took a knock on the door to interrupt it.

"Yes!" True called.

The door opened and Aelia danced in, followed by Dora, then Cass and Ellie.

"What do you think of my frock?" Aelia demanded of True as greeting.

"You're never anything but beautiful," True answered.

"Huzzah!" she cried. Then she asked cheekily, "Will you escort me to the wedding, Uncle True?"

He glanced my way, and when I dipped my chin, he looked to the girl, offering his arm, "It would be my honor."

"Will you accept me as an escort?" I asked Dora.

She grinned at me and linked arms, saying, "Of course."

I gave Cass and Ellie a smile, they returned them, and we moved out into the hall. Down it. Out of the building, mounted our horses, and rode down the avenue.

Our horses were taken at the base of the steps. We entered the temple, and with great fanfare, the royals were seated in a front pew.

But we would have been given that regardless.

Or Elena would.

For we were there to watch the first-ever official marriage of a priest of the Go'Doan.

And with it, the end to the position of acolyte.

Witnessing it, it made me happy to see how happy Liam and Saira were.

They were glowing.

Faunus of the Trusted
His New Manor, Fire City
FIRENZE

He had no idea what woke him.

But it did.

Thus, he untangled himself from the bodies sleeping in their bed, drew on some silk *ante* pants, and moved silently through the house.

When his feet hit the floor at the bottom of the stairs, he saw the mantles on the hooks by the door.

He'd refused his king's request to become a Trusted.

Saturn had as well.

They explained to their king they did this, for they would not be unfaithful to their lovers.

Mars had then surprised them by stating that, due to their explanation, that requirement would not need to be filled.

They'd performed the other rituals.

And earned their mantles.

He heard a whistling wind, like a whisper, come from the back of the house and his mind was turned.

As was his body.

He moved down the hall and out the back door to the courtyard.

The house was much more grand than he was used to, big rooms, and a lot of them.

They would need them, he hoped.

One day.

But the largest room was the kitchen, for she enjoyed cooking.

The courtyard, however, was small and intimate with a twinkling fountain tiled in green and peach and red and black, the ground covered in a stunning mosaic of cream and peach intermingled with shapes in bold colors. Yellow and red and pink flowers. Green swirls. An undulating black border broken with groupings of colorful pieces.

And here and there, small but not unnoticed...

There was an acorn.

The fountain was faced with one single, but large and deep-seated daybed covered in colorful blankets and pillows.

And this was what Faunus stood behind, halted by an overwhelming scent of honeysuckle.

That happened, even when those vines were nowhere around him.

And it happened a good deal.

His body jumped when the specter formed by the fountain.

Bloody hell.

What was the spirit of Queen Ophelia doing in his fucking courtyard?

"If you look, you can see," she said.

"See what?" he asked.

She tipped her head well back and repeated, "If you look, you can see."

He looked up into the starry skies.

"Toward Mar-el," she directed.

He adjusted his gaze.

And fucking hell.

He saw it.

Gods, it blinked very bright.

And he saw it.

He counted.

Three stars in the stem.

Twelve in the cupule.

Eight in the nut.

An acorn.

"You know him," Ophelia said, and his eyes cut to her. "He would never leave you and yours, Faunus. Not ever. He shines down on you always, warrior. Always."

He said no words, not only because he didn't have any, but because she faded from sight.

He tipped his head back and looked at the constellation.

Then he rounded the daybed, stretched out on it and pulled the blankets over him.

And that night, Faunus slept under the stars.

Nyx Chronis

Manor of the Captain of the Trusted, Fire City

Firenze

When she heard naught but men's murmurs in her entryway, and her husband did not call to share who was at the door he had answered some minutes ago, Nyx rose from the divan in their salon and moved to the hall.

She smiled brightly when she saw Faunus standing with her husband.

"*Ciao*, Faunus," she greeted.

His gaze came to her, and what she saw in it made her step falter.

He had found love, since they lost Teddy. He had found contentment, even happiness.

Thus, she did not understand why Faunus looked thrown back to before.

That before being when their loss was fresh.

"Nyx," he murmured, dipped his chin to her, lifted it to Lorenz, and then murmured, "Until another time."

And with a sweep of his mantle, he was out the door.

Lorenz closed it after him.

"What was that about?" she asked.

Lorenz turned to her.

She stood still, staring at his hands.

One held what appeared to be a broken off plank of old wood.

In the other, he held a book.

"Teddy left Faunus directions when Faunus was in search of him. Faunus liked the message, so he took it with him." He lifted the plank of wood. "And then later, Teddy rose a god." He lifted the book.

"I don't—" she began.

He turned the plank of wood and she quickly read the scratchings.

But as she read, her eyes only started prickling when she saw,

...tell Lorenz and Nyx I died the man they made me, thus I did such with a clear head and a full heart.

"Come, *amore*, apparently there has been another message left for us," Lorenz murmured gently.

She could barely tear her eyes from the wood, and only was able to do so when her husband caught her about the shoulders and drew her back to their salon.

He set the wood carefully, even reverently, aside on a table, and then he moved closer to her, holding the book up between them.

"Faunus says that we should read it all, but for the now, we must skip to the end," Lorenz said.

"Is that...the journal you gave Teddy?" she asked.

"It is," he answered.

"Faunus should keep it."

Lorenz shook his head. "He says Teddy left him his love in a number of other ways, and so he wants us to have these things. He says he feels Teddy would want us to have these things as well," Lorenz told her.

She shook her head. "I don't—"

"If it would be too much for you to take—" he began on a rumble, her protective husband.

"Read it to me," she whispered.

Her beloved held her eyes.

He then nodded, turned his handsome head down to the book, and opened it, flipping through to reach the end.

She watched Teddy's handwriting glide by and closed her eyes.

"Kindness," Lorenz started, his voice thick, and she opened her eyes and looked to his face, seeing it now was harsh with emotion. "There is no greater gift," he went on. "I know this, for when you showed it to me, it changed the course of my life. It changed the course of a continent. It changed the world."

Nyx swallowed.

Lorenz cleared his throat.

"I did not die loving you," Lorenz carried on, his voice now gruff. "I lived loving you. Now you live, knowing how deeply you were loved."

The noise she made she could not control.

Thus, she was in the tight embrace of her husband.

"Is that all?" she asked his chest.

"It is enough," he answered.

Her Lorenz was right.

It was.

~

King Cassius
Red Room, Sky Citadel, Sky Bay
AIREN

CASSIUS STARED AT HIS FRIEND.

"Things are getting boring, are they not?" Silvanus asked.

"I'm becoming enamored with boring," Cassius told him.

Silvanus threw back his head and boomed with laughter.

"You do this often?" Cassius asked curiously when he stopped.

Silvanus shrugged. "Every once in a while. It takes much magic. But, my man," he leaned toward Cass, "every time, it is *very* worth it."

"I can imagine, but even so..." Cassius let that trail, not repeating his declination of the invitation Silvanus had extended he and Ellie and the girls.

Silvanus sat back and grinned. "I see. The dark prince has become the king of the light. You wish to bask in that light. I would too, your sun queen is extraordinary. If I did not so much like the dark cleft that awaits me in my caravan, I would be most jealous of you."

"I'm pleased Ellie isn't here for this conversation," Cass muttered.

Silvanus grinned unrepentantly.

"I take the highwaymen with me," he shared. "They find thieving in the lands of kings they respect is not so much to their liking anymore. I have told them of that world, and they sense the challenge. So they will travel to new even greater adventures."

"They will be missed, they're good men. Their antics, not as much," Cassius replied.

Silvanus grew intense and stated, "And I take Macrinus."

Cassius stared.

"I have told him of the women there. Their boldness. Their audacity. You know. You have met Circe. Seoafin. Cora. Maddie," Silvanus said quietly. "You also know he enjoys boldness and audacity."

"Mac?" he asked.

"He wishes to go. He wishes to leave..." he hesitated before he finished, "his grief behind."

"You can't leave grief behind by chasing adventure...and skirt."

"There are many there who do not often wear skirts," Silvanus muttered.

"Silvanus, you can't take my captain."

"I'll bring him back."

"You can't take him."

"Cass, hear me. *He wants to go.*"

Cassius shut his mouth.

He opened it to say, "What will Hera do without him? They've barely..." He trailed off only to clip, "You can't take her too. Ellie would lose her mind."

"Well, before they left, your Hera had a situation with one of the Mystics. Her next journey will be by sea, not on a path between worlds."

"Shite," Cassius muttered.

"Love is freedom," Silvanus said softly.

It was annoying that he was right.

"They will return," Silvanus assured.

"What if they don't?" Cass demanded.

"Then you will have peace, for you know they have stayed because they have found happiness."

And he was even more annoying because he continued to be right.

Silvanus grinned like a madman, for he knew this as well.

"If you change your mind in future, we shall take you," he said to finish.

"I would not hold my breath."

That set the man again to laughing.

Soon after, they finished their drinks, Silvanus returned to his Patras, and Cass went in search of his wife.

He found her sitting atop their bed, cross-legged, wearing his shirt.

She had her cards spread out on the covers before her.

He stopped at the end of the bed and did not lead into it.

"Mac is going with Silvanus. Apparently, they journey back and forth between the parallel worlds with some frequency, for they enjoy being annoying on two different, but the same, planets."

She gazed up at him, her hair about her shoulders and down her chest, her long shapely legs practically begging him to uncross them with a purpose.

"And I hate to tell you this, but Hera—" he started to continue.

But Elena interrupted him.

"Journeys to The Mystics with the excuse to help Serena but instead she had some argument or something that wasn't an argument, it was her feeling guilt she was attracted to another woman so soon after we lost Rose, even though it wasn't that soon, but I think you understand her feelings about that more than I, so mostly, it's to see to that," she stated.

"You know?" he asked.

She nodded.

"About both?" he asked.

She hesitated.

And then nodded again.

He put his fists to his hips. "Why didn't you tell me?"

"Well, I thought it was Mac's to tell, which he intends to do, I only know because Hera told me when she told me her plans. I didn't expect Silvanus to share Mac's secrets."

He glowered at her.

"If they seek happiness, I champion it," she said gently.

"I do too, I just will miss them," he muttered.

Her face softened and her lips tipped up.

"Why are you doing a reading?" he asked.

And then he took in the cards.

All in a row, The Unicorn, The Moon, Eros, The Blood, The Star, and another Unicorn.

"And when did you add to your cards?" he asked after an additional Unicorn, for he knew there was only one in her deck.

"I didn't," she whispered.

His gaze cut to her.

"It's magic," she said.

He had no reply.

"Star is pregnant," she announced.

His body locked.

And he stared.

"And, um, well, apparently, unicorn magic beats pennyrium because, well..." She bit her lip, released it and asked, "How serious were you about not having any more children?"

The cards went flying not long before her panties landed on the carpet by their bed and he had his hand between their legs, his cock in his fist, seeking.

"Are you telling me you carry my child?" he demanded gruffly.

Then his groan drowned out her moan as he slid inside.

"Yes?" she asked as if he had the answer.

"Ellie," he growled his warning, thrusting inside.

She wrapped her arms and legs about him.

"Do you want a boy or girl?"

Gods.

She was carrying his child.

He closed his eyes and dropped his forehead to hers.

She truly *was* a powerful witch.

For he thought he was as happy as he could be.

But then she'd do something to make him even *happier*.

"Cass," she whispered, lifting her hips to take him deeper. "Do you want a boy or girl? The ritual has to be done early in the pregnancy."

He opened his eyes.

"No magic."

"Sorry?"

"We get what we make."

Her violet eyes melted.

"All right," she said before she tugged on his beard to demand his mouth.

He didn't make her tug hard.

He gave it to her.

~

HE ALSO TOOK MORE ink eight months later.

When they had a girl.

~

King Mars

Second Floor, West Corridor, Catrame Palace, Fire City
Firenze

"Tril," Mars called impatiently when his wife's friend saw him and tried to duck behind the door of her room.

She, and his queen, had been avoiding him all day.

He did not like this.

Not at all.

And he knew the reason behind it, one his wife was hiding.

She'd had a visit from her mother that morning.

The woman lived in a grand manse a good forty-five-minute ride away.

He would prefer it to be forty-five days, but he did not often get what he wished in regards to her mother.

His Silence was kind-hearted and forgiving.

Though he did not fail to note when a message came from her mother's manse sharing the woman wanted a visit, often Silence was most busy.

This usually doing something with his mother. Or Tril. Or Nyx. Or looking after Nyx and Lorenz's son so they could have time together, like she was a fucking nanny. Or she was with Zosime. Or looking after Guard and Zosime's child.

Or she was in the garden, reading.

Or off on a ride with Kyril.

Etcetera.

Further affecting his mood was that he had a missive to send to Aramus, but the servant came back sharing all the ravens trained to fly to Mar-el had been, that day, engaged by his queen.

There were bloody twenty of them.

When he'd asked after the message, the man had simply said she had called to Ha-Lah to get a communication to Jorie to make haste in visiting her in Fire City.

She had sent this same message *twenty times.*

He did not like her mother.

But it was *him* she would turn to if her mother distressed her.

Not her big brother.

"Oh, allo there, King Mars," Tril said false casually, dipping her chin and not meeting his eyes.

Allo there, King Mars?

He swallowed back a growl.

"Is my wife in our chambers?" he demanded.

"Um...yes, she awaits you."

"Tril?" he called.

"Yes," she said to the floor.

"Tril," he bit. "Look at me."

Her eyes came slowly to his, and when he looked into their bright, happy depths, his stomach flipped, and he strode away from her without a goodnight, covering the remaining lengths to their bedchamber door in fewer strides than it normally took.

He pushed through, went right, and saw her juggling Piccolina on her way to their bed.

Her gaze came to him and she smiled brightly. "Allo, my love."

"You carry my child," he declared.

She blinked and then frowned.

Then she asked him, "How did you know?"

"For that purpose," he began, "you haven't been taking pennyrium for weeks and I just saw Tril outside our door and she's about to burst with happiness."

She glared at their door and muttered, "Bloody Tril. She's the best friend of a queen and she can't keep a bloody secret."

"You wished to keep it a secret?" he asked dangerously.

"No," she snapped. "Of course not. But when my blood did not come and I asked mother here to ask after her symptoms when she was carrying me, and they mimic things I'm feeling, and I felt sure I was expecting, I decided to tell you."

She then lifted her arms out at her sides, and in doing so, Piccolina took that opportunity to race down one and leap toward Mars.

With practice, he caught the wee love, put her on his shoulder and continued listening to his wife, who was still complaining.

"I mean, I wore a new nightgown to celebrate after I told you and *everything.*"

She did not wear that nightgown long, for it was in tatters on the floor while she was naked and taking his cock in their bed.

"I'm reading...from this...you're pleased...with the news," she pushed out between thrusts, scraping his scalp with her nails.

"Bloody…*yes,*" he replied.

She grinned up at him.

He kissed the grin on her face and set about the serious business of cele-brating.

~

IT WOULD BE when Silence was recuperating after giving him their son that Mars would take the piercing in his cock that demonstrated his body was hers and hers alone.

It was an unnecessary gesture; she already knew that.

But it was important regardless.

So, it was done.

~

King True
Temple to Wohden, Notting Thicket
WODELL

"YOU DON'T SEEM VERY NERVOUS," Bram noted.

"Why would I be nervous?" Alfie asked.

"She's a handful, that one. Bossy," Florian stated.

"Thank the gods," Alfie muttered.

True grinned.

The door opened and the priest took one step in.

"She arrives. All is ready. If our future husband can take his place?"

He didn't wait for responses.

He moved out.

"Do or die," Luther said.

"True down, Alfie down, you're up next," Wallace said to Luther.

"Not a chance. Bram's up next," Luther retorted.

"I do not think so, it'll be Florian," Bram declared.

"I'll be last, for so many wenches, it would be a shame to tie myself to one and not let others have their piece of me," Florian decreed.

All of this nonsense came as they moved out of the door.

True walked beside Alfie as he wheeled.

They did this slowly, letting the others fall ahead in front of them.

"I know she carries your child and you two are not speaking of it, for you don't wish to take the light away from Bronagh," Alfie said quietly.

True studied his man intently as he asked, "You are loyal and wise and smart enough to fall in love with Bronagh, and you are also a healer who can sense a pregnancy?"

Alfie chuckled, shook his head, and replied, "Bronagh *is* a nurse."

"Ah," True murmured.

"And there is the added evidence that anytime she doesn't think someone's looking, she has her hand to her stomach. And anytime you're with her and you think no one is looking, you have *your* hand to her stomach."

It was then, True chuckled.

"I am happy for you, my friend," Alfie said quietly.

"I am as well. But today, I am happier for you," True replied.

He clamped his hand on his friend's shoulder.

When he did, Alfie lifted his and patted True's.

True walked, and Alfie wheeled, into the sanctuary.

He saw right away his wife, sitting in the front pew, did indeed give it all away for she sat with her hand as Alfie said.

Resting over their babe in her belly.

Her other hand, as it often did, was wrapped around the veneration to her mother that hung at her neck, close to her heart.

He liked that in the now, with his babe growing inside of her, her mother was that near to the both of them.

He smiled at her.

Farah beamed at him.

And then True stood by Alfie's chair and watched Bronagh practically run down the aisle to her intended.

He then proudly stayed where he was and watched them get married.

"Alfie knows," he murmured, watching his queen's face and enjoying how it expressed how much she liked what he was doing with his fingers.

"Oh dear," she muttered, pleasingly distractedly.

"Bronagh too," he said.

"True?" she called.

"Mm?" he answered.

Her back arched, her topaz eyes focused on his, and she whispered, "Please stop talking."

He smiled.

Then, in order to do that, he kissed her.

~

IT WOULD SEEM Sir Alfie and his lovely wife Bronagh were intent to take care of business early.

For their babe was born only two months after Queen Farah gave King True their first son.

~

King Aramus
King's Bedchamber, Keel Castle, Nautilus
MAR-EL

"YOU DO KNOW that mermaids don't lay eggs," his queen demanded irately.

"You've been sick all day, every day, for a *month*," he ground out.

"Auntie says this is because I need to get under the sea on a regular occasion."

"Do you know this for certain?" he asked.

"I have four cousins. You have met them. I think she knows," she answered.

Aramus simply scowled at her.

"I'll be fine," she assured. "We'll stay at Jorie's palace. He's welcomed us to do so as he's in Fire City to await the arrival of Silence and Mars's baby."

Aramus turned his gaze out the window, where he was standing during this (most recent, it must be said, his wife could fight her corner, brilliantly —it'd be bloody annoying, if he didn't admire it so much) argument with his wife.

He saw nothing but sea.

Normally, this soothed him.

Now, it did not.

"Aramus, you can breathe under the water. We go swimming all the time. You—"

He turned to her and gritted out, "You've been sick...all day...*every day...for a month*."

Her curls bounced as her head jolted.

She then unfolded her legs from beneath her, took her feet beside their bed, and moved to him.

She put one hand to his chest, the fingers of the other she curled around his neck, and she got up on her toes.

"Even non-Mer women retch and do it often during pregnancy," she assured.

His brows rose. "All day, every day, for a month?"

"Yes. Or for three months. Sometimes the entire pregnancy."

Fucking hell.

He did not know this.

He did not *like* this.

"But Auntie Ha-Zahlah feels The Deep will help," she said softly. "So I would like to try, but not without you."

"You go bloody nowhere without me," he decreed.

Her face grew gentle, and she leaned closer. "Of course not. And if it doesn't work, we will come back."

He grunted.

"Aramus, I will be fine."

"I am sure," he retorted. "You are strong and smart and give up on noth-ing. But this will be our only child."

She blinked, and when she was done, her crystal eyes were huge.

"Pardon?" she asked.

"I will not have you endure this another time. It doesn't matter. I've already decided, boy or girl, first born will take over the kingdom...or queendom as it were."

"As much as I very much like that, my darling, we are not only having one child."

He curled his arms about her and looked out to the sea, murmuring, "We shall see."

"Yes, we will," she murmured back. "Now, let us see about rectifying the fact you haven't made love to me in a month."

His eyes fell to hers. "You've been ill."

"I'm not ill right now."

"And I'm not *making* you ill."

She pressed to him and her siren's voice became a siren's song. "You won't make me ill."

His cock took notice.

It was his mind that refused. "Absolutely not."

She stared up at him.

"We will abstain until I am certain you are well," he announced.

"Have you gone mad?" she breathed.

"No," he stated the obvious.

"Aramus."

"Ha-Lah."

"Aramus!"

"Ha-Lah."

She frowned.

Then she grasped his head, pulled it down to her, and she kissed him.

She did things with her tongue and things with her hands that no man with an intent to abstain should have to endure.

Thus, he failed at enduring them.

Spectacularly.

HA-LAH DID NOT GET ILL during the festivities.

Though she stayed that way the first seven months of her pregnancy.

Two months later, she gave her king a boy.

The next two she gave him were girls.

Sisters of the Beast

THE ENCHANTMENTS

BLACK RINGLETS MIXED with locks of honey and chestnut and ebony in the grass as the women lay on their backs forming a cross with their heads together, their eyes aimed through the leafy trees to the blue skies.

Each had a wee babe snuggled asleep on their chests.

"He's ridiculous," Ellie was saying.

Silence giggled.

"You are not unaware he spoils his girls," Ha-Lah noted.

"Yes, well," she gently patted the rounded bottom of the wee one on her chest, "this one only has to chirrup and he's there, cooing at her and demanding an entire citadel meet her every whim, be it containing a draught or bringing a toy or changing a nappy."

"King Cassius Laird of Airen doesn't change nappies?" Farah asked.

"Hell no," Ellie answered. "Though he does stand over the nursemaid, or, say, *me*, scowling as he inspects we're doing it right."

There were chuckles all around.

"Does King True Axelsson of Wodell do it?" Silence inquired.

"We get into our chambers and the world melts away," Farah said serenely. "So yes, when it is us, our family alone together, and there is no one else to do it, for he allows no one there, my husband has no issue."

"Mars doesn't either," Silence said.

"Aramus has gained the skill of a noble Mer and becomes invisible when this one," she gave her son's round tush a tender shake, "starts to get smelly."

Low feminine laughter drifted into the skies.

Then they fell silent.

Silence broke it.

She did this with a whispered, "We did it."

"We did it," Farah whispered in return.

"We're here, together," Ellie said quietly.

"We're always together," Ha-Lah declared.

"Yes," three other women agreed.

Brothers of the Beast
THE ENCHANTMENTS

THEY STOOD IN THE TREES, tall, regal, shoulder to shoulder, and studied the women that lay on their backs in the grass, babes at their chests, eyes to the sky.

"Do we leave them be?" True queried.

"Fuck no, don't you hear my wee darling?" Cassius asked.

None of the men heard a thing.

"She fusses," Cass muttered. "She needs her father."

And then he strode into the glade.

Mars looked to Aramus then to True.

True looked to Mars then to Aramus.

Aramus grinned at the both of them.

"Cass!" they heard Ellie hiss. "We're having Sisters of the Beast time."

"Well, now it's Sisters *and* Brothers of the Beast time," Cassius retorted.

The remaining men looked into the glade.

Cass had wrested his sleeping daughter from her mother and was dropping to his arse, then falling back to rest his head on his wife's belly, his still surprisingly sleeping daughter wrapped in his arms.

Ha-Lah was the first to look their way as the rest started striding to them.

"We're being invaded," she warned.

"I don't mind," Silence said.

Mars grinned at his queen.

"I don't either," Farah added.

True winked at his wife.

Ha-Lah said nothing, but she smiled at her husband, who smiled in return.

The men claimed their children, and all settled in the grass, Aramus doing it much the same as Cass, though he had one arm around his son, the fingers of his other hand tangled in his Ha-Lah's curls.

And Mars arranged his Silence so her head rested on his stomach.

But when he did this, no one was surprised when a wee monkey came out from the curtain of her hair and snuggled into her papa's chest next to her beloved tot.

And True fell to his back with Farah curling down his side with her head resting on his shoulder.

After they had settled, they were quiet, eyes to the sky, and naught to be heard but the sound of the wind rustling the leaves.

And as all were peering at the heavens, no one saw two sets of eyes shade with a starry night. And two sets become a verdant green. And two, blue waves crashing. The last two, blithely dancing flames.

They lay, husbands and wives, sisters and brothers, in peace.

And no one paid any mind to the two unicorns and their wee babe pulling at the green blades not too far from their sides.

~

Faunus of the Trusted
Manor House of a Trusted, Fire City
FIRENZE

FAUNUS WOKE, and she was pressed down his side, her legs tangled in his, and behind her, his legs were tangled in both of theirs.

His eyes opened and he turned his head and tucked his chin in his throat.

This was because her hand was coasting down his stomach.

When she sensed him awake, she gave him a cheeky grin and wrapped her fingers around his morning erection.

He growled and reached to her, taking her hips in his hands and hauling her atop him.

Since she already had hold, she bent over him, planting a hand in his chest, and guiding his cock to her with her other.

Moira bore down and at the glorious feel of his woman's sleek, Faunus surged up.

They woke Saturn with their movements, and he moved as well.

He pressed a sleepy kiss to Moira's thigh as she rode Faunus and then he reached around her, gave Faunus's balls a squeeze, let go when he earned a pleasured grunt, and then he pushed up and touched his lips to Faunus's.

He then shifted back, got up on his elbow and watched.

Eventually, Faunus took the thick silk of her hair at the back of her neck in his fist and knifed up, taking control of the ride with his arm about her hips, doing this until he heard her gasp and whisper his name when she finished.

Then he allowed himself to finish.

Saturn gave them time for it to leave them both before he pulled Moira off Faunus's cock, rolled to his back and positioned her sitting over his face.

Her head fell back, and Saturn's name rushed from her lips.

Faunus slid down the bed, did his own roll, coming to his stomach between Saturn's legs.

Saturn ate Faunus's seed from Moira.

Faunus swallowed Saturn's direct.

～

It was night and the lovers were where they were often when the sky was dark, and the stars were out.

Tangled up together on their daybed by the fountain.

They were sipping wine and eating almonds dusted with Airen's golden salt, talking, lazily stroking, and letting go of the day so they could go to their bed and sleep peacefully in the night.

They all still wore their double wedding chains.

Faunus had Moira's leading from his right ear to his nose and lip.

Saturn's from his left.

Moira took Saturn's to her right, Faunus's to the left.

And Saturn took Faunus's to his right, Moira's to his left.

But all of the stones on Moira's were green.

"I have something you should know," Moira said from her place sandwiched between the men who were lounged into a corner of the daybed.

"Yes?" Faunus asked.

"Mm?" Saturn murmured into his wineglass.

"I'm pregnant."

Both men grew very still.

Moira carried on.

"And if it's a boy, we're naming him Teddy. And if it's a girl, we're naming her Teddy."

Suddenly, the air all around them smelled of honeysuckle.

Faunus's arms went about his wife, but his eyes lifted to the heavens.

"Are we all agreed?" Moira asked.

"Yes," Saturn said, and at his words, Faunus's gaze moved to him to catch him giving his husband a happy look before shoving his face in Moira's neck, his arms that were about her as well, tightening.

She tipped her head back to Faunus.

Faunus looked into his beloved *stellina's* beautiful face.

He smiled gently at her.

And he whispered, "Yes."

She returned his smile.

They all pressed together.

Saturn pulled his face out of his wife's neck.

Still tangled together in love and loyalty and hope for the future, they settled in.

And gazed at the beauty of the stars.

The End

THE RISING SERIES GLOSSARY

Terms, Words, Places

Abhainn Mouth – (AH-been) (n/place): Harbor city in the north of Airen located at the mouth of the Dunleth Abhainn (river).

Abyss (the) – (n/place): Large "bottomless" hole in the rock of a cliff on the coast of Mar-el fifteen miles down the coast from Nautilus, the capital city of Mar-el.

Airen – (Air-EN) (n/place): Country of Airen located in the northeast of the Triton mainland. The northernmost area is barren and craggy and made up of great boulders of black rock. The rest is mountainous or fertile and green, mostly pastureland, forests and rolling hills.

Airenzian – (Air-EN-zee-an) (adj.): Of Airen.

Alabasta – (Al-ah-BASS-tah) (goddess): Of Wodell. Goddess of Wisdom and the Earth. A goddess shared with Lunwyn in The Northlands.

Amphite – (Am-FITE) (n/place): Underwater capital of the Mer. Location of royal palace of King of the Mer.

Ancient Ritual Ground – (n/place): Area in the Lesser Thicket Forest of the country of Wodell where rituals were (are) conducted, including human sacrifice.

Argyll Forest – (n/place): Forest on the western border of Airen, butting The Enchantments, the city-state of Go'Doan and Wodell. The parts of it in Wodell are known as the Lesser Thicket Forest. Location of the Silbury Henge.

Ashesh – (Ash-EHSH) (n): Drug akin to opium. Available throughout Triton. Grown in Firenze.

Angmostros – (Aing-MO-stros) (n/creature): Sea creatures in the shape of enormous eels, some one hundred yards long, with two heads with long necks, very large mouths and very sharp teeth.

Aviast – (Ay-VEE-ast) (n): Keeper of a loft of ravens used for sending messages.

Bayzian – (Bay-ZEE-an) (n): Citizens of Sky Bay, the capital of Airen.

Birchlire Castle – (Birch-LEER) (n/place): Home of the King of Wodell. Located in Notting Thicket.

Bishop Cross – (n/island): Island off the southeast coast of the country of Airen. Temperate, but barren and very remote.

Bloody Boy Cove – (n/place): Deep cove to the north, across the wide bay (and hidden from sight) from Nautilus, in Mar-el.

Body stocking – (n): Worn by the Nadirii under tunics. More like a leotard or bathing suit. Can be tank/spaghetti strap/long-sleeved/strapless at top. Regular cut or high cut at the hips.

Bounden (The) – (n): Those taken into service on Mar-el as punishment for sailing the Triton seas without permission from the Mar-el king. This punishment is known and anyone who sails the seas risks it if caught doing so. The service of the bounden lasts a specified amount of time and those taken into it are guarded under significant strictures as by law as to their treatment. Once service is done, many of the bounden remain on Mar-el to make their lives there.

Cairngorn Lake – (KAREN-gorn) (n/lake): Very large lake located in the southeast of the country of Airen.

Carleigh Manor – (Car-LAY) (n/place): Royal manor house about thirty-five kilometers south of Sky Bay in the country of Airen.

Catrame Palace – (Cah-TRAME) (n/place): Royal palace of the King of Firenze. Located in Fire City.

Cells – (n): The room or rooms of a Go'Doan priest. In Go'Doan, they are quarters, with more than one room. For new priests or those in Go'Doan temples in other countries, the cell could be one room. However, they are not spartan, ranging from very comfortable (for a Go'Tish, a new priest) to luxurious (for a Go'En, a high priest).

Close – (n): A narrow, dead-end alleyway in a city. Mostly a footpath and not used for carriages or horses, etc. Opposite of "wynd" [see below].

Collected (The) – (n): Old or ancient books gathered and translated by the Go'Doan from all the realms of Triton. These were protected and kept safe in the Narration Hall (main library) of the Dome City.

Crittich Keep – (Crid-ITCH) (n/place): Royal prison and dungeons of Wodell, located in the capital of Notting Thicket. Also contains administration offices of the constabulary, prison and guard system in Wodell, interrogation rooms, cells for those held for questioning, and in the bowels of its depths, ancient torture chambers. Outside the Keep is the Lawn, where executions take place.

Cyrus – (SEAR-us) (n/place): Large merchant town to the northeast of Silbury Henge on the outskirts of the Argyll Forest.

Dahksahna – (Dahk-SAH-nah) (n/title): Means "queen" in Korwahkian, the language of Korwahk in The Southlands.

Dahlia Rooms – (n/place): Sex palace in the Heden District of Fire City in Firenze.

Dax – (n/title): Means "king" in Korwahkian, the language of Korwahk in The Southlands.

Dellish – (Del-ISH) (adj): Of Wodell (akin to English, Spanish, etc.).

Dome City – (n/place): Another name for the city-state of Go'Doan, named as such as it's known for its plentiful gold domes.

Doors (The) – (n/place): A magical gnome settlement in the Great Thicket Forest of Wodell where the gnomes live in the trees, the name referring to the many doors carved into the trunks.

Dune Desert – (n/place): Desert north of the Sheeonee Mountain range in Firenze.

Dunleth Abhainn – (DONE-leth AH-been) (n/river): Long, wide river running from an inlet in the northern shore of the country of Airen, southeast all the way to Cairngorn Lake. At the town of Kilcree Break, the Dunleth forks into Westfork River, which runs southwest to the Argyll Forest. (Abhainn means "river" in Gaelic).

Emerald Oil Asps – (n): Snakes in Firenze. Black with emerald-colored eyes. Highly venomous.

Enchantments (The) – (n/place): Forest in the center of the mainland of Triton with trees made magically tall and stout in order to house the Nadirii Sisterhood in their treehouses. Protected by fierce magic, The Enchantments cannot be breached by anyone other than one of the Sisterhood or unless given Nadirii permission. Regardless of the intensity of magic that protects it, it is patrolled constantly by Nadirii warriors.

Fire City – (n/place): Capital city of Firenze. Located to the north of the Sheeonee Mountain range that takes up the center of Firenze. Fire City is close to Fire Lake, the largest lake in Firenze.

Fire Lake – (n/lake): Very large lake to the east of Fire City in the country of Firenze formed by runoff of melted snow from the Sheeonee Mountains.

Firenz – (Fir-EHNZ) (adj): Meaning, of the country of Firenze.

Firenze – (Fir-ehn-ZAY) (n/place): Country of Firenze situated across the south of the Triton mainland. The largest country in Triton. Most of the country is desert or sand dunes with the middle of the country having a very large mountain range with high peaks that get great amounts of snow. When this snow melts, it floods Fire Lake, close to Fire City, and leads off into a large number of rivers and tributaries that cut through the desert and dunes with strips of fertile oases.

Firenzii – (Fir-ehn-ZEE) (n): Language of Firenze (much like Italian).

Fotiá Sea – (Foh-SHAH) (n/ocean): Body of water to the south of the continent of Triton.

Fumeria – (Foo-mare-EE-ah) (n): Water pipe. Akin to a marijuana bong but much more elegant and ornate.

Gairn Plain – (n/place): A stretch of plain southeast of Sky Bay and west of the Dunleth Abhainn in the country of Airen.

Go'Doan – (Go'Dōn) (n/place/religion):
   (1) City-state of priests, scholars and healers with temples, archives of the history Triton and a university. Also known as Dome City.
   a.   Go'Da (Go'DAH) (n): University in Go'Doan

   (2) Religion in Triton with temples across the continent where people worship:
   a.   Go'Bedi (Go'bed-EE) (god of obedience)
   b.   Go'Vicee (Go'vee-SEE) (god of service)
   c.   Go'Chas (god of faithfulness)

   (3) Orders of Go'Doan:
   a.   Go'Fell (order of priests as a whole)
   b.   Go'En (high priests)

c.   Go'Ar (Advanced priests, often are sent to do missionary work or teach in Go'Doan schools across Triton)

d.   Go'Tish (new priests/trainee priests)

e.   Go'Tec (priests who teach/scholars in the city-state)

f.   Go'Nis ("Keepers of the Records," priests who record history)

g.   Go'Ella (female acolytes that serve priests and the city-state)

Great Thicket Forest – (n/place): Massive forest in the middle of the country of Wodell, to the east of which is Notting Thicket, the capital city of Wodell.

Great Wohd (River) – (n/river): A very wide, very long river separating from the River Dorian in the north which runs from the Seil Sea. The Great Wohd cuts through the eastern part of Wodell, meeting the River Fae at Notting Thicket, the capital of Wodell, and continuing westerly nearly to the border of Wodell.

Green Sea – (n/ocean): Body of water to the east of the continent of Triton.

Gulliver – (n/place): Town in the south of Wodell located seventy-five miles from the Firenz boarder.

Hawkvale – (n/place): Country in the middle of The Northlands, south of Lunwyn, north of Fleuridia, ruled by King Noctorno and Queen Cora.

Heden District – (HEE-den) (n/place): Red light district of Fire City, Firenze. Where to find prostitutes (male and female), participate in orgies or other sexual games and play, consume smoke or *ashesh* or *koekah* and other forms of decadence.

Highgate – (n/place): Large gate at the top of the cliffs protecting Sky Bay, the capital city of Airen. Situated slightly to the southeast at the highest heights of the mountains that surround the capital city.

Ibex-whales – (EYE-bex whales) (n): Whales of which the bulls have enormous, ridged tusks that look like that of an ibex.

Irons – (n): Used in fireplaces or freestanding in rooms in Airen, Mar-el and Wodell, wood or other burning fuel in them or piled on them to heat them in order to heat a room.

kah rahna fauna – (n): Loosely means "my golden doe" in Korwahkian, the language of Korwahk in The Southlands.

Keel Castle – (n/place): Home of the king of Mar-el. Located in Nautilus, the capital city.

Keeper of The Lights – (group): A group of fairies who oversee and protect the area where The Lights (see: Lights (The)) can be viewed in the Greater Thicket Forest of Wodell.

Keerian Name – (description): The way Lunwynians (people of Lunwyn in the Northlands) describe a given name or as we know it Christian or first name.

Kilcree Break – (Kill-KREE Break) (n/place): Town in the middle of the country of Airen located at the break of the Dunleth Abhainn (river) where the Dunleth continues on to Cairngorn Lake and the Westfork River begins, running toward the Argyll Forest. A gentry seat.

Koekah – (koe-KAH) (n): Drug akin to cocaine. Available throughout Triton. Grown and manufactured in Firenze.

Korwahk – (n/place): Country taking up the northern part of the continent, The Southlands. Ruled by *Dax* (King) Lahn and *Dahksahna* (Queen) Circe of the Golden Dynasty.

Korwahn – (n/place): Capital city of Korwahk in The Southlands.

Lawn (The) – (n/place): Grassy area outside Crittich Keep, the royal prison and dungeons of Wodell, where executions take place. Located in Notting Thicket.

Lesser Thicket Forest – (n/place): Forest on the east border of the country of Wodell, west border of Airen. The parts of it in Airen are known as the Argyll Forest. Within it in Wodell is the Ancient Ritual Ground.

Leuthea – (LOU-thee-ah) (n): Sea goddess of sailors in distress. Worshiped by Mar-el.

Lights (The) (n/place): Atop the highest hill in the center of the Great Thicket Forest of Wodell where, on occasion, the sky illuminates with colored lights (akin to the Northern Lights). The reason for the phenomenon is unknown.

Lotus Den – (n/place): Bar and drug den with rooms for rent for a variety of hedonistic activities in the Heden District of Fire City in Firenze.

Lowgate – (n/place): Large gate in the downslope of the cliffs that protect Sky Bay, the capital city of Airen. Situated to the northwest in the lowest area where the cliffs meets the sea at Twilight Harbor.

Lunwyn – (n/place): Country taking up the northern part of The Northlands. Ruled by Queen Aurora.

Mar-el – (n/place): Country of Mar-el, island nation situated to the northeast of Triton (off the coast of Airen). Made up of dark rock around the shores, beaches, fertile land inland. Most of population works in some form of sea trade.

Marital Chain – (n): Firenz form of a wedding ring. It starts at upper ear, threads down to the lobe, across to the nostril and down to end at a hoop at the side of the mouth. In most cases, if it indicates marriage, it's worn on the right side. It's meant to signify listening to your mate, keeping them in mind, and communicating honestly with them.

McGarrity's Teahouse – (n/place): A brothel in Wodell.

Medusa – (n): Goddess of the sea. Worshipped by Mar-el.

Medusa's Gate – (n): Large, ornate monument to the goddess Medusa in which is the gate to the lane to Keel Castle in Nautilus, the home of the King of Mar-el.

Mer (The) – (n/people): Race of underwater charmed folk, including mermaids and mermales. Their fins split into legs and their gills disappear when they swim close to land so they can "pass" as human and move about on land.

Miet – (n/celebration/holiday): The celebration of the crop yield in Firenze, held as autumn subsides to winter. Celebrations mostly center around planned orgies, but they also include copious intake of liquor, food and drugs.

Mystics (The/the) – (n/place/spiritual practice):

(1) The continent to the west of Triton across the Triton Sea. Referred to with capitalized "The."

(2) Spiritual practice that includes personal reflection, transcendent study and deep training in various physical skills of defense and attack. Referred to with a lowercase "the."

Nadirii – (Nah-DEER-ee) (n): Sisterhood of warriors who live in an enchanted forest (The Enchantments) with no men. The veil around this forest was raised after the women of Airen revolted against their oppressors, magicking them to sleep, slitting their throats and escaping by stealing into the night to the newly established enchanted forest. No one can enter without Nadirii permission.
(1) "Nadirii" means "oppressed" in the old tongue.
(2) "Nadirii" means "sisterhood" in the ancient tongue.

Narration Hall – (n/building): Very large library that is very tall as well as built down deep in the earth in the Dome City where the tomes of history are recorded and kept, as well as all other books the Go'Doan have collected.

Nautilus – (n/place): Capital city of Mar-el, located on the southwest coast.

Night Heights – (n/mountain range): Range of mountains to the east of Sky Bay, the capital city of the country of Airen.

Nippenlas – (n/festival/holiday): A festival held midwinter in Wodell for the sole purpose of drawing the citizens out of their homes and to break the monotony of long nights and cold winters.

Northlands (The) – (n/place): One of two continents to the east of Triton across the Green Sea.

Notting Thicket – (n/place): Capital city of the country of Wodell, located to the east of the Great Thicket Forest.

Our Lady the Queen's Orphanage – (n/place): National orphanage in Notting Thicket, Wodell. Under patronage of the Queen of Wodell.

Pennyrium – (Pen-EER-ee-um) (n): A drug a woman can take through dissolving a powder in water in order to protect against conception.

Piercing Ceremony – (event): Done at age thirteen to boys and girls in Firenze, it is the ceremony where the right ear is pierced at the top and lobe, as well as the nostril and the side of the top lip. It is where the marital chain is threaded after a Firenz is wedded. Small hoops are worn in these piercings until a person is married and takes their chain.

Rayloo – (command): A Korwahkian word meaning [as it is in the imperative conjunction] "be quiet."

River Dorian – (n/river): Long, wide river running from Seil Sea through the eastern region of the country of Wodell, through the Lesser Thicket Forest, to the city-state of Go'Doan.

River Fae – (n/river): A river running from mountains to the north of the country of Wodell, through the mid-eastern part of the country to join with the Great Wohd at Notting Thicket, the capital of Wodell.

Royal Service Infirmary – (n/place): National hospital in Notting Thicket, the capital of Wodell, that treats all, but was created and caters to Dellish soldiers.

Seil Sea – (n/ocean): Body of water north of the continent of Triton.

Sheeonee Mountain Range – (SHE-oh-nee) (n/place): Large mountain range that makes up most of the central part of the country of Firenze. Very high peaks that get a great deal of snow. Snow melt feeds Fire Lake (outside Fire City) and five large rivers that run through the country, including the widest that flows north toward Wodell, the Tebes River.

Smoke – (n): Marijuana. Used mostly in Firenze but available throughout Triton.

Silbury Henge – (n/place): Standing stone henge in the forest on the western border of Airen where it meets The Enchantments and the city-state of Go'Doan. Made up of five standing stones and a sacrificial/ritual slab.

Sky Bay – (n/place): Capital city of Airen, located in a northwesternmost bay of Airen, close to the border of Wodell.

Sky Citadel – (n/place): Home of the King of Airen. Located in Sky Bay.

Slán Bailey – (SLAHN) (n/place): Royal prison in Airen, the building of which takes up a full, small island off the coast of Twilight Harbor in Sky Bay.

Soldier's Poison – (ritual): If a soldier is wounded gravely in the service of Airen or Wodell, he can request to be relieved of his life. This request is made of his commanding officer, and that officer can grant or refuse it. The ritual allows for a farewell from any loved one the soldier selects and making peace with his gods, before he's given a fast-acting, painless poison of a dense concentration of undiluted *taibac* to take, or if he's unable to drink it himself, it is administered to him by his commanding officer.

Southlands (The) – (n/place): One of two continents to the east of Triton across the Green Sea.

Strait of Medusa – (n/waterway): Narrow body of water that separates Mar-el from Airen.

Sparkles – (n): (When referring to a beverage) Champagne.

Taibac – (TIE-back) (n): Tobacco. Not smoked. Used as a poison to induce cardiac arrest. Can go undetected if poison is administered in small doses for a long time.

Tebes River – (TEH-behz) (n/river): Large river that flows from the Sheeonee Mountain range in Firenze, north toward the country of Wodell.

Temple to Wohden – (WOE-den) (n/place): National cathedral in Notting Thicket, Wodell where parishioners worship the god Wohden, the Dellish god of power and war. Also, where all royals are wed.

Trevor's Gorge – (n/place):

(1) A gorge south of Notting Thicket in Wodell that runs through a small, ancient mountain range (thus not high). It was formed by a narrow, but strong tributary that breaks off the Great Wohd River in Wodell.

(2) Also, the name of the large town situated at the west end of the gorge. This town is known for the making of sharp, but rich, goat's cheese that is renown throughout Triton.

a.   Trevor cheese (n/food): Cheese from this region.

Triton – (n/place):

(1) The continent to the west of the Northlands and Southlands, and to the east of The Mystics. It is surrounded by the Green Sea to the east, the Triton Sea to the west, Seil Sea to the north and Fotiá Sea to the south. It consists of one large land mass about the size of Australia and one large island (Mar-el) to the northeast. Countries include Airen, The Enchantments, Firenze, Mar-el, Wodell and the city-state of the Go'Doan.

(2) (n/god): God of the sea, worshiped by Mar-el.

Triton Sea – (n/ocean): Body of water to the west of the continent of Triton.

Trusted Ones (The) – (n): The elite guard that is commissioned with the safety of the King and Queen of Firenze. Also known as "The Trusted."

Twilight Harbor – (n/place): Wharf/dock in Sky Bay, the capital city of Airen.

Westfork River – (n/river): Short, narrow river in the country of Airen running from a break in the great Dunleth Abhainn at the town of Kilcree Break. The Westfork River runs southwest to the Argyll Forest.

Wodell – (n/place): Country of Wodell situated at the northwest of the Triton mainland. Very fertile and green, consisting of mainly farmland, forests, hills, dells and moors.

Wynd – (pronounced like "to wind your way") (n): A narrow, open-ended alley. Mostly a footpath and not used for carriages or horses, etc. Opposite of "close" [see above].

Zees – (people): A race of wanderers. Mostly in Wodell, but also some would travel around the westernmost border of Airen.

Full glossary, including character lists, tarot meanings, and gods and goddesses can be found on The Rising Series page at KristenAshley.net

WANT MORE KRISTEN ASHLEY PARANORMAL ROMANCE?

Until The Sun Falls From The Sky

Leah Buchanan's family has been in service to vampires for five centuries. Even so, Leah wants nothing to do with her family's legacy. But when she's summoned to her Selection by the Vampire Dominion, under familial pressure, she has no choice but to go.

Lucien has been living under the strict edicts of the Vampire Dominion for centuries but he's tired of these ancient laws stripping away everything that is the essence of the vampire.

This is because Lucien has been watching and waiting for decades for Leah to become available for a Selection and he will not be limited with what he can do with her. He will have her, all of her.

Therefore, Lucien is going to tame Leah, even if he gets hunted and killed for doing it.

What neither Leah nor Lucien expects is the strong bond that will form between them, connecting them on unprecedented levels for mortals or immortals. And what will grow between them means they will challenge their ways of life and their union will begin the Prophesies which makes them one of three couples who will save humanity...or die in the effort.

Keep reading for more of Until The Sun Falls From The Sky.

UNTIL THE SUN FALLS FROM THE SKY

Chapter One
The Selection

"Um, do you want to tell me what that was all about?" I asked.

Stephanie took my arm in her hand and moved me into the room all the while talking in a low voice. "The first bit, I'll let Lucien explain to you if he desires. The last bit, you must know. You haven't been to your studies, obviously, but I suspect your mother gave you *some* instruction. I don't know if you're ignoring it or have a death wish."

She stopped and turned to me, we were the same height and her eyes leveled on mine. Hers were serious as she continued speaking.

"Never disrespect a vampire, Leah. Cosmo and I, tonight, will be okay with it. Lucien, never. Don't *ever* disrespect Lucien. After you do your study, Cosmo and I'll not be patient with it either. You need to know this. And tonight any vampire that approaches you, you treat with respect. It's important, to your mother, your family, the legacy of your family past and present, and most of all, it's important to Lucien."

I had to admit I was getting more than a little bit sick of this Lucien business. Mostly not knowing what in the hell everyone was talking about and especially now that I'd laid eyes on him.

However, I wasn't stupid. Stephanie was being serious, she was also being real. She wasn't trying to scare me, she was telling me like it was. She

465

was trying to protect me. Even though she was a vampire, I decided not to throw that back in her face. I might be a lot of things but I wasn't someone who would do *that*.

"Now I'll introduce you to one of my old concubines," she told me, her voice back to friendly and cheerful.

She led me to a man who had to be seventy years old—and, I will add, Stephanie looked about twenty-five—but he was a fit, still handsome seventy-year-old with an even fitter, more handsome thirty-something man with him. The younger was the only man in the room wearing a red bow tie.

A blood-red bow tie. Another Uninitiated. A male one.

Wow.

I tried to be cool even though this was something Mom hadn't shared with me.

It was obvious Stephanie was fond of both the men. They laughed. They chatted. They drew me into their conversation.

After we said farewell, Stephanie led me away and I said, "I didn't know there were male concubines."

"There weren't," Stephanie replied. "But I lobbied The Dominion, which means I bitched and moaned so much that one hundred and fifty years ago they recruited males, thank Christ." She turned to me, plucked my empty champagne glass out of my hand and exchanged it with a full one from the tray of a passing waiter. "No offense." She grinned as she gave me my new glass.

"No offense?" I asked.

She was still grinning when she said, "Girls taste good. Boys taste better."

"Oh," I whispered, looking at the floor and going back to being flipped out by this entire business.

"Not surprisingly a lot of female vamps were pretty pleased at the new recruits. Also not surprisingly so were some males." She chuckled and the sound was nearly as beautiful as she was. So much so, I lifted my eyes to her as she carried on, "Though, some females still prefer their girls. It's the way of the world, no?"

I nodded because it was indeed.

Freakishly, I had to admit, I liked her. Therefore, I got closer to tell her something. Something I hadn't, until that moment, admitted to myself.

"Something's wrong," I whispered and she tensed.

"What?" she asked.

I shook my head and looked around.

Then I caught her eyes. "I don't know. I feel funny." And I did.

After Nestor left...

No, it was before that. After Lucien arrived, it happened. It wasn't the hands at the throat and heart thing. It was something else. Something that tugged at the edges of my consciousness. Something that was making me feel weird, like I was drugged.

I looked at my champagne. "I think I've been drugged," I breathed.

The rigidity left her body, her face grew soft, and she got close. "You haven't been drugged, Leah."

"I haven't?"

"No, you haven't. He's tracking you."

I blinked then *I* went rigid. "What? Who?"

"Lucien," was all she said.

My eyes flew around the room. It wasn't hard to spot him. He was standing with and talking to two men and a woman.

But his black eyes were on me.

"Tracking me?" I whispered, looking directly into those eyes.

Yes, my pet. Tracking you. Marking you. Mine.

I dropped my champagne flute.

Until The Sun Falls From The Sky is available now.

About the Author

Kristen Ashley is the *New York Times* bestselling author of over eighty romance novels including the *Rock Chick, Colorado Mountain, Dream Man, Chaos, Unfinished Heroes, The 'Burg, Magdalene, Fantasyland, The Three, Ghost and Reincarnation, The Rising, Dream Team, Moonlight and Motor Oil, River Rain, Wild West MC, Misted Pines* and *Honey* series along with several stand-alone novels. She's a hybrid author, publishing titles both independently and traditionally, her books have been translated in fourteen languages and she's sold over five million books.

Kristen's novel, *Law Man*, won the *RT Book Reviews* Reviewer's Choice Award for best Romantic Suspense, her independently published title *Hold On* was nominated for *RT Book Reviews* best Independent Contemporary Romance and her traditionally published title *Breathe* was nominated for best Contemporary Romance. Kristen's titles *Motorcycle Man, The Will*, and *Ride Steady* (which won the Reader's Choice award from *Romance Reviews*) all made the final rounds for Goodreads Choice Awards in the Romance category.

Kristen, born in Gary and raised in Brownsburg, Indiana, is a fourth-generation graduate of Purdue University. Since, she's lived in Denver, the West Country of England, and she now resides in Phoenix. She worked as a charity executive for eighteen years prior to beginning her independent publishing career. She now writes full-time.

Although romance is her genre, the prevailing themes running through all of Kristen's novels are friendship, family and a strong sisterhood. To this end, and as a way to thank her readers for their support, Kristen has created the Rock Chick Nation, a series of programs that are designed to give back to her readers and promote a strong female community.

The mission of the Rock Chick Nation is to live your best life, be true to your true self, recognize your beauty, and take your sister's back whether they're at your side as friends and family or if they're thousands of miles away and you don't know who they are.

The programs of the RC Nation include Rock Chick Rendezvous, weekends Kristen organizes full of parties and get-togethers to bring the sisterhood together, Rock Chick Recharges, evenings Kristen arranges for women who have been nominated to receive a special night, and Rock Chick Rewards, an ongoing program that raises funds for nonprofit women's organizations Kristen's readers nominate. Kristen's Rock Chick Rewards have donated hundreds of thousands of dollars to charity and this number continues to rise.

You can read more about Kristen, her titles and the Rock Chick Nation at KristenAshley.net.

facebook.com/kristenashleybooks

twitter.com/KristenAshley68

instagram.com/kristenashleybooks

pinterest.com/KristenAshleyBooks

goodreads.com/kristenashleybooks

bookbub.com/authors/kristen-ashley

ALSO BY KRISTEN ASHLEY

Rock Chick Series:

Rock Chick

Rock Chick Rescue

Rock Chick Redemption

Rock Chick Renegade

Rock Chick Revenge

Rock Chick Reckoning

Rock Chick Regret

Rock Chick Revolution

Rock Chick Reawakening

Rock Chick Reborn

The 'Burg Series:

For You

At Peace

Golden Trail

Games of the Heart

The Promise

Hold On

The Chaos Series:

Own the Wind

Fire Inside

Ride Steady

Walk Through Fire

A Christmas to Remember

Rough Ride

Wild Like the Wind

Free

Wild Fire

Wild Wind

The Colorado Mountain Series:

The Gamble

Sweet Dreams

Lady Luck

Breathe

Jagged

Kaleidoscope

Bounty

Dream Man Series:

Mystery Man

Wild Man

Law Man

Motorcycle Man

Quiet Man

Dream Team Series:

Dream Maker

Dream Chaser

Dream Bites Cookbook

Dream Spinner

Dream Keeper

The Fantasyland Series:

Wildest Dreams

The Golden Dynasty

Fantastical

Broken Dove

Midnight Soul

Gossamer in the Darkness

Ghosts and Reincarnation Series:

Sommersgate House

Lacybourne Manor

Penmort Castle

Fairytale Come Alive

Lucky Stars

The Honey Series:

The Deep End

The Farthest Edge

The Greatest Risk

The Magdalene Series:

The Will

Soaring

The Time in Between

Mathilda, SuperWitch:

Mathilda's Book of Shadows

Mathilda The Rise of the Dark Lord

Misted Pines Series

The Girl in the Mist

The Girl in the Woods

Moonlight and Motor Oil Series:

The Hookup

The Slow Burn

The Rising Series:

The Beginning of Everything

The Plan Commences

The Dawn of the End

The Rising

The River Rain Series:

After the Climb

After the Climb Special Edition

Chasing Serenity

Taking the Leap

Making the Match

The Three Series:

Until the Sun Falls from the Sky

With Everything I Am

Wild and Free

The Unfinished Hero Series:

Knight

Creed

Raid

Deacon

Sebring

Wild West MC Series:

Still Standing

Smoke and Steel

Other Titles by Kristen Ashley:

Heaven and Hell

Play It Safe

Three Wishes

Complicated

Loose Ends

Fast Lane

Perfect Together

Too Good To Be True